THE INDIGO REBELS

A FRENCH RESISTANCE NOVEL

ELLIE MIDWOOD

BOOK ONE IN THE INDIGO REBELS
SERIES

1

P aris, June 1940

GISELLE MADE A NEARLY impossible effort to open her eyes, but only managed to squint at the breaking dawn outside, groaned, rolled to the other side, hid her nose in her Pekinese's fur and fell back into slumber. All that crowd outside, her fellow Parisians, wouldn't let her sleep for a third night in a row; panic-stricken, disheveled, yanking their crying kids' hands and shouting at their wide-eyed husbands to mind the suitcases better, for "all that horde outside surely couldn't have been trusted," never mind that they belonged to the very same horde.

Parisians, so arrogantly waving off their neighbors' concerns just three days ago, stating haughtily that *their* capital would never be taken, that the Germans would never

1

make it here just because someone's *Gustave* was with the army, and he alone would teach their Prussian lot how to wander into countries they had no business with... *After all, didn't we show them what's what in 1918? And so we will again, mais oui, of course, we will!* Every such speech was always followed by pursed lips and up-and-down looks, which asked the silent question: *You aren't one of those, are you? The defeatist type? Because here in Paris we don't stand for that, Madame.*

Every time Giselle became an unwilling witness to such conversations in the café nearby or getting her new press in the kiosk on the corner, she could barely restrain herself from snorting with laughter and rolling her eyes at the women next to her. Unlike them, she hardly suffered from overly patriotic feelings and even more so from high hopes for their French army, which was retreating so fast that it seemed on certain days that the Germans were playing chase with them, and losing at that.

Giselle was more than convinced that the Germans would not only enter Paris any day now but would most likely stay for quite some time until they found a new country for them to conquer. Their celebrated *Wehrmacht* was probably already bored of France, which was far too easy to take. Giselle knew men a little too well for her thirty years of age: both in love and in war, it was the chase that they liked, the hunting element, the fight that their "prey" should put up. France fought off their advances with the reluctance of a farm girl, who only slaps her fellow farm boy's hands just for show, but then lets herself fall onto the hay with a contented sigh. And yet all these women – mostly the mothers of those poor boys fighting now at the front –

shouted their protests as soon as someone dared to voice their doubts concerning the fate of their country.

"It will never come to that! I will rather die than see those brutes walk the streets of *my* city!"

"Evacuate? Never! What our son, the hero of the war," (every son was the hero of the war, at least in these women's eyes) "what would he say if he comes home, and his parents have run off like rats off a sinking ship? No, Monsieur, Adolphe and I are staying in Paris and waiting for our Jean, and that's the end of it."

Giselle almost laughed when she woke up one morning alarmed by the shouts reverberating through the opened windows, climbed out of her bed, disturbing her dog who grumbled her discontent, and, leaning out of her window in her night slip, found all her patriotic fellow Parisians screaming their prices at the taxi cabs outside, begging them to take them to the closest train station because "the Germans were going to be here any minute now and slaughter them all!"

After nearly three days of panic, constant shouting and waves of refugees abandoning their city with more possessions than they could possibly carry on their backs, Paris fell silent for the first time. Last night was the worst one, when the last wave of the exodus, which consisted of the most obstreperous Parisians who tried to wait out until the last minute (for the train tickets were too expensive, or maybe hoping that the Germans would miraculously change their route and leave their city unmolested, just like a lava stream spares a condemned village at the last moment), they realized at last that the miracle wouldn't happen and tried to make it out of the city, keeping Giselle awake all night and Coco, her

Pekinese, growling and barking at the commotion outside, all the while pressing her trembling, well-fed body into her mistress's thigh.

At eleven o'clock in the morning, Giselle, even though she had slept hardly more than four hours, finally willed herself to kick the crumpled, sweaty sheets off her legs. She exhaled tiredly, rose from her bed and padded barefoot to the window to assess the situation outside. Paris had transformed into a ghost town overnight, completely devoid of any traces of life. Iron shutters sealed abandoned houses, restaurants and shops; no cars were honking outside, lifting the clouds of grayish summer dust which would grind like sand on the teeth; no children were playing in the deserted streets; no aroma of roasted chestnuts wafted through the air, tantalizing the senses of the passers-by.

And yet Giselle sighed again, only this time blissfully, like a cat who had been forgotten in the rush of a family hurrying to their vacation at the Midi, and who now had all the place to itself. After all, domestic cats, contrary to their masters' firm belief that their pampered creatures wouldn't last a day without proper care, managed perfectly well on their own and even preferred the newly obtained freedom to that of a golden cage to which they were ordinarily confined. And just like a cat, Giselle squinted her green eyes at the breaking day outside, raked her fingers through her short blonde hair leisurely and, purring a song under her breath, went to the bathroom to ready herself for the day that awaited.

KAMILLE WAS BRAIDING her daughter's hair absent-mindedly,

numbed by the silence of the big house, abandoned by both the maid and the cook, and pillaged by her in-laws. They appeared at the doors merely a day ago, swept through the house taking with them everything that was of a value – including the exquisite china set, table silver, two family portraits, fine embroidered linen – and left in their over-stuffed car, not forgetting to throw a scornful look at Kamille and little Violette, as if saying: "You should be grateful we aren't throwing you out into the street!"

The truth of the matter was that the Blanchards were too busy fleeing the city just like everyone else, and dealing with their "no-good" relative and her offspring ("who probably wasn't even our Charles's" as the matriarch of the family, Madame Blanchard, loved adding each time she spoke of her granddaughter) was the furthest thing from their minds. Kamille took all the looks and scorn as she always did, lowering her eyes compliantly and trying to stay as mute and invisible as possible while hiding her little daughter behind her leg.

She was used to such attitudes from the family that Kamille knew she hadn't been welcomed into from the very first day she had met Charles's parents. They met on the day when Kamille's father threatened to spread the scandal all over Paris if Charles didn't do "the right thing." Charles, with a sour face, had announced to his family that he and Kamille were getting married. Kamille, a docile girl of eighteen with sad blue eyes and porcelain cheeks that tend to blush too often, was two months pregnant at the time.

Charles, the only – and very spoiled – child of a wealthy, upper-middle-class family, cursed the day when he spotted Kamille at a picture gallery opening, of which his father was the benefactor, and to which Kamille's father had been invited so he could later write an article about the event. He wasn't a famous journalist at all, Monsieur Legrand, Charles knew it very well; nothing like his oldest daughter, who already had seven highly praised novels under her belt, a very good (even though somewhat scandalous) social standing and a nice sum in her bank account – an almost unspeakable thing for a single woman! That's who Charles would have loved to have gotten his claws into, but Mademoiselle Legrand, with her somewhat contemptuous sneer and cat-like eyes, was far above his reach, and Charles decided that Kamille, with her always frightened expression but very appealing body and luscious curves, would do nicely instead. Little did he know that Kamille was a virgin, whom he would have a misfortune to get pregnant during the short month that she thought they were dating, when, in reality, she was merely one of the many women Charles amused himself with, taking advantage of his handsome, fresh face and young age while he could.

Now, alone in their spacious house, which Charles rented right after their wedding, Kamille was recalling the eight years of their marriage with bitter-sweet emotion. She did love her husband endlessly at first and had tried her best to become an agreeable wife for him. But all her efforts were met with the same indifferent, distant and impenetrable expression, averted eyes and a dismissive shrug of the shoulders. Kamille blamed herself that Charles felt so trapped within the walls of his own family house, and not even once reproached him for not showing up at home for several nights in a row, or leaving before dinner dressed in his finely tailored tuxedo; for showing no interest in their newborn beautiful daughter who had his warm brown eyes and rosy cheeks; for snubbing her in their family bed, muttering under his breath that he was tired and that her perfume was making him sick. Kamille would only swallow more silent tears, alone on her side, feeling hurt, abandoned and ridiculous in the new chiffon nightgown that she bought so he would finally notice her, and for buying the same perfume that she smelled many times on his clothes after his nights in the city, in fruitless efforts to arouse his interest. Who was she trying to fool after all? She wasn't one of those women he liked, the mysterious, dazzling and frivolous women who would dance all night and drink champagne with the men who showered them with adoration and expensive gifts. Her sister was one of those women, but Kamille had never been like her.

Eventually, Kamille gave up on both Charles and their loveless marriage and concentrated on Violette, a lively little girl who thankfully didn't take after her, but more after her father, or her aunt for that matter. It was always easier for people like them to survive in this world. They didn't love anyone besides themselves, and therefore no pangs of conscience would stop them from enjoying their life, thought Kamille. *Just look at Giselle – she isn't even living like the rest of the gray mass around her, but flying like a butterfly from flower to flower instead; from one party to another; from one affluent aristocrat to an even wealthier foreign diplomat; and still she somehow manages to write her scandalous novels in between entertaining her high-class guests in her penthouse facing the Champs-Élysées. Giselle...*

Kamille glanced at her reflection in the mirror, in front of which she was braiding Violette's dark tresses and sighed.

She'd always been the golden girl, her oldest sister; she'd always been looked at with a mixture of awe and reverence by her parents for her defiant spirit and contagious laughter, as if Monsieur and Madame Legrand couldn't quite understand how it was possible that they, modest and God-fearing middle-class people, could possibly produce such a bright and fearless creature, who was nothing like them in her almost greedy love of life and all the pleasures it could possibly give, if one, of course, was bold enough to outstretch their hand and grab it. No, Kamille was nothing like her. If only she could pretend to be like her, for one day only even. If only someone would look at her with the same feverish adoration with which they looked at Giselle. If only someone loved her, actually loved her for one day only... She would die happy then. Yes, she would. Only, even her husband was dead now, killed in an air raid somewhere in the North where he used to vacation with his numerous mistresses before the war had started. So, it was her and Violette now, left to the empty, hostile, frightening city outside the tightly closed shutters.

MARCEL PULLED his legs up to his chest and squeezed his eyes shut, begging himself not to give in to the panic and to not start running, which would most certainly give him away to the enemy, passing by within mere steps from him. Pressing himself into the walls of a ditch under the road, on which German boots stomped the ground sending dust and small pebbles his way, Marcel willed himself to stay motionless until the whole regiment had finally passed, and the warm velvet night covered his hideout with a dewy blanket of musky June air.

Marcel slowly rose, probing and rubbing his arms and legs that had fallen asleep after being almost entirely devoid of moving for several hours. He threw an apprehensive, wide-eyed look around and, finding himself completely alone and one on one with the pearl of a moon in the sky, he slowly stepped away from the road. With the uncertainty of a newborn lamb, he made his first several steps on legs which were still shaky from both fear and lead-filled muscles, and then, as if it dawned on him at last that they were far, far away by now, far ahead of him and his scattered division, Marcel started moving faster and faster across the wheat field, trotting and then running as fast as he could, laughing at his newly gained freedom.

Even though the Germans didn't even bother taking prisoners of late and mostly did away with their French lot just by taking their rifles away and telling them to get lost, Marcel still didn't wish to find out for himself how many of these rumors were true. The war for France was lost, that much he had already admitted to himself, but being taken prisoner after the defeat seemed rather unjust for the young man; after all what was the point of surviving the war, even though it had been a short one, surviving the shelling, air raids and the whole approaching army if he would end his days in some *stalag*, in some German forest. No, he would shed his uniform at the first chance and go…

"Now where should I go?" Marcel stopped in his tracks and looked around once again, taking in the unfamiliar surroundings.

He was not far from Paris; he even knew this road, as it

was one his family always took when going up north to the little farm where their distant cousins lived. They were children back then of course, and those family outings stopped taking place many years ago, but Marcel still remembered how Giselle always rolled her eyes, moaning all the way along the road that they should have just left her home alone, that she wasn't a child anymore at twelve and that she hated countryside and had nothing in common with her cousins whatsoever... Marcel chuckled inaudibly, wondering if his older sister had left Paris together with the rest of the townsfolk or stayed in her apartment, shrugging off the whole German invasion like she always did with all the troubles in her life. Marcel had always admired that quality in her, and quite often wondered how Giselle would handle herself in his place, on the front, with a rifle in her hands – the rifle that he threw away as soon as he saw the first German tanks appearing at the bridge where Marcel and his comrades were stationed – he wondered if she would have run as well. No, she wouldn't. Giselle never ran. She would meet the whole squadron of the *Wehrmacht* with a smirk on her face in her assigned position, squinting at the sunlight reflecting off their helmets and buckles. Now, Kamille, she would run. Unlike her God-fearing family, Giselle for some reason didn't believe in death.

Giselle was the first person who came to his mind when Marcel contemplated where he should hide out before everything settled down. He had no doubt that his sister would help him with shelter and clothes, and maybe even temporary papers; with her connections – high standing lovers if he would call a spade a spade – she could get anything. But, then again, her social standing and her home being a sort of social club for both her literary friends and the Paris elite, might indeed pose a problem for his hiding arrangements.

Kamille and her in-laws, who came and went as they pleased, were out of the question. His own parents? Knowing them, Marcel dismissed that idea as well, knowing that they had most likely fled the city. The young man lifted his head towards the sky, which was unusually quiet without *Messerschmitts* cutting through the butter of clouds with their low, menacing roar, and patted his pockets looking for cigarettes. Remembering that he didn't have any left he headed to the nearest farm house on the other end of the field, its roof being his beacon as it reflected the luminous moonlight, luckily spared so far by the enemy air raids.

"There won't be any more air raids," the farmer's wife declared the following day, pouring fresh milk, still smelling of cows and grass, into Marcel's mug. Her two sons were both soldiers too; only her husband had been spared from the army this time after his right arm had been shredded by shrapnel during the Great War. It was their oldest son's clothes that Marcel was currently wearing. "The armistice has been signed, they say."

"And now what do we do?" Marcel, somewhat at a loss, looked up at the weary, tired woman with rough hands.

She glanced back at him and shrugged indifferently. "We live. That's what we do. We live, boy."

Live. The very meaning of this word changed for Marcel several weeks ago. From a history student with hazel eyes and russet bangs always falling on one eye, lively and curious, straightening proudly in his new uniform in front of the mirror of his family's apartment where he still lived since his parents didn't have enough means to provide him with a rented corner, to now, as he looked at his reflection in the farmers' kitchen, not even recognizing his eyes. With dark brows tightly drawn together, sunken cheeks covered with a shade of stubble and mouth pressed into a hard line, he had the eyes of a hunted animal, searching and wary, and the color of the sea at storm, having lost their innocent glimmer.

How could it be possible that only a few short weeks could transform him so? How could this uniform, stained with his comrades' blood and begrimed with layers of dust and shame after he had run for cover from the metal exploding nearby, make him into a different man; terrified, bitter and empty? Yes, that's exactly how he felt, empty inside, with nothing left – no pompous slogans, no national pride, no past, and no future in sight.

As if guessing his thoughts, as mothers always do, true mothers who are mothers to every soldier, the farmer's wife pressed Marcel's shoulder slightly.

"You should go to the Bussi's farm. It's not far from here, and my husband can even lend you a bicycle if you promise to return it of course. Their son, Philippe, is a communist as I heard. Maybe he can help you out. You know, for now. Before they," the woman motioned her graying head in an uncertain direction, meaning the government as Marcel guessed, "sort all this mess out."

Marcel, who had always been more interested in the politics of the past instead of current events, nodded obediently. After all, apart from the plan the farmer's wife had just presented, he didn't have any of his own.

2

The sun emerged from behind the clouds, delicately touching the tops of the trees as if ensuring that they were still in their place, where it had left them before going into hiding. Its rays dusted off the roofs, rendering their lustrous appearance once again just as it was expected to be at this time in June. Its beams discovered the dew on the abandoned flower beds and painted it in multicolored mosaic; it peeked inside the windows, navigating its way through the shutters and looking for life inside; and, finally, fearfully and with mistrust, it probed the metal of the helmets covering the blond heads of men marching in columns towards the capital.

Its curiosity growing, sunlight bounced off the helmets to the belt buckles, reflected off the silver buttons and crosses, sometimes blinding the soldiers and making them squint all while they sang their strange songs. Their high, melodic voices echoed off the walls of the narrow streets that they were passing, and made the contrast between their almost clerical singing and peculiar language, buzzing, deadly and cold like their *Messerschmitts,* even more pronounced. The calico cat cowered by the wall, pointed her ears, and glared at the invaders with her green eyes, her whiskers jittering invisibly as if tasting the unfamiliar sounds, smells, and noises. One of the marching soldiers noticed her, smiled and interrupted his singing to call her.

"Kss, kss, katze!"

The cat, mistaking his greeting for hissing, hissed in return, jumped under the stairs that she had been sitting on and disappeared from sight, just like the rest of the Parisians, who were now hiding behind bolted doors, tightly closed shutters and draped windows.

Giselle, having taken her morning shower, walked over to the window, pushed it wide open and inhaled a full chest of June Parisian air, which was still tight with electricity after last night's storm. She stretched her nimble limbs, smiled at the sight of the café being opened, where she usually took her morning coffee, and noted the visible hesitance of the frowning owner, who kept craning his neck in the direction from where Giselle could already hear the distant roar of approaching machinery, before she went to her dressing table.

Giselle was filled with a sense of perplexing agitation; agitation that made the air tingle in her lungs as it might if she had just made a bold bet in a casino, or as if she had expected a worrying verdict from her editor after sending him her latest novel. Rarely did something excite her like this, but when it did she envisioned the suffocating feeling of a condemned person on the gallows who doesn't know until the last moment if he is granted a pardon or whether he is going to be hanged in mere minutes. The feeling thrilled her to no end.

She had already wiped her sweaty palms on her silk stockings several times, as she sat in front of the mirror in her underwear, powdering her face with meticulous thoroughness, like that of a brain surgeon performing a life-saving operation in front of spectators.

At last, satisfied with her curled hair, painted lips and powdered neck, Giselle slipped into a bright yellow dress, tightened a leather belt around her waist making it even smaller, planted two dots of perfume behind her ears and on her wrists and, with a sly grin and with the gesture of a magician performing his most celebrated trick, lowered on top of her head her favorite straw hat with its green ribbon, bending it slightly sideways so that it covered one of her eyes.

With a confidence that the café owner silently envied when watching her approach the table that she always occupied outside, Giselle removed her white gloves finger by finger, arranged her purse on a chair next to her, crossed her legs and ordered her usual: a mocha without sugar and an éclair.

"Éclairs aren't fresh, Mademoiselle Legrand." The café owner's voice croaked against his will, and he rushed to clear his throat, bowing slightly to his one and only customer.

"They aren't fresh?" Giselle lifted her eyebrows with the incredulous smile of a person who has just been told that the sun doesn't rise in the east. "Come, Monsieur Richard, you must be teasing me. I know that you have only the best pastry in the whole of Paris on your counters. I wouldn't be so faithful to you if you didn't."

Monsieur Richard lowered his head and twisted the side of his mustache apologetically. "I'm afraid today is the exception to the rule, Mademoiselle. All the bakeries around have been closed for two days; no one is around to make fresh pastries…"

He spread his arms in such a helpless gesture that Giselle found it almost comical given the circumstances.

"Are they edible at all?" She tilted her head slightly to one side, looking at the man with her one mischievous green eye just visible from under her hat.

"They are… it's just that the crème… It's stale, I'm afraid."

"Oh, well… If I didn't die from what these gentlemen have been throwing at us from the sky lately, I suppose I will survive some stale crème. Bring it here!"

The roar of the machinery soon replaced the noise of Monsieur Richard's coffee machine, and Giselle promptly took a little notebook and a pen out of her purse and placed them on top of the table. *It's not every day an invading army is marching through our streets,* she thought, fixing her slightly squinted eyes at the plaza in front of her with curiosity. *Any minute now they will appear. Oh, who else can brag about witnessing something of this sort? What a remarkable novel I will make out of this!*

Indeed, barely five minutes after Giselle took the first bite out of an éclair (while glancing skeptically at the yellowish crème inside, before shrugging and continuing to eat it), the first German appeared through the arc, riding his horse, his back unnaturally straight. There followed several tanks and motorized divisions, all passing by their only two spectators, Monsieur Richard hiding wisely behind his blonde patron, who turned out to be much braver than he was.

Giselle was trying to keep her face straight after the first squadron of marching soldiers approached the spot where she was sitting, but the whole spectacle, as if it was played only for her entertainment given that there was no one else around, made her unwillingly give way to a smile. First it was just a sly grin, but then a contagious laughter emerged, which she couldn't suppress even though she genuinely tried to cover her mouth with her hand. Monsieur Richard watched her in utter astonishment, wondering if he should quietly walk inside his café and hide, because who knew if these Germans would take offense at such cheerfulness at their expense and shoot them both. But the Germans only smiled in response, some of them waving at the girl in the bright dress who was enjoying her coffee without a care in the world.

The last squadron that marched behind the long column appeared to be much more relaxed, for all the commanding officers were so far in front that they couldn't possibly see them. The young lieutenant, who was walking leisurely by his soldiers together with his adjutant, as Giselle assumed anyways, stopped from time to time to take pictures of the sights around him, trotting to catch up with his men after he spent a little too long in finding the best shot. As soon as he noticed Giselle he started pointing excitedly to his orderly, and they both approached her with interest and amusing reverence, like that of little boys who see a caged tiger for the first time in the zoo.

While the two exchanged hushed remarks in their language, which was impossible for her to understand, Giselle lifted her cup to her red lips, looking back at them with the same curiosity. The pair, in their pressed field gray uniforms and shining black boots – as if they didn't just march for hours! – walked over to her, still looking a little hesitant, until the lieutenant clicked his heels and bowed slightly, and in broken French asked Giselle for permission to take her picture. Giselle chuckled, shrugged slightly, put her cup down and graciously rested her head on her hand. The beaming officer quickly snapped his camera, clicked his heels again, thanking her profusely, and then, after throwing a last longing glance at her, trotted back to his squadron, his adjutant running behind him, exclaiming something.

"I wonder what he said," Giselle murmured, looking at the tail of the marching army as it moved away.

Monsieur Richard looked in the same direction and grinned with one side of his mouth from under his mustache.

"He said you're a true Parisian," he translated, trying to sound scornful towards the *Boches*. Only, Giselle still caught onto the carefully concealed pride in his voice. *Maybe you have conquered us, but we still have the best women.*

Giselle chortled and decided not to argue.

———

KAMILLE, with her dark hair put away neatly in a bun, covered her head with a navy blue hat which matched the color of the two-piece suit that she was wearing. She checked her daughter's appearance, smoothed out invisible lines on Violette's dress and took her hand firmly in hers before leaving the house.

"Now listen to me very carefully, Violette. The Germans are already in Paris. I doubt that they will venture to our outskirts today, but in case if they do, do not look at them, do not talk to them and under no circumstances let go of my hand. Do you understand?"

Despite her mother's stern expression and grave tone, Violette nodded eagerly because deep inside she was holding her breath in excitement, hoping that maybe, if she were lucky, she would see those mysterious Germans today. Her grandfather (her mother's father, the grandfather who talked to her unlike the other one who never deigned to pay any attention to the little girl apart from a cold, condescending nod in response to her greeting) had told her many stories about those *Boches* as he liked to call them: the men from the North in pointy helmets who he had fought for four years during the Great War, and who left him limping slightly on one leg.

"They were frightful, those fellows." Grandfather Gaspar would make big eyes at little Violette, his tone taking a theatrically dramatic note. "Even if you only show your head out of the trench – tra-ta-ta-ta-ta! Machine guns would blow the earth all around you. I was very young back then, younger than your mother now, and when I just went to war, I thought I would immediately beat them all by myself."

Violette always giggled when Grandfather Gaspar started aiming at a far off distance with his imaginary rifle, screwing up one of his eyes in a funny manner.

"I tried to jump out of the trench on my very first day, to show the *Boches* what's what. And had my commanding officer not yanked me down by my legs – you wouldn't have a grandfather now." He tapped the little girl's nose with his finger with a loving smile. "He saved my life then. They don't give second chances, the *Boches*. They shoot first and talk afterward. Did I tell you how one time a German plane was chasing me all over the potato field? No? Well, listen then…"

Violette grew up listening to Grandfather Gaspar's war stories, but just like all those fairy tales that he entertained his only granddaughter with, those war stories always had a happy end; after all, he survived the Great War to tell her about them, didn't he?

Violette looked up at her mother, who was walking in a rushed manner with her brows drawn in a frown, and wondered if she should be afraid of those Germans, just like she was taught to be afraid of an old witch that lived in a gingerbread house, or a giant who ate little kids who misbehaved. Her mother's sweaty palm should have persuaded her in this well enough, but her natural curiosity somehow still took over, and the little girl decided that she should see for herself, and make up her own mind about these Germans once she saw them.

Oblivious to her daughter's adventurous mood, Kamille was hoping that Madame Arnaud, the baker's widow who inherited her late husband's business and managed to run it quite successfully besides taking care of her five young children, would make good on her promise not to leave Paris with the rest of the townsfolk and have some fresh bread and flour that she could purchase in advance. Who knew what this German invasion would bring? Better stock up on all the necessities, because Kamille had learned all too well that it was only herself whom she could rely on.

A little relieved with the absence of any signs of the occupying forces in the silent streets that she was taking, Kamille slowed down her steps so that Violette wouldn't have to almost run alongside her mother. Paris was deserted, as if someone had taken a postcard and carefully erased all the people from it, leaving only bare sidewalks shadowed by blooming trees and empty houses, the eyes of their windows covered with white shutters. Strangely, but Kamille even preferred it this way; she was never too fond of the city's hustle and bustle, deep inside longing for a quiet piece of countryside instead.

Kamille breathed out in relief as she caught the first mouth-watering whiff of freshly baked bread as she turned around the corner. Madame Arnaud was not only at her usual place, not scared away by something so minor in her opinion as the occupying army, but loading fresh loaves of bread onto a little carriage, in front of which her sixteen-year-old son was smoking.

"Ah, Madame Blanchard!" The baker's widow, a plump, round-faced woman with cheeks that were always red and smiling, waved her greeting at Kamille as she saw her approaching. "Good thing you caught me in time. Louis and I are leaving in five minutes; someone has to cater to all those gentlemen who arrived without invitation, huh?"

The woman burst out laughing at her own joke while Kamille just paled slightly, gripping Violette's hand tighter.

"You're going to take your bread to the Germans?" she asked quietly, with an incredulous note in her voice. For the life of her, she couldn't understand how one didn't realize their blessing of not having any of those uniformed "gentlemen" in their streets but had decided to walk toward them willingly instead.

"Why, yes, Madame!" Madame Arnaud's voice gave way to her surprise at Kamille's reaction. "I have all this bread and no clientele to sell it to. I'm not letting it go to waste! And my sister Genevieve, the one from Strasbourg, she told me that those *Boches* pay in cash, and pay double and even triple price without asking. Now, why would I let such an opportunity go? I will be one stupid woman if I do, that much I can tell you."

"Aren't you afraid of them?" Violette voiced her mother's unspoken question.

The baker's widow laughed kindheartedly. "Now, why would I be afraid of a bunch of hungry boys?"

"Boys?"

"Why, yes, of course, they're just boys, my little one. Like this one," she explained to Violette, motioning her head towards her son. "But just in uniforms. There's nothing to be afraid about them."

Ten minutes later, carrying four heavy bags filled with fresh bread and flour, Kamille murmured under her breath but so that only her daughter could hear her. "Don't listen to Madame Arnaud, Violette. She doesn't know what she's saying. If they do come here, I don't want to see you near them, do you hear me?"

"Yes, *Maman*." Violette was shrewd enough for her age to agree with everything her mother said, which nevertheless didn't stop her from doing whatever she pleased behind the unsuspecting Kamille's back.

"Young boys," Kamille kept muttering as she panted

imperceptibly from her heavy load, feeling how her gentle fingers were gradually growing numb. "Those young boys were bombing us relentlessly for the past few weeks, but she's forgotten about that already. If they were as innocent as she says—"

Kamille gasped, not able to finish her sentence as she stopped in her tracks, startled and pale, with terror in her wide-open eyes. The soldier who she had run into as she turned a corner, smiled at her widely and offered his sincerest apologies in very good French. Violette kept turning her head from the soldier to her mother in utter excitement as Kamille tried to comprehend where the soldier had come from and what his intentions were.

Not getting any reaction from the apparently petrified woman, the German tilted his head slightly and asked with concern in his voice, "Did I hurt you, Madame?"

"No." Kamille found her voice at last, but apart from that one word couldn't bring herself to say anything else.

"*Gott im Himmel,* your bags, Madame!" he exclaimed, only now noticing Kamille's shaking hands and probably deciding that they shook because of the weight she carried and not due to her utmost terror, which covered her back with perspiration under her dark woolen suit. "Allow me to help you. You mustn't exert yourself like that!"

Ignoring her weak protests, the soldier, in his field gray uniform, shouted something to his comrades who were smoking next to their military car, which had probably arrived while Kamille was busy talking to the baker's widow, and proceeded across the street in his long, resolute strides. Kamille and Violette trailed behind him with Kamille's arm draped tightly around her daughter's shoulders.

"Where to, Madame?"

Little Violette, breaking all the rules of not only not talking to strangers but to the Germans even more so, chimed out their address in a heartbeat, receiving her mother's disdainful glare and pursed lips soon after.

"He doesn't look scary," the girl whispered in her defense, as Kamille's grip on her shoulder became tighter.

As if in confirmation of her words, the German turned around and beamed at the girl, giving her a little wink. He was indeed very young, barely twenty years old, Kamille thought. That, however, didn't change the fact that he was an enemy, and a feared enemy as it had recently been proven. Only after the soldier lowered the bags on the front porch of Kamille's house, clicked his heels, bowed respectfully and left, did she release the breath that she hadn't realized she'd been holding the entire time.

MARCEL SHIFTED in his seat uncomfortably. Philippe, a giant of a man, towered over his stooped frame, boring his coal black eyes into Marcel for a good several minutes. Marcel caught himself thinking (heavens only knew why such thoughts even appeared in his mind!) that the infamous communist – the first one he had seen in person – reminded him of Ernest Hemingway; only a young version, without a mustache, but with the same outstanding temperament. While all Marcel hoped for was to just secure some temporary papers so he could go back to Paris without arousing German suspicion, Philippe presented him with an almost third-degree interrogation, demanding answers to questions which Marcel had never even considered.

"Why did you join the army in the first place, boy?"

Why did he just call him a boy, Marcel wondered, when they were of the same age? Despite the hard, piercing glare, stubborn, chiseled jaw and interrogatory posture, Philippe was hardly older than twenty-five. However, the communist's power of intimidation could no doubt match that of a whole battalion of Germans, Marcel caught himself thinking again.

"I was conscripted..." he responded somewhat apologetically and felt the heat color his cheeks for some unexplainable reason as if the whole war was his fault.

"I was conscripted, too. It doesn't mean that I put on my smartest suit and went marching to certain death just because our rotten, capitalist government told me so," Philippe concluded sternly.

Marcel lowered his hazel eyes, feeling even more embarrassed. Philippe spoke with a soft, but powerful and magnetic voice, so that Marcel found it difficult not to fall under its hypnotic influence.

"Do you know who started this war, boy?"

Marcel lifted his head towards his interrogator, somewhat surprised. "The Germans?"

The snort which Philippe offered instead of a verbal reply clearly indicated that the communist found such a response quite ridiculous.

"The profiteers, boy. The profiteers, who right after the Great War started stuffing their pockets with everything they could get their hands on. You are far too young to remember the war, I suppose?"

"I'm twenty," he replied quietly, lowering his gaze again.

"That's what I thought. I grew up during the Great War, and I very well remember how we hardly survived the last two winters here on the farm, my parents and I, with no coal to fuel the stove, with all the livestock long gone, with threadbare clothes on our back. My older brother was killed in the war, my little brother and my little sister caught scarlet fever and died, because we had no means to take them to the city in time, and no doctor agreed to come to our farm in the middle of winter. But do you know which part about all this fascinates me the most? How our lot forgot our sufferings as soon as the armistice had been signed, and jumped on the opportunity to live high at any possible expense. And what did our government do? Not only supported such ideas but, more than that, decided that after the war they were entitled to the biggest piece of the pie and took whatever was left of Germany before the Allies could grab the rest of it. No wonder a blood-thirsty dictator was born out of it. I would have been quite mad at us if I were in that fellow Adolf's place, too. And all this," he made a gesture around them, "all this war, the new sufferings, the new occupation is solely due to our greed. If our government listened to our Party, if they supported our comrades in Germany like our leaders advised them to, if they treated them like brothers, all this could have been avoided. Communism would have won in Germany, and there wouldn't be any more wars between us. But no. We had to be greedy, and look where it led us. So, my question remains: why did you go fighting for this capitalist regime which is the very reason why this bloody, cursed war broke out?"

"I went to fight for France, not for the regime." Marcel

took on a defensive tone, visibly offended by Philippe's words.

"Until France becomes a communist state, you will always fight for the regime first, boy." Philippe finally moved the chair and sat across the table from Marcel, interlacing his long fingers. Marcel noticed how large his hands were, and yet much more graceful that he would have expected from a farmer. "What do you know about the main postulates of Marx and Engels?"

"Not much, I'm afraid." Marcel cursed himself once again as he detected bashful notes slipping into his barely audible whisper. The man who was sitting across from him had such a strong presence about him that Marcel couldn't help feeling timid and inadequate under his confident, powerful gaze. "I'm a history student, and I know more about politics of Ancient Rome than about current events in the country..."

Another snort followed, this time more amused than condescending.

"Do you want to go to a meeting with me tonight? My comrades and I are gathering in the forest nearby. There's a hunter's lodge there which is almost impossible to find unless you know exactly where you're going. You're not in a rush, as I understand?"

Marcel shook his head. What rush could Philippe possibly be talking about when Marcel had no place to go, and if Philippe refused to help him he would find himself alone and stranded again with only one option: head back to Paris, only to be caught by Germans at the first checkpoint.

"It's all decided then. You'll go with me and listen to what we're planning on doing. And if after that you find that our ideas don't suit your taste, I'll send you on your way with my deceased brother's papers. Putting the picture from your current military papers into his passport would be a five minute matter. Agreed?"

Marcel nodded eagerly, for the first time in a long time, a light, hopeful smile playing on his lips.

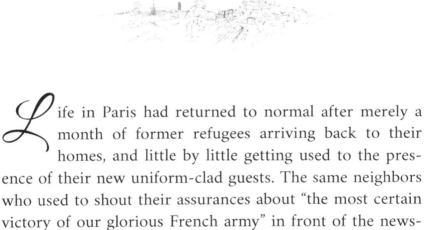

3

*L*ife in Paris had returned to normal after merely a
month of former refugees arriving back to their
homes, and little by little getting used to the presence of their new uniform-clad guests. The same neighbors
who used to shout their assurances about "the most certain
victory of our glorious French army" in front of the news-
stand near Giselle's favorite café just a few weeks ago had
returned to their respective apartments, taken the boards off
the windows and replied to all of Giselle's taunts about "the
glorious French army's success" by pursing their lips.

Giselle bit her tongue quite a few times, silently chiding
herself for her sarcasm directed towards her fellow French
folk, but couldn't help making more scornful remarks to yet
another matron's statement (expressed in a hushed tone of
course, so that "those gentlemen" wouldn't overhear them by
chance) that the loss of the army was most certainly not due
to the fact that their soldiers were simply unprepared, but

due to the government's failure to provide weapons, machinery, decent commanding officers, or diplomacy on a high scale. In the course of the several weeks after the beginning of the occupation, Giselle heard the most ridiculous excuses that the mothers – and it was mostly mothers who expressed them – brought up in order to justify their sons' shortcomings in the field, which had resulted in this very occupation.

"I know my Gaston; he would singlehandedly fight off those *Boches!* It's because they had no ammunition that their battalion had to give themselves up – he wrote to me describing it all in detail."

"It was not even that!" Another one would puff her rouged cheeks and wave the other woman off. "Their commanders were no good; ordered them to surrender as soon as they saw the *Boches* marching towards the town. My Gerome yearned to fight; they wouldn't let him!"

"It all would have been well avoided if only our President knew anything about diplomacy. There wouldn't be any war at all if he only knew how to peacefully arrange the matters to everyone's liking," the third one would state.

Giselle watched these sorts of debates almost daily under the striped green awning of Monsieur Richard's café, sipping her mocha and hiding her face from the sun. However, she could never keep quiet for too long and soon started amusing herself with word-fencing with women.

"And the idea that our army was simply too lazy and overfed after the former victory in the Great War never crossed your minds, I suppose?" she would murmur with a sly grin, but loudly enough for the women to immediately turn their heads to the insolent renegade, gasping all at once as if she had just offended each and every one of them personally.

"Aren't you ashamed of saying such things?!" they would start shouting indignantly. "Our sons, fighting there for our freedom and honor, losing their lives at those brutes' hands—"

"Shhh, or those 'brutes' will overhear you and kill you too, the savages that they are." Giselle would snicker and motion her blonde head towards the Germans sitting nearby and chatting amicably among themselves while enjoying the sun and their freshly-brewed coffee, for which Monsieur Richard charged them three times more than his fellow Frenchmen, according to the unspoken law that most of the vendors had adopted. "The sad truth, which I'm quite sure you don't want to admit to yourselves because it is a rather bitter pill to swallow – don't get me wrong, I agree whole-heartedly with you on this matter – the sad truth is that we dropped our guard a little too soon and falsely assumed that if we were lucky enough to beat our wurst-loving neighbors with the help of the Tommies and the Yanks, they wouldn't come back with a vengeance. More than that, not only had we decided to casually chop quite a big strip off their lands without any regard to their sentiments on this account, we also came up with a brilliant idea to slam them with the reparations, which, as a result, propelled their inflation to a point where the sun doesn't shine. So here we are, sitting pretty on all that money, sharing investments with the Yanks who also slammed them with the same reparations, drowning in caviar and champagne after shaking hands over yet another successful business deal. Buying yachts and summer houses in the Riviera, throwing all that money at each other in the casinos at night, signing more business deals with the Yanks during the day – and all the while our above mentioned wurst-loving neighbors watching us and getting a little upset on account of such arrangements. You see where I'm heading with this yet? And so, they're getting more and more upset, we're getting more and more careless and fat, until one day they finally slam their fist on the table and say that they have had enough. We snort in response, roll our eyes and tell the Tommy Prime Minister to deal with them. He waves his little paper in the air, everyone's patting themselves on the back about how we 'solved the conflict without a single shot fired,' and return to our deal signings and champagne drinking. And then one day during the lunch break we suddenly see their tanks on our border, and all of our wonderful boys who have been enjoying themselves these past twenty years, while our wurst-loving neighbors were actually preparing for war, try to stop them. I sincerely can't quite take it in, ladies, why exactly you're so surprised about the outcome? I personally would have been surprised if we did fight them off!"

"If you had somebody in the army, my dear, you wouldn't be saying such unpatriotic things!"

"Oh, but I do have someone in the army. My little brother Marcel." Giselle grinned at the women's surprised faces and added, "and knowing him I had actually thought of writing to his superiors asking them not to give him a weapon of any kind because that clueless brat would only end up shooting himself in the leg. I highly doubt that the rest of our 'brave boys,' without any kind of army training, differed from him so much. So, stop gossiping about why this happened, and accept the situation already. They're here, and judging by how comfortable they're acting, they're here to stay for quite a while. I heard they will even return all of our brave boys back to France soon, so get on with your lives instead of indulging in empty discussions that won't change anything anyway."

The women eyed her silently until one of them murmured before turning away and leaving, "It's because of people like you that we lost."

Giselle only laughed in response, shamelessly throwing her head backward under the Germans' inquiring glances, and lifted her cup in the air, sending a charming smile in Monsieur Richard's direction.

"One more and I'll head home, my friend. I think I have enough material to write about for today."

―――――

THE SUN WAS HEADING LEISURELY towards the horizon, making Giselle squint from the blinding light that reflected off the silver roofs. She lifted Coco off her lap, who growled her discontent at her slumber being disrupted, and padded to the window to drop the heavy, light-blocking drapes which she had used during the recent air-raids. The air-raids had stopped weeks ago, but Giselle opted to keep the shades so she could use them to block the sun from peeking directly into her room and bothering her while she was trying to write.

Sun-warmed wooden floors creaked mildly under her bare feet while she proceeded to turn on the lights in her spacious living room, in the corner of which she preferred to work. Even though Giselle had quite a grand study with extravagantly designed panels and a redwood desk that would garner any writer's envy, she rarely – if ever – paid the room a visit, using it mostly as a library. The living room with its French windows adorned by the white chiffon drapes, always brightly lit and commodious as Giselle didn't want to overburden it with furniture and kept it quite minimalistic, breathed the inspiration into her as soon as she moved her padded, light-beige chair to the table and put the first sheet of paper into the typing machine.

Even the table at which she worked was purchased for sharing a cup of coffee with a friend on a lazy afternoon; however, as soon as Giselle gave up on her mahogany desk, finding both the study and the innocent piece of furniture too dark and depressing for work, she moved her typing machine to the living room without thinking twice. The second light-beige chair was moved to the wall, and another table was purchased for drinking coffee and receiving guests, who had by now learned not to approach the other "working" table. Giselle had a habit of organizing her manuscripts in a certain way, separating each chapter by placing them in different stacks, and was known for immediately throwing fits if someone only touched a single sheet of paper. She didn't take too kindly to anyone reading her unfinished manuscripts either, and people who proved themselves to be too nosy for Giselle's taste were banned from entering her apartment for life. However, Giselle could afford to be picky about her acquaintances; as soon as she had bargained a deal for a hundred thousand francs for her latest novel two years ago the flow of people who were more than eager to befriend her had multiplied in a geometrical progression, much to her displeasure: Giselle wasn't quite a people person.

A loud knock on the door made her grunt in annoyance, as she detested being interrupted in the middle of work more than anything in the world. Trying to pacify Coco, who had burst into loud barking just as she always did at the sign of any "intruder," Giselle went to open the door while grumbling, "I know poppet, I know. I hate unannounced guests as much as you do, believe me. That's why I prefer your company to theirs any day of the week, and twice on Sunday."

Holding the dog under her arm, Giselle unlocked the door and lifted her eyes in surprise at the young German on the other side, who clicked his heels sharply and saluted her with such fervor as if he thought she were an army general. Giselle couldn't help but chortle in amusement.

"How can I be of service, young man?"

He was indeed very young, barely twenty years old, with eager blue eyes and light coloring.

"SS Unterscharführer Otto Reisinger, at your service, Madame." He clicked his heels once again and winced slightly at the loud disapproving barking from Coco, who made it difficult for him to be heard. "Allow me to come in?"

"Come in *here*? Are you a little lost in our beautiful city?" She motioned her head toward the suitcases near his immaculately polished boots. "I regret to inform you, but it's a private residence, not a hotel. Neither do I remember placing an advertisement in a paper about renting a room."

He nodded a little embarrassingly, as if having forgotten something, and quickly extracted a folded piece of paper from his pocket which he handed to Giselle with a slight bow, all the while eyeing the dog suspiciously. Coco bared her little teeth at the unexpected guest, clearly indicating that she meant business protecting her territory. The German clasped his hands behind his back wisely, away from the snapping animal, right after handing the paper to her owner.

"What is this supposed to mean?" Giselle's mischievous smile quickly transformed into a deep scowl as she studied the paper. "Order to provide a German officer with lodgings? You have *got* to be kidding me!"

"I'm afraid no, Madame." The young German lowered his eyes apologetically as a slight blush colored his clean-shaven cheeks, obviously in response to Giselle's reaction. "It's a high order from the *Wehrmacht* command which affects all French citizens, prescribing them to provide lodgings and necessary conditions for the *Wehrmacht* and *Waffen-SS* officers to fulfill their duties to the full extent—"

Giselle rather rudely interrupted his obviously very well-rehearsed speech by raising her hand in the air.

"Please, don't bore me with your high orders and unnecessary details. Even though I understand your army's need to accommodate your commanding staff in private residences, I simply *cannot* provide you with one for one simple reason: I live in the apartment which only has one bedroom; the second one was remodeled into a study by the owner a long time ago, before I even started renting it from him. Your people, who are in charge of providing officers with lodgings, must have had an old plan of the building and made a mistake assuming that there was another room – I assure you, there isn't. You can go and look for yourself, and then please go and find yourself something more suitable."

The German cleared his throat, looking even more embarrassed.

"I'm afraid there was no mistakes made, Madame. The room is not for me. The matter of the fact is that my commanding officer Herr Sturmbannführer put a special request in for this particular apartment as his future living quarters, for it is the only one which is occupied by a single tenant and which has such a magnificent view of the *Champs-Élysées* from the top floor." The German smiled bashfully for the first time. "He's rather fond of your Parisian architecture, I might add."

"Good for him, but where do you suggest I put him? On the sofa in the living room or on the floor? Or would your Herr Sturmbannführer rather sleep in my bed?" Giselle finished sarcastically, arching her brow.

"Even though I do appreciate the offer, that won't be necessary, Madame." A deep voice with a distinctive accent sounded from the stairs.

Giselle craned her neck to observe the tall, broad-shouldered man entering the staircase. Accompanied by Coco's incessant barking, his orderly saluted him sharply and froze at attention, while Giselle assessed the newly appeared man, looking rather sour. He was quite tall, almost a head taller than his adjutant (Giselle made her own assumptions concerning the young man's rank and position), and was somewhat somber looking. Or maybe it was because he had uncharacteristically dark features for a German: raven hair, almost black eyes which, together with slightly hollow cheekbones which were a little too sharply defined and a chiseled jaw, made him resemble an ancient Roman statue rather than that typical wheat-headed German which smiled out from multiple propaganda posters which had recently plastered the streets and every wall in Paris.

The newcomer also saluted Giselle, threw a glare at Coco who got strangely quiet under his stern look and introduced himself.

"SS Sturmbannführer Karl Wünsche at your service, Madame. And please, do not be concerned about my sleeping arrangements: I have already ordered my people to assemble a bed for me in your living room. The room is rather spacious as I could conclude from the plans, and I don't believe I would be of any inconvenience to you there."

With those words, he bowed slightly and stood still, calmly waiting for Giselle to let him inside. Realizing that he was going nowhere, she opened her door wider and gestured him inside in an exaggerated manner.

"Make yourselves at home," she muttered, as Otto walked past her with his superior's suitcases, before she slammed the door, purposely startling the young German fellow.

KAMILLE WRUNG her hands while observing how furiously Madame Blanchard was pulling all the linen out of the chestnut armoire and throwing it into open suitcases. Her maid, a frail young woman named Jeanine, with mousy brown hair and an invariably downcast gaze, patiently waited for her mistress to finish sorting out the sheets and moved swiftly away from her path whenever Madame Blanchard stormed to the other corner to yank more towels and table cloths out of the closet.

"Madame, I beg you, leave at least something—"

Kamille's faint objection only sent the already infuriated matriarch into an even bigger frenzy.

"What is it?!" Fists butting her wide hips and thin lips pinched into a contemptuous line, Madame Blanchard's bleak blue eyes shone with anger at her daughter-in-law. "You dare ask me to leave something?! Have you completely gone off your head? Or have you no shame left at all to insult me in such a manner? For whom are you asking me to leave the sheets – my sheets, finest Egyptian cotton – which I was generous enough to present them to you on your wedding because your parents had no dowry for their daughter; for whom, I ask you, do you want them? For one of those cursed *Boches*! I'll rather die than allow such an atrocity to happen – to let one of their kind sleep on the sheets on which my Charles was supposed to rest his head, God rest his soul! If you loved your late husband one bit or at least had some respect for his memory, you wouldn't dare even think of such a request! What if that very officer who they send to lodge with you was the one who killed our poor Charlie? Eh? Well, why are you silent now? Has that idea even occurred to you? Or do you, in fact, look forward to meeting your new tenant? How convenient it is, when the ground is still wet on your husband's grave, and you already turn to some *Boche*, like the shameless wenches who ogle at them through the windows and even dare to speak and laugh with them, as if it's not their fathers, brothers and husbands that are in their captivity now!"

Kamille did her best to blink away the hot tears clouding her vision which blurred Madame Blanchard's distorted lines, and spoke through the shame coloring her cheeks with a rosy blush. "Pardon me, Madame. I would never disrespect

Charles's memory in any way. I merely fear that the officer
who they're sending our way will get angry when I'm not
able to provide him with at least the basic needs such as
sheets and towels…"

"Nobody invited them here." Madame Blanchard softened her tone a little, observing her daughter-in-law's
unnerved state with a certain degree of satisfaction. "Let him
get his own sheets and towels."

Having stated her verdict, the black-clad woman turned
on her heels and marched out of the room, Jeanine barely
catching up with her, weighed down with two bursting suitcases. Kamille was more than assured that her mother-in-
law would order to commandeer the furniture as well if she
only had the place to put it in her house.

Kamille helped Jeanine bring one of the suitcases down
and, minding the steps in front of her so as not to lose her
grip of the heavy burden or to fall, she almost ran into
Madame Blanchard, who had come to a sudden halt at the
bottom of the steps. Kamille lifted her head and couldn't
catch her gasp in time, allowing it to escape her parted lips.
He was already here, the German whose arrival she feared so
and who she prayed hadn't heard her relative's scornful
rebuke on his account. However, he seemed to be too
immersed in an amicable chat with Violette and at first failed
to even notice the small procession descending the stairs.

He stood on one knee in front of the little girl, who
seemed to be quite taken by her new guest, judging by how
willingly she showed him and another uniformed man
behind his back her favorite doll.

"Violette!" Kamille found her voice at last and called out
to the girl, more fearing her mother-in-law's reaction to

such fraternizing than the possibility of the German actually harming her.

Violette turned her head with her neat braids swinging to her mother and ran towards her, catching Kamille by her hand. The German swiftly, and rather gracefully, straightened, beamed at the women in front of him and clicked his heels, following the greeting by a salute of his gloved hand.

"Mesdames, allow me to present myself. Hauptmann Jochen Hartmann, at your service. This is my adjutant, Unteroffizier Horst Sommer. The office told us that you have enough room to accommodate us both, however if it's of any inconvenience to you, please, do tell me and I'll arrange something for him elsewhere."

Hauptmann Hartmann's flawless French and soft smile was met with dead silence. Kamille fought the urge to welcome him to her house as any hospitable mistress of the household would, but Madame Blanchard's heavy breathing made the words stick in her throat.

Madame Blanchard stood for quite some time without uttering a word, only observing the two uniform-clad men with obvious hostility. Jeanine shuffled behind her back quietly. Kamille hadn't even noticed at first that the maid was trying to pull the suitcase out of her hand. Apparently, she'd guessed her mistress's mood correctly after being in her servitude for many years: Madame Blanchard, as if snapping out of her rigid state, thrust her pointed chin forward defiantly and proceeded to the exit, completely ignoring the two men, who politely moved out of her way.

Horst made a motion to help Jeanine with the suitcases, but the officer quickly stopped him with a slight shaking of his head and a knowing glance, which was, Kamille noticed, more amused than hostile. After the two women made their way out of the house, the German closed the door behind them and turned back to Kamille breaking into soft, barely contained chuckles.

"Please, do tell me she left for good, Madame!"

Violette was the first one to break into giggles, covering her mouth with one hand and sharing a look of conspiracy with the young officer.

"I doubt she will step through this door as long as you're here, Monsieur Hartmann," Kamille replied, trying not to smile as well. "I apologize for not introducing myself properly. You see, we have just lost Charles, my husband and her son, to the war, and she's still distressed seeing the men who... well..."

"No need to explain, Madame." He rushed to reassure her that he wasn't offended in the slightest. "I understand completely. And please, accept my sincerest condolences."

Kamille nodded and touched her wedding band out of habit.

"My name is Kamille," she said when realizing that she still hadn't offered him her name. "Kamille Blanchard. And this is Violette, my daughter. I believe you've already made your acquaintance with her."

"Yes, I did have the pleasure."

Violette broke into another fit of giggles after the officer winked at her.

"I have a niece about her age," Hauptmann Hartmann explained to Kamille. "Your daughter will remind me of the home which I haven't seen in far too long."

Niece, not a daughter Kamille noticed, and chastised herself at once for such unacceptable interest in his private life. What did it matter if he did have a daughter? Or a wife for that matter? He was handsome enough for any lucky girl to wed him, with his bright blue eyes and blond hair, neatly combed to one side and smoothed with brilliantine. He had removed his gloves, and Kamille threw a quick side glance at his hands. There were no rings on his fingers that had neatly manicured nails.

"Welcome to Paris, Monsieur Hartmann."

"Please, call me Jochen, Madame Kamille."

Only after showing him his room and closing the door leaving the two men to sort out their clothes did Kamille lean against it and allowed a smile play on her lips, tasting the new name in an inaudible whisper.

"Jochen."

4

*M*arcel sat motionless in the furthest corner of the small hunters' lodge so as not to attract any unwanted attention from the shouting men who had filled the cabin an hour ago, right after sunset. It was the fourth meeting he had attended, and yet he still felt rather awkward and out of place amongst the men with eyes which burned with determination. Most of them were of his age or even younger but had much more spirit and fearlessness in them than a sheltered "city boy," as they had mockingly baptized him at the first meeting. Maybe they were right in a sense, when alleging that life on a farm made them into adults much sooner than those who enjoyed the "lavishness of capitalistic civilization" in Paris – the words had also been spoken with obvious contempt.

Had he not made the acquaintance of these farmers, to whom Marxist ideas were much closer to their heart than to those residing in the city, Marcel probably would not have even considered what they had to offer. And in their eyes, it was nothing less but the salvation of their beloved France: from the *Boches*, from the rotten Vichy government imposed on the country by the same *Boches*, and the complete denunciation of capitalism and all the evil that it had brought with it.

"We must resist not only the *Boches* but the system itself," Philippe stated sternly during the very first meeting that he took Marcel to.

Not counting himself and Philippe, there were four other men gathered around a candle in a hunter's lodge, hidden deep inside the forest, its gray planks covered in strings of ivy, making it almost invisible to the eye until one stood right in front of it. Marcel caught himself thinking that if Philippe had left him there alone, he would never find his way back to the farm even if his life depended on it.

The dim night light provided by the single candle (for according to Philippe's directives flashlights and lanterns were strictly prohibited to avoid detection and capture) threw intricate shadows on the young partisans' faces. From the start, Marcel decided not to delude himself as to what they were: not only communists, but very real partisans, who expressed ideas which Marcel had found not only frightening but downright dangerous at first. But either it was due to Philippe's inspiring speeches and the audacious suggestions that followed them, or to their enthusiasm to stand up for what was right, but by the end of the first meeting Marcel had firmly decided to join their small group. However, as it is well known, an idea and a deed are two quite different things, and, therefore, Marcel still tried to find his voice in the ocean of others, much more intrepid than he had ever dreamed of being.

"The Vichy government is as much an enemy to us and to the people of France as the ones who imposed it," Philippe continued, as the other four men listened to him attentively. By now Marcel had already learned that the fifth one was always sent outside to stand on guard. "The so-called 'collaboration' is nothing but a deception, a lie fed to the regular citizens by Maréchal Pétain, who will do anything to be in good graces of his new German masters. The first thing they did was to shut up our press and appoint their mouthpieces, who speak in favor of collaboration, to the top positions. Listen to the radio, read a newspaper! They got rid of any free-thinking journalist, who was reporting the truth according to his conscience, and put their puppets in their place, which do the only thing they know: praise the new order and the Maréchal! Next thing they'll do is replace all the politicians and judges who still try to resist them. And when that happens, no one will be left in France to stand up for the truth. No one, except for us. The people. There are few of us as of now, but the tighter the noose becomes on the nation's throat, the more likeminded people, people just like us, will find their way to us. And together we will rise. And together we will march. They thought they had beat us. No, comrades. I say the war has just begun. And we, the people, will be the ones to win it. *Vive la France! Vive la Résistance!*"

"*Vive la Résistance*," Marcel whispered excitedly, for the first time in his life overcome with the feeling of belonging; belonging to a cause that was bigger than his life, belonging to a group of daredevils who refused to conform and submit, belonging to this time and place, set for him by destiny itself.

"I fixed you the papers," Philippe announced noncha-lantly as they made their way back to his parents' farm. The giant was treading confidently through the pitch-black forest in the moonless night while Marcel tried his best not to lose sight (or, more rightly, the sound) of him, as he stum-bled and tripped over unearthed tree roots.

"I won't be needing them," Marcel replied, out of breath after trying to catch up with his comrade's long strides. "I'm staying with you, aren't I?"

"Of course, you are. I wouldn't allow you to get to know us and our hideouts and ways for the whole month if you weren't," Philippe stated calmly. "But you'll still need them in case the *Boches* show up. Or if some business comes up in Paris. After all, you're the only one of us who knows the city fairly well and won't raise any suspicion, unlike us uncouth farm fellows."

Marcel for some reason imagined a teasing smirk tugging a corner of Philippe's mouth upwards as he said it. They all taunted him about his "refined upbringing" as they called it, even though he tried (each time in vain) to persuade them that he was just an ordinary student from an average middle-class family.

"If you need someone refined for your 'business,' you should seek my sister, not me." Marcel chuckled, recalling Giselle's remark that she had once thrown in response to their father, after he had all but refused to cover an opening of a new hotel near the *Champs-Élysées* because "it reeked of snooty, stuck-up people": *I'll cover it for you, Papa. I happen to like snooty, stuck-up people.* She was barely twenty-one then, and that one phrase, which soon defined her whole lifestyle, somehow stuck in Marcel's mind. "If anyone knows high-class society, it's her."

"Why, is she a big fish, your sister?" Philippe inquired with interest.

"In certain circles," Marcel replied evasively, but then, as a conceited little worm of pride at Giselle's social standing and achievements started to gnaw him more and more, as if fed by Philippe's silence, he revealed the truth at last. "My sister is Giselle Legrand."

"Giselle Legrand? The infamous Mademoiselle Legrand?"

At the mention of such an unexpected attribute next to her name, Marcel scowled involuntarily, even though Philippe, of course, couldn't possibly see his reaction.

"Why infamous?"

"Because you call someone *famous* when they have achieved something outstanding. And if that someone caught the whiff of easy money, wrote a couple of novels which were 'in' at the wave of the new life, and exploits the public just like the politicians and the rest of the 'selling' press and editors which she is friends with, that someone surely is *infamous,* boy," Philippe finished ruthlessly. "I'm sorry if it sounded rude, but it is what it is."

"You don't know her," Marcel muttered defensively, sudden heat flushing his face.

"I know of people like her. I understand that she's your sister, and you feel compelled to protect her, but answer me this: if she were a good person, a really decent person who you knew would have helped you, wouldn't you be on your way to Paris a long time ago? I offered to fix your papers if you decided not to stay here with us right away."

Marcel followed Philippe in stubborn silence for quite

some time, until he sniffled quietly and spoke at last. "She grew up in poverty, Philippe. Kamille – that's my other sister – and me, not so much. Kamille was too little to remember the war, and I was born after it. But Giselle, she still remembers it all: the hunger, cold, desperation... Just like you do. And you decided to fight for it to never happen again, only you joined the Communist Party, and she decided to follow a capitalist route and become as rich as she possibly could, no matter the price. You're right, she's not a good person. She clawed and bit her way into that world, with the same determination with which you're trying to transform your world. You both have the same goal, not to get caught in the past again, only you both chose entirely different paths to that goal. She's cynical and practical, she's your typical profiteer and a capitalist, but she has as much right to be one as you do to be a communist. She wouldn't like you and your way either if I told her about you. So even if you don't like her, I ask you to at least respect her, just like she would respect you."

Philippe snorted softly in response and caught Marcel midair after the latter lost his footing once again. "And that's where you're wrong, boy. Capitalists don't respect anyone or anything."

"Do Communists?" Marcel jerked his shoulder irritably, shaking Philippe's hand off. "What was with the execution of the Romanovs' royal family then? And with the destruction of the Winter Palace? And the recent collaboration with the Nazis?"

The two men faced each other, the top of Marcel's head barely reaching Philippe's chin. With eyes glistening in the dark as if asserting each other once again, Philippe with newfound curiosity and Marcel with newfound defiance, they silently stood their ground, each refusing to look away first. Finally, Marcel noticed a shadow of a grin on the communist's face.

"You have spunk in you, Marcel. I like it. You'll make a good fighter." A slap on the shoulder followed the unexpected compliment, and Marcel blinked a few times, wondering if Philippe had indeed just called him by his name, and not *boy* as he usually did. "I cannot promise that I'll respect your sister, but I surely will respect you. Now, hurry; no one needs to see us wandering around the village after the curfew."

As they made their way through the forest, Marcel couldn't understand the reason for a wide grin playing on his face, but some inward satisfaction made him square his shoulders more. Even Philippe didn't seem to frighten him that much anymore.

GISELLE THREW a glare in the direction of her former study once again, for the hundredth time that morning as it seemed. The study was now occupied by Sturmbannführer Wünsche, who turned it into its personal "headquarters" as soon as he finished his inspection of Giselle's apartment on the first day of his arrival.

"You don't use it, do you?" he inquired, turning on his heels towards the mistress of the household, who was standing in the doors with her arms crossed over her chest.

"You're observant."

"I have to be, Mademoiselle. I work for the *Staatspolizei*."

"I appreciate you warning me in advance. I guess it means that I'll have to ask the Marxists who I'm currently hiding in one of my closets to look for different living arrangements."

The German studied Giselle with his black eyes for quite some time, before finally giving way to a grin.

"In this case I'll tell Otto to move all of my documentation here if you're not using it," Karl Wünsche finally said, ignoring Giselle's previous ironic remark. "Also, I'll have to put a lock on the door to make sure that all the files inside are secure from any intruders while I'm away."

"Intruders meaning me?" Giselle arched her brow.

"Intruders meaning any kind of unauthorized person who might compromise the secrecy of the documentation, entrusted to me by the State," followed the impassive reply.

"I see. Well, I'll free one of the bookcases of all the Communist propaganda that I've been collecting for years, so you have some space to put your highly secret documentation there."

Sturmbannführer Wünsche snorted softly, exiting the study. "I've heard rumors that French women were impossible. They turn out to be true."

"You haven't seen anything yet," Giselle promised confidently, following him out of the study.

It turned out that German men were equally impossible, or at least it was impossible to work with one living under the same roof with her. The monotone staccato of Otto's typing machine following Karl's dictation in his unemotional, even tone, the metallic clanking of his boots on the hardwood floors – *as if he practiced his goose-stepping away from the carpet on purpose!* Giselle thought with a huff – and Coco's constant growling at the men in the other room made it unfeasible for

Giselle to concentrate on her writing. Even the tall clock next to the opposite wall seemed to mock her impotence with its emphatic ticking, measuring time that was wasted in vain – in drumming her fingers on the table, swallowing coffee that had long gone cold, in staring at the blank sheet of paper in her typing machine and at the thin stack of papers which consisted of the current chapter; a chapter which was supposed to be at the same level of its neighbors a few days ago. Fifteen minutes later and without a single word written, Giselle, at last, lost her patience and moved her chair angrily, getting up and headed in a resolute step towards the study, in which her new tenant was working with his adjutant. She yanked the door open without even considering knocking first and stood in the doorframe, her demeanor anything but amicable.

"I can't work like this!" Giselle shouted, startling the unsuspecting Otto who stopped his typing at once.

Karl Wünsche turned around and lifted his dark brows, expressing either mild surprise or annoyance at such an insolent intrusion.

"I can't work like this," Giselle repeated with the same firmness in her voice, which echoed from the walls in sudden silence. "When your office, or whoever it was, sent you here, they told me that you'd just be living here. Living, not working. Living as in going to work in the morning, to your own office or wherever it is that you're supposed to work from and coming back in the evening to sleep. That's all. End of story. I didn't agree to house a Gestapo headquarters in my apartment, *Mein Herr*. I have work to do, and I can't because *you* are doing *yours*. Now, I don't think it's quite fair. Do you?"

Her vexation and deep scowl seem to produce quite a different effect than the one Giselle was aiming at. Instead of offering her his apologies or even trying to argue with her as she had expected, Sturmbannführer Wünsche scrutinized the woman in front of him for a long moment before bursting out into unexpected laughter.

"You find it amusing?" Giselle snapped, even more insulted.

"Quite." The German approached her, took her by the elbow delicately but with a certain firmness, turning her away from the study. "Take your purse and your hat. Let's go."

"Go where?" Giselle asked, with suspicion creasing her brow as she wormed her arm out of his grip. Surprisingly, the Sturmbannführer released her at once.

"That will be all for today, Otto," he informed his adjutant over his shoulder while picking up his uniform cap and gloves from the mail table in the hallway. Seeing that Giselle didn't move from her spot, he picked up her straw hat and motioned his head towards the exit. "Come, I said."

"You didn't say where."

"You told me yourself that you can't work like this. So, if you can't work, and most likely you won't let me work either, we're going to have some lunch instead."

"You're inviting me to lunch?"

The skeptical look on Giselle's face seemed to amuse the German even more.

"Why? You expected me to take you to the Gestapo head-quarters and shoot you there for disrupting my work? Of course not, otherwise you wouldn't burst into my office like that. Although it baffles me a little, your reaction to my invitation."

"Well, I wouldn't call it an invitation, when someone orders you out in the manner that you just did." Giselle still had her arms crossed, but her grin was getting wider and wider, mirroring the one on her uniformed tenant's face.

He lowered his head, concealing a chortle, straightened up, fixed his jacket and clicked his heels. "I beg you to accept my sincerest apologies for my rudeness. Would you do me the honor of accepting my invitation to lunch, Mademoiselle?"

Giselle faked hesitance, moving her shoulder as if pondering her reply. "I don't even know... I'm not dressed to go out."

"You can change if you like, but I think you already look absolutely lovely." His gaze slid over Giselle's bright blue dress accented with a lace collar and a thin belt made of the same material.

She knew that she did. For several years now Giselle didn't have a single item in her closet that she would be ashamed to wear in public or receive guests in. Before Karl's arrival, she would wear silk slips and matching robes at home but she had to abandon that practice in view of her new lodger's presence in the apartment. Now she adopted a habit of dressing up and curling her hair every morning before leaving her bedroom.

"Well, I suppose we can share a meal if you insist." Giselle finally stopped her fake resisting and took her hat out of the smiling man's hands, placing it sideways on her platinum locks in a trained gesture, without even glancing in the mirror.

As they were stepping through the door, which Karl gallantly held for her, Giselle was grateful for the hat shielding the victorious smirk in her green cat-like eyes from the German. He might be the most feared man among his own kind, but she knew all too well that first and foremost he was only a man, and men she knew how to handle, German or not.

It turned out that Karl was an interesting conversationalist when put in a relaxing atmosphere and offered a bottle of famous French wine, Giselle noticed, while completely ignoring the astounded looks of matrons that passed the open café by; the same matrons with which she used to exchange her rather unconventional views on the French army and the situation in the country in general. Now, shamelessly enjoying lunch with one of the high-ranking uniformed occupants, her chances for redemption as a "good, conscientious citizen" were completely and utterly destroyed. Yet, being the careless creature that she was, Giselle only shrugged off the looks and whispers and turned all of her attention to the representative of the new species that she had never encountered before and who she was so curious about – one of France's "wurst-loving neighbors."

As the day progressed and coffee was finished, Giselle offered her guest a tour around the area, during which he indeed proved his knowledge of French architecture and history, even though he elaborated about them in a completely impassionate tone. Despite this last fact, Giselle was still rather impressed with his, if not passion for French culture (there was obviously no passion judging by his demeanor), but at least his vast academic knowledge. It even made her warm up to the somber-looking man a little, even though "warm up" was not the term that she fancied. Men were simply one of the pleasures of life for her and she used them as such, without any sentimental feelings attached. Accordingly, Giselle kept throwing evaluating looks his way, taking in the impeccable posture, refined speech, enviously handsome smile (on those rare occasions when he allowed it to appear), and calculated all the pros and cons of entering a slightly different sort of a relationship with the German than a hostess and her tenant would ordinarily have.

"I seem to have lost you with my ramblings about the Louvre, haven't I?" Karl Wünsche's voice interrupted her musings.

"*Pardon.*" Giselle couldn't help herself and sniggered. "I was just wondering about something... However, we aren't so well acquainted that I could ask you such things."

"You've intrigued me." He stopped and slightly tilted his perfectly coiffured head to one side. "What sort of things?"

With an impish gleam dancing in her eyes, Giselle looked up at him, grinning mischievously from under her hat. "Are Germans good lovers?"

He stared at her for quite some time in stunned silence, frozen under her amused gaze, wondering if he had misunderstood what she had said.

"I'm writing a book, you see." Giselle went on to clarify, hardly containing a fit of giggles at his reaction. "And I was wondering if I should write a German character into it, you know, as a lover that my protagonist might have an affair with. But to be sure, I need to know for a fact that it would be a believable move, that she would choose him over her husband, that is. Usually I write from experience but this time I'm afraid I'm completely ignorant and have to rely on independent opinion."

Karl regarded her a little longer, while Giselle kept her most impenetrable poker face on. Finally he replied, calmly saying, "No one has complained so far."

"Point taken."

Well, if she was already going *"renegade"* on her matronly French neighbors, why not do it to the full extent, Giselle decided, with the usual ease in her mind as she circled her arm through the crook of the German's elbow. After all, she had long ago abandoned all social conventions and vowed to herself to experience life to the fullest.

The German didn't lie, as Giselle found out later that evening when the two came back to her apartment. This time she offered him a "tour" around her bedroom, and she indeed had no complaints whatsoever on his account.

5

amille moved the lock up and pushed the windows open, allowing the fragrance-filled gust of the wind into the kitchen. She lingered there a little, resting her hands on the windowsill with some potted geraniums on it, while the cool breeze gently caressed her flushed skin. Cooking in such heat was pure madness, and even the light summer dress didn't lessen her discomfort in the slightest, its thin cotton sticking to her perspiring back. It looked like she'd need another shower before she could set the table, for the thought of her guests smelling anything but the elegant scent of her jasmine soap was only adding to Kamille's anxiety.

Why did she even bother, though? Kamille sighed dejectedly and went back to the stove to check on the fish, which she was broiling in mushroom sauce in the hope that maybe *that* would pique their interest. *Hardly.* Over two weeks had passed, and neither Hauptmann Hartmann nor his adjutant Horst bothered to appreciate her culinary efforts. No matter how much time Kamille spent in the kitchen doing her utmost to impress the two men, the only response she had gotten so far was a polite smile and reassurance that there was no need to worry about them and that they had plenty of food in the officers' quarters.

"But why would you eat army food when I'm more than happy to offer you my dining room?" Kamille argued meekly with a gentle smile. "I cook for myself and Violette anyway; it really is no bother at all to make two more portions…"

Jochen only pressed her hand in a courteous, but distant manner, and explained that they didn't want to impose on her more than they did already.

"After all, the less you see us, the better it is. Don't you agree?" He finished with yet another polite smile, and left Kamille alone and on the verge of unexpected tears, not even suspecting how deeply his words had hurt her.

"Maybe I do want to see more of you," she whispered under her breath when the echo of his steps had already been replaced by an indifferent silence.

The matter was even more complicated by the fact that her new tenant constantly sent her contradictory signs which Kamille never knew how to decipher. He would rush to her aid whenever they happened to return home at the same time and immediately relieve her of the heavy bags she carried; he would help set them on the countertop and even massage her numb hands gently, muttering for the tenth time that she shouldn't hesitate to ask Horst to take her shopping; and yet, at the same time, as soon as Kamille offered him tea in gratitude for his kindness, he would start shaking his head vehemently and disappear into his room at once, as if terrified of such a prospect.

Jochen would demonstrate infinite patience when answering Violette's incessant flood of questions about the army, Germany and anything else that came into her inquisitive mind, yet he seemed embarrassed to exchange even a few words with Kamille, resorting to polite questions about her day at the most.

And just when Kamille took his detached attitude for coldness, he expressed genuine concern soon after when he found Kamille crying quietly over her favorite tortoiseshell hair clips. After searching for them for a few days she had finally admitted to herself that her mother-in-law must have taken them out of spite, together with her wedding china set and the sheets, just prior to the officers' arrival. When Kamille gathered up enough courage to call Madame Blanchard, she received a stunningly nonchalant reply: "Yes, of course I took them. Charles gave them to you as a wedding gift; it would hardly be appropriate for you to parade around in them in front of those two Boches who lodge with you now."

Jochen tried to comfort her with such sincere gentleness that Kamille allowed a tiny glimmer of hope to ignite inside of her heart. Maybe he did care after all… But then, as soon as her tears dried and a small, hopeful smile replaced them, he once again stepped away and left her to her devices, as if completing his duty and leaving everything at that.

Who was she trying to fool with her girlish fantasies about this man who was clearly not interested in her? She shouldn't have had such fantasies in the first place, because he was a German, an invader, an enemy of her country and therefore *her* enemy, and yet her heart fluttered in her chest whenever she heard the front door open and his steps, first on the marble floor and then closer, muffled by the carpet in the living room. His slight bow and his soft *"Bonjour, Madame,"* to which she always replied with an almost inaudible *"Bonjour"* and an instantly lowered gaze were the brightest moments of her lonely days. If only he didn't leave her alone with her knitting, feeling even more rejected and lonely than before.

And what was the use dressing up for him, curling her hair in the hope that he would notice that she was a woman, and not just a faceless host in whose house he happened to lodge? Kamille slammed the door of the oven in uncharacteristic irritation, fighting back bitter tears once again. Now if Giselle were in her place, it would all be different. It would be him who would be following her everywhere with the lovelorn eyes of a puppy dog, striving for her attention, just like Charles did.

Kamille shook her head in disgust at the memory of her deceased husband. He never even had the decency to hide his longing for Giselle, who, truly speaking, wouldn't give him the time of day whenever they met, but that didn't change the fact that it was her older sister whom he so obviously desired and not his own wife. And her mother-in-law had the insolence to accuse her, Kamille, of infidelity and even go so far as to doubt Violette's parentage, when her son would jump into any woman's bed given the slightest chance. Charles even went as far as taking some twisted pleasure in comparing the two sisters, an ugly sneer marring his handsome face, while he would hint at Kamille's multiple "flaws" and suggesting that she should dye her hair blonde like Giselle did, or ask for her tailor's number because whatever she, Kamille, wore, was too... prudish, yes, that was the word he used for her. A prude. A frigid prude whose place was in a monastery.

Charles was dead, but his words still gnawed at her. Maybe she should go see her sister and ask her for advice? Kamille turned the stove off and left the fish inside to roast a little, while she prepared dough for her famous layered biscuits. Against those, even Charles couldn't say a single word of disapproval, and certainly, her guests would be too tempted by the sweet aroma to decline the offer.

"Violette!" Kamille called out from the kitchen, knowing how much her daughter enjoyed making the dough and even eating bits of it when her mother couldn't see – a habit that Kamille fought without success for as long as she remembered. Not getting any reply, Kamille stood in the door and looked into the hallway. "Violette! Where are you? I need you to help me with the dough."

Even the magic word – dough – didn't seem to work, and Kamille, with a worry creasing her brow, went from room to room in search of her daughter. Having checked the living room with its musky smell of heavy, dark blue drapes that Madame Blanchard (her mother-in-law, the *real* Madame Blanchard, unlike her, *the usurper of the undeserved title*) prohibited Kamille from touching, and the matching furniture, draped in the same gloomy, depressing colors, Kamille looked into the dining room. The long, gilt-rimmed redwood table with a red tablecloth and a candleholder in the middle was undisturbed, just like the eight padded chairs, perfectly aligned and just as untouched. Kamille brushed her fingers on the intricate design on the back of the chair, turning away to leave. All this furniture, and no one to use it. Charles had always dined someplace else, rarely deigning to oblige his wife and daughter with his presence, and the guests? He had never invited any, as if ashamed of her and Violette. And now Jochen, too…

Instead of going upstairs, where Violette probably played in her room, Kamille turned to enter Hauptmann Hartmann's study, in which he usually worked on some papers in the evening. Immersed in her melancholy, Kamille didn't even notice at first that something was out of place – or rather that something was actually in a place where it shouldn't have been. Her little girl, with the tip of her pink tongue sticking out in concentration, was sitting at Hauptmann Hartmann's desk and drawing something with a pencil.

Kamille gasped in horror and pressed her hand to her chest, rushing to take the paper out of Violette's hands.

"Violette! Who allowed you to… *Oh, mon Dieu!*" Kamille's throat went dry as soon as she turned the paper and saw exactly what her daughter had been drawing on.

It was most definitely some sort of official paper written in German and stamped with a dreadful eagle stamp with a swastika.

"Do you realize what you've done?!" Kamille screamed at the petrified child, who had rarely, if ever, seen her mother in such ire. "Do you understand how important these papers are?! Who allowed you to touch anything here at all, leave alone drawing on some official military order?!"

"But..." Violette blinked several times while shifting her sight from the drawing in her mother's hands to Kamille's face and back. "But... I turned it to the other side, *Maman*. I didn't draw anything on the important side..."

Kamille pulled the girl off the chair a little too forcefully, accidentally hurting her arm in the process. Little Violette burst into loud crying at once, and Kamille felt a pang of guilt for being too harsh in her punishment. She never hit the girl apart from very superficial spanking when occasion called for it and knew deep inside that if she hadn't been so upset about Jochen's indifference and the painful memories of Charles's treatment, she wouldn't have taken it out on the innocent child. And now, not only would he be indifferent, but angry on top of it for her being a bad mother and not paying attention to her daughter when she should have.

"You ruined it!" Kamille shouted once again, against her better judgment, almost crying herself. "You ruined everything!"

"Madame?"

Startled, Kamille turned to the door, in which Jochen stood, observing the scene in his study with his brows knitted together. Feeling like a criminal that had just been caught red-handed, she lifted the paper in her hand for him to see, struggling with words.

"She... She drew something on one of your documents. I... I was busy in the kitchen and..." Kamille's voice trailed off as Jochen approached her and took the paper out of her hand.

He inspected the official side with a disinterested look,

turned it to the side with Violette's drawing on it and grinned, much to Kamille's astonishment. Lowering himself on one knee to be on the same eye level with the crying girl, Jochen showed Violette her drawing.

"Did you draw this?"

"Yes," she whimpered, sniffling.

Jochen reached into his pocket and handed her his handkerchief. Violette looked at the offering curiously, but took it and wiped her tears at the unspoken request.

"That's a very nice drawing," the German continued in the same mild voice. "Is that you?"

Violette nodded as he pointed at a little girl figure in a dress and wearing her hair in braids, the smallest one of four people in front of the house.

"And this must be your *Maman?*" He shifted his finger to a taller figure in a dress.

Another nod followed in tow with a smile at the recognition of her drawing abilities.

"And this must be your father?" This time Jochen smiled back, pointing at the figure wearing a uniform. "Was he a soldier?"

"Yes…" Violette nodded but shook her head right after. "It's not him, though. It's you."

"Me?" He lifted his brows theatrically, however Kamille noticed that his surprise was more than genuine. No wonder, because she was rather surprised herself at such an unexpected explanation.

"Yes. See the tall boots?" Violette pressed her little finger to the figure's footwear. "Our soldiers don't have boots like yours. And there's a cross on your neck, too. See?"

"Oh, now I see."

"And this is Monsieur Horst."

"Indeed, I certainly see a resemblance."

Violette beamed at the compliment and pushed the drawing towards Jochen.

"You can keep it if you like."

"Violette," Kamille interrupted her daughter's innocent boldness. "I don't think Monsieur Jochen would be interested—"

"Of course I would love to keep it," he stated firmly, giving Kamille a pointed look. He smiled at Violette once again and nodded in gratitude, accepting her "gift." "As a matter of fact, I'll ask Monsieur Horst to find a nice frame for it so that we can hang it on this wall, right next to my desk. What do you think?"

"I think it would look lovely there," the girl agreed with enthusiasm.

"It's all settled then. And if you like drawing so much, how about we also ask Monsieur Horst to set up a little table for you over there in the corner, where you can draw while I work? I promise to provide you with clean paper and color pencils too, so you don't have to draw on these documents. They're no good for drawing anyway; the paper is too thin."

He winked at Violette and stood up, straightening his uniform. Kamille took it as a clue and gently placed a hand on her daughter's shoulder.

"Violette, why don't you go to the kitchen and wait for me there? I need you to help me with baking."

The girl nodded, beamed at Jochen once again and ran out of the study. Jochen's smile vanished at once, replaced by a stern look as he turned to face Kamille.

"Please, don't hurt the child again, and especially for such petty reasons."

She swallowed hard at the unusually harsh tone of his voice. "I didn't… I would never hurt her… I just thought that it was something important and that you would get in trouble with your superiors because of us…"

"Don't worry about me."

"Well, maybe I do worry about you!" Kamille blurted out before she realized what she was saying.

Jochen's face softened a little. They stood silently for some time before he spoke quietly, "You have a wonderful daughter, you know."

"I know." Kamille sighed, lowering her eyes, full of tears that were threatening to overflow.

"I'm sorry about her father," he said after another pause.

Kamille snorted softly. "I'm not. He never loved us. She didn't even draw him in her picture. Didn't you notice?"

"I'm sorry," he repeated.

"Me too." Kamille sighed again.

No, Violette didn't ruin anything. She, Kamille, had. She always did.

Just as she turned to walk out of the room, Jochen caught her wrist unexpectedly. He cleared his throat as if trying to conceal his embarrassment and silently handed her a box wrapped in paper, which he had extracted from his pocket.

"I doubt they can replace the original, but…" He stumbled over his words and lowered his eyes.

Kamille unwrapped the paper and opened the box, instantly gasping at its contents. Two of the most beautiful tortoiseshell hair clips lay there, the most precious present he could possibly give her, and not only because of their monetary value but simply because he didn't want her to cry over the old ones any longer.

"Oh, you shouldn't have…" Kamille pressed her hand to her heart, which fluttered ceaselessly in her chest. "They must have cost you a fortune."

"They made you smile. So, they were more than worth it."

6

"*Y*ou had to see the *Boches'* faces when they saw our French tricolor, flying from the bridge!" Pierre, a sixteen-year-old miller's son, the youngest of their group, sniggered with unabashed excitement. "They stood there with their mouths open as our *feldgendarmes* were scrambling to remove it as fast as they could!"

Marcel chuckled as well, picturing the astounded Germans, who must have been white with fury as soon as they witnessed such an audacious crime right in the heart of the conquered capital (as displaying any kind of national symbol had been strictly prohibited by the occupying forces). However, Philippe's hard glare silenced everyone in the spacious kitchen of his farmhouse.

There were only four of them, including Philippe and Marcel, sharing a Sunday lunch before setting back off to the field. The other two men were the tall, lanky Pierre with his still somewhat childish look on his healthy, young face and bright blue eyes under the tangled, wheat-colored bangs, and Philippe's father. Monsieur Bussi, a sturdy, imposing man with the same deep brown eyes as his son's, radiated the same air of unspoken authority as Philippe, and the deep-seated, profound lines of his face, hardened with weather, sun, and age, only enhanced that impression. Marcel caught himself thinking that he hardly ever heard the old farmer speak, which only asserted his previous assumption that Monsieur Bussi didn't take too well to his son's political views and his most recent partisan activities, which ran rather contrary to the Vichy policy of the collaboration.

"Why would you do something of the sort?" Philippe grumbled at last, pressing his stubborn mouth into a hard line and busying himself with smearing a thick layer of butter onto the freshly baked bread roll instead of looking at the boy.

Pierre even dropped his spoon, his enthusiasm seemingly deflated by his oldest comrade's reproachful remark.

"But... You said it yourself that we have to fight... You said that we have to show those *Boches* that we won't stand for their occupation, for the humiliation of France!" A former zeal was coming back to Pierre's voice as he spoke, until Philippe shushed him rather sharply.

"Yes, I did say that. I said that we need to organize and fight for the cause, Pierre. *Organize.*" Philippe bore his eyes into the blond young farmer, who had to lower his gaze, reddening to the roots of his hair. "What you did was moronic and reckless. What were you even thinking, going along with your brother's rabid idea? Do you not understand that you endangered not only yourselves but all of us here?"

"But no one saw us, Philippe!" Pierre protested, shaking

his head vigorously. "I swear to you! We took our father's flag that he always flew from the windmill on Bastille and Armistice Day, as he hadn't brought it to the post office as the gendarmes had demanded – neither had he given them his rifle – then we folded it, and I hid it under my shirt. We rode our bicycles at night, all the way to Paris, and left them in the field near the haystack before we entered the city. And from there we darted right to the nearest bridge, and there weren't even any *Boches* or gendarmes guarding it, imagine that! So, Jerome was holding me, and I tied the flag to the iron railings. We waited till the sunrise in someone's back-yard, and then came out together with the crowd once the *feldgendarmes* discovered our little present for their precious Nazis! Even the sub-prefect came in his car almost at once, with *Boches* on his heels! It was grand, Philippe!"

Philippe was chewing his bread slowly without inter-rupting the boy. For some reason, Marcel thought that silence to be the quiet before the storm. Monsieur Bussi snorted loudly and called for his wife to bring them more coffee. Philippe only prolonged the heavy, pregnant pause while his mother poured more steaming black liquid into their respective mugs.

"So let me get this straight," he spoke at last, concen-trating on stirring his coffee instead of looking at Pierre. Marcel realized that he did it on purpose, so as to keep his emotions under control and not to break into an angry tirade. "Not only did you ride into the city during the curfew, you didn't have any common sense to leave as soon as you committed your crime, which is punishable by imprisonment in case you didn't know. You actually waited until the *Boches* showed up together with our gendarmes, and – who knows? – maybe their infamous secret police in tow, and just like any stereotypical criminal stood in the crime scene and basked in your glory. On top of it, you flew not just any tricolor, but your father's. I don't even want to ask if you had any brains to check if that cursed tricolor was marked with your father's name sewn on it, like most of the flags are on any farm to prevent them from being stolen, because I assume that you dug it out of its hideout also at night, and therefore couldn't possibly do so."

Pierre gasped inaudibly, his blue eyes flying wide open as he had realized his mistake. Multiple mistakes, as Philippe had correctly pointed out. Marcel shifted in his seat, while the old Monsieur Bussi only snorted once again, picking up his mug.

"Grand is right," he muttered under his black mustache with obvious amusement.

"Father, please." Philippe waved his sarcastic remark away without any attempts to conceal his annoyance.

"What? Didn't I warn you that your propaganda, especially the one that you're spreading amongst the young, easily impressed minds, would get you in jail one day?" Monsieur Bussi arched his brow, giving his son a sharp glare. "And now the gendarmes or, even worse, the *Nazis* will come for the boy and throw him in jail, and all because of you and your ideals. A lot of good they did you. Should've just minded your business on the farm like I've been doing my whole life, and not run around the globe, first to Moscow and then to Spain!"

"I was sworn as a *politruk* in Moscow! And in Spain I was fighting for the cause, together with my comrades," Philippe retorted defiantly.

"You fought in the civil war in Spain?" Marcel inquired incredulously. So far he had assumed that among their small group he was the only one who had held a gun in his hands; yet it turned out that Philippe had also seen his share of fighting, and probably for a far longer period of time than Marcel had.

"Sure, he did," Monsieur Bussi smirked in reply instead of his son. "You heard him yourself: he fought for *the cause*."

"Nobody will arrest Pierre." Philippe changed the subject, dismissing his father's remark. Marcel wisely decided not to pry as the communist leader turned to him once again. "You'll take him to Paris today. Him and his brother."

"What?" Marcel thought that he had misheard him at first.

"We can't risk the Nazis coming here and arresting them both," Philippe explained tiredly, rubbing his forehead with his hand. "You'll have to take them to your sister's in Paris, and all three of you will have to hide there until I make other arrangements for them."

Pierre's arguments were drowned out in the stream of Marcel's protests.

"No, no, no, that's impossible! Giselle's apartment is a busier place than a market on a Saturday morning! And it's small on top of it!"

"I'm not talking about Mademoiselle Legrand's place," Philippe interrupted him at once. "I would rather risk Pierre being arrested by the *Boches* than sending him to that capital-ists' nest. I was talking about your other sister. You said that she lived somewhere in the suburbs, didn't you?"

"Kamille? Well… I suppose…" Marcel pondered out loud. "She does have a big house. Only, I don't know if her husband is there with her. He might pose a certain problem. He was drafted into the army together with me, but I don't know if he's back or not."

"It seems that you'll just have to improvise on the scene, Marcel," Philippe concluded calmly. "You're a smart man; I know that you'll come up with something. And I promise to do everything in my power to get the boys off your hands as soon as possible."

Marcel nodded as Philippe squeezed his shoulder slightly. He only wished he had as much faith in himself as Philippe had in him. After all, not only his own life but another two other lives now depended on him.

7

*K*amille had stood in front of the heavy wooden door for quite some time already, cowardly lowering her small, gloved hand each time she raised it for a knock. She had been rehearsing her speech all the way to her sister's house, and yet as soon as she climbed the last carpeted step leading to Giselle's door, her courage failed her. Kamille took a deep breath, smoothed out a non-existent wrinkle on her plaid skirt, fixed her hat in a nervous gesture and rapped on the door quickly before she could change her mind.

The steps on the hardwood floor behind the door were far too loud to belong to Giselle, who, Kamille knew, preferred walking around her apartment barefoot. Kamille had just mentally cursed herself for not calling prior to making a visit as it was obvious that her sister had company when the door swung open and Kamille couldn't suppress a gasp at the sight of who stood in the doorframe.

The German, and it was most definitely a German – jodhpurs, tall black boots and an immaculately white shirt all in place, only a uniform jacket lacking – looked her over assertively, with a scowl never leaving his otherwise handsome face.

"Can I help you, Madame?"

Even though his French was impeccable and grammatically correct, his cold, slightly hissing pronunciation lacked the warmth and charm that Jochen, *her* German, had.

"Yes, *pardon...*" Kamille stumbled under the scrutinizing gaze of his black eyes but forced herself to regain her composure. "I'm looking for Giselle Legrand."

He arched his brow at the inquiring intonation in her voice.

"And who would you be?"

Kamille felt heat coloring her cheeks at such a shameless interrogation.

"I'm her sister, Kamille Blanchard."

"A sister?" The German looked askance at her, studying Kamille's face closely. "I hardly see any resemblance between the two of you."

"Karl! Let her in! That's *ma petite Kamille!*" Giselle's melodic voice sounded from behind the tall German's back and in an instant a familiar arm moved him away from the door without further ceremony. Kamille grinned as Giselle flashed her brightest smile at her. "I haven't seen you in ages!"

Giselle squeezed Kamille in the tightest embrace and stepped away, still holding her sister's hands in hers.

"Look at you, how pretty you are!" Giselle turned her blonde head towards the grim looking German and beamed at him. "Karl, this is Kamille. Kamille, this is Karl... Oh, I beg your pardon; Sturmbannführer Wünsche for everyone around who is not *me*."

The German finally broke into a grin at the sound of Giselle's giggles and bowed his head slightly.

"It is my pleasure to meet you, Madame Blanchard."

As Kamille still tried to process Giselle's new acquaintance's mysterious appearance and why her sister acted at such ease in his presence, Giselle surprised her even more by clasping the German's arm with both hands and pecking him on his cheek.

"Karl, Kamille and I are going for a walk. Our girls' gossip will bore you anyway so..." Giselle moved behind his back to get her purse and a hat from the mail table. "Have you seen my sunglasses? The sun is blinding today!"

"I think they're in your purse. You put them away yesterday in the car, and I don't remember you taking them out."

Under Kamille's stare, who observed them both incredulously, Giselle indeed fished out a pair of sunglasses from her clutch and waved them in the air victoriously.

"He always remembers everything!" Giselle winked at her sister before hiding her green eyes behind the dark shades.

"Where are you going?" the German demanded as Giselle got busy with putting white sandals on her bare feet. "Shall I send Otto for you with a car in a couple of hours? I don't want you to walk all the way back."

"No need, *chéri*." Giselle caught his arm to steady herself while fasting the buckle on her other sandal. "I have no clue where we'll be heading or how long we shall stay out. And besides, if your people left us at least some gas which would allow us to drive cars, this wouldn't be a problem at all. I could have caught a cab back."

"It wasn't my decision to make."

"Right." Giselle snorted and waved goodbye.

"It was a pleasure meeting you, Madame Blanchard." The German nodded curtly to Kamille as Giselle began to already descend the stairs. Kamille nodded in response and followed her sister.

The heatwave washed over them as soon as the doorman pushed the heavy, gilded door outwards to the street, bowing his graying head to Giselle and her companion. Kamille pulled her hat slightly forward, trying to shield her eyes from the stinging sunlight, and Giselle started waving her face at once with her cherry-colored leather clutch.

"The Germans didn't kill us, but this sun certainly will!" The blonde circled her arm around her sister's, pulling her closer for a moment. "I missed you, *ma petite.*"

"Who is that man?" Kamille asked without acknowledging her chirping sister's words.

"Who? Karl? He's my new lover." Giselle flashed her another smile, nudging Kamille with her elbow slightly. "Did you like him?"

"Giselle, he's a German!" Kamille muttered reproachfully before she recalled what she had come to ask Giselle for, and bit her tongue at once.

She wasn't so innocent herself, longing for *her* German, so what right did she have to criticize her sister for her behavior? Or was it siblings' jealousy again, showing its ugly head? After all, it was Giselle who always dived head first into every new adventure that came her way, so was it really so surprising that out of them both that Giselle was the one who had quickly started a scandalous relationship with one of the uniformed occupants?

"So?" Giselle shrugged dismissively. "He's just a man. A little too *regimented* for my taste and tries to show his character a little too much, but I'll teach him how to behave eventually. He has…certain positive qualities that counter all the negative ones, if you know what I mean."

"Giselle, I don't want to hear about that." Kamille tried to ignore her sister's innuendo.

They walked in silence for a few minutes towards the *Place de la Concorde*, listening to the hustle and bustle of the city around them. Bicycles, dragging trolleys chained to them, had become quite an ordinary sight now after the new masters of the capital seized all the gasoline, and passed them by with a familiar ringing of the signal, sending dust up from the road into the hot, dry air. Street vendors, who usually got out of their way to sell their merchandise to the *Boches*, lounged lazily in their folding chairs, hiding from the scorching heat in the shadows of striped awnings.

A slight gust of wind ruffled the blond hair on the soldiers' heads in a group of them who initially strolled smartly on the opposite side of the sidewalk but then rushed like a bunch of adolescent boys to an ice-cream pushcart that stopped on the corner. Giselle snorted softly, motioning her head in the Germans' direction, who were storming the pushcart with the same fervor with which they had stormed their enemies.

"There are your terrifying Germans," she said jokingly. "Dreadful, aren't they?"

"I'm sorry, Giselle," Kamille spoke in a soft voice. "It

wasn't my business to judge you. I just… Didn't expect to see him there, that's all."

"Oh, in this case, you'd better get used to the sight of him, because you'll be seeing a lot of him in the future. He lives with me now."

"He lives with you?"

Giselle nodded and tugged her sister in the direction of the nearest café, which advertised ice cold lemonade on a bright sign.

"He does. Not that I invited him, of course."

The blonde dug in her purse for the money and handed several bills to the vendor, who eyed them suspiciously. Kamille noticed that they were Reichsmarks and not the usual Franks.

"What?" Giselle snapped at the merchant, almost shoving the money into his hands. "Take it already and stop staring at me like I'm the enemy of the state. It's the only currency that the bank had to give me when I went to cash my check."

The vendor muttered something under his breath about the *damn Boches* and handed the women two sweating bottles of the lemonade. Giselle opened hers with a bottle opener that hung on a string from the vendor's table, and took several greedy gulps, satisfying her thirst. Kamille was still struggling with her bottle and the opener which kept slipping from her gloved hands until Giselle took it from her and snapped the bottle open with virtually no effort.

"Would you really rather die from thirst than walk outside without your gloves on for once?"

Kamille had to laugh together with her sister, who shook her head mockingly.

"*And* you're wearing stockings! In this heat!"

"*Maman* always used to say that a lady should always wear stockings," Kamille replied defensively, but envying Giselle inwardly, who wore a thin white sundress revealing her shoulders and part of her back and which ended just below the knee.

"Yes, *a lady* probably should," the blonde conceded, looking over her bare legs and bursting into giggles once again.

"I have a German living with me, too," Kamille confessed at last, hiding her embarrassed gaze under the rim of her hat.

"You do? How exciting!"

"Two actually. Jochen and his adjutant, Horst."

"Oh? I see you're on first name terms with them both, little Mademoiselle Prim-and-Proper!" Giselle teased.

"I call them *Monsieur* Jochen and *Monsieur* Horst. And they call me *Madame* Kamille if that's the same as being on first name terms."

"Don't be so defensive; I'm just teasing you. Are they handsome?"

"They're...pleasing to the eye, yes."

"Which one do you like?"

"Giselle!"

"What? Is that why you finally graced my humble residence with your presence? You like one of them, but you don't know how to show it to him, right? Oh, please, do tell me that I'm right!"

Giselle was laughing contagiously, turning the heads of the uniformed men who also strolled along the *Place de la Concorde* in the direction of the Seine. Kamille was desperately trying to hush the blonde but to no avail.

"That is not what I came for at all!"

"Really?" Giselle arched her brow skeptically.

"Really. I came to... I wanted to ask you to give me the number of that salon that you go to... you know... to do your hair."

Giselle stopped in her tracks, studying her sister closely. "Why? What do you want to do with your hair?"

"I just..." Kamille tried to shrug, but the gesture came out contrived. "I just wanted to change something. I want to dye it blonde, like yours, that's all."

"You want what?"

Their conversation was interrupted by a group of officers, who approached them with cheerful banter and in pigeon French asked them if they could take a picture with them. Giselle broke into a wide grin at once, gesturing the beaming officers towards the railing of the river.

"*Bien sûr!* Let us all stand over there; the view here is breathtaking, don't you find? You don't have anything like that in your Prussia!"

Kamille watched the officers swarm around her vivacious sister, and once again felt left out; it was always like that with Giselle. She offered a tight smile to a German, who circled her waist with his arm and pointed her to his comrade, who was taking the picture. *Back home everyone will probably be asking them who the blonde is,* Kamille thought bitterly.

Offering bright smiles with overt generosity, Giselle apologized her way out of the officers' invitations to share a lunch with them, and pulled Kamille's arm further along the promenade, waving off her new admirers.

"So, why would you want to dye your hair?" she asked, as soon as they resumed their walk.

Kamille only gestured helplessly towards the officers,

THE INDIGO REBELS

who still turned their heads back to the two women, and gave her sister a small and apologetic smile. "I just want to be pretty like you."

"You want to be pretty like me?" Giselle repeated in disbelief.

Kamille stopped the speech that she knew was coming with a gesture of her delicate gloved hand. "Yes. You were right about everything. I do like Jochen. Very much. So much that I... I just want him to look at me with the same eyes that all those men have always looked at you."

"And you think that bleaching your hair will make him fall in love with you?"

"I shouldn't have come here," Kamille muttered and turned around to leave, tears stinging her eyes mercilessly. Of course, he wouldn't fall in love with her, Giselle was right. Her sister had a personality that matched her looks, and she, Kamille, didn't have anything.

"No, no, I'm sorry, it came out wrong!" Giselle caught her elbow and made Kamille face her. "All I wanted to say was that you don't need to change yourself to attract his attention. Pretty like me? Kamille, you're so much prettier than me, that I don't even understand why such a silly idea crossed your mind in the first place. Look at you, look how beautiful your eyes are! I always wanted to kill for those blue eyes of yours. And your skin, and hair... Look how gorgeous your hair is now! I never had such a lustrous, long, thick braid that you always have. I envied you so much because of your hair that I cut mine as soon as I turned twenty and have had to do a perm ever since, and my artificial curls still can't compare to yours! What are you even talking about, pretty like me? You're a natural beauty; you have no need for those masks, and powders, and blushes, and mascaras and lipsticks that I have to buy in tons. And when I wash all that stuff off my face in the evening? Do you think I still look pretty without it?"

"Your German doesn't seem to mind," Kamille muttered, grinning.

Giselle chuckled together with her. "He likes me because I challenge him all the time. Men are strange creatures; they're only happy when we start defying them instead of showing compliance."

"You've always been much more courageous than me. I'd never be able to do that."

"Well, maybe, in this case, *I* should tell your German about your feelings."

"Giselle, no!" Kamille opened her eyes wide in horror, clasping the blonde's arm. "Don't you dare!"

"Why? I say it's a date. When is he usually home? By dinner time?"

"You're not coming to my house!"

"You came to mine and met my Karl. Now it's my turn to come to yours and meet your Jochen."

"Giselle, you can't possibly be serious!"

"I'm very much serious, *ma chéri*. I have to meet my publisher tomorrow at five, so right after that I'll hop on the train and be right by you by seven."

"You'll never make it back home by the curfew." Kamille tried one last argument.

"Oh, don't you worry about that. Karl will send Otto for me with his car."

"I hate you, Giselle Legrand."

"That's not true. You love me very much. By the way, please, do not make fish for dinner. I hate fish."

"You're impossible; you know that?"

"Yes. I've been told quite a few times."

Giselle took her defeated sister's hand, and the two headed towards the nearest bench to enjoy their lemonade.

8

*M*arcel craned his neck, observing his surroundings from behind a tall stone wall, separating Kamille's garden from the cobblestoned street outside. He had wisely decided to leave Pierre and his four-teen-year-old brother, Jerome, at an open café two streets away, paying in advance for their tea and butter croissants with the meager money that Philippe had provided him with. Paris was swarming with Germans, and Marcel didn't want to run the risk of bringing the boys into the house before he checked for himself that it was safe to do so.

It was far too quiet, and Marcel soon realized that Kamille most likely wasn't at home. Or, he wondered, had she run together with the rest of her fellow Parisians two months ago and decided to stay behind the Demarcation Line, which had cut the country into two halves – Occupied France and the so-called Free Zone, with the Vichy govern-ment in the middle?

Marcel kept chewing on his lip that had long ago become raw without him noticing it, and concentrated his gaze on details behind the wall, through the crack of which he was peeking inside. The garden with Kamille's prized flowerbeds was in too much of an impeccable state to have been abandoned, with the ground freshly raked and the grass pulled out recently as it seemed. Golden leaves that had already started to cover the ground with a luxurious carpet were also swept away from the stone path, leading towards the back door. And one of the windows on the second floor – how had he not noticed it before? – was open, with sheer white curtains moving lazily in the wind. Only, it wasn't Kamille's bedroom, that much Marcel remembered from the few times that he had visited her house.

He never felt welcome here, not because of his sister of course, but because of her husband Charles, who seemed to snub all of the Legrand family besides Giselle. And so it had been decided, even though no one ever voiced the thought, that it would be more convenient to meet at their parents' apartment. Albeit small, it possessed a certain air of coziness and the most welcoming atmosphere, of which the Blanchards' mansion was completely devoid, despite all of the new mistress's desperate efforts to breathe some life into it.

Marcel wondered if Charles was back from the front, but would he actually take a separate room just for himself instead of sharing one with his wife? A motion in the window caught Marcel's eye, and he ducked his head instinctively, even though the man in the window couldn't possibly see him behind the tall wall.

"*Merde,*" Marcel cursed under his breath at his cowardice,

and reluctantly returned to the crack in between the stones, observing the man. "A *Boche!*"

A young German, who never suspected he was being watched, positioned himself on the windowsill comfortably, leaning onto the window frame to press his booted leg into the other side, while swinging the other leg in the air carelessly. He lit a cigarette, smiling at the azure, cloudless day outside – one of the last hot summer days, no doubt – and reached for something inside the room and placed the object (a notepad or an album as far as Marcel could see) on his lap. For the first time since he had returned from the front, Marcel saw a *Boche* from close quarters and in such a relaxed pose. He was young too, probably of Marcel's age, and had the same chestnut hair with bangs falling onto one eye. Even the slight build and outline of his face resembled Marcel's slightly. The young man caught himself gulping nervously, and turned away from the unwelcome vision as if an enemy had come to his house while he had been away and stole his very life. He had in a sense; Marcel wasn't even a Marcel anymore, but Claude Bussi, with Philippe's late brother's papers ready to confirm his new identity.

But what had happened to Kamille then? Marcel glued himself to the wall again, frantically searching for any signs of his sister. Realizing that he was looking on the wrong side, he got up warily and strolled along the wall, keeping as close as he could so as not to be detected by the *Boche* on the second floor. As soon as he turned around the corner and, not finding any visible cracks in the wall, he crossed the narrow street and looked up at where Kamille's bedroom was.

Her window was open as well, and to Marcel's big relief no more *Boches* were lounging in the window frame; only Kamille's favorite geraniums peaked their purple heads towards the sun. Marcel doubted that the Germans would look after her pottery with such devotion, which meant that Kamille still lived in the house. Only, the bad news was that he most definitely couldn't bring his two comrades here now. Marcel sighed, kicked a stone out of his way and turned back to fetch the boys, having no idea where to head from there.

***

A FAMILIAR, musty smell of old books and wood polish made Giselle smile as she stepped through the tall, heavy doors leading into the Demarche Publishing House. The concierge greeted her cordially and in a hushed tone confirmed that Monsieur Demarche was upstairs. Giselle nodded and proceeded to the vast, imposing elevator enclosed with a heavy iron cage, executed in the intricate manner of the beginning of the century. Giselle always begged Michel, for the esteemed owner of the Publishing House that bore his name was merely Michel to her, to get rid of the "ancient thing" that would break and kill somebody any day now. Michel Demarche only waved his long, elegant hand dismissively and replied in his placid tone that she, Giselle, would kill him first with her antics. Well, she might have been late quite a few times for the deadline, and did not necessarily care to submit at least a somewhat proofed manuscript, torturing the order-loving man with her typos and left out words, but she was still one of his best assets – a fact that

Giselle reminded him of at every chance she got, and rather unabashedly.

As the elevator made its way to the fourth floor, Giselle recalled the very first time she had stepped through the doors of the Demarche Publishing House, which had already made its name in the literary field. A young girl with hungry eyes and dark hair, pinned from both sides, much too thin as she had spent the little money she made writing odd articles under false names for newspapers on paper and ink rolls for her typing machine. She sat across the desk, which was bigger than her parents' dining table, from this earnest, dignified man with dark mustache and a monocle sparkling in his sharp blue eye, in this beautifully paneled office of his, trying to cover a patch on her faded dress that had been mended over and over.

"You wrote this?" Michel Demarche had asked her in the tone of a schoolmaster who had caught his student cheating during the final exam.

Giselle held his gaze firmly and nodded, trying not to look at the manuscript that lay between them on the polished, redwood surface, with the editor-in-chief's manicured hand on top of it.

"Yes, I did."

"All of it? By yourself?"

"Yes," Giselle confirmed once again, forcing herself to steady her breathing.

"Hm. Fascinating." Monsieur Demarche cleared his throat and reached for his silver cigarette case. "And… Have you studied writing somewhere?"

"Mais oui," Giselle replied even more assertively, now wanting to put this arrogant snob and his condescending

attitude in his place. "I just graduated from the Sorbonne with honors, Monsieur Demarche. I majored in Journalism, just like my father did. I learned how to read when I was four years old, and hardly remember spending a day without a book in my hands. This particular novel, even though I understand that it's rather modern and expresses quite unorthodox ideas, was influenced by the works of Dostoyevsky and Nietzsche. Both Dostoyevsky's and Nietzsche's concepts of a man who has the power to evolve into a higher being than the rest of his kin only if he finds strength in himself to reject the burdensome chains of the past that stop him from such progress have always fascinated me. Outdated moral restraints, imposed by religion and social conventions that don't have the right to exist in our progressive century are exactly the demons that my protagonist, Jean-Marc, is fighting on his path to an ultimate transcendence and an eventual deliverance from an abyss to which many of his comrades fell victims. He's a very atypical hero, I know, but can you really blame him for his views that changed so radically in the course of the four years that he spent witnessing his comrades die in his arms? *God is dead,* as Nietzsche said; well, God had died for Jean-Marc on the very first day when he wandered around the field after the battle, collecting what was left of his regiment, with which he marched, sang songs, exchanged jokes, slept and ate with to then just bury them in a ditch, dug out in a foreign land. That was the day when he reevaluated life itself, and his inner self. That was when a human life lost its value for him in the old, Christian sense and became merely a notion, an obstacle on the path to survival. As for my ending, you were probably surprised by it, for it is also rather unexpected.

There was no path for redemption because Jean-Marc refused the notion of redemption in its philosophical sense. It's a concept of the past for him. You probably figured out that just like my protagonist I firmly reject the highly regarded Monsieur Dostoyevsky's idea of undergoing the necessary suffering in order to atone for one's sins. Therefore, Jean-Marc doesn't regress to his past self after he returns from the front; on the contrary, he returns a stronger man, a man who relies on his mental abilities instead of his emotions, and only thus is he able to continue his life, unlike his comrade, Luc, who drinks himself to death eventually. It's a rather nihilistic novel, I am very well aware of that. But the public has acquired a taste for nihilism lately, so I'm afraid I'm merely the voice of my cynical, post-war generation."

Michel Demarche tilted his coiffured head with his dark, pomaded hair to one side, curiosity shining from behind his monocle for the first time instead of mistrust.

"You wrote about the war as if you've been to one, Mademoiselle Legrand. It feels like a man wrote it, a tired, angry man, who's been through hell and back."

Giselle couldn't suppress a grin at such a compliment, even though it was aimed to shame her into confessing that it wasn't really her who authored the novel.

"You're partially right, Monsieur Demarche. The war stories are my father's; however, what the character of Jean-Marc eventually evolved into is very far from my kind-hearted *Papa.*"

A faint smile, just visible from under his dark mustache, turned the corners of the man's mouth upwards at last.

"And do you believe you can produce more of such novels in the future, Mademoiselle Legrand?"

Giselle grinned, a triumphant light playing in her green eyes. "It depends on how much you're willing to pay me."

THE ELEVATOR DOORS opened in front of her, and Giselle stepped onto a soft, green carpet leading towards the publisher's office. Michel Demarche had a habit of meeting his writers, who he became close friends with over the course of several years, after his regular working hours, and therefore the whole fourth floor, where the even buzz of the typing machines usually prevailed over any other noise, was now deserted and silent. Giselle paused for a moment, hearing indistinct voices from behind the closed door of Monsieur Demarche's office, and checked her watch, wondering if she had arrived too early.

No, it was five fifteen, all right; she was actually "fashionably late," as she always called it in response to Michel's discontent sighs. Shrugging, Giselle pulled the door open without knocking and raised her brow inquisitively as not only Michel himself but several other writers who she knew quite intimately almost jumped in their seats at her unexpected appearance.

"I apologize. Have I interrupted something?" The blonde tried to suppress an amused grin at the comical sight of the four grown men, unanimously letting out a sigh of relief. "Why is everyone so jittery? They declared the armistice two months ago, in case you haven't heard. The Germans aren't coming to get you."

"Ah, Giselle, stop your jesting and sit down, please!"

Michel Demarche patted his forehead, which seemed to have suddenly broken out in a sweat, with a stark white handkerchief with his initials embroidered in the corner. "We were discussing... some pressing matters here."

"Oh?" Giselle took a seat in a leather chair, chivalrously offered to her by Antoine Levy, a young blond man with sad, honey-colored eyes.

Just like Giselle, Antoine had also been discovered by Michel Demarche almost ten years ago, and, just like everyone else who had stepped through the doors of Demarche's office, he pledged his undying allegiance to the man, who, unlike many others in the industry, cared deeply for the authors under his wing.

The air inside the room was heavy with cigarette smoke, but Giselle's suggestion to open the window was met with a collective protest.

"We don't want to risk anyone hearing what we're discussing here," Michel explained, carefully selecting his words.

"Something tells me that you weren't discussing literature," Giselle probed, noticing how the other two men, Pascal Thierry and Gilles Le Roux, both in their early thirties, started shifting uncomfortably in their chairs. "Or our profits for the past year."

"Giselle, can you be discreet about something I would like to suggest to you?" Michel Demarche rarely expressed amusement at hers, or anyone else's jests, preferring to reply to them with seemingly cool irony and a stony face, which suited him much better than belly-shaking laughter. However, this time Giselle noticed that he was uncharacteristically serious.

"Of course I can." She decided to take on a serious note as well. "You know well enough that you can fully trust me. I owe you nothing less than my very life, the way I have it now."

"Yes, that…" The publisher lit a cigarette, his brows getting knitted together once again in deep thought. "I want you to think twice and even thrice about the suggestion that I'm about to voice, because that frivolous, beautiful life of yours might change, If you agree with my, I must say, rather daring proposal."

"For God's sake, Michel! You have intrigued me enough; speak already!"

Monsieur Demarche squirmed in his chair a little longer, obviously searching for the right words to begin.

"What do you think of the policy of the collaboration, Giselle?"

The blonde shrugged, smiling at the obvious answer. "What do I think? Probably what everybody else thinks. I am relieved that they don't bomb us anymore, but if they picked up and left tomorrow, let's just say I wouldn't cry."

"Right, right." Michel Demarche nodded his approval. "And what do you think of Général de Gaulle's call?"

"Général de Gaulle's call?" Now Giselle was really at a loss. She remembered the name of the decorated officer of the Great War, but for the life of her couldn't come up with anything having to do with him or his recent mysterious "call."

"Didn't you hear his speech?" Antoine inquired in disbelief.

"What speech?"

"On BBC, they still repeat it sometimes. Every morning at 8.15," the writer went on to explain.

"Antoine, my morning starts at 10.30 at its earliest." Giselle shot him a glare.

"Well, that explains it," Michel muttered while the other men chuckled quietly. "In short, Général de Gaulle proclaimed Maréchal Pétain a traitor of *la République,* and called to all the French patriots to raise their voices and resist."

"Resist as in…" Giselle motioned her hands demanding further explanation. "Take up machine guns and try to shoot as many *Boches* as possible? Our troops tried it; didn't succeed that much."

"Resist as in refuse to give up on our freedom and reject the collaboration." Demarche ignored her previous sarcastic remark. "In any way possible."

"And how would we do that?" Giselle laughed. "We're writers only! What can we possibly do? Write a satirical play about them?"

"No. A satirical play wouldn't be staged, so that would be a waste of everyone's time." Demarche patiently fenced off another jab from his blonde, sharp-tongued novelist. "What we can do is start printing a weekly newspaper, in which we would not only tarnish the Vichy government's cowardly decision to submit to Hitler and his henchmen, but also call for everyone, who thinks alike, to unite and follow the *Général's* call. We, like no one else, would be able to unite our people as they will be passing the newspaper from one to another until the whole nation will turn on the aggressors, and liberate France from every last one of them."

Giselle sat quietly for some time under the awaiting gaze

of her colleagues, pondering her options. "And where are you going to print it, Michel? Not on one of your book presses, most certainly. The Gestapo will be here in no time."

"No, of course not. We have an old, portable printing press in the basement. We haven't used it in ages, but I'm quite confident that with some oil on its gears it might actually still be in working condition. It's not big by any means, but big enough to print several hundred copies on it. All that is needed from you four is to submit one article each week. It doesn't have to be lengthy or too political; on the contrary, the clearer you make it for the ordinary man in the street, the better. Just write about current day affairs, of what bothers you personally, about your fears and concerns. Be truthful and sincere, that's all I ask of you."

"What if we get caught?"

"We'll be using aliases, of course, and I'll be the only one who puts the newspaper together. After all, I started with that some thirty years ago," Demarche recalled with a rare dreamy smile. "You aren't risking much. I'll be working the press one night a week, alone. After all, the Germans don't care where you spend the night after the curfew as long as you're indoors. So, I'll just stay after work on certain days like I do now."

"But what if we do get caught?" Giselle insisted.

"In that case, they'll most likely arrest us and send us to jail," Demarche replied calmly, and then added in the same leveled tone, "or shoot us."

"Fair enough." Giselle slapped her knee eagerly as if those last words of his were the only thing lacking for her decision to be made. "Count me in!"

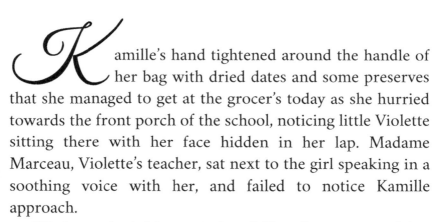

*K*amille's hand tightened around the handle of her bag with dried dates and some preserves that she managed to get at the grocer's today as she hurried towards the front porch of the school, noticing little Violette sitting there with her face hidden in her lap. Madame Marceau, Violette's teacher, sat next to the girl speaking in a soothing voice with her, and failed to notice Kamille approach.

"Violette, *chéri, Maman* is here." Kamille announced her arrival trying to sound cheerful. The girl, however, raised her tear-stained face to her only to lower it back onto her folded arms.

Madame Marceau rose, sighing. She was a young woman just a few years Kamille's senior, yet she already looked weary beyond her age. Her deep, almond-shaped brown eyes were shadowed with dark circles and her beautiful olive skin, of which Kamille was always secretly envious, had taken on a grayish tone, obviously due to the new amount of work that was imposed on her in recent months.

Reluctant to leave children to play without supervision in the streets as they usually did, French parents had unanimously decided to put them up for summer schools, away from mischief and antics that could get them in trouble with the new occupants of the city. Needless to say, Madame Marceau, just like many female teachers, had to embrace a double and sometimes triple workload, as their male counterparts were all, for the most part, gone, locked away in one of the German *stalags.*

"What happened?" Kamille mouthed to the teacher.

Madame Marceau took her gently by the elbow and moved several steps away from Violette.

"We had an unpleasant incident today in the drawing class," she started to explain in a soft voice. "You are aware, of course, that we had to combine three groups in one because we lack staff; well, apparently one third-grader decided that it was acceptable to taunt a little girl over... nothing, really."

"Why would he taunt her?" Kamille inquired, astounded. "My Violette is a darling. She's never had any problems with children before."

"I know that, Madame Blanchard. And you know that Violette is one of my favorite students, even though I'm not supposed to single anyone out." Madame Marceau pressed her hand to her chest to emphasize her sincerity. "Apparently what happened was that Violette completed the assignment that I gave them last week better than anyone in the class. As a matter of fact, her drawing was so well-done that I felt compelled to ask her whether she made it herself. Violette confirmed that she did, but she also admitted that... a certain gentleman showed her some techniques that he learned in his art school."

Madame Marceau paused, biting on her lip as if embarrassed to continue. Kamille shrugged her shoulders slightly with a confused look. She didn't know anyone who could possibly show her Violette any art techniques.

"Monsieur Horst taught me, *Maman*," Violette, who hadn't been oblivious to their hushed conversation as it turned out, went on to explain. "All the trees in my forest, when I started painting them green, all morphed one into another, and when Monsieur Horst saw me taking my painting to the waste bin, he told me not to throw it away but to change the shades of the green instead. He showed me how to move the brush to create an illusion of the leaves, and how to mix the green with water so that some trees would look darker, and some lighter. It came out beautiful after I finished it."

Violette finished her sentence with a shaky voice and a trembling lip and hid her face in her lap again, overcome with a new wave of grief. Kamille rushed to hug her daughter, lowering to the stairs next to her and rubbing her hair and back.

"Violette was kind enough to explain to the class how to do it, and even offered to show some students on their drawings," Madame Marceau spoke again. "And then during the recess, Jacque, that third-grader who I mentioned – he's always up to no good – took Violette's painting off the wall to which I pinned it, and tore it in front of her, saying that no one needed her 'Nazi art' in the school. It was such a despicable thing to do... I punished him, of course, but Violette was devastated. It was indeed a beautiful painting."

Madame Marceau lowered her eyes apologetically, seeming sincerely upset over the situation.

"I graded it excellent, of course," she rushed to add. "I was trying to tell her that she will make many more beautiful paintings like this one in the future because she has already learned how to make them, but she was distressed over that particular one. I'm sorry that I couldn't prevent this from happening."

"No need to apologize," Kamille reassured the guilty looking woman, even though everything was boiling inside of her from a purely maternal, instinctual desire to punish the ruffian who had dared upset her sweet little girl. "I understand it perfectly that it's impossible for you to watch over every single child at school. You're overworked as it is."

"I still am sorry."

Kamille pressed her hand standing up, picked up her bag and pulled Violette's hand. "Come, *chéri*. No need to cry over it; I'm sure that Monsieur Horst will help you make many more drawings, even better than this one."

Violette stood up reluctantly, wiped her face with her sleeve and bid her goodbyes to her teacher, who smiled at her warmly.

"I wasn't crying over the painting that much," Violette said as she took her mother by the hand and the two started making their way home across the sunlit square. "I know that I can make more, I'm not stupid."

"No one would dare call you stupid, *chéri*." Kamille smiled, relieved that her daughter's tears had dried, at last, to be replaced only by the occasional sniffle.

"I was more upset over what he said about Monsieur Horst."

"What did he say?"

"He called him a Nazi and all sorts of things that I don't want to repeat. He said that Hitler was a failed artist too, and most likely that was the reason why both of them ended up in the army because they both couldn't draw. And then he added that Monsieur Horst was probably Hitler's bastard child from some... lowly woman." Violette changed the expression that her offender used to a more decent one, having been taught by her mother from an early age not to repeat any word that was 'unladylike.'

"Some children just have foul mouths, Violette. You know better than to listen to the mean things that they say." Kamille tried to sound level, but deep inside she promised herself to get to the bottom of this with the boy's mother the following day.

"I know, but what I don't understand is why he was saying such nasty things about Monsieur Horst when he doesn't even know him. Not all Germans are like Hitler. Monsieur Horst is very nice," the girl finished somewhat defensively.

"Yes, he is," Kamille agreed pensively, her thoughts trailing back to the first days of the occupation when her opinion of the invading army wasn't much different from that of Jacque's.

"He was saying bad things about you, too."

Lost in her musings, Kamille didn't catch her daughter's words at first.

"He said that we are collaborators for taking in the Nazis and that we should be ashamed of ourselves. He said that we have food and all the ration cards we want just because you're..." Violette paused, trying to recall the unfamiliar phrase which Kamille had already heard spoken on account of other women and dreaded to hear it now from her own daughter. "A horizontal collaborator. What does it even mean, a horizontal collaborator?"

"Nothing, *ma petite*, nothing at all," Kamille muttered, not noticing how her grip tightened on her daughter's hand. "Just silly, meaningless words, that's all."

"That's what I thought." Violette nodded, reassured.

Kamille silently fought the tears that were ready to over-flow from her eyes. She did hear women spit the term while squinting at some of the young girls with curled hair and painted lips, strolling hand in hand with a German; she heard mothers scorning their daughters for throwing appraising glances at the soldiers, playing ball only in their breeches and boots, their muscular, tanned torsos glistening with sweat in the sun. "Horizontal collaboration" was as much a crime in her fellow peoples' eyes as any regular crime, such as when a neighbor sold out a neighbor fearing reprisal; or when a merchant pointed an accusing finger at a competitor across the street, whispering *"Un Juif"* – a Jew – to the plain clothed men with piercing eyes – one of the characteristic features of their kind, the Gestapo. And now Kamille was branded to be one, even though she was most innocent despite what everyone around thought.

Or was she, really? Shame colored her porcelain cheeks as she recalled her less than innocent longing for one of the occupants who was currently sharing a house with her. The only reason why he didn't share her bed was his decision not to, that much Kamille admitted to herself bitterly. It wouldn't be so sad to be accused of the deed if it was done indeed. But it seemed that even Germans who weren't too picky around local women didn't want her. Maybe Charles was right after all, and she was indeed unattractive and uninteresting... *And all I want is to be loved,* Kamille thought gloomily to herself. *Am I asking too much? Is it too much of a sin, my desire to be loved? Ah, how I would give everything in the world to just be loved once, like in a romance novel, madly and deeply, and after that, come what may!*

Kamille jolted at the sound of the church's bells striking seven as if she'd just made a deal with the devil that would turn her whole life upside down. She shook her head slightly, clearing it from the premonition, and winked at her daughter, who had all but forgot about her recent ordeal, in the way that children do.

"*TAUNTE* GISELLE!"

Those were the first words that Kamille heard as soon as she stepped through the doors of her house. It looked like Violette had some sixth sense trained on her favorite aunt's presence, or maybe she'd heard her joyful laughter, coming from the living room. Whatever it was, Violette rushed past her mother and disappeared into the living room. Kamille took a deep breath and followed her daughter inside, still clenching the bag with unpacked products in her gloved hands.

As soon as she stopped over the threshold of the living room, Kamille felt like an intruder in her own house, for the jovial banter and occasional bursts of laughter ceased at once as if her very presence had killed the joy in the room. Giselle, her scarlet dress and lips to match, beamed at her first, exchanging mischievous glances with the two men next to her. Kamille caught herself thinking that she had never before seen Jochen nor Horst in such a relaxed state and, more than that, drinking before dinner. Each time Kamille tried to offer her tenants refreshments, they only bowed politely and refused, explaining that they either couldn't drink during service hours or offering her some other senseless excuse.

They put away their cognac glasses awkwardly at once and jumped to their feet to greet her, but Kamille found herself even more upset over the sudden demeanor change that it seemed she'd provoked; she would prefer them lounging on their sofa and laughing like they had been, exchanging jests with Giselle. At least Kamille now knew that they could laugh if they actually wanted to.

"We were just talking about you," Giselle said instead of a greeting and, to Kamille's horror, winked shamelessly at Jochen. Kamille's handsome tenant only lowered his gaze in response.

She really couldn't have been here more than half an hour, and they're both all over her already, Kamille thought, but she bit back her temper and forced a smile back at her sister, who was bouncing Violette on her knee playfully.

"You were?" she muttered, feigning interest. Most likely Giselle was telling her new admirers some embarrassing stories from their childhood, and, heavens knew, Kamille was the most timid and awkward child in the whole of France. Thank goodness, Violette didn't take after her.

"Why, yes." Giselle flashed an even row of white teeth at

her, scheming gleam not leaving her eyes. "And as a matter of fact, I almost talked Jochen here into taking us out on a double date this Saturday. If Horst agrees to escort me, of course."

Another playful wink followed, only in Jochen's adjutant's direction. She was certainly no expert in amorous affairs, but even Kamille could tell that the young man was already smitten with Giselle.

"It will be my utmost honor to escort you, Mademoiselle Giselle," Horst breathed out, his eyes not leaving Giselle for a second.

"If you aren't going to ditch that *Mademoiselle* thing, I refuse to go anywhere with you," she reprimanded Horst playfully, this time making him blush in the most adorable way.

Kamille fought the desire to leave the joyful company to their own devices and head to the kitchen, where she belonged, as Charles had pointed out so many times. He used to always send her away on the rare occasion when guests visited them, not hiding the fact that he was positively ashamed of his wife. 'Don't you have anything in the kitchen to check?' – it was his signature remark signaling that she should disappear out of sight and not to 'embarrass him' for being such an 'utterly useless hostess.'

"Don't worry, Madame Kamille." Jochen's soft voice distracted her from her unhappy musings. "I have absolutely no intention of putting you in such a compromising position. Your lovely sister was only joking, of course, so please rest assured that you have nothing to worry about."

"Joking?" Giselle had turned to her victim before Kamille had a chance to interject anything. "I was most certainly *not* joking, my dear friend. *And,* as far as I remember, I told you that if you try to back your way out of this, I'll bring some communist propaganda, stuff it all over your room and call the Gestapo on you. They'll come fast, too; their chief is billeted in my apartment."

Violette together with Horst burst into hardly suppressed chuckles while Giselle addressed her sister once again.

"It turns out that the *Wehrmacht,*" she started with a nod in the direction to the two men, theatrically covering her mouth and whispering like a conspirator, "fancy those *Staatspolizei* no more than we do. Did you know that?"

"Speaking of *Staatspolizei,*" Kamille spoke with a shy smile, trying to help Hauptmann Hartmann out of the uncomfortable situation. He clearly didn't want to go anywhere, with her as his company at least, but her stubborn sister would force him, of course, like she did with everyone, and everything would become even worse and more awkward between them. Jochen tried to avoid Kamille as it was and less than anything she didn't want to deal with straightforward rejection. "I doubt that your... tenant will be pleased with such arrangements."

"What arrangements?"

"Your plans for Saturday evening," Kamille clarified in response to her sister's genuinely confused look.

"But *ma chéri,* nobody's going to notify him in written form about our plans." Giselle chuckled.

"There's still a chance that he'll find out," Kamille muttered, already sensing her defeat. It was impossible to argue with Giselle and win.

"He's not as high and mighty as he tries to seem." The blonde rolled her eyes in mock contempt, which drew more chuckles from her receptive audience. "Besides, let me worry about him. I like Horst much better, anyway."

The young officer beamed such a radiant smile at her that Kamille felt sorry for him that very instant. The poor thing, he was too young to understand that Giselle was only toying with him; not out of malice of course. She was just... being Giselle.

"I'm sorry, I have to go make dinner." Kamille had just turned to make her leave when Giselle jumped to her feet at once.

"We'll all help you then, won't we gentlemen?"

"No, no, I really can manage by myself—"

Kamille's protesting was cut off by Giselle's categorical raise of a hand.

"We will. No need to worry." She turned to the startled Germans, who seemed to be partly surprised and partly amused by such a suggestion. "I have as much of an idea of how to make dinner as you do, but Kamille will be giving us instructions. Right, Kamille? And I know that my dear niece knows her way around a pastry like no other pastry chef around. Together we'll make such a feast, that you'll be writing home about it, trust me."

With those words, she marched resolutely in the direction to the kitchen with both men in tow, just like little geese following the piper in that fairy tale that she used to read to Violette. Kamille only shook her head in admiration of Giselle's commanding abilities and regretted that it wasn't her sister who had led the troops against the Germans just a couple of months ago. With such a leader, their enemies wouldn't stand a chance, that's for sure.

GISELLE HAD LEFT LONG AGO, escorted by Otto, who she had simply introduced as her 'personal driver' and her *high and mighty tenant's* adjutant to the company at the table, almost dragging the young man in the SS uniform to meet her new friends from the *Wehrmacht*. All three men exchanged crisp salutes, not forgetting to look each other over apprehensively however. After Otto had, for the third time, refused the bubbly blonde's offer to a drink, explaining that Herr Sturmbannführer would shoot him personally if he caught even the slightest whiff of alcohol on his breath, Giselle departed, blowing a last kiss to her sister.

Kamille was busy with the dishes in the kitchen and almost dropped a plate into the aluminum sink, startled by the voice behind her back.

"The dinner came out lovely, Madame Kamille. You truly are a great instructor."

She cast a bashful gaze over her shoulder in Jochen's direction. He had placed the cheese platter with what was left of their small feast next to her, but lingered in the kitchen instead of retiring to his room like he always did.

"It seems that my poor Horst is utterly and madly in love with your sister," he spoke again, chuckling softly. "He left me as soon as you cleared the table. Most likely he is busy drawing his new beloved's portrait in his room."

"It's difficult not to fall in love with Giselle," Kamille admitted, smiling, trying her best not to become affected by his presence so near to her.

"You think?"

Kamille turned to him, tilting her head to one side curiously. Jochen's cheeks had acquired a faint rosy glow from the wine, which Giselle had made them all drink in adamancy, raising her glass in one toast after another. At one point they even drank to the Führer, as Kamille recalled correctly; that was Giselle's latest trick that she used after the men refused to drink. Now, Hauptmann Hartmann resembled an ordinary young man much more than a feared occupant, especially now after he had shed his uniform jacket and casually rolled up the sleeves of his white shirt.

"Of course. You saw her. She's beautiful, vivacious, intelligent, funny, successful... She's everything I'll never be," Kamille finished quietly.

"Why would you want to be like your sister?" Jochen sounded genuinely surprised.

Kamille gestured helplessly. "Come, now. I saw how different you acted around her! You are always so distant and cold and standoffish with me, and if Giselle didn't appear today, I would probably have never learnt what the sound of your laughter is like! And you don't have to go anywhere with me out of pity, or just because she coerced you into it. I'll tell her that you're not feeling well, or that something came up with your...work, and she'll just go with Monsieur Horst."

With those words, Kamille turned back to the sink to hide her eyes from him, which were glistening with unshed tears, and started lathering a plate ferociously.

"What makes you think that I don't want to go?"

Kamille only shook her head instead of replying, fearing that her voice would betray her with its trembling if she spoke even one word.

"Kamille?" His voice whispered right in her ear this time,

and Kamille's heart faltered as she realized that Jochen had called her by her name for the first time, without the pretentious title 'Madame' attached to it first.

Jochen lowered his hands gently on her shoulders, and Kamille's slippery fingers lost their grip on the plate she was holding. It fell into the sink, knocking down glasses and silverware. Ignoring the cacophony of tumbling dishes, Kamille turned swiftly to face the German. A soft grin was playing on his face.

"You're a beautiful woman, Kamille. A most beautiful woman."

"You're just saying that because you've been drinking," Kamille retorted coldly, trying to get a hold of her feelings which were all over the place.

"I have." The German lowered his head in a somewhat comical manner, like a reprimanded child. "I shouldn't have. Your sister made me."

Kamille pursed her trembling lips and waved him off with his apologies, leaning against the sink and wishing for him to just leave her alone to her misery. Nobody needed his drunken apologies or compliments here.

"Kamille."

"Go away!" She had had too much wine herself; if she had been sober she would have never allowed herself to speak with such rudeness.

"No. I have to... how do you say it?" He was searching for the foreign words which kept escaping him. "I have to express my feelings."

"Please, don't."

"No, I insist that I explain myself, because... there has

been a misunderstanding. And you're upset with me over it, and I can't leave it this way."

Jochen winced at how disjointed and *German* his speech likely sounded due to the wine, as if the soft, purring language itself was against him that night. As if to make her understand him better, Jochen held her delicate arms again, turning her towards him a little too forcefully, to see that she was crying. Kamille pushed against his chest, leaving wet marks on his white shirt, trying to worm her way out of his arms, and then, all of a sudden, he caught her face in his palms and pressed his mouth to hers. Kamille froze, as all of her thoughts suddenly disappeared into thin air, and dissolved into his warm breathing mixing with her own and drowned in the unsteady rhythm of her wildly beating heart. He had just parted her lips slightly with his and then moved away as unexpectedly as he had kissed her, stopping himself before it was too late. Wiping her tears with his thumbs, Jochen kissed Kamille's eyelids with infinite gentleness while she stood there, both terrified and elated at the same time.

"You're a most beautiful woman, Kamille," he repeated quietly, whispering his words into her hair, covering the top of her head with soft kisses as he spoke. "But you've got it all wrong. I've been so distant with you, as you put it, only because I've been so drawn to you from the first day that we met... I worried that it wouldn't lead to anything good. You just lost your husband to war, and less than anything do I want evil tongues to tarnish your good name because of me. You're right: you're nothing like your sister, Kamille. She could pull this sort of a stunt, and no one would bat an eye because she's a different type of a woman. But you... You're sweet and kind, and fragile; you wouldn't be able to deal with all the hatred directed at you. It would break you eventually, ruin your whole life, and all because of some man, who couldn't fight his infatuation? I would never let this happen to you, my dearest, dearest Kamille. You mean too much to me to use your kindness in such a manner. Yes, I know, I'm drunk and I'm babbling all sorts of nonsense that I will be embarrassed to even remember tomorrow, but I'm glad that I told you this tonight. You are a most amazing woman, Kamille, and please, never, never change. One day you'll make some lucky man so very happy."

"I don't want any other man," Kamille muttered, stunning herself with her boldness. She stood on her tip toes, wrapped her wet arms around his neck and found his mouth once again.

"Kamille, please—" Jochen tried to sound stern, not realizing that his fingers were already unbuttoning Kamille's pearl buttons on her blouse. "You don't know what you're doing. You'll regret it tomorrow."

Kamille pulled him close again in some kind of desperate gesture, refusing to let him go. "No, I won't. I most definitely won't."

arcel walked purposefully along the street, keeping his head high and back almost unnaturally straight, even though his heart betrayed him by skipping a bit cowardly each time a group of uniformed Germans passed him by. There were fewer of them here, in this residential area of Paris, where narrow streets were connected into an endless labyrinth of row houses, stitched together by garlands of laundry, stretched out from one window to another, and hidden backstreets, which the *Boches* tried to avoid.

Marcel breathed in the familiar air of starched sheets, cabbage and naphthalene, and smiled to himself. It was the air of his youth, his childhood when life itself was much simpler and he didn't have to glance over his shoulder fearfully, making sure that the two young charges, who were following him within twenty steps hadn't been stopped and interrogated by the Germans. Marcel was home. He had just turned the last corner leading to his parents' house; only it didn't feel like home anymore, more of one big prison of a city, in which all of them had been incarcerated.

Marcel waited for Pierre and his brother Jerome to turn the corner as well and waved them to follow him inside a dark doorway, leading to his parents' apartment on the third floor. He saw from the outside that the shutters on the windows were closed, and breathed out in relief, guessing that his mother and father had most likely run from Paris during the exodus and either hadn't returned yet or, better yet, decided to stay with their relatives behind the Demarcation Line.

Marcel came to a stop in front of the familiar door with its small and clean, albeit worn-out, mat in front of it and knocked indecisively. Listening to the stillness inside and the shuffling of the boys behind his back, Marcel turned to them at last, admitting that now they faced a new problem.

"Just like I thought, my parents aren't home. They probably left for the South, and now the *Boches* won't let them back across the line."

"But that's good, isn't it?" Pierre fixed his cap, trying to look older than he really was in his baggy suit, no doubt borrowed from his father before the two brothers set off on their journey to Paris with Marcel. "It means that we have an apartment all to ourselves."

"How are we going to *get inside* that apartment?" Marcel crossed his arms over his chest, becoming irritated with the kid's inability to see the obvious, which had landed him and his brother in trouble in the first place.

Having returned to his childhood home, Marcel experienced a sudden pining for that old, comfortable life, which he could have resumed now. He could have come back to the Uni and continued his studies, become an ordinary citizen again, and not some criminal on the run, which he was made into against his will. It was Philippe's hypnotic influence that made him fall for his dangerous ideas, join some communist cell, and become a part of a movement which had been prohibited. And now he was with these two scoundrels on his hands, having to care for them when he didn't know how to care for himself...

His uneasy thoughts were interrupted by Jerome, who shrugged nonchalantly, moving Marcel out of his way with his shoulder, even though that shoulder of his barely reached Marcel's.

"We'll pick the lock of course. What's the big deal?" the youngest of the scoundrels proclaimed casually, extracting a pin out of the pocket of his pants with a knowing look.

Under Marcel's incredulous stare the fourteen-year-old kid squinted his eyes slightly, feeling his way inside the lock with his pin, and in only a few seconds declared a victorious *"Voilà!"* before pushing the door open. Pierre snorted under his breath at Marcel's dropped jaw and pulled his brother aside, allowing the master of the house to enter it first, giving him the chance to somehow restore his dignity.

"Thank you," Marcel muttered, wiping his feet before stepping through the door.

"Pas de problème," Jerome replied, throwing the pin up in the air and catching it swiftly.

Right, Marcel thought grimly. *No problem at all.* Except that they had no money left and the boys were wanted by the *feldgendarmes* and Marcel was implicated in the anti-governmental activities. Apart from that, everything was peachy.

GISELLE STARED at the ceiling for so long that her neck went numb. She sat on her chair in front of the typing machine with her head thrown back, and with her mind as blank as the ceiling in front of her eyes. The coffee had long gone cold, and Coco had fallen asleep on her lap. At least someone benefited from her idleness, Giselle smirked to herself.

"Would you like to hear my opinion?"

Karl's voice made her wince imperceptibly. The thrill and novelty of her latest romance hadn't passed yet, but those details about him that seemed insignificant at first had started to gradually irk her. His manner of speech, too accented and coolly disjointed; his habit of herding her to the bedroom as early as eleven in the evening, completely ignoring her protests that she was a nocturnal creature and liked writing at night; his autocratic manner, in which he always expressed his opinion on subjects that no one had asked him about...

"Concerning?" Giselle asked, still staring at the ceiling.

The tall German stepped forward, his dark features coming into the periphery of her vision. She outstretched her arm and caressed the smoothness of his immaculately shaven cheek.

"Concerning your writing. Or, actually, the lack of such."

"Oh?" She grinned, humoring him. "I didn't know that you were a literary critic. But go ahead."

"I read your manuscript."

Giselle's smile dropped, together with her arm. "I usually don't allow anyone to read my unfinished manuscripts."

117

"I read all of your books," he continued, ignoring her remark. "They're all good. Especially your very first one."

"Why, thank you very much." Giselle hoped that it didn't come out too sarcastic. "It's nice to be acknowledged internationally."

"I don't read for pleasure. It's a rather useless pastime if you ask me."

Giselle arched her brow.

"Why bother with my novels then?"

"I was studying you."

"Studying me?"

"Yes. Your personality, your views and your ideas on different subjects. As I've said, I rarely read without purpose. This time my purpose was to better understand you. I'm very aware of the fact that writers project their personalities on their characters, so I decided to learn who Mademoiselle Giselle Legrand really is."

"And who is she?" This time Giselle sounded genuine. He was strange, this somber Karl with his invariably poised demeanor, too collected and impassionate even for a German, but one thing she had to give him: he was a highly intelligent man. She was curious to hear his opinion.

"You're a rebel. A rebel and a nihilist. Your first novel was so good because you wrote it while in need. I believe you wrote it under the influence of the Great War even though you wrote it years after it had ended, and most likely your circumstances differed slightly from the lifestyle that you're leading now. Correct me if I'm wrong."

"Were you investigating me, Monsieur *Staatspolizei?*" she asked, slightly unnerved by such a correct characterization.

"I asked you not to call me that."

"You haven't answered my question."

"No, I wasn't investigating you. I made my conclusions solely based on what I read in your novel."

"Maybe you should have become a literary critic." Giselle leaned forward and busied herself with fixing a new sheet of paper in her typing machine. The waste bin next to her was filled with crumpled pages.

"You can't write because you're too comfortable," the German behind her back spoke again with almost infuriating calmness.

Giselle fought the urge to get up and storm out of the room, away from him and his opinions, which didn't interest her in the slightest anymore. *Who the hell does he think he is?* Only, the problem was that she had no place to go – he occupied her apartment just like the rest of their German lot occupied her whole country, and now all of them had to listen to what they had to say.

"You are too comfortable, and you've lost your edge, your voice, with which you made Jean-Marc, your protagonist, the hero of the war, take an axe to the new age, which was born out of that war. It was a little too... revolutionary and unnecessarily loud, in my opinion, but it was... What's the word?" He snapped his fingers sharply several times. "Fascinating, *ja*. He was heading to the gallows with his ideas, your Jean-Marc, but it was impossible not to watch him until the last moment, when the rope was sprung, metaphorically speaking. That first novel of yours was written with passion, with feeling... Your other books were all right I suppose, but this last manuscript... It's too contrived. The characters are flat and overfed. They want for nothing, and they have nothing to fight for. They're bored, as you are. Bored and comfortable. That's why you can't write. Not because I'm here and interfere with your thinking process – I even spend most of my day in the *Kommandatur*, like you asked me to. *Nein.* You can't write because you have no conflict, and therefore no plot."

Giselle bit one red painted nail angrily, trying her best not to throw some venomous remark back at him. What angered her even more was that the *damned Boche* was right through and through, and he had just shoved her face into what she had refused to acknowledge to herself. She pondered her options, collected herself and turned in her chair, facing him with an overly sweet smile.

"If you're such an expert in writing, maybe you can advise me on what to do?"

Karl shrugged, either not detecting or purposely ignoring the irony in her voice. "If you can't write anymore, maybe it's time to think about family?"

"About family?"

"*Ja.* You understand, husband and children," he clarified as if to a child.

"You know what, Karl?" Giselle said in a menacingly leveled tone, getting up and putting her dog on the floor. She straightened and stepped as close to him as she could. "Why don't *you* find yourself a husband?"

The German frowned slightly, confused with her response. He followed the seething woman with his gaze until she disappeared behind the door of her bedroom, which she slammed with force. He leveled the typing machine so it would be perfectly paralleled to the edge of the desk, reorganized randomly thrown pages in a neat stack and picked up her mug with unfinished coffee, satisfied with his arrangements. She could throw tantrums all she wanted, just like her fellow countrymen did at first before they came to the realization: the Germans were here to stay, and they would discipline them into the correct order, either willingly or not.

'CONFLICT, you say? I have no goddamn conflict?'

Giselle's fingers were flying over her typing machine, to which she had returned to just as soon as both Karl and Otto left to go to the *Kommandatur*.

'I'll show you conflict, you bastard!'

The article was coming along so nicely and effortlessly that Giselle burst into a fit of giggles, elated with the sudden flow of inspiration, which that *damned Boche* had triggered, not even suspecting it. Just two hours ago she had no idea what she could possibly submit to Michel's first edition of his underground newspaper. Now, the words were flowing from under her fingers in a forceful stream of defiance and pure provocation, targeting not only the Vichy government and the *Boches* in charge but every single policy imposed on the nation by the new order.

"They think that they can march in here and make us submit to their will like some defenseless sheep going to the slaughterhouse? They believe that they can tell us what to do in our country, and treat us like secondary citizens while they are acting like rightful masters in each house, each *arrondissement* that they so insolently took over? Well, that, bloody hell, is not going to happen! We'll raise our voices first, and soon our weapons will follow, until the very last one of the blood-sucking occupants stops muddying our streets with their black boots." She muttered, outlining a rough draft of her article, out of which she would most definitely have to weed out all the curse words and exclamation marks. "No conflict, you say? I'll show you such conflict that you'll be spitting fire for the next few weeks after this paper comes out!"

11

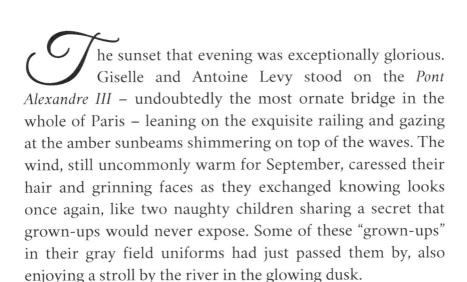

The sunset that evening was exceptionally glorious. Giselle and Antoine Levy stood on the *Pont Alexandre III* – undoubtedly the most ornate bridge in the whole of Paris – leaning on the exquisite railing and gazing at the amber sunbeams shimmering on top of the waves. The wind, still uncommonly warm for September, caressed their hair and grinning faces as they exchanged knowing looks once again, like two naughty children sharing a secret that grown-ups would never expose. Some of these "grown-ups" in their gray field uniforms had just passed them by, also enjoying a stroll by the river in the glowing dusk.

"Can you believe that we're actually going through with this?" Antoine whispered to his colleague, as soon as the Germans were far enough away.

Giselle brushed a platinum lock of hair away from her eyes and turned to face him, resting her elbows on the railing and leaning onto it with her back. "No. I won't believe it until I see the paper with my own eyes."

"Michel is staying overnight tonight to print a thousand copies, he said."

Giselle grinned at the novelist. From the perspective of others, the two looked like an ordinary couple on a date. Both were dressed with discernible taste – he in a striped woolen suit (custom made undoubtedly) and wing point and immaculately polished shoes; she was clad in a powder chiffon blouse matched with a brown skirt and holding a masterpiece of a hat with an ostrich feather in her hands. They spoke in hushed tones, but still enjoyed that certain feeling of satisfaction that comes to people who know that they can get away with anything just because they belong to a particular class that never raised any suspicion in the Germans. Dubious looking factory workers with begrimed hands and worn out shoes were subjects to regular checkups, but Giselle and Antoine, so far, were spared from the necessity to produce their *cartes d'identité* at the first demand, for no one would ever suspect them in something so utterly audacious and criminal as to contribute to an underground newspaper, which called for the support of Général de Gaulle and advocated any form of resistance to the occupying forces. Communists were expected to do such a thing, but definitely not successful novelists, who even in the eyes of the general public didn't suffer from the hardships of the occupation.

"I read your article before Michel approved it for print," Antoine whispered in Giselle's ear as another couple passed them by, and all four exchanged acknowledging nods. "It was so raw and emotional that I admit I felt a slight sting of professional jealousy."

"Pfft." Giselle rolled her eyes dismissively and waved him off. "Flatterer! You out of all people shouldn't feel any professional jealousy because you're a much more gifted writer than I am. I can write my whole life and never get to the level of your poetic language and use of metaphors no matter how much I try."

"Your writing wouldn't be half as good as it is now, muddled with my metaphors. And my poetic language as you call it would entirely and completely destroy the naked, undisguised feelings that your characters so proudly display. I'm more of a… an American, romantically inclined Fitzgerald. And you, my dear, are definitely the disillusioned and cynical Guy de Maupassant."

"I don't want to be de Maupassant! I want to be Tolstoy!"

"You can't be Tolstoy; His Excellence Count Lev Nikolaevich was too soft for you. If we're switching to Russians, you can be Mayakovsky, if you like."

Giselle snorted with laughter and play-swatted Antoine on his forearm. "I'm no communist, Monsieur Levy!"

"We were talking literature, not political ideology," he countered, raising his brow.

"Can I ask you something, Antoine?"

"Of course."

"Why did you decide to go along with this… project?" Even though Giselle was still smiling, her green eyes were now serious.

Antoine dropped his playful mask as well, threw a last glance to the golden water and offered his bent arm chivalrously to his friend. "Let me walk you to the train, for it's a long story and I don't want you to be late."

"I'm only going to stop by my parents' apartment to check if everything is fine. I finally got a postcard from them a day ago. They're in the Free Zone, just like Kamille and I thought, so at least they don't get to see these fine gentlemen," she motioned her head in the Germans' direction, "in the streets daily. If I'm late for curfew, I'll just stay there for the night. So, why?"

"Why did you?"

Antoine's smile came out a little pained this time, and Giselle already regretted asking. It seemed that, unwittingly, she had struck a nerve in his gentle, sensitive soul, capable of producing such magnificent novels which she could only dream about.

"For fun." The blonde shrugged off the serious question, being almost sincere.

She didn't know herself yet why she had initially said yes without giving the rather dangerous idea a second thought. The occupation almost didn't affect her. She still cringed inwardly, of course, each time a German officer was given a better table in a café than her fellow French countryman. She tried to ignore the sighs and complaints about the endless lines and the talk about the lack of food that she couldn't help but overhear in the streets. Her food was delivered by the housekeeper who came twice a week to clean the apartment and collect the laundry. The food rations? Karl had Otto speak with the housekeeper only once about what exactly he preferred to see in his (why, it might as well be called his now) fridge, handed her some paper, and since then Giselle started seeing even more food at home that she usually cared to buy for herself, dining mostly outside.

Out of rebellion probably, or boredom. Or because of both – that her austere looking *Boche* with his sharp, analytical mind was right about, Giselle admitted at last. Oh, well, out of boredom or not, at least she did something for the cause and something that wouldn't land her in any real trouble if caught. Shoot them? No one would shoot them; it was just a silly little newspaper only. Something to later tell her children about, if she ever decided to have any.

"You still didn't answer my question," she reminded her friend in a mild voice after they had walked a long way without speaking a word.

Antoine sighed and lifted his honey-colored eyes to the sky, which had just started turning from a magnificent shade of pink to an ominous purple.

"I'm Jewish, Giselle. You heard already what they do to their Jews in Germany. Now they have come here, and I don't think it will be any different. They made Michel break contracts with all Jewish writers working for his publishing house. I'm officially dismissed until further notice, with no means of existence. Well, in my case I've been lucky, to be completely honest. Michel still pays me a salary and my percentage of the sales every two weeks, even though he has to take the money out of his bank account. My accounts have all been arrested 'until further notice' as well. We're lucky they aren't making us wear yellow stars yet. But I feel that the change is coming, and fast. So, the answer to your question as to why I agreed to go along with this project is that I have nothing to lose. And I'll try to do as much as I can against them while I still can."

Giselle was silent for some time, all the words of comfort which would be suitable in any other case now tasting sour and insincere on her tongue. What could she possibly tell him to make him feel better? Nothing. Nothing at all.

"Michel is a good man," she spoke at last, giving his forearm a reassuring squeeze instead of meaningless words. How ludicrous was it that the two renowned novelists had no words in this new world?

"Yes, he is. Without him, I wouldn't last long."

"I would take care of you. We all would. My bank account is fine and is more than plenty for the two of us."

Antoine smiled the warmest smile and hugged her gently, planting a friendly kiss on Giselle's temple. "I know. Thank you."

"With me, you will always have a place to go to, if you need one."

"With your new tenant there? I'll try my chances elsewhere, but thank you for the offer." He chuckled.

"You know what I mean, silly." Giselle nudged him with her elbow in mock contempt. "My parents' apartment is vacant at the moment, and they're not planning to come back anytime soon – not that I blame them. So just give me a call if things go south with the *Boches*, and I'll give you the key."

They stopped in front of the *Champs-Élysées – Clemenceau Metro* station, pausing at the steps that lead underground. Antoine took Giselle's hands in his and kissed each ceremoniously. She smiled at the incorrigible romantic; despite the constant flirting and playful jokes, the two shared a most innocent, almost sibling-like attachment to each other, and never crossed the line that would ruin their friendship.

"Here we are, Mademoiselle."

"Merci, Monsieur."

Antoine planted a kiss on her cheek and waited until Giselle descended the stairs, only then turning around to go back to his apartment, facing the Champs-Élysées, just like Giselle's only from the western side. Heavens knew how long he would be allowed to enjoy that grand, majestic view.

12

*G*iselle cursed under her breath, almost losing her footing on the cobbled road, slippery with evening dew, for the third time in five minutes. *Bercy,* the residential area in the 12th *arrondissement,* despite being considered middle-class and well looked after, apparently lacked lampposts where they were needed most. Giselle almost regretted not seeing *feldgendarmes* around *or* their German bosses.

"Of course they don't patrol this area," she kept muttering so as to embolden herself with the sound of her voice to go through the dark, narrow street. "They only patrol where it's light, and where the pretty girls swarm around in the evening. I'll be lucky if I don't mugged here, or killed by some communists. *Merde!* Damn *Boches* and their curfew! And why the hell did they commandeer all the gas so that we can't even use taxis now? Is it so dangerous for the occupying forces when people try to get to their destination in one piece, like me? Ah, *bordel!*"

She regained some confidence as soon as she turned the corner and stepped in the dingy light of the lamp, hanging above the door of the building where her parents had lived for the most of their life, and where she was born, and later her sister and brother. Giselle caught herself shaking her head, suppressing a lopsided grin. She would have forgotten the road here if Madame and Monsieur Legrand hadn't asked her for the favor to check on their home while they were away, and maybe rent it to someone, had she needed the money. That must have been *Papa's* idea; he was always the most resourceful one, always trying to accumulate some *savings*. Giselle despised the very idea of this typical lower-middle-class mentality of 'saving' and 'putting away for a rainy day.'

"Instead of saving, why not just make more, so that you don't have to choose between paying rent and feeding your family? And so that your daughter isn't ashamed to go to a Uni in her mother's old dress; or so your wife doesn't have to miss out on church because she's embarrassed to go to God's house without stockings. We could have it all you know if it weren't for your highly valued principles. A lot of good they do," she told him off angrily once when overhearing *Maman* complaining quietly about not having enough money to buy shoes for little seven-year-old Marcel.

Papa only paled then, looking at his oldest daughter as if she were a stranger, and didn't say a word in response. It was the day when she packed all the meager possessions she had into one small rucksack, grabbed her typing machine – her parents' present for her seventeenth birthday – and walked out, to work day shifts in a Uni café to pay her own rent and to make her own living, away from all that misery that was poisoning her life and draining her while everyone around was making fortunes. It was the day when Giselle swore to herself that she would do anything, no matter how low or unethical, to make her own living; a life filled with beautiful things that she had only seen in magazines, with influential friends and fine dining, and let them all rot with their 'savings.'

She didn't speak with her parents for a few months, and only came back to proudly demonstrate to them her very first article, published under an alias, but still hers, for which she got paid her first salary. They almost had a fight again, when her father refused to accept the money that Giselle tried to give them.

"Don't be mad at me, *Papa*," she said that day with a conciliatory smile, putting the money under the teapot, before getting up to leave. "I know that you would never write for that *filthy press*, as you call the commercial news-paper that I work for. I know that you will never be proud of *what* I write. But you can't keep me here either, *Papa*. I wasn't born for this misery. I was born for bigger things. I feel that I can do such great things, things that people will talk about for years after I'm gone… Please, don't be mad at me. You'll be proud of me one day, you'll see."

Giselle was hit by a wave of deja-vu, stepping through the door leading to the staircase, which hadn't changed in the slightest in the past thirteen years. She had refused to come back here after her first novel was published, and always invited her parents to either some restaurant or to her newly rented apartment on the fourth floor of a building with a doorman, who her mother secretly feared.

She stood indecisively on the bottom step as if making that step would somehow miraculously transport her back into old times, and the poverty and hunger of the post-war years, which seemed to be forever imprinted in these very wooden steps, shuffled by too many feet in need, hurrying to ungrateful and lowly paid work.

After making her way upstairs, Giselle dug for a key in her leather purse, smiled at the familiar rustling of the lock, and stepped inside.

"Don't move."

A firm grip on her shoulder, pushing her inside the apartment, and an apparent gun shoved in between her shoulder blades made Giselle raise both hands instinctively, cursing her decision to come back here in the first place. *Great, now some burglar, or worse, a runaway criminal who they had released from the prisons during the exodus, and who had most likely taken up residence in a seemingly vacant apartment, would rob and kill her in her childhood home.*

"Make a sound, and I'll make my trigger happy." The intruder, whose face she couldn't see for he had caught her completely unawares hiding behind the door, had shut it closed as soon as he had his victim on aim, judging by the sound of it. His hand released her shoulder only to slide down her waist and back while he searched her for weapons. However, Giselle still slapped his hand hard, gun or no gun pointing at her back.

"You try to lay your dirty hands on me, and you're dead! The chief of the city's Department of *Staatspolizei* is living with me, and he will be here within thirty minutes if I'm not back in time. And when he finds you – and he will find you – he'll cut you into such fine pieces that you will resemble a Union Jack, flying from the gallows the next morning!"

Instead of a reply, the same strong arm turned her around forcefully, and Giselle came face to face with a giant of a man, well over six feet tall, with dark brows knitted together and black eyes shining with anger. Giselle, nevertheless, quickly regained her composure, glowering as well and doing her best not to look intimidated.

"What the hell are you doing in this apartment?"

"How the hell did you get in here?"

They spoke at the same time, the man's gun still pointing at her chest. Giselle crossed her arms over her chest, thrusting her chin forward in a defiant manner.

"Unlike you, I obviously used a key."

"Do you work for the Gestapo?"

"What?" Giselle arched her brow, to which the man jerked his wrist with the gun impatiently.

"I don't have time to play games with you, Madame. Are you their agent, yes or no? Who gave you this key? That Gestapo chief, your *Boche* lover? Are there people outside waiting for you? How many?"

"Yes. The whole brigade of the finest, vilest and best trained Gestapo agents are waiting outside. Even Heydrich and Himmler are there, too. To take pictures, you know. You're so important, after all. They came all the way from Berlin to arrest such a famous criminal, whatever it is you were in jail for. You uncovered our plot. Bravo."

Giselle pronounced the whole tirade with such a dispassionate face and in such a flat tone that "the criminal," no matter how much he tried to contain himself, snorted with laughter, demonstrating two rows of enviously even, white teeth. Even Giselle felt the corners of her red mouth curl upwards in a grin.

"Did you seriously think that even if the Gestapo were onto you, they would have sent a woman here first? And a woman like me, on top of it? You're twice my size, for God's sake!"

"All right, I admit, it was a rather foolish assumption."

"It certainly was."

"Still, what are you doing here?"

He had lowered his gun but was still blocking the doorway. Regardless, Giselle had decided by now that he was harmless and relaxed her shoulders, toying with the keys in her gloved hands.

"It's my parents' apartment. They have gone to the Free Zone, and I came to check if everything was in order." She looked the man over apprehensively. "It's obviously not."

"You're – Giselle Legrand?" the man inquired, much to her surprise.

Her portraits were printed inside her books of course, and she was recognized by the patrons of theaters or restaurants from time to time, but Giselle could never complain that people bothered her in the streets. And it was a wonder that this lumberjack could read at all, to recognize her from her portraits.

"What makes you think so?" She squinted her green eyes slightly.

"You said it was your parents' apartment. So, you're Marcel's sister, I suppose?"

"You know something about my brother?" Giselle stepped forward, her face lighting up at once.

"Yes," the man grumbled, and went to the closed door that separated the living room from the bedroom. He opened it, and in several long strides crossed the room that used to be her parents' bedroom and opened another door, which led to a separate bathroom.

Only when he stepped aside did Giselle see Marcel behind his giant frame, and the two rushed to hug each other, meeting in the middle of the bedroom.

"Marcel! *Mon petit!* I'm so happy to see you! When did you return from the front?"

"Giselle! What are you doing here?" Marcel beamed at her, after kissing his sister on both cheeks.

"Who's that?" Her face fell into a scowl once again, when she noticed two teenagers, lingering in the door of the bathroom.

"These are…" Marcel threw a glance over his shoulder in a futile attempt to come up with something credible. "Just my friends. They… erm… they're former soldiers, from my regiment. They had nowhere to stay, so… I invited them here."

"Nowhere to stay?" Giselle repeated skeptically.

"Yes… They're from the South, which is the Free Zone now," Marcel lied quickly, while the trio behind his back tried their best to look disinterested in the unraveling interrogation.

"Marcel?" Giselle tilted her head to one side, giving her brother one more chance to correct himself. He stubbornly kept quiet, studying the carpeted floor under his feet.

"Those two are still kids, so they obviously couldn't have been in the army with you. And this… gentleman," she threw another glare at the dark-haired man, "speaks like a typical Parisian. Unrefined maybe, but native nevertheless."

"What makes you think I'm unrefined?" The giant fired back, knitting his brows together. *He took offense,* Giselle snickered to herself, surprised. "The absence of the fancy suit and pomade on my hair?"

She glanced him over once again, feeling more and more amused.

"Precisely."

He was dressed in a gray shirt with its sleeves rolled up, and flannel trousers, reaching his worn boots, and not in a "fancy suit," but his clothes were still well-kept, and his dark hair was also neatly brushed to one side. No "fancy pomade" either, but he was clean shaven and spoke very well for a working class representative, for which Giselle took him, promoting him to that rank from the label of "petty criminal" in her mind.

"That's a very superficial idea, to judge a person's cultural and intellectual abilities by his look, Mademoiselle Legrand."

"I didn't say anything about your intellectual abilities. I said you were unrefined in the sense of lacking higher education, and education and intellect are two very different things, Monsieur..?"

"Bussi. Philippe Bussi. And you're very mistaken about him; he's very smart! He was promoted to a *politruk* in Moscow, and you have to be educated for that." Marcel blurted out in his friend's defense, immediately drawing a wrathful glare from the latter.

"I told you that to any outsiders we must use aliases," Philippe growled through gritted teeth. "And we definitely mustn't, under any circumstances, reveal any personal information."

Giselle gasped in theatrical excitement. "Ah! A communist! I should have guessed as soon as I heard the whole anti-capitalistic 'fancy suit and hair pomade' agitprop!"

Philippe narrowed his eyes at the blonde.

"At least I don't cuddle with the *Boches* at night, Mademoiselle."

"Something tells me that it was intended to be an offensive jab in my direction." She sneered, unfazed. "Only, I regret to disappoint you, I, for some reason, don't feel offended in the slightest."

"Of course you don't." Philippe snorted with contempt.

"They're very cuddly," she hissed back, taking the last word.

Philippe only pressed his mouth into a thin line and looked away in disdain.

Marcel, who kept turning his head from his sister to his comrade and back while they were exchanging retorts, got a hold of his voice at last.

"What does it mean, cuddle the *Boches*?"

"Nothing, Marcel, my little innocent lamb."

"Your sister got herself a chief of the local Gestapo as a lover," Philippe spoke again, trying to somehow get to the arrogant socialite – the embodiment of everything he despised about their class. Most of the likes of her also shamelessly demonstrated their high-ranking *Boches* in broad daylight, strolling hand in hand with them, when ordinary people had to live on meager rations according to their ration cards. If it wasn't for Marcel, he would have shot her, and wouldn't bat an eye. To think of it, he had even liked the feisty blonde at first.

"Is it true?" Marcel breathed out, looking at his sister in dismay. He always looked up to her, boasted before his university peers of his famous sibling, and she did...this? Betrayed him in the worst way, warming the bed of an enemy, who was shooting at him and his comrades in the front?

"Why?" Giselle shrugged nonchalantly. "Such connections come in handy nowadays."

"How typically capitalistic. Profiteering on the blood of your countrymen," Philippe threw out the accusation, which again broke against the invisible wall of the blonde's indifference.

"He was billeted in my apartment," she explained to her brother, completely ignoring Philippe's heavy breathing behind Marcel's back. "I didn't invite him if that's what you want to know. And why didn't you call me or come to see me as soon as you came back? It must have been months! And how did you come across these people? Please, do tell me that you didn't fall for their propaganda and didn't join the Party, or I'll officially disown you."

"I couldn't come see you, Giselle. I wasn't released from the army; I deserted. I must stay as far away from the *Boches* as possible for now because even the papers I have aren't my own. I was in hiding this whole time, and it's only thanks to Philippe that I'm alive now. Offering him and these two boys this apartment was the least I could do. Philippe and I are going to work in a munitions factory here in Paris, and we—"

"Oh no." She raised her hand, shaking her head. "No, no,

no. I won't hear a word of it. You? Living and working with these people? No. I'll find some other apartment for them, and I'll provide you with food, and maybe I'll even persuade Karl to do something concerning your situation. But you won't be playing around with these criminals."

"They aren't criminals, Giselle!"

"They're communists, and therefore criminals. I won't have you arrested and jailed because you fell for their propaganda."

"I appreciate that you care for your brother so much, Mademoiselle Legrand, but he's a grown man and can make his own decisions," Philippe interjected.

"And I appreciate your efforts to get a new member into your Party, but I won't allow it, and that's the end of it!" Giselle fought back.

"It's not about the Party." Marcel frowned, feeling like a child whose parents were fighting over what was better for him. Despite what Philippe said, he still didn't consider himself a grown man, regrettably. "And they aren't criminals. They're patriots. And we're all Resistance fighters, whether you like it or not. We all swore!"

Philippe pinched the bridge of his nose with a pained expression on his face. The boy was so smart when he wanted to be, but so unbelievably dense in the simplest of the situations.

"You dragged my brother into the Resistance?" Giselle spoke in a menacingly quiet tone, stepping close to the communist leader.

"I didn't drag him anywhere. I offered him a choice, and he chose us. Why, are you going to sell us out to your *Boche* now?" He growled, also pulling forward.

Only, Giselle didn't move away, and the two stood nose to nose with each other, like two army generals, refusing to concede even the smallest piece of gained territory to the opponent. He noticed that she had hazel eyes, and not brown as he had thought at first, and that she would have been pretty if she washed off all that powder and blush accenting her high cheekbones. The bright red lipstick was also horribly distasteful. He wondered if her *Boche* liked her red lips and if he kissed her often on her full mouth. *Hussy.*

Giselle thought that he smelled surprisingly good for a communist, of soap and his own masculine scent, strangely pleasant even without any expensive colognes and after-shaves. He had the same dark features as Karl, only while the German looked impenetrably cold, this one's eyes burned with passion, and his facial expressions changed every second, as if the energy, brewing inside, had to find its outlet somewhere. *Shame he's a communist.*

Suddenly, Giselle tilted her head to one side, an impish light illuminating her eyes. Philippe felt that he was losing ground again, unable to figure out his opponent and there-fore counter her next move before she made it.

"Of course not," she spoke finally, and her mint-scented breath caressed his mouth. He pulled back again. Her grin became wider. "Exactly how serious are you about that Resistance idea?"

"Pardon me?" Philippe cleared his throat, keeping on guard.

"How important are you? Do you have many people? Are you organized at all? Do you have access to the channels in London? How close are you to Général de Gaulle? What exactly are your plans? Who's in charge?"

Philippe opened and closed his mouth while Marcel and the boys' eyes shone with admiration at their new guest's knowledge of their cause and their leaders.

"Why are you asking?"

Giselle rolled her eyes. "Because if I decide to deal with you and supply you with information from my *Boche*, I want to know how exactly you will be able to use it."

13

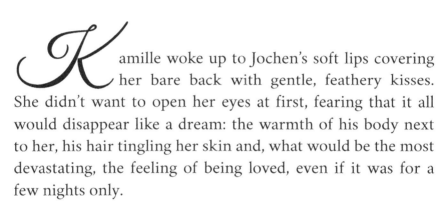

Kamille woke up to Jochen's soft lips covering her bare back with gentle, feathery kisses. She didn't want to open her eyes at first, fearing that it all would disappear like a dream: the warmth of his body next to her, his hair tingling her skin and, what would be the most devastating, the feeling of being loved, even if it was for a few nights only.

"I have to go before Horst wakes up," he whispered in her ear, as he found the corner of her mouth to kiss her once again before sliding out of bed.

Kamille felt cold at once and sat up, pulling the blankets over herself. Jochen gathered his military identification tag with its chain from the bedside table, collected his clothes from the chair and kissed Kamille one last time, before heading to the door.

"I'll take a shower and help you with breakfast."

"You don't have to. I'll get up right away, and everything

143

will be ready before you know it." Kamille made a motion to reach for her robe, but Jochen stopped her, placing his hand on top of her arm gently.

"No need to rush. Sleep some more. We'll fix something together later." He grinned, giving Kamille's arm a playful squeeze. "I like doing things together in the kitchen with you. It appears that your sister comes up with good ideas."

"No, she doesn't. She just has to do what no one else would even think of, and she has a tendency to involve everyone around her in her 'activities.'" Kamille chuckled. "Giselle has always been an instigator. She's one of the few women who graduated from the Sorbonne, too. She probably told the dean that she would burn the place down if they refused to award her with the degree."

Holding the door ajar, Kamille ensured that the hallway was empty and motioned Jochen outside. The two exchanged another quick kiss, chortling like two mischievous children before Jochen darted to the door of his bedroom. Kamille closed hers and leaned on it, almost painful bliss filling her lungs with every new breath.

"A German..." she whispered, noticing how different her intonation was from just three months ago when she uttered the same word with fear and overwhelming anxiety. Now the same word tasted sweet and dreamy, rolling off her tongue. She frowned, recalling the recent incident in Violette's school, but then shrugged, all of a sudden not caring one bit about anyone's opinion on her account. "A German. So what?"

"I'm not a German," Jochen declared later in the kitchen, confusing her.

The two stood next to each other, Jochen stirring oatmeal for Violette, and Kamille flipping the eggs over.

"What do you mean, not a German?"

"I'm an Austrian." He smiled. "Just like Horst. He's from Austria, too. That's why I picked him to be my adjutant. Only I'm from Salzburg, and he's from Vienna. He went to the Academy of Fine Arts there, too; before the war, that is."

"I'm sorry, I didn't know." Kamille caught herself blushing with embarrassment.

"How would you know?" Jochen grinned. "We all sound alike to you. We wear the same uniforms. We serve the same country."

Kamille bit her lip reluctantly for some time, before gathering enough courage to ask him a question that she had never thought she would dare ask.

"Why did you join the army?"

Jochen gave her a one shoulder shrug, pondering his response. "All of my family members were in the military. I followed my father's footsteps and joined the academy for future officers to later join the Austrian army. Only, Austria ceased to exist after the *Anschluss*, and so did the sovereign army. We became a part of the Reich. We were offered two choices: join the *Wehrmacht*, or pursue a civil career. Given that I only had a military education, I had no other choice than join the German army. And so, here I am."

"Do you like it?" Kamille pressed further, a little emboldened by his openness.

"It's all right, I suppose. Better than civil service. I would make a lousy civil servant. Horst, on the contrary, he doesn't belong in the army."

"No?"

"Not at all." Jochen shook his head, laughing. "He's too much of a hopeless romantic for that. He only went into the army because he fell in love with all the outer beauty of the parades, uniforms, wreaths and flags that flew all over Austria after the *Anschluss*. I bet he regrets it now."

"You think?"

"Not that he would admit it to me. But I can tell that he's… unhappy."

"And you?"

"Not anymore, I'm not." He pecked Kamille on her cheek with a playful wink.

"But you were?"

"I was, a few months ago. My fiancé left me in March. Naturally, I was rather upset over it."

Kamille bit her tongue inside her mouth, instantly regretting her nosiness.

"I'm sorry. I didn't mean to pry."

"You weren't prying. And besides, I'm over it now. I don't blame her either," he added quietly. "We got engaged in February 1938, and after that, I got deployed to Germany before we could get married; then to Poland, then to Finland, then all over Europe. With only a week-long leave once every six months it doesn't leave much room for any family life, you see. So, I can't really reproach her for not waiting for me."

"It doesn't excuse her," Kamille muttered somewhat defensively, as if hurting the man whom she cared for that other woman had hurt her as well. "I would have waited for you."

Jochen stopped his stirring for a moment and beamed at her.

"You would?"

She nodded.

"If I get deployed somewhere else tomorrow, you will wait for me?"

"I will. Only if you promise to write."

"I promise."

"Then I promise, too."

———

GISELLE LINGERED in the door of her former study, where Karl was perusing some papers with a look of deep concentration creasing his dark brow. Giselle sometimes found guilty pleasure in scrutinizing him without him noticing it; he was a dashing man after all, in his always immaculate uniform, with his raven-black hair always neatly parted and sleeked to one side, and the profound eyes of a scientist.

Giselle had only recently found out what that mysterious "Dr." stood for, preceding his signature, written in exquisite cursive on multiple papers, neatly stacked on the side of his desk: *SS Sturmbannführer Dr. Karl Wünsche.*

"ARE YOU A LAWYER?" she teased him on one of those rare occasions when he didn't force her out of his study, politely as always, but in a tone that didn't leave any room for discussion. Giselle rested her head on his shoulder, pointing her manicured finger to the "Dr." part of his signature under some order, which she couldn't possibly understand, for it was written in German. "Or are you indeed a literary critic? Doctor of German Literature and Fine Arts?"

She sniggered at her own joke.

"Do I give you such an impression?" He indulged her with a tight smile.

"No." Giselle gave up her attempt at playfulness and straightened, studying his face closely. He was enviously handsome, but at the same time emanated almost graveyard coldness. Giselle traced her finger from his chiseled chin to his high cheekbone, almost surprised that his skin felt warm, and not stony and lifeless, like that of a marble statue that he reminded her of. "I will go with my first guess. You're a lawyer."

"And why do you assume that I'm a lawyer?" His smile reflected interest this time.

"You have a phenomenal memory. You always analyze everything. You're very organized." Giselle kept count on her fingers. "And you always keep talking about this law, or that law, or this order, or that one. A typical lawyer."

He snorted softly, shaking his head.

"I'm not a lawyer. I talk about laws so you will be the first one to know about what is illegal and so you won't get in trouble. I talk about them because I care about your well-being."

Giselle's brows shot up, but she decided to refrain from her usual sarcastic remarks. She doubted that he would take too kindly to her saying something like *That's an interesting way to care about someone, threatening them with a firing squad if they walk around past curfew time.* It seemed that he didn't understand irony whatsoever.

"So what are you then?"

"I'm an actual doctor. A neurosurgeon, to be precise."

Well, that explained his aristocratic hands with long

fingers, which he had a habit of washing every half an hour. Giselle tilted her head to one side curiously.

"What on earth are you doing in the Gestapo then? It's a rather rare and noble profession, being a surgeon. I don't understand why you would forsake it for something so... petty."

Karl gave her a long, pointed look before replying. "An in-depth knowledge of the human body's anatomy, brain functions and nerve endings, in particular, allows me to be much more efficient in the course of an interrogation than my colleagues who are not educated in a medical field."

Giselle fell silent, for the first time in her life not finding something with which to reply.

"You mean... You studied neurology so you could... torture people more efficiently?"

"*Ja.*"

A pregnant pause followed, the grave silence in the room interrupted only by the clock counting seconds next to the wall, under the portrait of the Führer. Karl's lips slowly moved into a grin.

"Don't look so terrified, my beautiful *Gisela*. I'm only joking with you. I got my medical degree long before I became a member of the Party."

"You still didn't answer my question. What are you doing in the Gestapo?" Giselle didn't laugh with him and only cringed when he called her by the German version of her name – one of his recently adopted habits which irritated her to no end.

"It's a long story." He kissed her hand gallantly and rose from his chair to escort her out of his study. The conversation was obviously over. "You need not worry your pretty head about such matters anyway. Why don't you go for a walk with Coco? Maybe your muse will visit you after some fresh air."

GISELLE RECALLED that recent conversation while lingering in the doors until Karl lifted his head from his papers and obliged her with a polite smile.

"Did you want something, *Gisela?*"

Giselle swallowed her annoyance and ignored him pronouncing her name once again in his German manner. Instead, she put on her most charming smile and walked over to the officer, gracefully perching on the edge of the desk in front of him.

"As a matter of fact, yes, I did." Giselle took his hand in hers and lowered it onto her lap, studying his fingers. "I told you that my sister, Kamille, lost her husband to the war, didn't I?"

"Yes, you did."

"Well, you saw how she is after that, all sad eyes, and so subdued, the poor thing." Giselle threw a quick glance from under her lashes to see his reaction. The German's face remained immobile. Giselle sighed deeply, trying not to overplay her words, and continued. "I want to cheer her up a little. She deserves it after all she's been through, the poor, devastated widow of a war hero..."

"I hate to cut you short, but what exactly do you need from me? I have a lot of paperwork to finish, and I need to be done with this by five if you still want to get to *Maxim's* for dinner in time."

Giselle barely suppressed her indignation at his dismissive tone, a malicious green ire igniting in her eyes, but for a fleeting second only. She lowered her gaze, hiding her defiance from him the best she could, even though any other man in his place would have long been kicked out into the street, and the doorman would have been told to give his hide a good tanning if he dared to solicit a meeting with her ever again. Giselle always refused to put up with such condescending treatment, and cut short any of her lovers, no matter how handsome or influential they were, if they dared try to express any sort of dominance on her territory. Only, with the new masters of the house, it was all far too different.

"Mais, Charlie," she purred his name, changing it into French as well, like he did it with hers, satisfied with the seemingly innocent act of rebellion. "That's exactly what I came to ask you for. You and me, we go to different restaurants, to *Maxim's,* to the *Ritz* even, at least twice a week; we go to see shows and plays, all the while *ma petite* Kamille sits at home, locked away under that cursed curfew of yours, and withers away day by day. She's sad as it is after the loss of her beloved husband, and I can't even do my sibling duty for her and entertain her a little."

"Süße, I can't possibly cancel the curfew. What do you want me to do?"

Was he really that thickheaded, or just really good at acting? Giselle tried her best to suppress her temper once again.

"I know you can't, *mon coeur,* but you can write an *Ausweis* for each of us. This way I will be able to be a dutiful sister and take my poor Kamille out once in a while. When you have your own plans for the evening, that is."

"Nein." He took his hand out of hers and picked up his

pen again, turning back to his papers. "I don't want you walking around at night all alone, without an escort. It's too dangerous for a woman to be alone in the streets at night. There are a lot of communists and other criminals who roam around when they shouldn't, and despite our utmost efforts, we, *die Staatspolizei*, still can't wipe the streets of Paris clean of them. We will, most certainly, but with time. Until then you tell me where and when you want to go with your sister, and I'll send Otto with you. He'll drive you there, and he'll take you back home after that."

Those streets were perfectly safe before you Herren showed up. Giselle bit back her thoughts. But she still refused to move and retreat to her room just because some *Boche* has spoken his weighty *nein*.

Even though he had already shifted his attention back to the documents in front of him, Giselle slid off the table and circled his chair. She lowered her hands on his shoulders and rested her chin on the back of her hand, pressing her cheek to his immaculately shaven one.

"But *Charlie, Charlie, mon amour*, it's not fun for two girls to be out with a military escort. We'll look ridiculous as if we're two kids who can't be trusted to go outside without an adult. Besides, Otto will be bored to death with us, and our girls chat..."

"He won't be escorting you inside. Think of him as your personal driver. He'll do just that," Karl retorted, cutting the conversation short once again.

A driver is not good enough, Giselle huffed angrily, *if I want for us to be alone with Jochen and Horst. He'll see us together, most definitely.*

She had her own plans for Kamille's lodger's young adjutant. The boy was clearly infatuated with her, and she could milk him for information during the dinner, just to prove to that uneducated leader of the Resistance, or whoever he imagined himself to be, that she was a far better leader and organizer. *And then let's see how he starts singing about her "cuddling the Boches." Communist, all right. He probably doesn't even know what communism means.*

Giselle shook her head slightly, clearing it from distracting thoughts, and decided to press the matter further.

"Karl." She tried his German name this time, thinking that maybe that would coax him into a better disposition. That and her arms, which she slowly lowered down to his waist to start undoing his belt while covering his neck and jawline with soft, seductive kisses, bit by bit approaching his lips. "I really would like to have that *Ausweis*. And I'll be forever grateful, every single night, I promise."

He caught her hands in his and gently but firmly removed them from his belt, readjusting it in its place.

"I said no, *Gisela*. It's non-negotiable, *Herz*. Now, why don't you get ready for dinner? I really am busy and would like to finish everything in time."

Straightening behind his back, Giselle gestured desperately, barely containing herself from swatting him on his perfectly coiffured head.

"Très bien, Charlie," she replied sweetly instead. "You know better."

He beamed at her with a rather uncharacteristic smile. Giselle replied with a lopsided grin.

This is not over, Charlie, Giselle promised to herself, leaving his study. *Not by a long shot. I'll still get that damned Ausweis, with your help or without.*

14

Marcel pulled his cap down to his eyes, doing his best to avoid the *Boches'* beady eyes, which surveyed everyone coming and going from the munitions factory. Due to Philippe's contacts, Marcel was fortunate enough to secure himself a position as a press worker, and even though the job was exhausting and physically demanding he felt much better having a task to do, a certain purpose, instead of lingering in the apartment together with two teenagers. The boys grew restless, just like he did, and started voicing their suggestions to do some sabotage work more and more often, but Philippe had already stated his attitude on the matter, strictly forbidding the two brothers to leave the apartment without his permission. However, both he and Marcel knew very well that Pierre and Jerome had reached that age when they defied any authority: parental, governmental and even their comrades.

"Those kids are trouble," Marcel recalled Philippe grumbling when they were walking towards the factory one day, lowering their eyes each time a German lorry filled with ammunition passed them by. "They'll get into something before you know it. We need to move them, and fast."

Marcel only nodded, shifting his satchel on his shoulder and catching a whiff of the two ham sandwiches that he had packed as his lunch at home. Thanks to the money that Giselle had left (*Reichsmarks* even, not the devalued Franks!), Philippe was able to obtain some food which they could only dream about for the past few weeks, together with the rest of the population. However, *Le Marché Noir* – the Black Market – thrived and flourished, distributing prohibited or unobtainable goods for a price that exceeded their actual value five and sometimes ten times more. Philippe kept grumbling about the profiteering traitors of *la République*, who didn't give a damn about their fellow countrymen but still paid the price for ham, bread, and eggs to feed the boys. Even though he and Marcel had their ration cards as factory workers, they weren't enough by any means to feed all four of them.

Today, walking out of the factory after a blaring siren had signaled the end of the day shift, Marcel noticed at once that something troubled Philippe. The communist leveled his steps with Marcel's as the crowd of workers slowly made their way through the checkpoint, where every single one of them was checked for stolen parts or scrap metal, which they could later sell at the Black Market. The German soldiers with their machine guns paced leisurely near the exit, supervising the process.

"We need to talk," Philippe spoke inaudibly above Marcel's ear.

"Something happened?" Marcel replied in the same manner.

"Yes. Let's have a walk before we head to the *Metro*."

After they were both thoroughly searched and waved away to the exit, Marcel could barely contain his anxiety. Philippe was a seasoned fighter, and rarely ever exaggerated the gravity of the situation. Now, however, he looked as grim as the sky above them, which was ready to burst into September, bone-chilling showers.

"Well? What is it?" Marcel demanded impatiently, catching Philippe's sleeve as soon as they had walked away enough from the crowd.

"The boys' father has been arrested by the Gestapo. A comrade delivered the news from the village. Apparently, the flag was indeed marked and brought them to him."

Marcel swallowed hard, already foreseeing the reaction of the two brothers. Both Pierre and Jerome didn't fancy the *Boches* as it is, but now they would most definitely do something utterly stupid either to avenge their father or to try and rescue him.

"I know what you're thinking," Philippe spoke again, motioning Marcel to a small bench with a newly screwed plate on top of it saying *'Nur für Arier'* – 'For Aryans Only.' "I'm wondering myself if we should tell them at all. On the other hand, they're both members of the *Komsomol* and it's against the code to use a situation against your fellow comrade. We don't deceive each other to profit from it, no matter how grave the situation is."

Marcel dug in his satchel and fished out the last sandwich from it. He sunk his teeth into it and took a hearty bite, while Philippe chewed on his lip, scowling and staring into the distance.

"What do you suggest we do then?" Marcel spoke with his mouth full, forgetting all the good manners that his mother had taught him. He was certain that she would forgive him now: he could have hardly been blamed for feeling almost starved after a hard day's work. After all, his parents raised him as a future bourgeois, a history professor, and not a factory worker. The war had turned everyone's world upside down.

"Tell them as it is and try to reason with them." Philippe opened his satchel and offered Marcel his daily ration, completely untouched and still carefully wrapped in news-paper. "Here, have mine too. You must be starving."

"What about you?"

"I'm used to going without food when needed. Don't worry about me. Eat. Manual labor doesn't seem to agree with you just yet." He smirked, but kind-heartedly.

Marcel reddened but took the offering with gratitude.

"Thank you."

"You don't have to thank me. Communism isn't as bad as you think. It's not about 'stealing from the rich and giving to the poor.' We share everything with the ones who need it more than us, willingly. Now imagine if our society were built on the same principle, the world would be a much better place."

"I suppose," Marcel muttered, working on Philippe's sandwich. "What about my sister then? You still think she's a typical profiteering capitalist? She shared her money with us. Gave us all she had in her wallet, actually."

"It wasn't her money; it was probably her *Boche's*."

157

Marcel chuckled, finding it amusing that Philippe downright refused to accept the very idea that Giselle could possibly have at least one redeeming feature. His brows knitted together soon after though, as soon as he remembered the topic of their conversation.

"What do you think the Nazis will do to the boys' father?"

"Who knows? Maybe jail him, maybe shoot him. Maybe send him to Germany to one of their working camps. Either way, he won't end up well."

"But he probably doesn't even know about the flag. Can't he tell them that it was stolen from him?"

"And you think they'll believe him?"

"Why not?"

"Because when you're guilty of something, and the police find evidence against you, that's the first thing you do – say that it was stolen by some crooks who later used it."

"The boys will not sit idle as soon as they learn. They'll do something preposterous."

"I know, Marcel." Philippe sighed. "Trust me; I'm trying to figure out what to do myself."

GISELLE TOOK on the task of ordering food for everyone at the table, as the two Germans (*Austrians!* Kamille had corrected her earlier, making big eyes. Giselle did her best not to snigger in response, realizing at once that one of those *Austrians* had most likely already completed his own *blitzkrieg* with her little sister) admitted their defeat, at least when it came to knowledge of sophisticated French cuisine. In *Café de la Paix*, the famous restaurant within walking distance to the Paris Opera House, Giselle was like a fish in water. Her guests didn't conceal their admiration of the extravagant frescoes and rich gilding reflected in multiple mirrors, and exchanged excited exclamations switching to their mother tongue without realizing it.

"Escargot and oysters," Giselle declared as soon as they were seated at the round table, which was covered with an immaculately starched tablecloth with another, red one, showing its luxurious material underneath it. "You have to try them. They're the best here, and even the shameless plunder, which you lot have been doing in our beautiful country for the past month, didn't change that fact."

The two officers lowered their eyes apologetically, murmuring some suitable excuses. Under Kamille's accusing stare Giselle only flicked her wrist effortlessly, placing a napkin on her lap and laughed in her charming manner.

"Oh, don't be so embarrassed. I'm just teasing you two."

They beamed at her, Jochen from across the table, where he sat next to Kamille, and Horst right next to her. The four had sat in the same manner in the Opera House as well, from where they walked to the restaurant, in which Giselle insisted they had to dine. After the two glasses of champagne that they enjoyed during the intermission, Horst babbled away about the Vienna Opera House, museums and the army, mixing the words from time to time, not noticing how closely his blonde date was watching him, waiting for the right moment to pounce on her victim.

Giselle had already realized that unlike the experienced and more reserved Jochen, Horst would tell her anything she'd ask him about when combined with the right amount of alcohol and her feminine charms, so she could later rub all that information into that horrid communist's face.

Giselle moved her padded chair closer to Horst, pressing her knee into his as if by accident. He beamed even wider and scooted closer to her as well, readjusting his plate and cutlery.

"So tell me more about your service, Horst. What exactly do you do now, except for dining with pretty French girls from time to time?" she asked him teasingly.

"There is no time to time, Mademoiselle..." Horst stopped himself mid-word as Giselle's shoe caught his boot under the table, and cleared his throat, grinning. "I meant, Giselle."

Giselle nodded approvingly with a mischievous smile, only now moving her foot away.

"I'll kick you every time you make that mistake," she warned him playfully.

"Then I'll only keep making it again and again." Horst breathed out, not even noticing the waiter, who had placed a plate of escargot in front of him. "I was saying there is no 'from time to time' and there is definitely no other French girls. This is the first time Herr Hauptmann and I have escorted French ladies out since our service brought us to Paris. We used to dine alone before that, in the officers' mess mostly. Herr Hauptmann didn't want to impose on Madame Kamille."

"Oh, what silliness! I'm always telling you that you're no imposition by any means," Kamille spoke quietly, smoothing out the skirt of her dress once again in a nervous gesture.

Unlike Giselle, she wasn't used to places of such fine dining and, besides, she couldn't even recall when was the last time she was out on a date with a man. Charles never took her anywhere, apart from a few rare times in the very beginning of their relationship. Jochen caught her hand and gave it a reassuring squeeze, adding in a quiet whisper that she looked stunning – for the tenth time that evening.

Giselle watched the two exchange their hushed words and lovelorn glances with a knowing smile on her face. More than anything, Kamille deserved to be happy after that no-good husband of hers, and Jochen seemed to be a nice enough man for her. Alas, he belonged to the occupying forces and who knew where his fate would land him tomorrow. Giselle caught herself frowning, hoping deep inside that he wouldn't break her sister's heart.

"…and then, when Herr Hauptmann promotes me to a higher rank, I'll be in charge of it." Horst's voice broke her concentration and Giselle chastised herself for not paying his words enough attention.

"Really? That is fascinating," she gushed and picked up an escargot on her small fork. "Here, try it."

Horst eyed the mollusk suspiciously, without making any attempt to take it from her. Giselle moved the fork closer to his mouth.

"Come, stop being such a scaredy cat. I won't poison you, I promise." Seeing his reluctance, Giselle added with a scheming gleam in her green eyes, "And if you don't like it, I'll make it up to you with a kiss."

The young man took a deep breath under his commanding officer's amused stare and bravely allowed the blonde to navigate the fork into his mouth. He chewed a couple of times while everyone at the table awaited his verdict and then smiled brightly, raising his brows.

"Delicious, isn't it?" Giselle clapped her hands excitedly.

"No, I hated it." Horst gave Giselle an impish glance from under his long lashes.

Jochen burst out laughing together with Kamille. Giselle noticed that they did everything together now, the emotions of one reflecting on the face of the other immediately.

"You have to kiss him now!" Jochen exclaimed, and even Kamille joined him in his teasing, her eyes shining brightly with joy.

"Yes, kiss him, Giselle!"

"No, I can't kiss him; I'm a lady after all, and we're in a public place. But he can kiss me if he likes." Giselle gave Horst a playful wink, pointing at her cheek.

Horst leaned forward readily, but when he was just about to peck Giselle on her cheek, she turned her head unexpectedly, and his lips met hers instead.

"Giselle, you're incorrigible!" Kamille squealed with delight at the latest of her sister's antics. She had already forgotten that Giselle was always up for any possible shenanigan, and ladylike behavior wasn't something she honored or followed.

Both men only laughed, Horst looking positively delighted. Giselle watched her carefully orchestrated play, wondering when she had become such a schemer.

Just the manner in which she had obtained the necessary passes for Kamille and herself, allowing them to be outside after the curfew, spoke volumes. Giselle never told Karl about the second key to his study that she had, so opening the door to his home office while he was at work was a piece of cake. She would have preferred it much more if he had simply given her the papers, but she justified her shameless intrusion by the fact that he had left her no choice. Giselle rummaged through his papers carefully, opening drawer after drawer until she found what she was looking for – a stack of *Ausweis* blanks. She filled two of them out – one for herself and one for Kamille, copying Karl's writing and signature from one of his handwritten letters that lay right there, on top of his desk.

Then she just as shamelessly lied to Karl that she would spend the evening at Kamille's at a game of bridge, and now she had manipulated this poor boy into almost falling in love with her, and all for what? To learn what they were working on, so later she could manipulate that cursed communist into giving her the leading position. And for what? For fun, like she told Antoine? All those people had a goal, and her? *Well, she might just get a new and very entertaining novel out of it,* Giselle thought with a small laugh, as she shrugged off the doubts gnawing on her restless mind and turned back to Horst.

15

As soon as the four returned to Kamille's house, Giselle headed straight to the bar. Violette was spending the night at Lili's – her teacher Madame Marceau's daughter and her best friend from school – as it had been previously arranged by Kamille, and so the blonde wasn't afraid to make noise with her contagious laughter and the clinking of the glasses. Horst was right by her side, of course, offering her help despite his commanding officer's wary looks.

Jochen, just as Giselle suspected he would, had caught onto his adjutant saying a little too much during the dinner. He even interrupted him harshly once, when Horst started explaining to Giselle about the "highly important operation" that they were working on, and some wire net that was supposed to stretch around the one hundred kilometer radius around Paris…

"Horst!" Jochen's sharp voice cut into the boy's chatter in

tow with a stern glare. "We aren't supposed to talk about that with civilians, and certainly not in public places."

"*Jawohl*, Herr Hauptmann." Horst lowered his head guiltily, even though Giselle guessed that he was more disappointed that he couldn't impress his date with the details of the "highly important operation" than with upsetting his superior.

Giselle wisely changed the subject then, deciding that she would get to the chatty adjutant when they were back at Kamille's. Only, Jochen apparently feared the same happening again and had therefore ordered Horst to go up to his bedroom instead of staying with Giselle downstairs.

"We have to be up early tomorrow, Horst."

"But tomorrow is Sunday…" the young man protested weakly.

Giselle tried her best charming smile on Jochen, pointing at the two glasses on the silver tray near the bar.

"Oh, come now, don't send my Horst away! I've already mixed us drinks. You don't want them to go to waste, do you? That would be a true atrocity in times like these!"

"I'm sorry, Giselle." Jochen smiled politely, but she had already guessed his answer before he uttered it. "I'm afraid he has already had his fill. I'm responsible for him as his commanding officer, and I don't want him to suffer from a headache tomorrow."

Horst didn't even bother to suppress a disappointed sigh, turned to Giselle and kissed her hand gallantly.

"I'm sorry, Giselle. Maybe next time. Goodnight."

"Goodnight, Horst," Giselle replied, and added very quietly, pressing his hand in a conspiratorial manner. "Don't lock your door, will you?"

Horst's head shot up, and his face lit up at once.

"I won't," he whispered, kissing her hand once again ardently and leaving the room, wishing everyone good night in a cheerful tone. Jochen eyed him with suspicion.

"Don't worry about me." Giselle waved off her sister, who made a motion to take a seat on the sofa near her. "You two should call it a night too; you're both tired, I can see. I'll stay here and read for a while. I'm a night owl and most likely will be up all night. So, go ahead and rest. And tomorrow we'll all have a nice breakfast together."

Both Jochen and Kamille obviously couldn't wait to go upstairs together, and Giselle didn't want to embarrass them by being witness to the fact that they would likely share the same room. Not a word was spoken of it, but she knew all too well by the telltale signs as to what was going on between the two. And besides, she needed them to sleep soundly together, so when she tried to sneak into Horst's room, no one would hear her.

Giselle stalled for a good thirty minutes downstairs and then soundlessly ascended the carpeted steps, pausing on the landing and still playing with the amber liquid in her glass. Her calculations turned out to be correct as it seemed, as she heard soft snoring from behind Kamille's door. Trying not to chuckle at her prim and proper sister who always prided herself on doing everything by the book, Giselle took her shoes off and padded to the opposite side of the landing, where Horst's bedroom was.

She opened the door softly and slid inside, feeling her way in the dark. The poor boy had fallen asleep too, she guessed by the heavy breathing coming from his bed. Giselle placed the glass on top of the nightstand silently, removed her dress and stockings and slid under the warm covers, shushing the young man's audible gasp as he woke up.

Horst instantly pulled her close, covering her mouth and neck in rushed, greedy kisses, and promising her everything she wanted in a fervent whisper; even to take her to the field, where "the highly important operation" was taking place.

"Let's run away tomorrow morning. Before everyone wakes up?" Giselle purred in his ear as he moved on top of her.

"Yes… Of course, we will… Whatever you want, Giselle, I'll do it."

It was almost too easy.

———

THE RISING SUN had barely painted the sky in pale blue at break of day as Giselle and Horst pedaled away on two bicycles, brazenly "borrowed" from one of the *Wehrmacht* barracks nearby; which, according to Horst, no one would use on Sunday. The golden carpet of fallen leaves rustled under their wheels as the two sped away from the city, which was still immersed into its tranquil slumber behind its blacked-out windows.

"This way!" Horst shouted to Giselle as they approached a crossroads, with the sign *Verboten* under an arrow, which was pointing to the right.

"Are you sure we won't get in trouble for trespassing?" she inquired, leveling the speed of her bicycle with his.

"Are you afraid?" Horst teased.

"Of you Germans?" Giselle snorted, rolling her eyes. "You wish."

He laughed, throwing his head backward, and soon pointed to a pathway leading to the forest.

"We'll have to leave our bicycles there."

"Whatever you say. You're leading the way today." Giselle winked at the young man.

Reaching the edge of the forest, which seemed impenetrable with its growth and bushes completely cutting off the trail from entering its emerald kingdom, Horst jumped off his bicycle and helped Giselle get off of hers.

"Let's lead the bikes with us as far as we can," he suggested. "This way the patrol won't notice them right away and won't raise the alarm."

Giselle nodded and sighed as soon as they started making their way inside the wood, wishing that she had some sort of sandals on her feet and not these pretty, but oh-so-uncomfortable pumps. Horst kept checking on her every few steps, making sure that she followed and didn't get caught in the spiky bushes, which caught onto their clothes relentlessly.

Just as Giselle was beginning to regret her decision to set on such a physically demanding adventure, Horst took her hand in his and warned her quietly to keep her head low.

They were climbing up a rocky hill, having left their bicycles halfway from here, but Giselle still frowned, deciding that the young man just wanted to impress her and was being overly dramatic. Most likely they would have to walk another hour before they reached—

"Quiet!" He shushed her suddenly, interrupting her thoughts, as a twig snapped loudly under her foot. "There are sentries out there, and if they hear us..."

Giselle had just decided to roll her eyes emphatically when they reached the top of the hill, when she indeed saw a small figure in its green-grayish uniform, sitting at the bottom, almost in a field that spread out in front of him, with his rifle resting casually nearby.

Giselle heard Horst hissing something in his language. He snorted in response to her inquiring look and shook his head with disdain, pointing at the sentry in the distance.

"He's napping, the lazy good-for-nothing! Don't you see?" he whispered, motioning Giselle to lower on the ground. Sensing her reluctance, he quickly took off his uniform jacket and placed it in front of her, gesturing to it chivalrously. As soon as the two took up their positions, Giselle on top of Horst's uniform, he motioned his head towards the private, who was supposed to be guarding the perimeter. "It's a secret object as of now, the whole field. The *Wehrmacht* aren't allowing the locals to use it. See how over-grown it is? It's all because we're stretching the wire through it, from over there to – see that border? – to that side, you see?"

Giselle squinted against the rising sun, trying to make out what he was pointing at. She saw it at last, barely noticeable due to it being camouflaged: a reel of thick wire on the neighboring side of the woods not too far from them, near where another sentry was resting. This one was busy reading a book at least, and not shamelessly sleeping like his comrade at the bottom of the hill. The thick wire itself disappeared from the reel into the dense growth of the field.

"I told you we were working on a secret operation." Horst beamed at her with a smug look, satisfied that he could finally impress his new lady friend, who wasn't usually so easy to impress.

"Yes, you most certainly are," Giselle replied, playing with his chestnut hair. "What exactly does that wire do, did you say?"

Horst tensed for a moment, his face taking on a guarded expression, but only until Giselle sprawled out next to him with a content sigh as if forgetting her question.

"It must be so boring anyway. I wish you could take me to Vienna instead. I bet it's a beautiful city with plenty of entertainment."

Horst's expression brightened again, and Giselle released another soft sigh, treading carefully. "Ah, if only you were stationed there, and not forced to walk daily through the middle of nowhere, minding some stupid wire. Most likely it doesn't even do anything; your superiors are just trying to keep you busy this way."

"Of course it does! It feeds our communication lines!" Horst argued, swallowing the bait. "I told you already. As soon as it's set up, together with several other parts of the net, it will be able to not only unify all the telephone and telegraph lines of the city but will also help us in gathering intelligence. The Gestapo have been fighting tooth and nail to gain control over it, but our *Wehrmacht* command won't hear a word of it. We want to apprehend the remaining rebels on our own, without their meddling in our affairs. Those rebels rescue and hide downed British pilots, and who knows how soon they will be able to communicate with London if we don't stop them in time. And you're saying it's not doing anything."

Giselle shrugged dismissively as if showing a complete lack of interest in the wire and its purpose and pulled Horst closer to silence him with a kiss.

"I didn't come here for some stupid wire of yours. I just

wanted to be with you away from that stern, commanding officer of yours, and my sister, the prude." She was lying obviously, and judging by his eyes, glowing with adoration, rather convincingly. "Have you ever made love in the woods?"

GISELLE ASCENDED THE STAIRS, almost dragging her feet from the exhausting first half of the day. Having returned the missing adjutant to Jochen, Giselle refused Kamille's offer to share lunch together, citing other plans. No one needed to know that those "other plans" included their "missing" brother and his newfound friends/communists, whom she decided to pay a visit before returning home.

She opened the door to her parents' apartment with her key and cast a pointed glare Philippe's way as he emerged from the living room, aiming a gun at her.

"Will we ever have a normal meeting, *comrade?*" Giselle didn't even hide the irony in her voice, locking the door after herself.

The communist tucked the gun back into his belt and looked Giselle up and down, taking in her shoes, which were covered in dust, and the creased clothes and hair, which framed her face in gentle waves without being perfectly styled in comparison to the first time when he had met her. She also didn't wear any makeup besides lipstick, which strangely made her look much more attractive, despite her somewhat pale complexion and the grayish circles under her tired eyes.

"What happened? The Nazis occupied all the beauty

salons around?" He asked with a lopsided contemptuous smirk.

Surprisingly, she decided to ignore the jab and proceeded into the living room to lower herself onto the old sofa, on which she used to curl up with a book when she was a teenager. Now, instead of books and newspapers, an over-flowing ashtray rested on the small coffee table with faded whitish spots from hot coffee mugs, for which her mother used to chide her father, and several leaflets with some communist propaganda – of course.

"Could you be a lamb and bring me a glass of water, comrade?" Giselle asked, taking off her shoes and massaging her aching ankles.

"You're not my comrade, and I don't remember being hired as your personal lackey," the harsh reply followed.

She sighed, lifting her legs onto the sofa, and offered him a surprisingly gentle smile.

"For once, why don't we not make it about communism and capitalism, and pretend that I'm just a very tired woman and can't possibly make it to the kitchen myself, and you're a man, who won't let me die of thirst? Please?"

Philippe frowned but nevertheless turned on his heel and headed to the kitchen to fetch her water.

"Thank you."

"You look like you've walked for miles. Did your *Boche* kick you out of your house?"

"Drop that tone so that we can talk like two adults, will you?" Giselle muttered after downing the glass.

Philippe snorted but refrained from making another retort.

"Where is my brother?"

"He's out with the boys. They should be back any minute now."

Giselle caught him throwing a sideways glance at the leaflets on the table, which he clearly wished she hadn't seen.

"Please, don't tell me that you sent them out to distribute those communist flyers of yours."

"I didn't send them out. They volunteered," he replied defensively and quickly grabbed the remaining papers off the table to take them to one of the bedrooms.

"What if they get caught?"

"The boys needed something to do," he replied, returning to the room, and picked up an unfinished cigarette from an ashtray. "The Gestapo have just arrested their father. They couldn't possibly sit idly without doing anything, and it was the only way to keep them out of trouble because they were ready to steal your kitchen knives to hunt the *Boches* at night. This way I can at least offer them some task that gives them purpose with minimal risk. And, besides, Marcel is watching over them so that they can't do anything stupid."

"I'm sorry to hear that." Giselle lowered her eyes. "What did they arrest him for?"

"For something he didn't do," Philippe replied curtly. "You better go before they return. They don't take too kindly to collaborators, especially now. And particularly those who share the bed of the man who will possibly send their father to Germany in the near future."

"Is that why you're so angry with me today?" Giselle grinned faintly. "I have no control over what he does, you know."

"I know. And I'm not angry. I despise people like you, that's all."

"I don't like this collaboration policy any more than you do, Philippe."

He looked up at the woman in front of him, who had just called him by his name for the first time, instead of her usual sarcastic titles like "comrade" and such. She was leaning on the back of the sofa, upholstered in dark burgundy material, with her legs tucked underneath her. Her smile seemed sad this time. She held his gaze for some time and then returned to studying the empty glass in her hands without saying a word.

"Do you want more water?" Philippe asked, not even knowing why he would ask such a thing. A feeling of guilt started to overcome him for some reason.

"No, thank you, it's all right." Giselle reached for her black leather clutch and, after rummaging through its contents, pulled several *Reichsmarks* out of it and put them on the coffee table.

Philippe had just opened his mouth in protest, but she shook her head, stopping him. "It's for all of you. For food. Or whatever else you need. And please, do tell me if you need anything; I can get almost everything for you."

"Thank you, but I don't want to accept charity from..." Philippe didn't finish his sentence, cursing inwardly once again at a sense of conscience striking him unexpectedly for insulting the young woman in front of him. She probably meant well.

"From the collaborator?" Giselle grinned with a corner of her mouth, not showing any signs of being offended. "What if I'm collaborating with you now? And it's money for the cause?"

"The cause?"

"Mais oui. La République libérée."

Philippe recognized the mischievous gleam shining in her eyes, which had seemed dull and indifferent just moments ago. She grinned wider, and he caught himself doing the same.

"I have information for you," she proceeded, taking up a sitting position and patting a spot on the sofa next to her, offering him a seat.

Philippe faltered for a second but decided that no harm would come out of sitting next to a collaborator.

She had enough tact not to tease him for it and continued. "Today one German soldier took me to the forest near the *Fontainebleau*. Apparently, they're setting up some wire net around the city for communication purposes, and also to gather intelligence. I saw the exact location of one of those wires, but, according to him, there are more of them somewhere else. I didn't want to press the matter, but what if we find a way to somehow damage this one? It will disrupt the work of the others, won't it?"

"Which *Boche* in his right mind would take you to the forest to show you a secret object?" Philippe narrowed his eyes in mistrust.

"He was not precisely in his right mind; you're right about that." Giselle chuckled softly. "But that's not what's important. What's important is the question of whether you know people who could carry out this plot, and whether they have access to that part of the wood. It's being guarded, of course, and so is the wire. However, the sentries don't seem to take their task seriously. One of them was sleeping, and another one was reading a highly compelling book. Let me warn you before you ask: I'm not going back there, and you are not mentioning my name to your comrades. Deal? I'll show you the location on a map, and describe how to get there, but that's where everything ends. You can all die like martyrs if you like, but leave me out of it. Yes, I know, I know – this is typical profiteering capitalist collaborator talk, or whatever you call it, but take it or leave it. I'm not getting physically involved with your Resistance."

Philippe studied her a little longer, getting more and more confused with her behavior. No, that's where she was mistaken. She was everything but a typical "profiteering collaborator." Whatever the hell she was, he still couldn't figure her out for the life of him.

"I don't blame you. It's much more dangerous for a woman than for a man," he concluded quietly. "And yes, I do know the right people."

16

*M*arcel once again lifted a finger to his mouth, trying to pacify the fuming boys together with Philippe, who's been whisper-yelling at them for a good ten minutes now. Together with the robust communist, he was able to herd Pierre and Jerome into the furthest bedroom, which was once the Legrand children's room, to ensure that no neighbors could overhear their indignant shouts.

The shouts stopped rather fast, though, as soon as Philippe clasped his wide palm on top of Pierre's mouth after the boy started to raise his voice to a dangerous level.

"How dare you preach to us the principles of a Free France and talk about the Resistance when you take money from a collaborator?!" Pierre's blue eyes were shining with angry tears while he was hurling the tirade at Phillipe. "Her *Boche's* money! Dirty *Reichsmarks*, from the very man who took *our Papa* away! You're no better than her! I'd rather starve than use that bloody money! Let go of me! I'm not staying here with you!"

"Pierre, one last time I'm warning you: keep it down," Philippe growled.

"No! Let go! You can't order me around! You're not my father!"

Jerome, the younger brother, was biting his bottom lip nervously, watching the confrontation unravel. Giselle had left barely minutes before Marcel returned with the boys. However, the faint smell of her perfume and the German currency still laying on the table were a telltale sign as to whom the recent visitor had been. Needless to say, the brothers didn't take too kindly to fraternizing with a person from a differing social class and a political enemy on top of it, which they considered her to be.

"You're lucky that I'm not. Otherwise, I would tan your hides at every chance possible, and, who knows, maybe you wouldn't grow into such hot-headed, irresponsible scoundrels!" Philippe hissed without releasing his firm grip on Pierre's arm. "Allow me to remind you that it's not her who's at fault for your father being arrested in the first place; it's you! You went ahead and did an idiotic thing without considering the repercussions, and now you blame someone else for your deeds! She's helping us, even though she has all the reasons not to. She's not the nicest person in the world, I agree with you, but we don't have the luxury of being selective when it comes to accepting help from the few who are ready to offer it to the cause. So, you will shut your mouths, and you will listen to me and obey me. If not, I'm getting you new papers and putting you on the train to the Free Zone tomorrow, and you can sit together with the rest of the collaborators while we're fighting for freedom here. I won't repeat it twice."

"That's the whole point!" the boy argued, a long-contained tear finding its way on his cheek. "We aren't fighting! We aren't doing anything at all! What good will spreading these flyers do? Nothing at all. The *Boches* don't even bother with them anymore. We need to start doing something. Doing!"

"And what do you suggest you 'do,' young man?" Philippe arched his brow skeptically.

"Going out and actually killing them! We don't have the numbers, but why not ambush them, when they return from their clubs and whore houses at night? Let's set up an ambush and kill one or two. It doesn't have to be the whole battalion! And we don't need too many people for that – two or three is more than enough. I'll go if I need to. And Jerome will go with me. I'll prove to you that I'm not afraid."

"I know you're not afraid, Pierre." Philippe sighed, releasing the boy's arm at last. "Only, as Général de Gaulle said himself, leave the fighting to the army. Killing even one *Boche* will end up in such havoc, that the rest of them will make our lives impossible here. Killing one of them? Really? Do you think the *Boches* will just shrug it off and go on with their lives? Do you not think they will not want to retaliate?"

Pierre lowered his wheat-colored head with its matted hair and pursed his lips, without replying anything.

"We will not sit idly anymore, comrade."

The boy's head shot up when Philippe addressed him in the official Party manner for the first time in his life.

"Mademoiselle Legrand didn't just come here to bring us money. She also learned some very important information, and if we succeed with the plan concerning that highly valuable information, the *Boches* will have their hands full for the next few weeks. But, if you want to be a part of our cell – a responsible, sensible part that is – you will have to promise me right now that you will not throw tantrums anymore, and you will listen to everything I tell you. Deal?"

Pierre fumbled with the button of his worn cardigan for a few moments before raising his eyes, with resolution in them, to the communist leader and nodded firmly.

"Yes. It's a deal. Comrade."

The next morning Philippe and Marcel stepped out into the street, which was damp with a September mist that shone on the cobblestone road, making it even more slippery than usual, and completely blocking the sun. Just a few months ago a similar street in the residential area would be empty and quiet, with its habitants snuggling peacefully in their beds. Only the workers, like Marcel and Philippe, would disturb the silence with their steps and usual banter, heading to the morning shift in the factory. Now, the street was crawling with life even at such an early hour, with mothers pulling their crying children by the arm, muttering that if they wanted their dinner that night, they'd better move their feet before the shop run out of meat. *God knows the line over there must be tremendous already!*

Men, with sunken cheeks and defeated looks on their gaunt faces, walked by to their respective working places as well, trying their best not to look around. Few of them were young people; instead, they were mostly the veterans of the Great War, who loathed seeing their country under the occupation of ones whom as they thought they had beaten once and for all some twenty years ago. The Great War mangled all of them, in one respect or another – if not in a physical sense, then in psychological ways, that's for sure. Marcel sighed, thinking of his father, whose face he kept seeing in every single man that passed him by. And just like his father, these men were all too weary and old to start a new fight, which meant only one thing: it was now his, Marcel's young generation's task to step up, to pick up the tricolor and carry it proudly to absolute victory, so that their fathers wouldn't be ashamed to walk the streets next to them.

"You think the boys will keep their word?" Marcel asked Philippe as the two shared the match to light their harsh, cheap cigarettes – the only ones that they could afford.

"For now they will. But we'll still need to keep an eye on them and keep them occupied."

They walked in silence for some time, until Marcel nudged his comrade with his elbow slightly. "Thank you for speaking up for Giselle before them. I know you don't like her, so I appreciate it even more."

Philippe grunted instead of a issuing a reply, and with that, the subject was dropped.

———

GISELLE OPENED the door to her apartment with her keys and crouched to rub Coco behind the ear. The Pekinese rushed to her, shivering and squealing with excitement, obviously relieved to have her mistress back.

"You missed me, didn't you, my little one?"

Giselle picked up the dog into her arms and laughed as Coco feverishly licked her face.

"I missed you too, my precious. Otto didn't forget to feed you, did he now?"

Expecting to be alone, Giselle was surprised to hear steps as Karl walked into the living room, looking even more austere than usual. Giselle took in his stiff posture with arms crossed over his chest, mouth pressed into a hard line and a deep scowl in place, and touched her hair self-consciously.

"Oh, hello. I thought you were at the Prefect's."

"Where have you been?" The question was given without a reciprocal greeting.

"At my sister's, I told you."

"I called her this morning. No one was home."

Giselle glowered, not liking his interrogatory tone nor the fact that he was checking on her whereabouts as if he had any right to do so.

"I left early," she replied curtly, passing by the stern-looking German and heading into her bedroom. She heard his steps following her, and added, without looking back, "Kamille probably left with Violette for a walk, or went shopping. That's why no one was home to answer."

"Where were you all day today then?"

"I was walking, enjoying the weather. You said it yourself that you would be spending Sunday at the Prefect's house, and I didn't want to be stuck here alone all day. Are Sunday walks prohibited as well now?" Giselle snapped back, not able to contain the sarcasm.

He was standing in the doors of her bedroom, refusing to allow her any privacy to change her clothes. Giselle tried to avoid the apprehensive look of his black eyes while taking off her watch and earrings. However, when he didn't move, even when she undid the zipper on the side of her dress, she turned to him sharply and spoke with an authority to her voice which had never failed to intimidate her former lovers, "Do you mind? I'd like to take a shower."

"I do mind." Karl didn't budge. "And you will not go anywhere until you tell me where you were these past twenty-four hours."

"I have told you exactly where I was. Karl, you're being ridiculous now. Move, please."

They stood face to face, her scowling irritably, and him unmoved and menacing as always.

"One more question, *Gisela*. What were you doing in my study?" His accent sounded even harsher now, interlaced with ice.

Giselle caught herself swallowing involuntarily. She wasn't prepared for this question by any means. How did he know that she had stolen two *Ausweis* passes from that thick pile? He didn't recount them one by one every morning most certainly, and she had pulled them out of the middle of the stack. They weren't even numbered in succession!

"I don't understand what you're saying." She offered him a sheepish smile, wisely deciding to drop the arrogant tone for now, or at least until she found out what he knew exactly. "I couldn't possibly enter your study – you have the only key. And besides, why would I go there in the first place?"

"That's what I'm trying to figure out," he replied calmly. "And I will."

"Karl, come now, be reasonable. You know perfectly well that I was not in your study." She traced her fingers on top of his uniform, feverishly trying to worm her way out of the very unnerving situation. "You made this up only to get to me. You most likely are simply jealous, thinking that I was somewhere out with another handsome compatriot of yours. But *Charlie, mon amour,* I truly was just enjoying my sister's company. Why don't you call Kamille again? She's probably home by now, and she'll tell you that I was with her."

For the first time in her life, her playful tone and a sweet smile didn't produce any effect on the man in front of her. He brushed her hand off his uniform jacket and repeated slowly, separating every word, "What were you doing in my study?"

"Karl, I was not—"

He clasped her forearm with enough force to leave bruises. Giselle couldn't suppress a startled yelp.

"Don't lie to me. We both know that you were there. Now tell me what were you looking for?"

"Karl! Let go of me!" She struggled to yank her arm free, which only resulted in him holding it tighter. "You're hurting me!"

"If you call that hurting, you haven't been hurt in your life yet," the German replied with a threatening sneer. "Now answer me: what were you looking for in my study?"

Coco's relentless barking made him raise his voice even more. "Answer me!"

"I didn't go into your study!" Giselle yelled back, struggling with his unyielding grip.

Coco snapped at the man, who was attacking her mistress, and received such a hard kick with a polished black boot that she let out a loud cry and disappeared into the living room.

"You heartless bastard!" Giselle screamed, furious, but the man in front of her refused to let go despite her attempt at releasing herself.

"Fine. You'll go with me. Maybe a more suitable place will help you loosen your tongue."

He almost dragged her by the arm out of the bedroom and into the living room, while Giselle frantically tried to find her little pet with her eyes, fearing that the vicious kick could have easily broken the little dog's ribs. Coco was nowhere to be seen, probably shivering uncontrollably in some hideout.

Karl meanwhile opened the door and pushed Giselle onto the staircase, slamming it behind him.

"Where are you taking me?" Giselle hissed, discarding the idea of making a run for it just out of spite. He would have caught up with her in no time anyway, but even if that wasn't the case, she simply refused to back down even though she had long ago admitted to herself that the situation was out of control. Well, fine indeed; she never backed away from a confrontation, and wouldn't do it now because of some *Boche's* threats. *What would he do to her, really? Throw her in jail?* She didn't think so.

"You've always been curious about my work. I think it's about time I show you what exactly I do when people question my authority." Karl clutched her forearm again, leading her downstairs.

Giselle started laughing. "I'm intrigued, truly. Please, do tell: are you planning on throwing me into some dark cell and to have your people torture me?"

"By all means, no. It's such a cliché, and you as a writer should know it. *Nein.* I'm planning to take you to my office and to question you myself."

"I'm all attention. Maybe I'll get some nice material for my manuscript out of such an exciting experience. My main villain is falling a little flat, but maybe you will be able to inspire me to breathe some life into him." Giselle spoke with poisonous irony oozing out of every word as he led her to his black car which had little red flags above its headlights.

"It'll be my pleasure." He opened the passenger door and pushed her inside rather rudely.

Giselle was still fuming about him hurting her dog but set her mind on doing anything in her power to show him that he didn't frighten her. He didn't, for now, anyway. She had heard about the Gestapo, she had heard about arrests and German camps, but those were for the hardened criminals, not for someone like her. Since the beginning of the occupation, there were hardly any shootings. Most certainly the governments of both countries wished to keep peace and calm by every means possible, and would hardly do anything to a woman on top of it.

Of that – them hurting a woman that is – Giselle had never heard talking of. So, he was bluffing, nothing more, just like some of her previous lovers, who had tried to threaten or manipulate her on several rare occasions. She was too opinionated and strong-willed for them all, and even if her compatriots couldn't have the upper hand with her, some *Boche* would never be the first one to do it. Giselle swore to herself that she would die first before she would submit to him or his threats. She didn't mind him or their occupation before that, but now that he had shown his true face, he had made it personal.

Immersed in her thoughts and still breathing heavily with barely suppressed anger, Giselle didn't notice how they stopped at 93 *Rue Lauriston* in the 16th *arrondissement* which the local Gestapo had turned into their headquarters. She refused to even grace the *Boche* with a single look when he opened the door for her. They walked in silence along the marble-floored hallways with overpowering crimson swastika banners decorating each wall around them. The orderlies and officers snapped to attention at the sight of her guard, while he only nodded his acknowledgment to a rare few of them. Giselle snorted with contempt each time she heard the familiar *Heil Hitler* being shouted instead of a greeting.

One of Karl's orderlies opened the door for the two of them after giving his chief a crisp salute and disappeared as soon as Karl said something quietly to him in German.

Giselle looked around the spacious room, which served as his personal office no doubt. Apparently, it used to belong to some French official before that; some diplomat or city council representative, who she maybe even knew. Extravagant cherry wood panels decorated the walls and the silky dark green wallpaper above them. Rich Aubusson rugs covered the hardwood floor, velvet window panels embellished the windows, and in the center of the room stood an imposing gilded mahogany desk, surrounded by three padded chairs.

Karl moved one of them with a false chivalrous grin and motioned his head towards it as if inviting his guest to take a seat.

"How do you find my working arrangements?"

"The portrait has to go." Giselle thrust her chin towards the picture of Hitler, marring the sophisticated office just with its overpowering size. Needless to say, Giselle didn't fancy the man on it either. "Apart from that, I'm glad you kept our French interior intact."

She sat on the offered chair gracefully, smoothing the skirt over her lap.

"You see, that's what I was afraid of, Giselle."

She pricked her ears as he called her by her real name without twisting it into a German version, and in such a mild tone on top of it. He was onto something, that damned *Boche*, digging in one of his drawers under her watchful eye.

"I was afraid that with your rebellious nature it would come to this. That you wouldn't be satisfied with a good life and the freedom that I offered you – we all offered you, the French people – and that you would want to defy me in one way or another. Why can't you be content with what you have? All of you? Is that some national pride of yours showing its ugly head? Why do you feel compelled to challenge our authority day by day? Why all this?" He lifted his hand with a communist leaflet in it, one of those that she had seen in Philippe's hands. Giselle suppressed a smile, trying to keep an impassionate face. "What for? Do you want to live in a communist state now? I think not, so you're just doing it out of spite, like spoiled rotten children. Do you know what my father used to do with me if I tried to come up with something of this sort? He would belt my back until I screamed for mercy."

"And look at you, you turned out just fine, didn't you?" Giselle arched her brow sarcastically.

Karl paused for a moment, giving her a hard glare, and returned to the papers on his table. "Yes, we did. We all did. We are disciplined and know our place. And so should you."

"You haven't taken into consideration that the French aren't Germans. We are unruly, stubborn and disobedient people who value our freedom above all. So, good luck trying to discipline us."

"Oh, but we will discipline you. We'll discipline you into submission like our father disciplined us. Then I would be able to read a nice, normal newspaper in the morning and not something of this sort."

He thrust an outstretched arm in front of her eyes, holding a paper with an unfamiliar name on it. *La Libération* it read, in proud black letters, and under it – Giselle wasn't able to contain a victorious grin this time – she recognized the title of her article, submitted to her editor under the false name, Jean Moreau. So, Michel Demarche, her fearless publisher and a fellow "unruly, disobedient French," was able to not only print the copies but somehow distribute them so that even Karl got one on his table. She only regretted that she didn't see Karl's face when he realized exactly what he was holding in his hands.

"Have you read it?" he demanded, misinterpreting her smile.

"No. Just glad to see that at least someone has the guts to point out that nothing is as peachy in our beautiful Occupied Zone as you depict it to be in your state propaganda news."

"What do you have to complain about, Giselle?" he asked somewhat tiredly. "Why did you have to go against me?"

"How did I go against you?"

"Sneaking into my study, disappearing somewhere for twenty-four hours. What do you suggest I think if not betrayal?"

"Ah, so we're back to that, are we? First, I didn't sneak into your study, and second, I didn't disappear. I was at my sister's."

Karl shuffled through one of his drawers again and took out a pair of handcuffs without uttering a word. Giselle straightened in her seat warily.

"You were in my study, Giselle." He circled her chair and pulled both of her arms backward, cuffing them behind the back of the chair. "Working for the intelligence, or the Gestapo, you learn certain tricks which come in very handy. One of those tricks is to attach a string in between two drawers, which won't fall off by itself and will only move if someone pulls the drawer open. There are other options, which I won't reveal to you in the event of you coming up with another stupid idea about rummaging through my papers once again – if you're still alive by then of course. And now that we have both agreed that you were indeed in my study, I would like to know the reason why exactly. Have you been foolish enough to get involved with one of those criminal cells? Did you sneak in there with the purpose of obtaining information for them?"

Giselle watched him with caution as he pulled out a pair of pliers from the same drawer. She hated to admit it, but her palms started to sweat.

"Well? Why are you so quiet all of a sudden?" He glided behind her back, but she refused to turn her head to follow his moves no matter how much this maneuver unnerved her. "Speak, Giselle. What were you looking for?"

Giselle pondered her options for a few short seconds and decided to keep her mouth shut, calling his bluff.

"Giselle?"

She only smirked in response. "Well? Proceed. You wanted to interrogate me, didn't you? Go ahead. Interrogate. I'm waiting."

"I would really hate to hurt you, Giselle." She felt the cold metal squeeze a phalange of her forefinger slightly. "You know that I'm a surgeon, don't you? And I know just the right amount of pressure needed to crash a bone."

The pliers dug into her skin painfully. Giselle flinched but decided to play along with this twisted game of wills. Only, she wasn't so sure anymore as to what his intentions were.

"If you keep being stubborn, I'll have to go from one phalange to another, one finger to another, until I break all of them." He pressed the pliers tighter, and Giselle had to press her tongue against her teeth to bite back the hot, stinging tears already pooling in her eyes. It started to hurt like hell as her finger went numb, with its end pulsating violently. "Do not doubt me. I'll make you speak one way or another."

Suddenly, he pressed the pliers together with such brutal force that Giselle could swear she heard her bone crack. She screamed out in agony as he twisted the ends of the instrument around her finger, adding to the searing pain.

"Speak, I said!!!" he yelled in her ear, squeezing the pliers even harder.

"I was looking for the letters from your wife!" Giselle shouted back the first credible lie that came to her mind, and burst into tears, dropping her head on her chest.

"What letters?" he demanded, sounding a little confused, but at least he stopped his tormenting, for now. Giselle was grateful for that.

"The letters… You know, the personal letters…" She kept sobbing, feverishly trying to make her words sound as plausible as possible. "I kept asking you about your wife, and you kept telling me that you didn't have anybody at home, and I thought that you were lying to me... So I wanted to look for myself..."

"How could you look for yourself if you don't read German?" Karl spoke again, slightly releasing the grip on the instrument.

"Of course I don't, but you know us women." Giselle sniffled, trying to look as miserable as she could. Taking into consideration how much pain she was in, it wasn't a hard task. "We know these things, and I don't need to read German to recognize a handwritten letter, smelling of perfume and starting with *'Mein Lieber Karl.'* That's how I would know that it's from your wife."

"Well? Did you find something smelling of perfume?"

She could swear that he sounded almost amused. The pliers suddenly disappeared from the top of her finger. Giselle breathed out in relief.

"No, I didn't."

"Why didn't you tell me that before?" He moved to stand in front of her again, his arms crossed over his chest.

Giselle managed a one shoulder shrug.

"Didn't want you to think too much of yourself," she grumbled in response, convincingly, judging by his reaction that followed. He burst out laughing.

"And to think of it, you were the one accusing me of jealousy just thirty minutes ago."

"I'm not jealous. It was just curiosity."

"It killed the cat."

"I guess I should be grateful for getting away with a broken finger." Giselle wiped her wet cheek on her shoulder.

"Your nail is probably broken, but apart from that your

finger is perfectly fine." He moved behind her back to undo the handcuffs. "I told you I'm a surgeon, and I know anatomy too well to hurt you by accident."

Giselle pulled her left hand to her chest at once, inspecting the damage. The tip of her forefinger was visibly bruised and still red, and the nail had already started to turn blue, but apart from that it indeed seemed to be all right. It wasn't getting swollen, and she could bend it at least.

"Connard," she hissed under her breath. "You'll pay for this."

He either didn't hear her words, or decided to ignore them. "You did it to yourself, *Gisela.* I didn't want to do this to you."

She refused to utter a word when he helped her upwards and offered her his handkerchief. She even allowed him to take her downstairs, and into his car; but as soon as they stopped at a red light close enough to the entrance of the *Metro* for her to make a run for it, Giselle pushed the passenger door open and rushed outside, to the welcoming darkness of the underground.

17

*K*amille made her way along the street in between the German lorries, pulling her daughter's hand and urging the girl to walk faster.

"Violette, you need to put some pep in your step, *chéri*," Kamille spoke, after glancing at the big clock, which was crowning the bell tower of the church. "Madame Marceau will be very upset if we're late again. You wouldn't want your favorite teacher to repeat the beginning of the lesson just for you personally, would you? That would just be rude and inconsiderate."

"I'm hurrying, *Maman*," the girl argued, tucking a loose strand of hair back under her navy blue beret. "My feet are smaller than yours, that's why I can't walk as fast."

"You can walk – and even run – fast enough when you play with Monsieur Horst and Monsieur Jochen outside, mademoiselle. So, don't give me that."

They crossed the street almost running, and Kamille dived under the heavy iron gates of the school together with a few other parents. Nowadays, children mostly walked to school and back by themselves, rarely escorted by their mothers, and even more so fathers, and Kamille praised God daily that she didn't have to worry about her little girl wandering the streets alone because her mother had to rush to work or to buy food and didn't have time to take her to school.

"Ah, Madame Marceau, I'm so glad you haven't started yet." Kamille rushed to greet the teacher, who stood on the steps of the school together with her daughter, Lili. Violette waved at her friend and the teacher, smiling widely. "I was afraid that we would be late again."

"Bonjour, *maîtresse*," Violette chirped, standing next to the woman, who gave her a sad smile in response.

"Bonjour, *chéri*. Only, I'm afraid I'm not a *maîtresse* anymore," Madame Marceau spoke softly. "You better get inside, girls. I heard your new teacher is very strict when it comes to being late."

"But…" Violette's searching eyes wouldn't leave the woman, and Kamille hurried to push the girls towards the doors before they both could see the tears that stood in Madame Marceau's eyes. She looked even gaunter and wearier than when Kamille had seem her last.

"No 'buts.' Do as you're told," Kamille spoke with authority, nudging the girls further. "You don't want to get in trouble with your new teacher on the first day, right?"

As soon as Violette and Lili disappeared inside, Kamille took the teacher by the crook of her arm and pulled her away from curious ears.

"Madame Marceau, what happened?" she inquired when they both took a seat on the bench in a school yard.

"The headmaster told me this morning when I came to work." The woman sighed, brushing the tears away. "Apparently there is a new law, according to which Jews can't be teachers from now on. So, I was dismissed, together with the rest of the Jews."

"I didn't know you were Jewish," Kamille muttered, not knowing what to say.

She had seen all the new posters with anti-Semitic propaganda, which had started to appear not that long ago, and there were more and more signs every day in the front windows of stores and cafés, declaring that Jews were not allowed inside. She even read it in the newspaper that all officials of Jewish descent had been fired from their positions... But this was simply unjust. Madame Marceau was everyone's favorite teacher, not just Violette's, and she cared deeply about every child in her charge as if they were her own. And now they had replaced her with some discipline-demanding collaborator, most certainly, who would demand that the little children sing that cursed *Maréchal* song and brainwash them into being sympathetic to the new regime as well. No, that was just... wrong.

"I'm so sorry." Kamille pulled off her glove and covered the teacher's hand with hers, offering her at least this silent support. "Is there anything I can help you with?"

The woman, who stared into space without blinking for some time, as if taking in her new situation, slowly shook her head at last.

"No. There's nothing that can be done. It's final and isn't a subject for discussion, as I was explicitly told." She shook her head again, with a bitter look in her eyes. "It's only, I can't imagine how we're going to survive this winter, Lili and I. Without a job, without money... What am I going to feed her with? I could start offering to do laundry for those who can afford it, *bien sûr*... But who would want to hire a Jew nowadays?"

She pulled her hand towards her mouth and started chewing on her nail, still staring at the ground in distress. Kamille sat next to her for some time, as shaken up as Madame Marceau herself, and wondering what she would do if she happened to lose her job and fearing that her little Violette would have nothing to eat in as little as the next few days. Then, as if suddenly remembering something, she quickly opened her purse, dug out all the unused food coupons she had and dropped them in the stupefied woman's lap.

"Please, take these for now. It should last you for a month at least. I'm not going to use them anyway; I have German officers lodging with me, and I'm sure they have their ways when it comes to getting food, and these coupons for that matter. And I'll bring you new ones next time when I bring Violette to play with Lili, if you don't mind of course. And clothes and money, too. You just tell me what you need, and I'll try to get it. I'm sure that Monsieur Hartmann won't refuse to help me if I say that it's for a friend."

"Is that the one who taught Violette how to draw?" A faint smile brightened Madame Marceau's pale face.

"No, that was his adjutant, Monsieur Horst." Kamille smiled back. "But they're both very nice people, I assure you."

"I don't know how to thank you, Madame Blanchard."

"You don't have to. I'm sure you would do the same if this happened to me. And please, call me Kamille."

"Augustine." Madame Marceau offered Kamille her narrow, delicate palm and two women exchanged handshakes. "Thank you."

Kamille brushed her tears away and, as if a simple handshake wasn't enough, they hugged each other firmly and held it for several moments.

GISELLE KNOCKED on the door in the peculiar pattern which Philippe had taught her, just in case if she forgot her keys one day. Today, she hadn't forgotten them, she simply didn't have them, after running out of Karl's car with only the clothes on her back. The good thing was, the sympathetic teller in the *Metro* bought her story about being robbed and allowed her inside without a token.

The door creaked open just enough for her to recognize the face of one of the young boys, who Marcel and Philippe took care of – the older one. He didn't bother unbolting it as soon as he saw who stood in front of it, only furrowed his light brow.

"What do you want?"

Apparently, Philippe had already left for some business together with her brother, leaving the boys in charge of the apartment. Giselle thought of putting the little insolent scoundrel in place, reminding him that it was her apartment and that he ate food bought with her money, and that he was lucky in the first place that she hadn't reported them to the gendarmes yet... Only, that old, haughty Giselle who used to do such things had momentarily disappeared somewhere along the way from the Gestapo headquarters to her old apartment; the apartment in which she grew up and had become the woman she thought she should always strive to be – arrogant, independent and having enough money to buy everything and everyone around her. This new Giselle, in wrinkled clothes and with a look of deadly determination forever emblazed into her green eyes, only cocked her head and whispered quietly, so only the boy behind the door could hear her, "Still want to exact revenge on the *Boches?*"

The boy's eyes widened in obvious surprise and, after looking her up and down apprehensively, he closed the door to unbolt it.

MARCEL BIT into the thick slice of rye bread still smelling seductively of ham. The ham itself had been consumed with envious speed by one of the youngest members of their group – a lanky, pale-faced man named Nicolas. He was only a year younger than Marcel and yet he looked barely seventeen with his patched-up clothes hanging loose on his scrawny frame, his pants held in place only with the help of two strings. With his father gone somewhere in the German *stalags*, Nicolas was the only one left to feed his ailing mother and three siblings. As soon as Marcel heard from one of his fellow workers that almost all the food he earned went to his family, he and Philippe made it their task to feed the young man while at work, at the least, sharing their lunches with him.

"That's what the communism is about," Philippe told him

soon after they learned of Nicolas. "Sharing everything within the community."

Marcel nodded his agreement. He still wasn't an ardent supporter of the communistic doctrine, but he liked how Philippe always explained everything to him. He made it sound appealing, and not as alien and hostile as his university professors used to present it to him.

"Of course they did," Philippe scoffed nonchalantly, when Marcel mentioned the attitude of his professors. "The bourgeois class."

Their group consisted of Philippe's comrades: old ones, who Marcel had met at the Bussi's farm and who had moved to the city as well, knowing that they would be of better use to the cause here in Paris; and new ones, recruited just recently from common acquaintances. Now, they all huddled together near the wall of the factory, resting their aching legs during a short thirty minute lunch break. German supervisors didn't take too kindly to such comradery and always frowned upon any tight-knit group of men sitting together (suspecting some anti-governmental activity, most certainly; however, Marcel couldn't smirk at the thought that for once they were right). Nonetheless, given the size of the munitions factory and the impossibility to separate each worker during the lunch break, they soon started ignoring them, which suited Philippe and his men just fine.

"My connection said that he could point out the exact location of the wire net on the map." Philippe, the leader of the group, spoke quietly, all the while watching for movement around them. He had warned Marcel a long time ago that he should be on the alert not only for the *Boches* but the French as well; nowadays no one could be certain of whom to trust. "He won't be coming along, but he will explain in detail how to get there."

Marcel gulped some water from his canteen, hiding a knowing smile from his comrades. Besides Philippe, only he knew that the mysterious "he" was his big sister, but of that Philippe had warned him too. *Never reveal your sources, not because you don't trust your men, but because they might reveal them in turn, in case if caught and interrogated.* The less everyone knew, the better.

"We need a group of two, or better, three people. There are two sentries there, and your task is to immobilize them quietly and simultaneously, so no one will hear a peep out of them. *Immobilize* is the key word, not kill."

Philippe narrowed his black eyes, shifting them from one man to another, making sure that they all understood the message. Sabotaging the wiring was one thing, killing the occupants was another, and less than anything Philippe wanted the Germans to organize a massive manhunt and executions in retaliation. It was too soon for such actions. They were too weak and unorganized. With time, maybe… But not now.

"The mission is high risk, I understand that. If there aren't any volunteers, I'll go myself—"

"I volunteer," Nicolas interrupted him before he could finish.

Philippe, judging by his look, wasn't too enthralled with the idea.

"Nicolas, you're far too young, and maybe—"

"No, please, allow me to do it. I'll prove myself worthy, I promise." The young man's face flushed with emotion. "I couldn't go into the army because of my weak lungs, so at least now I will serve my country the best I can. So my father will be proud of me when he returns, so the *Boches* leave sooner, and my family doesn't starve anymore, together with the rest."

"Very well then." Philippe nodded after a moment's thought. "Who else?"

"I'll go." Marcel surprised even himself with how naturally it came out.

Philippe knitted his dark brows together.

"You're sure?" he asked after a long pause.

"Yes. Haven't been surer in my entire life." Marcel smiled brightly.

It was strange how just a few hours ago he was thinking of picking up his father's torch, just like this boy next to him, and proceeding with fighting for his France – a free France, an independent France – to restore its dignity and to be able to hold his head proudly before the following generation, knowing in his heart that he did everything in his power to rid them of the German plague. And now, when a very real opportunity presented itself, saying this simple "yes" seemed like the most natural thing to do. He had run from the frontline once, and he still bore the shame of his personal defeat in his heart, but now the time had come to prove what he was really made of. If his sister didn't fear them, he wouldn't either. He would prove himself, to everyone around him, and what was more important, he would prove to the fearful, young Marcel inside that he could leave him behind, because he had no business in this new country anymore.

GISELLE ACCEPTED a piece of ice from Jerome's hands with a grateful grin.

"From the ice box. For your finger," he muttered, before disappearing into the living room and leaving her alone with a very cross looking Philippe.

He towered over her with his arms folded on his chest while Giselle sat on the bed in her former bedroom, rolling the ice cube around her forefinger. It didn't really bother her anymore, but the bruising still looked rather ugly, so the boy's concern was more than understandable. Giselle spent the night at Kamille's after having a little chat with Pierre the day before, thinking over her situation. Her sister gasped at the sight of the wound as well and insisted that Giselle should go to the hospital to have her injury inspected. Giselle, however, declined with a smile, reassuring Kamille that it was nothing to worry about and that it was her own fault, being so clumsy and catching her finger in the door. Reluctantly, Kamille decided not to press the matter.

"What's gotten into you, saying something of this sort to the boys?!" Philippe growled as soon as Jerome left the room and headed to the kitchen to help Marcel and his older brother Pierre with dinner. "Didn't I tell you just yesterday that they're very vulnerable right now and as little as someone's words, spoken unwisely, can encourage them to do something foolish, which will most likely end up with them being shot! And you go ahead and offer them the chance to go on a hunting spree for the *Boches*! Why not try and assassinate Hitler then?"

"That would be simply impractical, for the *Boches'* beloved Führer is in Germany, not in France. Now had he been within our reach..." Giselle offered the communist an impish smile, her eyes twinkling with mischief.

"You're insane," Philippe stated calmly, shaking his head. "I understand that you had a little... falling out with your Nazi lover, but please, be so kind as to leave us out of it. I'm not going to risk the lives of my men, and especially two very young, vulnerable boys in my charge, just to exact revenge on some *Boche*, who scratched the nail polish off your little finger."

Giselle lowered her head, suppressing her chuckling. For some time she watched the tiny droplets of water fall onto the faded rug under her feet, before she spoke again, taking on a serious tone this time.

"Who cares about the nail polish? And it's not about him and me, Philippe, that's where you're mistaken. It's about all of us, the French people, and them – the occupants, who have the right to do anything they like to us without the slightest repercussion. Do you not understand that it's only going to get worse? Do you not see that the more we submit to them, the more at home they feel? I don't know about you, but I for one am sick and tired of them being in my personal space, interfering with my work, and following my every step. I want my freedom back. I want my apartment back. I want my nights out back. I want my taxi cabs back. I want my damn country back!"

"And how are you planning to get it back?" Philippe smirked. "Obtain a machine gun in the *Marché Noir*, walk outside and try to shoot as many *Boches* as you can before they shoot you?"

"No, of course not. We tried that already, our whole French army I mean, and we failed miserably. No. Blunt force is not going to work with them; they'll beat us again in no time." Giselle bit her lower lip for a few moments, deep in thought. "What we need to do is to outsmart them. Outsmart, and strike when they least expect it. Small assassination groups, at night: one, two, three – done and gone."

"No. It's a terrible idea. They will retaliate."

"They won't if they don't know who is behind it. How can you execute assassins if you don't know who they are?"

"Oh, they'll think of something."

Giselle played with the ice cube some more, twirling it around her finger, and smiled serenely at Philippe.

"Don't worry, I'm not going to force you into anything. I'll do it all by myself. The first one will be mine. And then we'll see how they react."

"Giselle, don't do it," Philippe warned her once again.

"Oh, don't fret, you. I'm not so stupid to shoot him in the open." A predatory smirk twitched the corners of her mouth. "No. If I sell my life, I'll sell it for a high price, and I'll make sure to take as many *Boches* with me as I can. Getting executed after the first one isn't in my plan."

"Think about your brother…" Philippe lowered his gaze as soon as he heard the words that he had spoken.

It was very unlike him, warning someone off a dangerous undertaking, and even more so to bring up family members to talk them out of it. Only, despite all his contempt for the woman in front of him, he had quickly grown to respect her for her bravery and didn't wish anything to happen to her. She was a woman after all… And the war, even though it was a partisan one, was men's business.

"Did my brother think of me when he agreed to go on that assignment?" Giselle raised her brows, grinning, and then waved Philippe off as soon as he tried to interject something. "I'm just saying. I'm actually very proud of him. Good for him, volunteering for such a task. It'll make a man out of him, a man that he himself will be proud of."

"What if he…"

"What? Dies?" Giselle shrugged nonchalantly. "We'll all die one day, won't we? Why not die standing with a gun in our hands than to wither slowly, starved to death and beaten into submission by the Nazis?"

Philippe's eyes met hers, and he smiled at the woman in front of him – sincerely, for the first time.

he doorman appeared to breathe out in relief when he noticed Giselle walking wearily towards the steps of the building. He pushed the heavy door open and stepped outside, grinning widely. The day before, when the *Boche* had led her outside, the man was convinced he wouldn't see one of his favorite tenants anymore. He didn't care so much about all the generous tips she always snuck into his gloved hand, discretely and with taste during a gentle handshake, and only when they were alone, unlike the suit-and-tie wearing snobs, who only did so to impress their ladies. He didn't care about the presents that she always handed him, wrapped in shiny wrapping paper (*for little Olivier's birthday. You did tell me he liked trains, didn't you?*). He didn't care for the material things, no. He cared more for the small talk she always shared with him on her way in or out, for her kind smiles and reassurances that she would be more than happy to write a recommendation letter for his youngest son, Alphonse, when he announced his desire to study in the prestigious Sorbonne. And lastly, for treating him almost like a most intimate friend, and not a blank face, which many of the tenants living here, considered him to be.

"Mademoiselle Legrand." He bowed his graying head respectfully, holding the door for her. "It's good to see you back."

Even though he pronounced the last words as softly as possible, breaking protocol with speaking more than just a necessary greeting, Giselle beamed at him and pressed his hand with both of hers for a second, before sliding into the cool marble hallway of the building.

"It's good to see you too, Didier."

"*Ça va?*" he whispered, with barely concealed concern.

"Couldn't be better," she whispered back, giving him the wink of a conspirator.

He sighed in relief, following her resolute steps with his gaze as she headed towards the carpeted steps.

Giselle paused at the door of her apartment like an artist before stepping onto the stage before an audience. She smoothed her hair with her hands, pinched her cheeks to add some rosy blush to her complexion, carefully faked innocence and compliance on her face, redid the bow on the collar of her dress and put on her most charming smile before rapping on the door.

Karl opened it himself, even paler and more somber than usual, and stepped aside to click his heels in his military greeting.

"*Bonjour, Charlie,*" Giselle murmured, walking inside. She helped him close the door when he hesitated to do so, and stood in front of him calmly, while he was thinking of what words to say.

"*Bonjour.*" His gaze traveled to her hand, and he faltered before taking it into his to look at the wound which he had inflicted. "I was afraid that you wouldn't return."

"Now, don't be silly. Where would I go, and why? My home is here."

In a gesture that she never anticipated from him, he brought her sore finger to his mouth and kissed it with infinite gentleness. Giselle barely restrained herself from yanking her hand away.

"Please, forgive me. I didn't want to hurt you."

"It's all long forgiven and forgotten, *Charlie.* It was my fault after all, as you pointed out correctly. I know that you did it only in my best interests, so next time I wouldn't do something as careless and irresponsible as putting my nose where it doesn't belong. You were right all along: I do have a terribly rebellious side, and I don't like it any better than you do. It always lands me in trouble, and I suppose I failed to realize that now is not the right time to show defiance just to prove something to myself or the people around me. I am actually grateful for the lesson – it is well-learned, I assure you – and I promise that you won't see any problems from me from this day on. You were right: you have given me a wonderful life. You care about me and my well-being even though you are under no obligations to do so, and yet I treated you so unfairly and disrespectfully in return. I was mad at you earlier, I'm not going to lie. But then I realized how fortunate I am for having you in my life, and how you did what you did only to save me from my reckless self in the future. I should thank you, but taking into consideration that you bruised my finger, I decided against it. Or you might take it the wrong way," she finished with a carefully played-out, coy smile.

The German stood silently, scrutinizing her every facial muscle as it seemed, but Giselle didn't even flinch. He breathed out at last, after several long, agonizing moments during which she was awaiting his "verdict," and wrapped his arms around her.

"I'm so glad to hear that, my dearest Giselle…"

Her hand rested on top of his holster as she embraced him in return. Giselle inhaled deeply, to smell the woolen, almost sterile fragrance of his neatly cleaned and pressed uniform which always carried the faint remnant of alcohol or some other disinfectant. The hard, well-oiled leather with a gun hidden in it tingled her careful fingertips, and she slid them back onto his back, pressing him tighter.

"I was mistaken about you after all," he said with a relieved smile, after placing a soft kiss on her temple.

"Yes, you were, *mon chéri*. You have no idea how mistaken you were."

THE AUTUMN CAME to Paris without warning, just like the Germans a few months earlier, and set up its own occupation, only adding to everyone's misery. Gusts of wind tore into wet swastika flags – the only bright spots, dotted in bloody sputters throughout the faded, bleak city. A permanent foggy haze traveled along the river, its murky waters splashing against the cold concrete. The lines along the walls of stores grew even longer, with despondent, scowling

Parisians waiting for their daily rations, their heads pulled into their shoulders and rubber galoshes stomping in rhythm with their fogged breathing in a futile attempt to keep warm.

Giselle passed them by daily, grateful for the rainproof, black cloak that helped conceal her face, not so much from the weather as from her fellow countrymen. She had heard their disapproving murmurs even before the occupation, for Giselle had always been quite far from embodying the exemplary citizen in their eyes. Now the whispers were becoming louder and bolder, fueled by the very fact that she passed them by instead of sharing their plight to get their scanty rations, clothed and fed – "a *Boche's* whore" whom they were slowly growing to hate.

It was a strange thing that the occupation did, when the people of France learned how to pour out their resentment and detestation on just about anyone when baring their teeth at the real enemy was not an option. The *enemy* made everything worse for her already unfortunate situation, that very *Boche*, who was the reason for all the unwanted attention and grumbles. After their "reconciliation" as he called it once, not coming up with a better alternative in the French language, Karl made it a habit to take walks with Giselle along the Champs-Élysées, her arm on the crook of his, as if parading another one of his war trophies with the same conceited look with which he put on his crosses and other signs of recognition every time the maid delivered his uniform, pressed and in immaculate state. Only the typical Parisian dog was missing from the "idyllic" family portrait on such walks, but Giselle didn't think twice before scooping the pooch up together with her bed, leash, and bowls and handing Coco into Violette's awaiting arms two days after the vicious kick. A glare stopped Kamille's protesting all at once.

Today, Giselle marched along the drenched streets alone, stepping over puddles and passing the few German sentries, also miserable in their melancholic state, in soaked raincoats with the hoods pulled on top of their helmets. She pressed the brown leather valise towards her chest under the cloak, guarding it against the rain. A most precious possession was hidden inside, smuggled from right under her watchful tenant's nose – a new article for *La Libération,* Michel Demarche's pride and joy which had already gathered quite an audience, as he announced himself during their last meeting. It was her third article already and even more poisonous and revealing than her previous ones.

Giselle gathered little snippets of information from all sources available to her: from Karl during their dinners (even though she was trying to be as watchful as possible with him); from Otto, when he would carelessly blabber something during an amicable chat to which she invited him from time to time; and, finally, from Horst and Jochen whenever she went over for dinner.

It was through her that the people of Paris, and soon several other cities to which the copies of *La Libération* traveled, discovered that the food was lacking due to most of their farm produce going to the south – to North Africa to be precise, to sustain a rather big German *Afrika Korps.* It was Giselle who revealed that most factories worked for Germany now and that due to the Vichy government's collaboration policies the British proclaimed them, the French, an enemy nation and announced their plans to start bombing those factories, killing more French people in the process. People owed it to Giselle that they learned to be careful and not to trust their acquaintances and neighbors so readily, for the *Staatspolizei* employed more and more agents from the local population, promising them money and ration cards for collaboration. But, it was also due to *La Libération* that they learned not to lose hope, for each issue always ended with good news from the North about the undefeatable British navy, with more encouraging words from Général de Gaulle, and with calls to resist in spirit until they were able to resist with weapons in their arms.

Giselle ran up the stairs to the Demarche Publishing House and smiled at the doorman gleefully, shaking the raindrops from her cloak and hair, which still got damp even under the protection of the hood.

"Some weather today, eh?" she remarked, pulling her valise out from under the cloak. "Is everyone here yet?"

"Yes. I was just waiting for you to lock up, Mademoiselle Legrand."

After more and more rumors about unexpected raids by the Gestapo circulated around the city, Michel wisely advised his loyal concierge to lock the front door as soon as all members of the group, who gathered for "discussions" every week, were inside the building. This way, in case the Gestapo agents did show up, the concierge would at least have time to make a call before unlocking the door, thus giving Michel a much needed chance to hide any fresh articles brought to him by his writers.

Hearing the loud clink of the heavy front door being bolted, Giselle pulled the iron doors of the elevator closed and waved at the doorman through them. Upstairs, Michel's office was full of cigarette smoke and muffled chatter. Giselle waved at the men gathered around the desk, deeply immersed in some heated discussion, judging by their concerned looks and the number of cigarettes they must have smoked.

"How's everyone doing?" the blonde chirped, heading to her seat.

Michel took the article from her hands and placed it together with the others, in a separate stack on the side of his table.

"We have some important news, Giselle," Demarche announced, his hand still resting on top of the newly submitted articles.

"What is it?" Giselle cocked her head curiously and smiled at Antoine, who gallantly offered her his silver cigarette case. *"Merci."*

"A man from the Free Zone came to see me last night," Michel continued. "A son of an old friend of mine. His father and I used to work for the same newspaper many years ago... The father died during the summer campaign, I'm afraid... The son, Etienne, was fortunate to be in the Free Zone with his mother and sisters when the new government was established, but now he believes that he owes it to his father to continue his fight."

"That's understandable." Giselle nodded. "Many young men feel the same way."

"Yes." Michel cleared his throat, pondering something. "Somehow our little *Libération* made its way to the South."

"That's great news, isn't it?" Giselle's eyes gleamed with pride.

"It is, and it isn't. You see, Etienne kept asking me if I

knew who published the newspaper. After I admitted that it was I, he offered to distribute the newspaper among the population of the Free Zone, not just in Paris and its surrounding towns."

"You agreed, didn't you?"

"I promised to give him my answer tomorrow night." Michel shot Giselle a sharp look in response to her enthusiasm. "It's good news in one sense, and bad in another. And being the cautious and responsible people that we are, we have to weigh all the pros and cons before agreeing to something of this sort."

"What do we need to discuss, Michel? It's a brilliant idea! And if he has the means of copying and distributing *La Libération* in the Free Zone, I say that's just grand! We couldn't even dream of this a month ago!"

"Giselle, the Nazis are already searching major newspaper headquarters, looking for the people behind *La Libération.* We are quite a big thorn in their side as it is. Now imagine how rabid their reaction will be once they get wind of us distributing *La Libération* in the Free Zone as well!" Michel clasped his hands together and tilted his head to one side, awaiting Giselle's response.

She took a drag on her cigarette, squinting through the gray cloud of smoke. Antoine paced the room behind her back while the other two men – Pascal Thierry and Gilles Le Roux – shifted in their seats, also deep in thought.

"I still say that it's a chance we've got to take," Giselle announced resolutely. "If we can distribute even several issues in the Free Zone before the situation here gets too dangerous for us to continue – it's still better than nothing. People across the border need to know what is really happening to their friends and relatives in the Occupied Zone, because now they're all being fed Vichy government propaganda, according to which the German occupation is the best thing that could happen to France next to the Second Coming."

The men chuckled at the joke and then sighed almost in unison.

"It's going to be a very dangerous undertaking," Michel warned. "Etienne will be risking his life smuggling *La Libéra-tion* through the border, and then establishing the cell which will help him copy and distribute it. I don't want his mother to mourn not only the loss of her husband but also an only son."

"But you can't stop him either if that's what he wants to do. It's his decision, Michel, not yours."

"What if the Gestapo double their efforts in looking for us though?" Pascal inquired, searching Giselle's face.

"If the Gestapo is on to us, I'll be the first one to know," Giselle promised confidently with a cynical smirk. "Some-times it can be very convenient keeping such an enemy in your house."

"Let's vote then," Michel spoke, drawing everyone's atten-tion back to himself. "Raise your hand if you're for the idea that *La Libération* travels to the south. I'll vote the last."

Giselle was the first person to raise her hand. Antoine followed suit, after which there was a moment of hesitation among the other two writers. Finally, Pascal lifted his arm, and after him Gilles, who shrugged carelessly.

"I'm voting as everyone else is voting. If you all say yes, I say yes too."

"It's all decided then," Michel concluded, after raising his arm as well. *La Libération* will make itself known in the Free Zone, and from there – who knows? – maybe even in Britain. Etienne says he has connections within the army as well, among the ones who ran to the UK to join de Gaulle. Only, be careful, my friends. Be very careful from now on. The Nazis won't let it slide."

19

The heavy rain was coming down in buckets, turning the ground underneath in mud. Pearls of raindrops bounced off leaves in a never-ending, angry shower, soaking clothes to the bone. Marcel lay down on his stomach, shivering both from cold and anticipation, as he peered into the distance through the thick wall of bushes. The picture in front of his eyes was the same as it was during the other four times Nicolas and he had come here to observe, to assess the situation and to learn the schedule of the patrolman so that they could carefully plan everything. After all, sabotaging a German operation, no matter how facile it seemed, was no easy feat, and especially for two inexperienced young men. Philippe had twice offered to go instead of him, but Marcel was determined to execute this plan on his own.

After spending four consecutive Sundays watching the movement in the former wheat field, Marcel and Nicolas learned that the patrolman only checked on the two sentries, guarding the reel and wire, every three hours, after making his round on foot around the wood. Then the other patrolman changed him with him and also appeared to call out to the two guards every three more hours. The Germans all seemed to be bored out of their minds (that much Giselle was right about, Marcel noticed to himself), especially the ones who manned the wire.

One of them, who stood guard down the hill (even though the word "stood" would do him too much of an honor given that he spent most of his time napping, and woke up only to shift position and to take another swig from his flask) would be Nicolas's guy, Marcel decided. Immobilizing an intoxicated man would be much easier than a sober one, and Nicolas was too frail to fight him off if he put up a fight.

The other one posed a bigger problem, for he was positioned on the edge of the wood, and a dense one at that, so getting close to him without making any suspicious noise would be much more challenging. Besides, unlike his schnapps-loving comrade, this one took his task more seriously, shifting his eyes from the book that he carried with him all the time to check the perimeter with irritating regularity.

"We'll have to do it in the rain," Marcel had announced during one of their meetings a couple of weeks ago, when the five of them, including Philippe and the boys, sat in a tight circle on the floor, their heads lowered above the map. "This way they won't hear us approach. The noise from the rain will be a perfect guise."

"Good idea," agreed Philippe. "Also, it would be better if

you take care of yours first, and Nicolas takes care of the drunkard after you give him a signal. This way the *Boche* with the book won't notice Nicolas coming down the hill and won't be able to warn his buddy. The latter I'm not worried about; he'll most likely be sleeping and won't see what's going on across the field when you're dealing with his comrade."

Working out the details of the plan in a warm, secure apartment was one thing, but lying flat on his stomach for several hours in the pouring rain, preparing to go along with it, was completely different. Marcel clenched his jaw so that his teeth didn't chatter so loudly. He'd checked his watch only a few minutes ago: the time on which they had agreed to carry out an attack was nearing. Marcel felt the firm handle of Philippe's gun pressing into his stomach with every ragged breath he took. The terror, the animalistic, frantic terror which had sent him off running without looking back several months ago, further and further away from the frontline, was coming back in disgusting, sweaty waves. That terror saved his freedom – or maybe even his life – back then. Now, it might turn into his worst enemy.

The *Boche* sat within a few steps of him, now that Marcel had crawled so close to him that he could hear each time the man in his army issued raincoat cleared his throat. He could hear his quiet cursing in his strange, harsh language whenever his newly lit cigarette died from an unfortunate raindrop falling on its tip. Marcel stilled himself, prohibiting himself from panicking, and crept even closer, clenching a bottle with chloroform in one hand and a handkerchief in another: Philippe was more than clear on this point – *immobilize them, don't kill.* The only issue that Marcel had with that order was that "immobilizing" meant getting in direct contact with a German, covering his face with that chloroform-soaked cloth, fighting off his struggling hands until he would still in his arms… But what if he managed to fight *him* off instead? Then what?

"Then you use your gun," Philippe concluded with a deadly calmness in his voice.

Merde, he should have agreed to switch places with Philippe! He should have known he didn't have the guts to proceed with it… he was a coward, a lousy coward and nothing else; what was he doing in the Resistance at all? Who was he fooling with all this newly found bravery and patriotism?

Marcel noticed a movement on top of the hill across the field and realized that it was time. Yes, it was time, and also there was a young boy, a very young boy in his charge carefully treading his way down the steep surface. *What about that signal,* flashed in Marcel's mind, but then he forced himself to take a deep breath and carefully uncover the bottle, holding his breath and ensuring that the wind was blowing in his direction, away from the *Boche's* nose. He poured the clear liquid onto the handkerchief, soaking it completely, and slowly rose to his feet, ready to pounce on the *Boche*, who sat only two steps away from him.

The pouring rain shielded his steps from the sentry's ears, and all the German did was release a startled yelp when Marcel's hand with a chloroform-soaked cloth landed on his face from behind his back. Marcel held both hands as hard as he could against the writhing man's head, feeling the man's hard helmet through the hood of his raincoat, pressed against his chin. And then, just as Marcel hoped that he had overpowered his enemy at last, the German's hand found the rifle laying on the muddy ground, and, with his last power and on the verge of losing consciousness, the sentry pulled the trigger.

A powerful, warning shot reverberated across the field, and Marcel, with a sense of horror that sharpened each of his senses, saw the second sentry bolt upright and grab his rifle, knowing where the shot had come from. Marcel dropped the unconscious man's body from his arms and stood on the spot as if he was glued to it, already giving in to his fate.

"Run, comrade! Run!!!" A desperate shout pierced the cacophony of the rain together with several shots of Nicolas's gun. Unfortunately, neither one of them even grazed the German, who now switched his attention from his fellow guard's assailant to the small, frail figure on top of the hill.

Marcel's lips moved in silent denial as the *Boche* lifted his weapon and took aim with the trained eye of a soldier. The boy didn't stand a chance, and yet he continued to shoot just to die fighting, to protect his comrade even though it was his, Marcel's, duty to protect him from a disaster like this.

"Nicolas…"

The scrawny figure was already falling, sliding down the hill in mud, to halt right under the iron-lined boots of his murderer.

"No." Marcel's trembling fingers clenched the handle of an ax that was tucked in his belt on the small of his back. He charged forward before he even had a chance to consider his options. "You haven't died for nothing, Nicolas, I promise."

The wet ground exploded under his feet, but Marcel had already swung his arm with a determination that he had never experienced before, and landed on top of the thick cable, cutting it in two with the blade of his ax. Another shot followed, sending chunks of mud into his eyes, but Marcel had already pivoted and taken off as fast as he could, sliding in dirt and scratching his arms and face with the spiky branches of thick growth and bushes, that clawed into his clothes as if nature itself collaborated with the *Boches* to prevent him from escaping.

He ran, without looking back. He ran from the soldiers as he had done several months ago, also leaving dying comrades behind; comrades, who gave their lives so he could live. For a second, stopping to catch his breath as soon as he was out of the woods, a thought crossed his mind to put Philippe's gun to use and to shoot the traitor with his own hands, who had just sent another innocent soul to the devils to buy several more precious hours of life for himself. But, he was too much of a coward to shoot. And so, Marcel kept on running.

THE BASKET WAS ALREADY full to the brim, yet Kamille struggled to stuff a bag of flour inside. A red and white checkered napkin lay on the counter next to the basket, to cover all the food items, neatly stacked inside, from curious eyes. Giselle's dog barked relentlessly near the front door, and Kamille shouted at the animal without turning away from the countertop. Apparently, it was due to that high-pitched barking that Kamille didn't hear Jochen's steps when he entered the house and jumped like a criminal from his voice behind her back, caught on the spot red-handed.

"I thought the food goes inside the house, not the other way round."

He stood in the doors of the kitchen, leaning on the frame and observing her with a slight frown.

"I thought you left for work," Kamille muttered breathlessly, not thinking of anything better to say.

She could have lied that she was only restocking the shelves or taking the excess food to the pantry under the stairs, but since she was dressed in her coat and wearing a hat, her attire was a giveaway sign that she was up to something quite different.

"I forgot my papers." Jochen glanced her over and then shifted his gaze to the basket. "I thought you complained that you couldn't get any of this even with ration cards, and that was the reason why you asked me to bring it to you. Only, judging by the fact that you're planning to take all this someplace other than your own kitchen tells me otherwise."

"Jochen, I..." Kamille stumbled, feeling the heat slowly flushing her cheeks with a bright red color. Unlike her sister, who would dare lie at her last confession had she not been an agnostic, Kamille had never been good at lying. "I was only..."

She touched the handle of the basket nervously, noticing the irritation in his tightly pressed lips. Jochen had not been in his best disposition during the last two weeks, after an attack on men in his charge had happened. He was either constantly absent, spending all of his time trying to investigate the matter in order to find the perpetrators, or he came home exhausted and in a foul mood after dealing with another reprimand from his commanding officers. Kamille could only imagine how this stunt of hers would anger him now.

"Where are you taking this food?" he demanded, sighing.

"I..." She dared raise her eyes to meet his and saw bitter disappointment in his gaze as if she had betrayed him in the worst way possible. *No, please, don't be mad at me, I beg of you*, flashed in her mind while she fought the tears already gathering in her eyes. *Not you now, not like Charles back then...* "I was going to take it to the church."

"The church?"

"Yes." Lies again. She loathed herself for deceiving this man, who was always so open and honest with her, yet how could she tell him that all the food was for Violette's former teacher and her little daughter, who were both Jewish? They never discussed that subject matter, but Kamille assumed without asking that Jochen shared the views of his fellow countrymen. So, lies it was; she simply had no other option. "There are so many displaced, poor people in need going there daily for their rations that I just felt compelled..."

"You're sharing our food with them?" Jochen finished her thought and shook his head in reproach. At least he was smiling, just a little, but it was still something. "Kamille, you can't possibly feed every person in need in Paris."

"I know that. But at least I know that I tried..."

He snorted softly and walked over to her. Kamille readily stepped into his embrace as soon as he opened his arms to her.

"Such a wonderful, kind woman you are," he said, placing a gentle kiss on her temple. "But, Kamille, really? A church?"

"They have orphans there... And I'm a mother myself, and I can't stand seeing children suffer."

At least this statement was true. The way Lili's eyes lit up every time Kamille produced a candy or a butter croissant from under the checkered napkin made all the deception and anxiety worth it.

"I understand, but, my darling, understand me too: I'm not supposed to bring you food at all, and especially in the quantities I've been taking recently – all because you told me that a lot of food items were unobtainable. And here I am, stealing butter, flour, sugar from under my commanders' noses for you, and you go and take it all to the church? And what if someone sees you on the street with all these goods, what will you tell them? That it came from your generous tenant? I'll get another administrative punishment on my list, that is getting far too long already, and we still haven't caught those communists, who sabotaged one of our paramount operations. Maybe the *Kommandant* will have enough of it and will send me away to the front. I'm ready to go back into fighting of course but is that what you want?"

He sounded reproachful again. Kamille didn't blame him, so she only hid her face on his chest, clenching her hands tighter on top of his leather belt with its holster on top of his military overcoat.

"No, of course not. Please, forgive me. I won't do it again, I promise. I didn't mean to upset you."

"You didn't upset me, Kamille," he replied in a mild voice. "In other circumstances, I would be even proud of you and your generosity. But not now, not during the war... It's just... irresponsible."

"Yes, you're right, it is." Kamille nodded several times readily. "I wasn't thinking what I was doing, and I certainly didn't know about the possible ramifications my actions might have for you. I'm sorry, I truly am!"

"Hush, not a word anymore." He kissed her lightly on the lips and moved a lock of dark hair away from her brow. "I have to go get those papers and run back to the *Kommandatur*. Horst must be getting antsy waiting for me in the car."

"Will you be back for dinner?" Kamille held her breath, hoping for a positive reply.

"I don't know." He lowered his eyes. "But I'll try my best."

Kamille waved at him through the window, after he had left the house with a folder under his arm, and turned back to the countertop, eyeing the basket with a pained expression on her face.

She paced the kitchen for several minutes, trying to decide what was worse: risking Jochen's fate and his feelings towards her (as she wasn't sure how lenient he would be if he happened to catch her doing the same thing a second time), or leaving Augustine, who had already become her close friend, and her little girl Lili to fend for themselves in this cruel world, where they most likely wouldn't survive the winter.

Kamille recalled the immense gratitude with which every basket was met, and how relieved Augustine looked whenever another portion of supplies was handed to her, meaning that her little daughter wouldn't go starving for another two weeks. It seemed that ration cards weren't doing her any good either, as, being Jewish, Augustine was allowed to stand in line for food only within a certain time period, at the end of the day, and by then all the meager rations were long gone. Kamille remembered how excited Augustine had been to proudly tell her that she had managed to get chicken insides the other day, and what a delicious soup she made with them. *With real meat!* she exclaimed, her eyes sparkling.

Kamille grabbed the basket resolutely, threw a napkin on top of it and proceeded to the exit, coming to terms with her decision at last. Tears stood in her throat as she pictured Jochen's disappointed face in her mind, and the way he would walk out of the door without uttering a word. However, he was right about one thing: it wasn't time for such sentiments now. It wasn't time for egotistical sentiments, when another mother and little girl, who could have been her daughter, were struggling to stay alive. Walking out of the door, Kamille knew she'd made the right choice.

20

*G*iselle set the table absent-mindedly, going through long-forgotten motions. That was something her mother taught her, the always soft-spoken, always smiling, kind and sweet Madame Legrand. *The tablecloth needs to be smoothed out so that there are no wrinkles; the candles go in the middle, together with a crystal decanter with wine; plates and silverware need to be perfectly parallel to each other, and the napkins have to be folded in a way that they can stand on top of the plate without leaning to one side, or (God forbid!) falling. Of course, the secret to a perfect napkin is to starch them thoroughly...*

Seven-year-old Giselle was still interested in her mother's – a poster housewife's – teachings; at fifteen, not so much.

"Why on earth would I want to waste my time on starching napkins day after day if they end up being dirty after the first meal?" she would argue, much to her mother's dismay.

"What do you mean, why?" the gentle woman would inquire, confused by the strange question that had apparently never even crossed her mind. "My dear, it's your duty as a future wife and a mother: to create a home for your future husband that he will want to come home to. To set the table for him when he comes from work, to make him feel comfortable so he can rest after an exhausting day…"

"Well, what if I don't want to get married?" Giselle would shrug dismissively, leaving all the dishware on the table for her little sister to sort out.

Unlike her, Kamille had always had much more interest in domestic affairs, preferring to help her mother around the house instead of staring out of the window with a somber look, like Giselle often did, dreaming of the day when she would have a much better view than the wall of the neighboring building.

"You're saying such nonsense, Gigi, really. What will you do without a husband?"

"I know what I won't do: I won't have to spend my life cooking dinners and starching damned napkins every day," Giselle would grumble in response.

Kamille, little *Maman's* twin, with two neat braids, in contrast to Giselle's always messy bun, would start laying out the cutlery with intentional noise to show *Maman* that she, unlike her big unruly sister, was a good daughter and did everything by the book.

"But, *chéri*, that's a woman's natural place in this world, to be a wife and a mother."

Her mother never gave up her attempts to convince her, God bless her heart. Giselle would only shrug again. "I guess, I will have to respectfully disagree."

"My dear, you're being plain silly now…"

"I wasn't born for starching napkins, *Maman*."

"What were you born for then?"

"To do things that actually matter."

Kamille always shot her wary glares after such statements, statements that she couldn't quite comprehend. Giselle would only turn away back to the window. She sometimes wished that she was born a normal girl, like Kamille. She wished her poor mother didn't have to cross herself and whisper a prayer whenever her oldest daughter spouted some blasphemy about the uselessness of the Church, or start another dispute with her father with a cynicism that was far too harsh and unbecoming for a young girl of her age.

Giselle wished that she didn't have that fire burning inside of her, which wouldn't let her sleep at night and made her strive for things that others feared or shunned. She admired people who others avoided – the ones who shamelessly made their fortunes in the new age right after the Great War. She never felt a pang of conscience when defending those new people's "atrocious" ideas, that were too forward or too immoral for people like her parents. She read "Crime and Punishment" when she was only fifteen and calmly proclaimed at a family dinner that she didn't understand Raskolnikov and why he chose to give himself up… She for one wouldn't. Her mother gasped and crossed herself once again, and her father only looked at her strangely.

"What? A crime is not a crime if you're not caught, is it?"

"You're too young to understand Dostoyevsky, daughter," her father spoke, and his voice trembled slightly for some reason, maybe from a horrifying realization that his daughter was indeed a very different child from the other two, and on the contrary, understood Dostoyevsky all too well, and simply disagreed with him. "It's not about not being caught. It's about the inner struggle, about a human being's morals, about... conscience at least."

"You killed men on the front, *Papa*. Did you have moral qualms about that?"

"Of course I did," he barely whispered in reply.

Giselle went quiet for a few moments, pondering something, and then proclaimed in the same calm voice, "I don't think I would."

"It's a human life you're talking about..."

GISELLE WAS SO IMMERSED in her memories that she didn't notice that she was sitting for some time without moving, holding a sharp knife in her hand that she had ready for cutting meat. Its edge glistened seductively in the candlelight.

It's a human life you're talking about...

I don't think I would...

The door opened, sending amber candle flames into a dancing frenzy. Ominous shadows scattered around the table as Giselle's lips slowly moved into a crooked grin. She hastily hid the knife, placing it next to the platter with a silver lid on top of it, which preserved the meat, just delivered from the nearby restaurant, from getting cold, and stood up to greet her guest.

"Smells delicious." Karl planted a kiss on her lips, sliding an approving glance over the table.

"You know perfectly well that I didn't make it."

"You'll learn with time." He offered her an encouraging smile, moved her chair up and headed to the bathroom to wash his hands.

"Do I look like an exemplary German *hausfrau* yet?" Her eyes took on some strange, almost feral look in the uneven light of the candles, but the smile was in place when Karl returned to the table.

"Not yet," he jested, not noticing anything, too busy pouring blood-red wine into their respective glasses. "But you will. With time."

He smiled and raised his glass in a toast. Giselle sipped the ruby liquid, observing him over the rim of her glass.

No. I definitely will not.

"My mother would be delighted with the changes you're making in me," Giselle responded, unfolding a perfectly starched napkin over her lap.

"Maybe I'll get an *Ausweis* for them both one day. I think I'd like to meet them."

Giselle didn't reply but noticed yet another subtle hint on her account. Recently he had started asking her all sorts of rather strange questions, such as whether her relatives were healthy, who worked where and who was married to whom (*"Shatsky? Not Jewish, is he?" "Mais non, bien sûr non, Charlie. A white Russian émigré, which my cousin was lucky to meet right after that terrible Revolution. An Orthodox Christian turned Catholic and a Count on top of it. Such a refined gentleman. You would love him."*). He also wanted to know if anyone among her relatives were sympathetic to the Communist Party (*"What nonsense! We're all proud representatives of the intelligentsia; who would want to deal with that red flag-wielding riff-raff?"*).

He was planning something about her, thinking that he was always twenty steps ahead of her. Only, he didn't take into consideration that his opponent also did the same, and if she were right in her assumptions, soon the chance would present itself to find out *if she really would.*

MARCEL SAT RIGIDLY, watching himself closely, trying not to give himself away by a twitching of his leg or nervous gulping, which would show how terrified he was. The local *Wehrmacht* headquarters was swarming with the *Boches*, and seeing all these gray-clad men marching along the wide hallway in their shiny boots was more than enough to make even an innocent person nervous. And Marcel was anything but innocent, and who knew how insightful his interrogator would be.

Forty agonizingly slow minutes passed before Philippe finally came out from the room used for questioning, grinning and unharmed, to confidently stride up to the row of chairs where Marcel sat.

"You're up next, brother," the communist leader said, with that single word reminding Marcel, who was already pale with fear, to keep up with their ruse, according to which the two were blood brothers.

It was the late Claude Bussi's papers that he carried to prove his identity after Philippe had generously offered them to him all those months ago, when the Resistance was just a newborn idea. It all seemed so far away and impossible even to conceive now.

"Don't fret, just answer their questions. You have nothing to hide."

As if on cue, a female secretary, also wearing a uniform, called out his name, and Philippe slapped Marcel on his shoulder as if sharing his courage and confidence with him. It was easy for Philippe to be confident; he had gone through similar interrogations many times, even before the war had started and France was still free and independent. It was just routine questioning, Philippe reassured him a day earlier, when a German soldier showed up at the factory and read out the names on his list who were prescribed to appear at the *Wehrmacht* headquarters the following morning for questioning. They had called the others for a similar examination before, and everyone had managed to return unscathed so far. The *Boches* were looking for communists in particular and called out the names of those who were on government lists dating back to the times of the Republic. Philippe and his comrades were on it of course, but Marcel wasn't.

"Why are they calling me then?" he had whispered to Philippe in a trembling voice the day before. "They're onto something. They know it was me…"

"They know nothing. Otherwise, they wouldn't bother to invite you in such a kind manner to the *Kommandatur*. They would have simply dragged you outside and shot you, my friend," Philippe replied with almost infuriating calmness. "The only reason why you're on that list is that you're a brother of a 'notorious communist' and a friend of his communist friends. They think you might also be a communist, that's all. There's nothing to it, so stop panicking. You'll give yourself away in a second if you do. Just stay calm and feign ignorance. They'll let you out in no time."

Marcel recalled Philippe's encouraging words as he walked along the hallway, approaching the doors of the room where his interrogator awaited him. The carpeted floor felt like the road to the gallows, and Marcel hardly managed to collect himself before entering the small anteroom.

A young orderly sat at a table typing something and lifted his head, with chestnut hair neatly parted on one side, to look at the newcomer.

"Claude Bussi?" he inquired, checking the list sitting in front of him.

Marcel blinked a few times, breaking into a cold sweat as recognition washed him over in a nauseating wave. It was the same German he had seen lounging on Kamille's windowsill when he had first arrived in Paris with the two boys in tow, looking for a place to hide them. A few seconds passed before he realized that there was nothing to be afraid of and that the German couldn't possibly recognize him because he had never seen Marcel before. He answered as confidently as possible. "Yes."

"Herr Hauptmann awaits you." The young man got up and proceeded to open the door to *Herr Hauptmann's* office, motioning Marcel inside.

Marcel faltered at the door, waiting for the man at the table to acknowledge his presence. So, if the young officer, who he saw in his sister's window was his orderly, this one was the *Boche* who lived with Kamille. He was rather young and handsome, in that German blond-hair-blue-eyes way. The uniform suited him well; better than Marcel's had suited him (back when he still wore it, that is).

"Sit down, please."

Even his accent was soft and barely noticeable. Germans, who spoke French in the same manner as this one, came from well-educated, upper-middle-class families, Marcel thought with relief, remembering Philippe's teachings for the millionth time. They weren't savages like the ones who used the Nazi Party to swiftly rise from poverty and abuse the higher echelon of power by being brutally vicious in pursuing their higher command's twisted desires. And this man was wearing a *Wehrmacht* uniform, not an SS one, or plain clothes, which was the Gestapo agents' trademark. Marcel noticed a child's painting with some other documents under the thick glass, which was covering the German's table, and let out a soft sigh of relief. Hardened Nazis, who tortured people for a living, would hardly display such sentimental items in their office.

The German noticed his look and quickly moved a sheet of paper on top of the drawing, covering it.

"You're Philippe Bussi's brother?"

"Yes, I am." Marcel nodded his affirmation.

The German squinted his eyes slightly, scrutinizing his face.

"You two don't look alike. Your brother is a veritable giant."

Marcel offered him a bashful smile.

"Everybody says so. He took after our father. And I – after our mother."

"I see." The German proceeded to study Marcel's papers closely, marking something down in a notepad next to him. "Are you aware of your brother's activities within the Communist Party?"

"I do know that he has a fascination with it, yes. But I never understood why, to be honest."

"Is that so?" The German's brow shot up in surprise. "Usually when a family member belongs to a certain party, he drags everyone else in too, especially younger brothers who strive for approval."

"That was not the case with our family. Philippe traveled a lot, and I stayed on the farm and took care of it together with my father. I never understood why Philippe found communism so attractive. It's too... vague and idealistic, in my opinion."

The German got back to his scrutinizing.

"So you have read about their main ideas, have you? I must say, you sound very well-educated for a farmer. Where did you go to school?"

Marcel bit his tongue inside his mouth, realizing his mistake. Philippe had warned him to speak like a factory worker, not a former Sorbonne student, and he had gone and done just that. *Moron!*

"There's a school for farmers' children that I attended for nine years... But it was mostly Philippe who taught me other subjects and gave me books to read."

"Communist manifests?"

"No. French classics mostly."

"Interesting choice." The German grinned.

Marcel almost thought that the worst part was over when suddenly his interrogator took a photo out of his folder and put it right in front of Marcel's eyes. From the black and white surface, Nicolas's face looked at his with his unseeing eyes, his wet hair matted and blood streaks marring his young, innocent face. Marcel pulled back at once.

"Did you know this man?"

"Yes." Something caught in his throat, and Marcel forced himself to clear it under the German's attentive stare. "Yes, I did. He worked in the same factory with us."

"Do you know what happened to him?"

"He just failed to come to work one day… We thought that something happened in his family, or his failing lungs got the better of him. He was coughing quite badly."

"You see now that it was not the case."

"Yes, I do."

"Do you know why he got shot?"

"No, I don't."

"He and one of his comrades organized an assault on two of our army soldiers. He got killed, while the other one was lucky to escape." The German held a very long pause. "You wouldn't be, by any chance, the one to know who that second comrade was?"

"I assure you that it was not my brother," Marcel spoke fast, wiping sweaty palms on top of his trousers under the table. "He wouldn't do something of this sort…"

"I know for a fact that it was not Philippe Bussi," his interrogator replied, nodding. "He has a firm alibi of being at work on the day when the assault happened. Just like the rest of his comrades, with whom he is seen with most of the time. Only one man was absent from work that day."

Marcel swallowed hard, already knowing what the German would say next.

"You."

21

*H*umming a tune under her breath, Giselle didn't notice Karl clearing his throat behind her back. Her fingers were flying over the keys of the typing machine, apparently not fast enough to follow her thoughts. Only when he brushed her hair gently did she turn towards him, beaming.

"Your muse has returned to you, I see?" he inquired, observing a small stack of papers filled with black text on the corner of her table.

"It has indeed." Giselle shifted in her seat, impatient to return to work. "You wanted something?"

Karl nodded and produced a stack of papers from behind his back.

"I found these in the waste bin and realized that it was your manuscript. You must have thrown it away by mistake." He held his hand out, but Giselle only shook her head, not making any attempt to take the papers from him.

"I don't need it anymore. I started a new project."

"Just like that? There are a lot of pages in this one… Surely, you can make something suitable out of this."

"You said it yourself that my characters were bored and overfed. I reread it and realized that you were right. That manuscript is no good. Now this one," she motioned her head towards her typing machine, "this one is simply brilliant. I've written five chapters already, in one sitting."

Karl glanced at the stack of papers near the typing machine with curiosity, placing both hands with the old manuscript behind his back once again.

"What is it about?"

"Oh. I decided to try the noir genre. Literary fiction has become a little too overused for me." She scrunched her nose.

"Noir?"

"Yes. You know, murders and femme fatales," Giselle whispered in a theatrical manner, narrowing her eyes. "Only, I changed it a little. In my noir novel, a femme fatale is a killer, not a beautiful victim. The public should be intrigued, what do you think?"

Karl didn't reply and only straightened his back a little more. Giselle noticed his movement, and grinned more widely.

"Yes. You know me, I'm an innovator. Ordinary noir bores me. So, I made my main protagonist a woman instead of a man, like I used to do before and like everyone else does. Present day, the war is raging… And she's just an ordinary French housewife, right? An exemplary one, of course, not like me." She laughed, but her playful laughter sounded artificial. "And what do you know? Behind her perfect façade, this exemplary housewife plans her husband's murder. He's a no-good husband too; he cheated on her, and she found out. Only, when she demanded a divorce, he hurt her, not much, but just enough to threaten her to stay in the relationship. And so she stays, only in her mind she's scheming such things, from which the hair on his neck would have stood up if he had the ability to read her thoughts."

A meaningful silence lingered for what felt like a minute until Giselle turned on her chair and started humming again, gently caressing the keys with her fingers instead of hitting them with force, as she did it before.

"And so?" She heard Karl's voice, tense with barely detectable emotion, behind her back. "Does she kill him?"

"I don't know yet. So far she's in the planning phase, making sure that she can get away with it. As soon as she ensures that she can..." Giselle threw another impish glare over her shoulder at the German. "Then she will."

He slowly circled the table and stood in front of her, placing her old manuscript on top of the new one.

"It's a rather dangerous idea."

"Trying to get away with one's husband's murder? Most certainly."

"No," Karl replied coldly. "That new novel of yours."

"That's a chance I've got to take. With my name and my connections I'm quite sure that, just like my protagonist, I can get away with anything."

A pointed look of her green eyes unnerved him, she could see it in the thin blue vein pulsating above the high collar of his uniform jacket. Giselle sighed contentedly and offered him her most radiant smile. His guarded look remained in place.

"Do you think that people will like something of this sort?" he inquired quietly.

"Oh, my darling, people will absolutely love it! They'll be in ecstasy, I promise!"

Another pregnant pause followed.

"So, what, if you don't mind me asking, inspired you for such a... dark undertaking?"

"Oh. Promise not to tell anyone." Giselle pressed both palms on her chest in a play-pleading gesture, mischief dancing in her gaze. "I reread 'Crime and Punishment,' and inspiration just overcame me. Can you believe it?"

Karl replied with a tight-lipped smile. "That's prohibited literature you're playing with."

"Are you going to bring me up on charges? Come, *Charlie*, even you couldn't bring yourself to throw away that book. It's a first edition, a rare, collectible item, and besides, you know my weakness for Russian classics. You said it yourself: even your highly praised Goebbels loves it."

Karl studied her face a little longer. "I'd like to read it when you're done."

"*Pas de problème, chéri.* And, knowing how impatient you are, I'll put these first few chapters on your bedside table this very evening."

"*Danke.*"

He turned around sharply on his heels and proceeded to his study. Giselle stretched her arms over her head, moved her tense shoulders front and back a few times, and attacked her typing machine with a renewed vigor.

***

243

KAMILLE PUSHED MORE paper into the fireplace, trying to get the damp wood to start burning. Thankfully, they still had wood, only due to the German officers' presence in the house. From her neighbors, she heard that all firewood had been confiscated, unless a uniform-clad tenant was lodging with the owners. The others, who weren't so fortunate, had to warm themselves with multiple blankets in their unheated houses. And it was not even winter yet.

Violette lay on the carpet in front of the fireplace, mixing her aquarelles in an emptied-out ink bottle, drawing some *chef d'oeuvre*, judging by the look of deep concentration on her face. Kamille smiled at her daughter and shifted the wood with an iron rod, allowing it to finally start catching fire. She had just moved to lower herself onto the carpet next to Violette, when the latter, together with Giselle's Pekinese, who seemed to have taken a liking to the girl and wouldn't leave her side now, scrambled to her feet and rushed to the hallway.

"Monsieur Jochen!"

Kamille caught a quiet gasp escaping her lips and hurried after her daughter. Violette was already hanging off his neck, her bubbly enthusiasm being most contagious.

"I haven't expected you so early," Kamille admitted, stopping within a few steps from him and fighting the desire to greet him with a tight embrace as well. Despite their relationship, they still maintained decorum, at least in front of Violette, even though Kamille had long suspected that her savvy little girl was more than informed about the true nature of their 'friendship.' "I haven't even started making dinner…"

"Don't worry about dinner." Jochen put Violette down,

planting another loud kiss on top of her head, causing the girl to giggle. He rubbed Coco behind the ear and straightened, positively beaming. "Horst is bringing something for us to feast on. We stopped at the café nearby and ordered some food to take home with us. I thought that some real red meat would be most welcome in this cold."

"You're in a good mood," Kamille noticed, rushing to help him remove his overcoat.

"I'm in a great mood," he agreed cheerfully. "We got our terrorist, at last!"

"You did?" Kamille breathed out with relief, almost as elated with his success as Jochen himself. "That's great news!"

"Indeed." Jochen caught her hand in between the folds of the overcoat when Violette couldn't see and pressed it in the most affectionate manner. "My superiors are most satisfied."

"Everything will be back to normal now?" Kamille's voice was a mere whisper, full of hope. Maybe, if he were in a better mood than he had been recently, he would overlook her little 'church trips.'

Jochen only nodded his reassurance and moved away from the door, when his adjutant walked in, carrying two heavy paper bags which produced a mouth-watering smell.

"Good evening, Madame Kamille."

"Good evening, Monsieur Horst."

"Good evening," Violette chimed in with her high voice and outstretched her arms in an attempt to offer the young man help with one of his bags.

"No, no, it's far too heavy for a young lady like yourself," Jochen protested and took the heavy burden from Horst himself. "You better go help you mother set the table instead, and I'll go get a decent bottle of wine from the cellar for us to celebrate."

"What are we celebrating?" Violette's natural curiosity showed itself once again, despite all of her mother's reproaches, calling it un-ladylike behavior.

"Monsieur Jochen and Monsieur Horst caught a very dangerous criminal today," Kamille explained, placing her hand on her daughter's shoulder and nudging her towards the dining room. "Go put a tablecloth, the red one, on the table, and I'll go fetch plates and silverware."

The two officers waited with infinite patience while Violette carefully smoothed all wrinkles out of the rich, cherry-red tablecloth.

"What did he do? The criminal?" the girl inquired, pulling one end of the tablecloth down so it would be perfectly in line with the other end. She observed her job with a critical eye and smiled at the men, inviting them to place their bags on the surface.

"He attacked our soldiers together with his comrade," Jochen explained, taking the heavy dishes out of the paper bag. The seductive smell intensified.

"Why?"

"He..." Jochen pondered his reply for a few moments. "He wanted to sabotage a major operation for the German army. And, so, he attacked the soldiers who were in charge of this operation."

"Did he kill them?"

Horst snorted softly, apparently finding this little inter-rogation rather amusing. Jochen shot him a glare, and the young man doubled his efforts in taking care of the food platters.

"No, he didn't. But he did… damage our property."

"Why? Aren't we friends now?"

"Friends?"

"Well, yes. We signed the armistice, didn't we? So we're supposed to be friends now, the Germans and the French. That's what our new *maître* says."

"Your new *maître* is right," Kamille joined in, returning to the room with a stack of plates, folded napkins and silver-ware neatly laid out on top of them. "We are friends; only some people refuse to acknowledge it."

"Why?"

"Because they don't like the occupation. Enough questions, Violette, you're being rude," Kamille lowered her voice in reprimand.

Violette nodded with a solemn look. "I know. Some people are just being mean for no reason. Just like Jacques, that boy, who tore my drawing apart, just because Monsieur Horst helped me draw it. But I like Monsieur Horst…"

"How can you not like Monsieur Horst?" Jochen replied jokingly, making his adjutant chuckle. "He's an absolute charmer."

Violette nodded her agreement and climbed into her chair after the last plate was set.

"What are you going to do to him now?"

Kamille thought of chiding her daughter once again for her questioning, but she was curious herself.

"Nothing." Jochen shrugged, after sending Horst for a bottle of wine. "I'll try to question him myself tomorrow, but if he refuses to speak about his reasons or accomplices, I'll have to hand him over to the Gestapo."

"Giselle's tenant will be delighted at such a prospect,"

Kamille tried to hide a bashful smile after her little jab at the Chief of the local *Staatspolizei*.

"Oh, he called me already on the terrorist's account." Jochen picked up a steak knife and started cutting into the thick, bleeding cut of meat. Violette wetted her lips, pulling forward in her chair.

"He did?" Kamille repeated.

"Mhm. Quite a… friendly gentleman." The sarcasm in his voice was more than obvious. "So amiable that the least I deal with him, the better. So, I'll just let him have his terrorist and return to my usual duties."

Horst returned with a bottle of red wine and popped it open with a practiced move. Kamille raised her glass in toast together with the two men, only for some reason Violette's voice kept repeating her questions over and over, the questions that only children had the courage to ask. The parents preferred to seal their lips when it came to the occupation and to pretend that they indeed were "friends." Suddenly, at the thought of that "terrorist's" brave, even though foolish, actions, the steak tasted foul in her mouth, just like a gag that the Germans were trying to impose on the whole nation. Had she indeed become one of them now? A collaborator, eating from the enemy's hand and allowing the same enemy to offer one of her countrymen for execution at the hands of the brutal Gestapo? Kamille stabbed another piece of bloody meat with her fork, angry at her own impotence. Even Giselle seemed a lesser collaborator to her than her reflection, accusingly staring at her from the mirror across the room, framed by the two uniform-clad men. But what could she do, really? She was under occupation as well.

22

*P*hilippe pulled his cap lower over his eyes, hiding from the inquiring looks of the Germans that kept passing him by. He was sticking out like a sore thumb here, dressed in his ragged attire, so different from the usual habitants of the area. He'd been sitting here long enough to start attracting attention: a factory worker, casually lounging on a bench in the middle of the Champs-Élysées, on a working day, with a day-old newspaper in his hands. But that was the risk that he had to take, for Marcel's very life depended on him. He'd dragged the boy into all this, after all… Now he had to get him out.

Philippe glanced up from the paper in his hands and finally spotted Giselle, walking on the opposite side of the street with a small leather valise in her gloved hand. She didn't notice him, of course, looking straight ahead in her black overcoat, hiding her eyes behind the veil net of her exquisite hat. Philippe quickly got up, folded the paper and proceeded to follow her along the street while throwing occasional glances over his shoulder to make sure that no one followed her. Who knew if her *Boche* lover had her followed?

Sensing no danger, Philippe quickly crossed the street and caught up with the woman in a few short strides. She gasped in surprise when someone caught her shoulder from behind, but Philippe quickly silenced her, pressing his finger to his mouth.

"It's just me. No need to alarm the authorities."

His attempts at humor missed the spot, judging by her look.

"You don't need me to alarm the authorities. You're doing a perfect job by yourself. My windows oversee the street, and my *Boche*, seeing you with me, is all I need now." Without further ceremony, Giselle grabbed his sleeve and almost dragged Philippe into the nearest antique store, favored by the local officers. The Germans took particular pride in strutting inside and, after throwing half-bored, half-appreciative looks around, would leave with some purchase to send back to their families, who in their turn would put the said antique object on the shelf to proudly demonstrate to their guests.

As soon as the two stepped inside the dimly lit shop, a small silver bell above the door announced their presence. Giselle exercised her most gracious smile at the owner, a part-time university professor with a passion for history, who, however, despised her immensely for buying his antiques solely based on how they would look in her living room, and not showing even the slightest interest in their origin. The professor nodded solemnly in response, pressing his mouth into a hard line under his enviously thick mustache, and returned to studying a new catalog, not deeming the strange couple a second look, which suited Giselle just fine.

"Good morning, *Monsieur Professeur*," she still uttered in a sweet, sing-song voice, just to disperse any last doubts on their account. "I'm in desperate need of a new clock and a bookcase. If you don't mind, I'll take a look around, and if I fancy something I'll leave my delivery man here to talk details with you."

"By all means, Mademoiselle Legrand. Take your time." With that he left them to their devices, ignoring them completely.

Giselle pulled Philippe to the furthest corner and stopped in front of the cherry wood bookcase, admiring the carved details.

"What do you want?"

"Well, I didn't come because I missed seeing you, obviously," he threw back sarcastically, a little wounded on account of her "delivery man" remark.

He was dressed like one, and deep inside he understood that it was a clever reply in this scenario, but it still made old feelings stir inside; like back to the times right after the war, when he would ride to Paris with his father to deliver fresh vegetables to the market – he couldn't stand the haughty, condescending looks that the gentry threw their way.

Those looks, and the inequality in general, propelled his desire to fight for an idealistic state, praised by the communists in their leaflets, where everyone would share everything, and the world would be a much better place, in which no one would suffer from hunger or be homeless while others gorged themselves with food and resided in palaces. Giselle didn't belong to the gentry, but came from the ordinary middle class, just like Marcel, but she had chosen to become one of those arrogant people, and Philippe didn't fancy her one bit for that choice. She was a writer on top of it and could have used her talent (*all right, she did have talent,* he had admitted to himself a long time ago, only he would never share that confession with anyone) to bring some good ideas to the masses, but she chose to write about high class issues, for high class. Philippe reminded himself that it was none of his business anyway, what she did with her life.

"Do you need money?" she whispered back, ignoring his previous remark.

"No, I don't need your money. Even if I did, I wouldn't ask you for it. Whatever you gave me before went to buy food for Marcel and the boys."

"Are we starting the whole class-struggle argument again?" Giselle touched the intricate carving on the small coffee table, pretending to assess it.

"No. I'm sorry." Philippe quickly collected himself. She unnerved him, and much too often, and these very conflicted feelings didn't help him think straight, much to his annoyance. He took a deep breath and whispered close to her ear, trying not to notice the smell of her perfume invading his senses, "Marcel is in trouble."

"How big of a trouble?" Giselle whispered back, her gloved fingers tensing on the polished wood.

"Very big." He hated breaking the news to Marcel's sister, who had warned him on the day of their very first meeting not to drag her brother into his Resistance activities. Now, Philippe had not only gotten the boy in trouble, but he also had to ask her for help because…well, frankly, he had no one else to go to. "He never returned from the interrogation yesterday. They dismissed all of us after questioning, but him… They haven't announced anything yet, but I suspect that the *Boches* arrested him."

"On what grounds? Do they have anything in particular on him? Was it the *Wehrmacht* or the SS that were conducting the interrogation?"

Philippe looked her over with newfound respect. Instead of breaking into hysterics and starting to accuse him, as he had expected from her, Giselle took on a look of utter concentration, moving straight to resolving the situation with a composed, coolheaded tone. Maybe, he was mistaken about her after all, and she was a much tougher cookie than he had imagined her to be.

"The *Wehrmacht*. They called us to the *Kommandatur* and this young officer… What the hell was his name? Hartmann, I think. Yes, Hauptmann Hartmann interrogated us. I don't think he has anything particular on Marcel, but if he starts interrogating him intensely…" Philippe lowered his eyes, chewing on his lip vigorously. "I'm sorry that I dragged him into all this. I shouldn't have. You warned me not to."

Giselle only sighed deeply, and shook her head, surprising him with her reaction once again. Her brows were drawn together under the veil as she pondered something in her mind.

"I also said that it would make a man out of him. Don't blame yourself. It's not your fault. Besides, your remorse is of no use to us now; now we have to figure out how we can help him."

Philippe nodded eagerly, a little relieved and grateful for her approach to the matter.

"Hartmann, you said?" She turned to him suddenly.

"Yes... I believe his name was Hartmann."

"A handsome, blond man, right? Wears his hair sleeked to the left side, but his bangs are wavy, and he keeps fixing them from time to time?"

Philippe nodded once again, wondering if the infamous Mademoiselle Legrand knew all the *Boches* in town.

"And he has an adjutant, a very young man, with dark hair and blue eyes? He has a very nice voice, but his accent is a little stronger than Hartmann's?"

"That's him, all right."

She breathed out in relief as it seemed.

"I know them both. They lodge with my sister, Kamille," Giselle explained. "I'll go visit her tonight and talk to this Hartmann."

"He thinks that Marcel is my brother! He has my late brother's papers—"

Giselle interrupted his protests with a simple shake of her head. "He'll just have to find out the truth then. This way, Marcel has much more chance. Maybe he'll just agree to send him as a forced laborer to Germany and won't execute him. Marcel didn't kill anybody, after all."

"You think he'll agree to that?"

"He seems to be very much in love with my sister. So, yes, I'd say he'll agree to this small concession concerning Marcel's punishment to please Kamille. Men do such favors for their mistresses, you know."

She winked at Philippe, catching him off guard again.

"Your brother is in jail, and you're joking," he grumbled in response.

"I will joke even standing on the gallows, my friend." Giselle shrugged off his accusations. "I'm a fatalist, you see. Whatever is destined to happen, will happen. I see no reason to tear my hair and bawl my eyes out, no matter the situation. I learned that from the very early age either I will change the situation, or accept it; there are no other options. It's much easier to live this way. So, given that Marcel is in jail, I accept that he might never leave it, or even die. But it doesn't matter, as I will do my utmost to save his life."

"That's very... unorthodox thinking, I must say."

"Suits me just fine."

"I didn't say I don't like it." Philippe smiled. "It's just...I didn't expect it from you."

Their eyes met for a short moment until Giselle dug into her pocket and produced a small notebook. She wrote something down, tore a page out, folded it in two and put it into Philippe's pocket.

"Don't come here anymore," she whispered, pressing his hand as if apologizing for her words. "It's very dangerous for the both of us. Next time call this number, and if it's not me who answers the phone, just say that you're Philippe from the Demarche Publishing House and that Monsieur Demarche needs to see me urgently. I'll come and meet you in his building, where we'll be able to talk discretely. I put the address there as well. And don't worry, I'll warn Michel, the owner, about you. He's in it with us, too."

After that Giselle gave him another warm smile, nodded at him reassuringly, and spoke with intentional loudness. "Lovely, but too dark for my living room. Monsieur

Professeur, will you be so kind to give me a call when you receive anything beige or caramel?"

"Rest assured, Mademoiselle," followed his curt reply.

Philippe exited the store, following Giselle's steps, and the two parted ways. He willed himself not to turn around to look at her once again.

UPON HER RETURN from the Demarche Publishing House, where she submitted yet another article for Michel, Giselle put her valise, not containing anything compromising anymore, next to her desk and went into the study, shedding her coat along the way.

"Karl." She knocked on the opened door with a most cordial smile. "Would you mind lending me Otto's services as a driver tonight? Kamille and I are planning a small family dinner."

"Of course."

Giselle had just turned around to take her leave, beaming with success, when he added, "I'll be coming with you, as a matter of fact."

Giselle pivoted on her heels, facing her gray-clad tenant, who was grinning coolly.

"She won't mind you bringing a guest, I'm sure." Karl slightly tilted his head to one side. "You'd better call her in advance though. It's rude surprising a host with someone's appearance like that, after all."

"But Karl," Giselle spoke, carefully selecting her words. "It's to be a family dinner. Not that you're not welcome to join us, *bien sûr*, but you'll be bored out of your mind…"

"You always say that," he reprimanded her with a somewhat sly grin. He had some ulterior motive for this visit, most certainly. "And besides, aren't her *Wehrmacht* guests going to be dining with her as well?"

"I don't know," Giselle replied honestly. "I suppose they will."

"*Gut.* It's all decided then. I need to speak to Hartmann anyway. He owes me a prisoner."

"A prisoner?" Giselle caught onto how her voice faltered slightly, and quickly composed herself. "How intriguing. Anyone I know?"

"Perhaps." He was already deep into studying some papers in front of him. "A terrorist who attacked one of our posts a couple of weeks ago. They finally found him; he's been in their custody for two days, but they didn't get anywhere with him. That *Wehrmacht* are utterly useless when it comes to interrogations. They just sit and talk to their prisoners, like good old friends. And when they don't give them any names, they simply reprimand them for mischief and send them to jail, or even worse, to work in Germany. And who guarantees that from there they won't run and start their terrorist activities once again?"

"No one, you're right," Giselle agreed with a carefully faked smile. Her mind, contrary to her perfectly calm demeanor, was a buzzing beehive as she feverishly thought what could possibly be done to save Marcel from Karl's clutches. "So what is the deal between you two?"

"High command in Berlin was infuriated not only with the act of sabotage itself but with how the *Wehrmacht* handled the case. It took them two bloody weeks to just catch the terrorist when the idea that I suggested – taking twenty civilian hostages and threatening the population with their execution if the terrorist doesn't come forward – would get him into our hands in just two days. But it was rejected for its 'severity.'" Karl snorted with contempt, shaking his head. "Pathetic weaklings, all of them, the *Wehrmacht*. Can't stand that."

"You're right," Giselle repeated, her hands squeezing into fists under the coat that she was still holding.

"And now on top of everything, Hartmann refuses to hand over the terrorist for interrogation, even though it's clear as day that he will never get a single name out of him. I called him yesterday, but he rejected my request for a transfer, citing that 'the *Staatspolizei* would only torture him to death.'" Another snort followed. "The *Staatspolizei* at least gets the job done. One day and I would have a full list of names of all his accomplices. But Hauptmann Hartmann obviously has some humanitarian qualms on this account. Very well then. I'll address all of his qualms tonight." Karl lifted his black eyes towards Giselle. "Make sure he'll be there when you call Madame Blanchard, please."

Giselle nodded, smiled once again and headed to her bedroom. There she lowered herself tiredly on her bed, deep in thought, for the first time in many years doubting her strength.

*T*he tension at the table was palpable. Karl was all smiles and charm as soon as he stepped through the doors, handing the mistress of the household a bottle of wine and even a bouquet of roses, which were almost impossible to get for ordinary citizens. He kissed Kamille's hand ceremoniously under Jochen's hard glare, exchanged sharp salutes with two *Wehrmacht* officers, and even lifted little Violette's chin and, after studying her face with the detached interest of a scientist, complimented Kamille on her beautiful daughter.

"I see good genes run in all of your family members," he noted, grinning mysteriously at Giselle for some reason.

She forced a smile in response and tried to ignore the fact that her little Coco, who she was very much looking forward to seeing, had retreated from the hallway at the first sight of her date.

Now, they all sat at the long, redwood dining table thoroughly pretending that it wasn't the most awkward gathering that each of them had ever encountered in their lives. Kamille sat unnaturally straight and looked both alarmed and guilty – a habit that all law-abiding citizens shared, Giselle had noticed a long time ago. The criminals always managed to keep the most impenetrable poker face whenever they encountered an authority figure of Karl's rank, while people like Kamille sported the most guilt-ridden air even when they didn't do anything that could be considered even remotely criminal.

Violette ate her food silently, from time to time checking under the table in hope of seeing her little four-legged friend; Giselle did too, but the Pekinese was nowhere to be found.

Horst barely touched his plate, looking flushed, and pushing the food around, refusing to even look at the man who was sitting next to Giselle. Jochen drank a little too much wine, obviously in an attempt to fuel much needed courage when the time came to face the Gestapo chief face-to-face. He knew all too well what it was all about, even though not a word had been spoken about anyone's work or politics.

"The chicken is delicious, Madame." Karl finally interrupted the uncomfortable silence, even though he seemed to be the one who reveled in it, enjoying his meal in the most relaxed manner.

This man makes himself at home no matter where he goes, Giselle thought sulkily, cutting her chicken breast without any desire to eat.

"*Merci,* Herr Sturmbannführer." Kamille nodded embarrassingly, using the German form of address for he detested the French one, and Giselle had wisely warned her about it.

There was no need to rub him the wrong way with what Giselle had in mind. Well, truth be told, so far she didn't have anything particular in mind, but hoped to conceive some quick plan along the way, as soon as the opportunity presented itself. Keeping her options open was one of the qualities which had helped her immensely in her life.

Karl inquired about Kamille's late husband and offered his almost sincere condolences concerning the "brave death of a true French patriot."

"Soldiers are the only true patriots of this country, Madame." He spoke with the calm confidence of a man who was used to his opinion always being the correct one, or that everyone would accept it even if it wasn't. "Those worthless terrorists, who call themselves patriots, with that General in exile as their leader, are nothing but the worst that French society has to offer. They are all either communists or ordinary criminals, who are happy to have any reason to do some malice, not only to the new government – that was welcomed with gratitude by all the citizens – but also to those very citizens. I finally received a cable from Gruppenführer Müller's Berlin office just a couple of hours ago, and he promised me full support in my suggestion of using hostages to seize the fugitive terrorists sooner. This one is in custody, of course, but for future cases, Gruppenführer and I agreed that such a tactic would prove itself most effective."

Giselle noticed how Jochen's gaze shot up, boring into the SS officer sitting directly across from him and smiling at him in the most sinister manner. *So, he got what he was after,* Giselle sighed. No wonder; Karl could be very persuasive when he wanted to. And she knew how rational and logical he always sounded while presenting his arguments to the other side. Karl always prepared for such conversations with a meticulous obsession with details, and there was not a single matter that he didn't investigate and take into account before starting to drive his point across. No wonder that his superiors supported him.

"Most definitely the Gestapo authority will not override the authority of the governing *Wehrmacht* administration," Jochen noticed coolly. "And the governing administration will never allow using innocent civilians as human bait for the terrorists."

"You're so idealistic, Hauptmann Hartmann, it's worth admiration." Karl raised his glass in a mock toast. "Only, your ideals and faith in humanity don't mean a thing during the war. And to answer your previous question: yes, it will override the administration's authority, for we're talking about 'extreme circumstances' here, of which Gruppenführer Heydrich spoke just recently – you still have the memo, I hope – and in any case, such 'extreme circumstance' ensure that the authority will come under the SS jurisdiction, and the Gestapo namely. Gruppenführer Müller will also send the cable, which I mentioned earlier, to all the offices, in the course of the next few days."

"Cable or no cable, with all due respect, Herr Sturmbann-führer, such practice is most condemnable in my eyes, and all of my fellow officers will agree with me." Jochen's cheeks reddened slightly from both the wine and emotion.

Karl remained enviously calm.

"Condemnable or not, it will prevent the terrorists from their activities. In this case, the end justifies the means." Karl shrugged his shoulders as if he didn't comprehend why his compatriot couldn't understand such an obvious thing. To him, everything seemed more than logical and conclusive. "But, I don't want to discuss such matters in front of the ladies. We'll have plenty of time to talk about it after dinner. Talking politics during dinner is distasteful, and we don't want our beautiful hostess to think we are barbarians without manners, do we?"

"By all means, don't mind us." Giselle quickly made use of the situation and got up to help Kamille clear the table before the dessert could be served. "We'll be in the kitchen, so talk all you want. Only, no longer than ten minutes, please."

Karl laughed at her little jest in the most charming manner and kissed her hand gallantly before she reached for his plate. Horst lowered his glass on the table rather loudly and muttered his apologies. Giselle threw him a remorseful glance, but he was too busy studying the pattern on the tablecloth.

"Violette, would you be so kind as to take Monsieur Jochen and Monsieur Horst's plates, *chéri?*" Kamille asked her daughter, so the girl wouldn't be in the same room with the men when they renewed their discussion. No child needed to hear that, no matter how much the adults thought she understood, and Violette was a very smart girl.

"*Oui, Maman.*"

In the kitchen, Giselle disposed of the dirty dishes by dropping them into the sink in the most careless manner, much to Kamille's dissatisfaction, and turned to face her sister.

"Kamille, it's Marcel," she whispered, pulling the remaining plates from Kamille hands, despite her protests.

After the plates had joined the uneven pile in the sink, she clasped her sister's elbow and pulled her towards the window, away from Violette.

"What about him? Did you manage to find out where he is?"

All this time Giselle had played along with Kamille's version that Marcel was missing in action and that no one knew what happened to him. For some reason, Giselle thought it unwise to reveal to her vulnerable sibling about her and Marcel's recent highly criminal activities. Only, now she didn't have a choice but to tell her the truth.

"Marcel has been living in Paris all this time. In our old apartment."

Kamille gasped softly, covering her mouth with her hand.

"What are you saying, Giselle?"

"I'm saying that he didn't go missing; he deserted. He ran and stumbled across one man who offered him his late brother's papers to conceal his identity because he would have been arrested by the Germans if he were caught with his real ones. The man who helped him turned out to be a communist, and Marcel..." Giselle waved her hand impatiently, deciding to come right to the point. "Making the story short, the terrorist in Jochen's custody is our Marcel. We need to intervene to prevent Jochen from handing him over to Karl. Because if he does..."

Giselle shook her head, pressing her mouth into a firm line. She had never told Kamille about Karl and his methods of interrogation, and when he had almost broken her finger, even though she was nowhere near the same charge that Marcel currently faced.

"You knew all this time? You knew, and you didn't tell me?" Kamille asked, sounding wounded with such a betrayal.

"It was for your own good, Kamille." Giselle put both hands on her sister's shoulders, but Kamille stepped away.

"You knew all along. You knew about him and some communist, and you never did anything? You didn't help him? How could you, Giselle? He's our only brother. He's your little brother, and you allowed him to get involved with communists? What's gotten into you?"

"Kamille, I promise, I'll answer all of your questions when the time is right. And when the time is right, you can hurl all the accusations you like at me. Now, please, pull yourself together and let's think about how to get him out of this."

"No. You're always like this, Giselle. You dive head first into any new adventure that comes your way, and your drag everyone else after you. You should have looked after him, not encouraged him to do something of this sort! What is it, is your new fad with communism? Are you that bored?"

Giselle hushed her and smiled encouragingly at Violette, who was busy bringing *Limoges* china from the kitchen to the dining room.

"No. Don't try to silence me when we both know that it's your fault," Kamille hissed crossly in resignation, very rare for her usual mild demeanor. "You've always been like this, thinking only about yourself. And now look where it's got poor Marcel! You don't care about anyone at all... Not even poor Horst! Nothing even stirred in you to bring your lover here and have him sit at one table with the man who obviously has feelings for you. How can you be such a callous, cruel person, Giselle?"

Giselle squinted her eyes slightly, processing a new thought that had just flashed through her mind. Accusations and shaming, frankly speaking, had never bothered her that much, for she saw her share of it while growing up. Kamille didn't call her anything she hadn't already been called before.

"Horst. It might actually work... Yes, Horst. Quickly, go fetch him for me. Tell him that I need some help in the kitchen. Karl is probably so deep in argument with Jochen now that he won't even notice that he's gone."

"Giselle, what do you—"

"Do you want Marcel to survive, or not?"

Kamille left in a huff, but at least she did as she was told. Giselle winked at Violette, who moved a little stool next to the sink and busied herself with the dishes.

HER UNEXPECTED GUEST'S presence still lingered in the room long after the Gestapo chief had left with Giselle. Kamille finished clearing the table and paused in the doorway. Jochen stood with his back to her, pouring himself a glass of brandy. Judging by the fact that he hardly ever drank, he was obviously in the same morose mood as she was. Kamille watched him nurse the amber liquid in his glass and thought of what possible words she could say to him.

How could she possibly tell him, her lover and yet a representative of the occupying forces nevertheless, that the terrorist in his custody was her little brother? Could she count on his loyalty and support in the most desperate of moments, or would she ruin the only relationship she cherished, one which had blossomed against all odds? What reaction would prevail in him: a sense of loyalty to his country, something instilled in him long ago, or compassion and a desire to help someone, even if he was not supposed to help by any means, for such "help" would not only go against army policy but even land him somewhere on the frontline in Africa?

He noticed her at last, turned to face her, and smiled with such habitual gentleness that Kamille was suddenly overcome with the feeling of guilt, as if it was her who committed the crime, and not Marcel. She was feeling guilty for the words she hadn't pronounced yet, for they would decide not only Marcel's future but her own as well; her future with this man, whose smile in the course of the short six months that they have known each other seemed to have become as essential for her as the air she breathed.

"You look upset," Jochen noticed as he approached her. "Don't be. I don't want you to worry about Wünsche. I'll deal with him, I promise."

He cupped her cheek. Kamille pressed into his warm palm and whispered, closing her eyes because she simply couldn't bring herself to look into his, "Don't hand your prisoner over to him, please."

"I don't want to, but Kamille… He left me no choice," Jochen explained in a soft voice.

"He'll kill him, just to set an example for the rest. I know he will."

"I know it too." Jochen let out a sigh and added after a pause, "I didn't want to tell you, but he gave me an ultimatum: I surrender my prisoner to him or he makes a report to the *Kommandant* of Paris that a certain Hauptmann Hartmann is involved in an indecent – and illegal – relationship with a Frenchwoman. The *Kommandant* will take his side, too; they're longtime friends from what I've heard. It's very unfortunate of course. The 'terrorist' is just a young boy whose only crime was trying to protect his country... I've even come to like him during our interrogations. He seems like a very nice fellow."

"He is. He's a very, very nice boy and such a gentle soul!" Kamille clasped Jochen's hands in hers. "He's my brother, Jochen. Giselle told me tonight. My little brother Marcel. I've told you about him so many times, remember?"

"But..." He seemed to be caught completely off guard, just like Kamille was when her sister had announced the news. "How is it possible? You said Marcel was missing in action. I was looking for him through my channels..."

"My little Marcel was never cut out for fighting. He deserted apparently. Was afraid to go back home. Stumbled across some communists who dragged him into their cell, provided him with papers and coerced him to participate in their criminal activities. I don't even know what the story is, I only know what Giselle told me." Kamille gestured desperately. "But one thing I can vouch for: Marcel would never harm a soul. He's not a criminal, nor is he a terrorist... And if you hand him over to Wünsche, he'll die. My little brother will die."

"*Gott im Himmel*, Kamille, what can I possibly do?" Jochen muttered, stroking her hair and back as she cried quietly on his chest, pressing her cheek to the cool metal of his medals.

The old clock was counting the minutes.

"I can give him two days for now. And I'll try to make

some calls tomorrow. I can't promise you that I'll be able to save him because it would be dishonest, but what I can promise is that I'll apply all my efforts to do so. Will that do?"

Kamille looked up at the sound of his voice, a faint smile barely touching her lips.

"Yes. That is more than I ever hoped."

———

THE FIRST SNOW covered the ground during the night, the first signs of winter biting into Giselle's cheeks, rosy from the frosty weather, as she braved the cold, heading towards her old apartment. Philippe let her in, anxiously awaiting the news.

"It's not good," Giselle declared right away, unraveling the scarf from around her neck. "I spoke to Kamille this morning. Jochen agreed to hold him in the *Kommandatur* prison for a couple more days, but Karl apparently threatened him last night, when they spoke alone, that if Jochen doesn't agree to hand over his prisoner, he will report Jochen's 'indecent relationship' with a Frenchwoman to the city *Kommandant*. And the *Kommandant* eats from Karl's hand."

"*Putain*," Philippe cursed under his breath.

Pierre and his brother were also there, chewing on their nails, concentration creasing their foreheads.

"We only have today and tomorrow, as that's how long Jochen can milk the story that he's supposedly trying to interrogate Marcel before he has to transfer him into Karl's custody. So, we have to act fast," Giselle stated with determination.

Philippe nodded. "Any ideas?"

"I did think of something last night, when I was still at Kamille's," Giselle admitted and then paused, wondering if she should voice the idea. "It's a very daring plan though, and I'm only fifty percent sure that it will work."

"Your plan is already better than mine because I have none."

She motioned her head towards the boys. "Can we use them? We won't be able to pull it off with just the two of us."

"Yes, you can," Pierre replied before Philippe had a chance to open his mouth. "Just tell us what to do, and we'll do it."

"There's a catch, as I've already said," Giselle warned, looking Pierre intently in the eye. "We can either get Marcel out, or we can all die. I honestly don't know how everything will turn out."

"So? Won't we all die one day anyway?" Jerome shrugged, seconding his brother, too nonchalantly for a boy his age. "I'd rather die young and doing something remarkable than old and helpless in my bed."

"Can't argue with that logic," Giselle joked grimly. "Here's the plan. You tell me what you think."

24

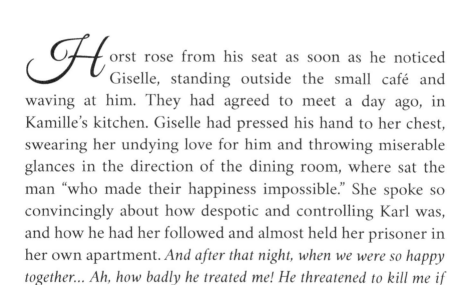

*H*orst rose from his seat as soon as he noticed Giselle, standing outside the small café and waving at him. They had agreed to meet a day ago, in Kamille's kitchen. Giselle had pressed his hand to her chest, swearing her undying love for him and throwing miserable glances in the direction of the dining room, where sat the man "who made their happiness impossible." She spoke so convincingly about how despotic and controlling Karl was, and how he had her followed and almost held her prisoner in her own apartment. *And after that night, when we were so happy together... Ah, how badly he treated me! He threatened to kill me if I ran away in that manner again... I dream of you, my dearest Horst, every single night I do, and he is a tyrant, I tell you, a tyrant!*

Well, she might have embellished the story a little, but her final goal had been reached: she was back in Horst's good graces, and, even though she did feel a slight pinch of conscience for distorting the truth, Horst was her only chance at getting her brother out of jail. He promised to meet her at the place she indicated, kissed her greedily and hurried back to the table, to prevent "the tyrant" from going to look for her.

Horst threw money on the table absentmindedly, without even asking for the bill, and rushed to put on his overcoat, all along eyeing Giselle through the window, who was beaming at him from under her veil. They had agreed that they had to meet discretely, and the further from any place that the SS favored the better. And what was a better place than a small café not too far from the *Wehrmacht Kommandatur*, and a better time than the sunset?

Horst walked outside and made a motion to embrace the woman, who had occupied his mind and heart for the past few months, but Giselle shook her head in warning, taking him by the crook of his arm instead.

"Just in case that despot has his people following me, let him think we met by accident," she explained, her voice intentionally low. Horst nodded solemnly and looked over his shoulder, just in case. "Walk with me, please."

"Giselle, how I wish I could hold you again in my arms," he whispered to her, and caressed her fingers discretely with his gloved hand before moving his hand right away.

"I know." She sighed. "I keep thinking about our night..."

"Me, too! Not a day passes by that I don't think of you."

They kept exchanging hopeless expressions of desperate and impossible love, like two heroes of some romance belonging to the nineteenth century. *Eighteenth even,* Giselle noted to herself with the bored mind of a novelist. *Such a cliché, Michel would say. Antoine would love it, though. Two*

lovers, separated by an oppressive husband. But Antoine's charac-
ters would both die in the end if he scripted this story. He loves
drama a little too much, my sweet Antoine with his sad, caramel
eyes. I hope for my characters to live a bit longer though...

She threw a wary glance around, before pulling Horst
into a narrow side street, approaching the spot which she
had marked on a map with Philippe a day ago. Now, if only
everything went as they planned.

Making sure that they were alone in the deserted narrow
alleyway, sheltered by two high stone walls, Giselle stepped
in front of Horst and threw her arms around his neck.
Delighted that he could kiss her at last – just as she had
expected he would – the young man pulled her close and
pressed his lips to hers, completely oblivious to the quiet
steps behind his back.

"Don't move."

The words, spoken with deadly calmness, and the soft
click of a cocked gun right next to his ear, were more than
enough to convince Horst to follow the instructions. Giselle
saw a silent question in his blue eyes, and she shook her head
slowly, replying it in the same silent way.

Someone's arm was already opening his holster to relive
Horst of his personal weapon. Alarm flashed in his gaze, but
the man behind his back had already turned the young
officer by the scruff of his neck to face him.

All Horst could see were the eyes of the man, deep, black
eyes burning with determination, as the rest of the man's
face, who was at least a head taller than him, was wrapped in
a thick scarf, completely concealing his features. Two other
terrorists – and Horst had already abandoned all illusion as
to what they were – also stood behind the tall man's back,

and also had their faces disguised in the same manner: under multiple layers of scarves and caps, pulled onto their eyes.

"Now, if you and your lady friend want to survive this night, you'll do exactly what I say," the terrorist leader spoke in a low, menacing voice. The gun was now pressing directly into Horst's chest. Horst noticed that his gun had already made its way into one of the accomplice's hands, and was aimed at Giselle.

"Let the woman go," Horst demanded quietly. "She's your compatriot. Surely you don't want to hurt her."

"I don't care for that *pute à Boche*," the man in front of him said dismissively. "I'd shoot her right now if I didn't have need for the both of you. And enough of this empty talk. You're not in a position to negotiate as you have probably realized by now. So just do as I say, and I'll let you both live."

"What do you want?"

"I want you to stop asking questions and dragging time. Now, be a good fellow, take your lady friend by the hand and walk to the *Kommandatur* like the two sweet doves you are. Walk slowly, and don't even think of attracting any sort of attention or giving any kind of signal to your military brethren, if you happen to encounter them on your way. Don't forget that my comrades and I will be walking ten steps behind you, and that's more than enough to shoot you both before you can even think of running for cover. Do you understand me?"

"Yes."

"You don't want your little lady friend to die, do you?"

"No, of course not."

"*Bien.* I suppose, we have an understanding then. Now, walk."

Giselle noticed how Philippe stepped back and put his gun into his pocket so that its muzzle was still aiming at his victim, only now it was carefully concealed from curious eyes. Jerome also had his gun hidden in the same manner. Horst sighed, turned around, and, with a helpless look on his face, took Giselle by the hand.

"Don't be afraid," he whispered to her, trying to sound reassuring. "They won't hurt you."

"I'm not," Giselle whispered in response.

No, she wasn't afraid of the men behind their backs; she was much more afraid of the one who would decide their fate very soon.

The street, leading to the *Kommandatur*, was never crowded. Few ordinary citizens wanted to stroll around these quarters, preferring to stay away from the Germans as far as possible. Even the Germans themselves were missing from the scene at this hour, as most of them were already enjoying their first glass of wine in the restaurants after a long working day, wine which the French could hardly afford nowadays.

Night had already ascended on the city despite the early hour, and the small procession soon came to a halt at Philippe's demand, spoken quietly so that only Giselle and Horst could hear him.

"Walk over to that lamppost across from the entrance and stand next to it, facing each other. It would be nice if you keep your hands on your lady friend's waist, so your comrades think that you brought her here to impress her with your working quarters."

Horst obediently walked towards the tall, three-light lamppost, and glanced at a single private, smoking in his booth next to the entrance. No one expected the *Komman-datur* to be attacked, so the Germans didn't really bother with tight security.

Philippe followed Horst and Giselle and spoke softly, before heading towards the wide stone balustrade of the *Metro* entrance to sit on top of it right behind the couple. "Remember: behave, and nobody suffers. You try something stupid – I start shooting."

Jerome joined Philippe on top of the balustrade. Pierre meanwhile walked straight to the entrance and showed some note to the sentry. The German read it under the light of the lamp, scowled, read it again and looked at the young man in front of him and then at the couple standing near the lamppost. Horst glanced at him and turned away. Who knew what was in that note, and he most definitely didn't want to provoke the terrorist, who – he was sure of it – meant business when he said that he would shoot them both. He looked like he would, like one of those fanatical patriots who didn't care about dying as long as they could take a few of their enemies with them. He was probably a communist, too...

The sentry shifted his rifle on his shoulder, but, noticing Philippe shaking his head deliberately, only motioned for Pierre to go inside.

"I wonder what's in that note," Horst whispered to Giselle, holding her waist firmly. He had intentionally turned his back on the terrorists, even though he would rather see what they were doing. But this way if they indeed started shooting, he would be able to protect her from their bullets.

"They're probably that terrorist's friends," Giselle whispered back with a small wry grin.

She knew perfectly well what was in the note, for she and Philippe had composed it together.

Do not raise the alarm. We are holding the Boche and the woman at gunpoint. You blow the whistle – they die. Let our messenger inside so he can show the note to the night guard.

You have five minutes to release Claude Bussi from jail. If he's not out in precisely five minutes after our messenger walks inside – your Boche and the woman die.

The woman's name is Giselle Legrand, and she's the mistress of Gestapo Chief Wünsche. Contact him immediately so he can grant you the release of the prisoner. In case he refuses – the Boche and the woman die.

As soon as Claude Bussi walks free, we'll take the Boche and Mademoiselle Legrand with us and will release them at a location of our choosing. You have our word they will be unharmed. But in case if you try to pursue us – they both die.

Vive le Parti Communiste! Vive la Résistance!

"You're probably right," Horst muttered. "Do you think they want to get him out?"

"I don't see any other reason why they would drag us here."

"They will never succeed. Whoever stands on guard with prisoners tonight would never agree to release him. They'll just hold that other one with the note hostage, and refuse to cooperate."

"So you're saying that your compatriots would rather see us get shot? Because I'm rather convinced that those two behind us will do it without blinking an eye."

"Don't worry." Horst pulled her a little closer, warming her face with his breath. "I'm in their way. They won't get you."

What a horrible person I am, doing this to you, Giselle thought, looking into his trusting eyes. *Kamille was right. This is plain heartless. I'm risking his life for my own goals, and here he is, ready to shelter me from the bullets with his body. If I believed in hell, I would be dreading death, because that's exactly where I will be heading.*

Just as she opened her mouth to speak some soft words of reassurance, Pierre walked out with Marcel and another German in tow. The sentry and the other officer stopped in the entrance, looking very tense, but remained motionless, while Pierre and Marcel quickly walked in Horst and Giselle's direction.

"Come," Pierre commanded to Horst and headed briskly towards Philippe and his brother, who were already getting up from the top of the balustrade.

As the small procession turned the corner, Giselle expected to hear whistles or gun shots, however only their rushed steps and heavy breathing disturbed the silence. They changed from one street to another, Philippe following behind them to make sure that they weren't being pursued. Finally, as Giselle noticed the bright light of the letter "M" at the other end of yet another narrow street, Philippe suddenly pounced on Horst, hitting him on the back of the head with his gun.

He caught the young officer, who started falling to the ground with a soft moan, in his arms, and carefully lowered him onto the cobbled street.

"We're going. Give us a few minutes and start screaming bloody murder right after."

Marcel rushed to hug his sister before Philippe pulled his sleeve with force. "Come, there's no time for it now!"

"Be careful. I'll meet you Friday at Michel's, just as we agreed," Giselle said to Philippe.

He nodded and before leaving he threw over his shoulder, "Good luck with your *Boche.*"

"Thank you." They disappeared from sight, as Giselle sighed and lowered to the ground to put Horst's head on her lap. "I'll need it."

GISELLE SAT in the chair with her shoulders hunched and studied the pattern of the carpet inside the *Kommandatur* building. Horst sat next to her with his hand on the back of his head holding an ice pack that the medic had given him after inspecting his rather superficial wound.

"Just a bump really," the doctor, who was wearing a uniform under his white gown, proclaimed with a smile. "You're very lucky they didn't shoot you."

"I thought they would," Horst admitted, replacing the hand with the ice pack back to the swelling.

"At least they had the decency not to hurt the lady," the doctor noticed.

"They just told me to shut up and to not to make any noise until they leave." Giselle shrugged her shoulders indifferently.

The adrenaline rush had passed, and she felt extremely exhausted, even though she was yet to face the main battle of the evening, and this time all by herself. The *Wehrmacht* officer who had released Marcel, according to Karl's orders (Giselle was still surprised that he valued her life slightly higher than the opportunity to torture or execute the terrorist in custody), lowered his hand gently on her shoulder and promised that *Herr Sturmbannführer* was on his way. Giselle would have preferred it better if he wasn't. So far, all the *Wehrmacht* staff were more than sympathetic to her, but she knew Karl all too well to suspect that he was most likely seething with fury and would give her a dressing down which she wouldn't forget for a very long time. After all, technically it was because of her that he had lost a prisoner who he couldn't wait to get his hands on.

Karl walked in, immediately sending all the officers in the room scrambling to salute him and stand at attention. He hardly deigned to nod his acknowledgment and stopped in front of Giselle, and Horst, who also rushed to get up, but had to lower back onto his chair, fighting a dizzy spell.

Karl noticed the ice pack that the young man was holding and waved dismissively at his apologies, already turning to Giselle. She sighed, not even bothering to fake a guilty smile.

"Did they hurt you?" was his first question.

"No." She shook her head.

"Let's go." He offered her his hand to help her get up, and barely glanced at the officer in charge, already turning to leave. "I'll deal with all of you tomorrow."

"Heil Hitler!" The men shouted behind his back, but he didn't bother replying.

*K*amille kept wringing her hands, opening her mouth to say something, and then just ending up saying nothing at all. The tea had long gone cold in their cups, both Jochen and Kamille hardly touching it. He sat opposite from her at the small, bare kitchen table, with his gaze transfixed blankly on something in the distance. His hair was disheveled from him raking his fingers through it too many times in the past few hours, and subtle growth had already started shadowing his face, for he had spent the past night and day with his men and hadn't had the chance to shave. Even his uniform, always immaculately cleaned and pressed, was now wrinkled and didn't look as smart as Kamille was used to seeing it.

Kamille cleared her throat and shifted in her seat, still afraid to talk. It was her fault after all, that the man whom she had grown to love so dearly was now facing the consequences of her brother's escape. After learning about the true identity of the man in his custody, Jochen had agreed not to hand him over to the Gestapo for at least a few days. He even promised to try and reach out to one of his contacts in Vienna – his father's old friend, who was not only a decorated hero of the Great War but also a highly skilled diplomat. *He will think of something,* Jochen had promised Kamille two days ago, before planting a gentle kiss on top of her wet eyelashes. Now, Marcel was gone, and Kamille was not entirely sure that her sister was a mere victim of the circumstances related to his daringly orchestrated escape.

"Now what?" she finally breathed out in such a soft voice that for a few long moments he didn't respond. Kamille thought that he didn't hear her.

Jochen shifted his position at last, rubbing his eyes, red from lack of sleep.

"Now what?" he repeated, sounding terribly enervated. Kamille's heart ached for him, but she still didn't dare to outstretch her arms to take his hands in hers. "Now – nothing. If we fail to find him in the next twenty-four hours, he's long gone from the city by now. Maybe even from the Occupied Zone altogether. My office cabled his description to all the posts of course, but there are hundreds of young men out there fitting that description. He doesn't have anything remarkable about him for them to look for. Just an ordinary young man, with ordinary papers. His comrades had them ready for him, I suppose. They aren't stupid enough to hide him here."

"No. I meant, what's going to happen with you." Kamille bit her lip, fearing his answer. "Are they going to… reprimand you in any way? They shouldn't, I mean. It's not your fault that he escaped after all! And you didn't even authorize his release – Giselle's Karl did."

"That's what bothers me the most," he pronounced, thoughtful. "How easily he agreed to it."

"She's his mistress." Kamille lowered her eyes, feeling her cheeks blush at the word that she was always so ashamed to utter. "He didn't want to risk her life, most certainly."

"Him?" Jochen smirked cynically. "No. Men like him are cold, calculated and completely devoid of any human emotion. Wünsche authorized your brother's release because he can profit from it somehow, not because some terrorists were holding his mistress at gunpoint. He had some other motive in mind, trust me."

"But he can't possibly harm you, can he?" Kamille inquired with genuine alarm in her voice.

She had naively assumed that Karl, despite the fact that he terrified her without any obvious reason, had at least something human about him when he had chosen Giselle's safety over keeping a terrorist jailed. That should have accounted for something... Only, now Jochen had shattered all of her illusions with one single, no-nonsense statement.

"I don't know," Jochen replied honestly. "I don't know if he wants to, that is. But if he does – yes, he can, and easily."

———

HIDING HER CHEEKS, rosy from the brisk walking and the frost biting into them, into the thick, blue fox collar of her coat, Giselle soon switched to running after she ascended the stairs of the somewhat warm *Metro* to the brightly lit square outside.

She flew up the stairs of the Demarche Publishing House, stomped her feet on the thick red carpet, smiling at the doorman, and dove into the buzz of the familiar atmosphere that excited her just as much as on the very first day she had stepped through the doors. Today, instead of holding a new manuscript, she carried a new article in her valise, an article in which she had written a story about a brave young man – a true French patriot – and his several comrades, who refused to bow to the conquerors and who had outsmarted them in the most daring manner.

For the first time, the French people would be able to see for themselves that the Germans weren't as tough and impenetrable as their carefully created image suggested they were, an image concocted by the propaganda that was being shoved down the population's throat on a daily basis. *Instead of food,* as Pascal Thierry, another writer from their group, noted in one of his articles.

Giselle had typed it as fast as she could, not paying any attention to typos and misspellings (*Michel would correct them all later*) before Karl could appear for lunch and she would miss her chance to deliver it to Michel in time; a new issue was supposed to be printed that evening.

Having checked with his secretary that Michel was alone in his office, Giselle rapped on the heavy door and pushed it open, not waiting for permission to enter. Michel Demarche lifted his coiffured head from the manuscript he was reading and removed his tortoise shell glasses, a welcoming smile appearing on his lips at the sight of his *l'enfant rebelle.*

"Good afternoon, Giselle." He rose from his chair to greet her properly. "I didn't expect you today."

"I know. I have something for you." Giselle opened her

valise and extracted a single sheet of paper, which was carefully concealed in between the pages of her manuscript. "You still have time to put it in today's issue, don't you?"

Michel replaced the glasses back onto the bridge of his nose and started reading instead of responding. As his eyes followed the lines of the text, he began nodding to his thoughts. Giselle's grin was growing as well, as she had learned by now that nodding meant one thing: Michel liked what he was reading.

"I'll have to rearrange the layout, but..." He nodded several more times, before quickly hiding the paper in the top drawer of his desk, which had a double bottom in it. "I'll put it on the front page. *First Strike of the Resistance*. The public will love it. It'll inspire more people to join the underground."

"I hope so." Giselle glanced back at the door before asking, "How are our guests?"

"Given the situation – they're fine. Would you like to pay them a visit?"

Giselle agreed eagerly, and Michel proceeded to open the door for her, not forgetting to lock the office after following her into the corridor, filled with the unceasing buzz of typing machines.

"Write down a message for me if someone calls," Michel instructed his secretary. "I'll be back in a few minutes."

"*Oui, Monsieur Demarche.*"

He grudgingly agreed to take the stairs instead of waiting for the ancient elevator, which he knew Giselle detested with all her might, especially when it was crammed with people like it always was during the day. Nodding his greeting to the man with the formidable mustache who was guarding the entrance leading downstairs, Michel inquired about his wife's knee that she had unfortunately broken a few weeks ago, tsked several times sympathetically, and patted the man's shoulder, insisting that the man should immediately let him know if *Madame* needed anything. Michel Demarche prided himself in knowing all of his employees by name, no matter if they were successful novelists or simple janitors, and treated everyone with equal respect, thus ensuring not only the most welcoming of working atmospheres but the employees' undisputable loyalty. *The latter they needed the most now,* Giselle thought to herself, descending the stairs after Michel.

"Mademoiselle Legrand presented me with something utterly remarkable today," he said to the guard, before heading downstairs. "I think such fine writing calls for an equally fine bottle of wine."

The building itself, which Michel had renovated right after purchasing, dated back to the eighteenth century, and, just like most buildings of that era, had the most impressive underground chambers, corridors and secret passages, one of them even leading as far as the Catacombs of Paris. Rumor had it that the original owner was a *Huguenot* preacher in hiding, who made it his mission to hide and transport to freedom the arrested congregants of his faith. Two hundred years had passed, and now Michel Demarche was hiding Resistance members while managing his little press enterprise from the same basement. *The French and their love for free spirit and defiance will never change,* Giselle thought, with the somewhat conceited pride of a typical Frenchwoman.

Michel headed further into the catacombs, as Giselle

mockingly called the underground system under the building, passed the wooden door leading to the wine storage and confidently turned corner after corner, easily navigating his way in the labyrinth of corridors. At last, when Giselle found herself to be completely and truly lost, Michel came to a sudden halt at one of the doors and knocked in a certain pattern, before fitting a skeleton key into the lock.

"Your friends are armed," he explained in regards to his precautionary measures.

"I know. By now I am used to their leader meeting me with a gun aiming at my chest," she replied, not trying to conceal her irony.

Michel pushed the thick iron door open with visible effort, and Giselle scrunched her nose at the smell of mold and humid air, which was even more pronounced here than in the corridor. All four men – Marcel, Philippe, Pierre and his brother Jerome – rose from their seats, which they had occupied around a small wooden table which was covered with the remains of their lunch.

"Giselle." Marcel rushed to embrace his sister, positively beaming. "I never got the chance to thank you."

"I did nothing," she replied with the same radiant smile. "Thank your friends over there."

She nodded at Philippe, who responded with a nod which looked slightly awkward.

"I see you're feeding them here quite well," Giselle addressed Michel, who stood behind looking out of place, not only among the poorly dressed men but also in the general environment with its bare, stone walls and scarce furniture.

"I hardly bring them anything," he confessed. "These

enterprising gentlemen correctly pointed out to me that carrying sacks of food to work daily, would raise suspicion and reassured me that they had no trouble walking to the Catacombs, where a lot of Black Market sellers operate. I only give them money, and they take care of themselves."

Giselle removed her gloves and pinched her brother's unshaven cheek affectionately.

"I'm so glad that you're safe and sound."

"Me, too. I admit I was ready to say my farewells to life in that prison." Marcel took his sister's hands in his and noticed a ring on one of her fingers where he had never seen any rings before. "What is this?"

"An import from Germany." Giselle smirked.

A long, pregnant pause followed.

"Are you saying...You're engaged? To *him?*" Marcel whispered, refusing to believe his own eyes. But the ring was there, golden and very real, with two rubies in an intricate setting.

"I suppose I am." She shrugged with almost infuriating carelessness.

Philippe, who was also scrutinizing Giselle's hand from behind Marcel's shoulder, spoke with sudden emotion, "How could you agree to something like this?!"

Giselle arched her brow, surprised with the reaction which was even stronger than her brother's, but only waved it off dismissively, with the same smirk in place.

"You see, he didn't particularly ask me."

In meaningful, accusing silence, she raked her memory for the events, which followed that memorable night of Marcel's escape.

KARL WAS STRANGELY quiet on the way home, only asked her what she was doing with Hartmann's orderly. After she had presented him with a long ago prepared story about meeting Horst incidentally in the street, from where the *damned terrorists* kidnapped them, he only nodded, and the car was once again immersed in silence. The silence disturbed Giselle much more than accusations and reprimands would have, which she, frankly speaking, had been expecting.

As soon as they stepped through the doors of her apartment, he proceeded to the bathroom and drew a hot bath, almost ordering Giselle to get undressed and get into it despite her protests.

"You were sitting on the frozen ground for over twenty minutes before they found you," he said, with an edge of authority that was not meant to be questioned. "For women, it's especially dangerous. Didn't your mother warn you against sitting on stones?"

"She warned me against everything, but I never listened," Giselle grumbled, lowering herself into the almost painfully hot water.

Karl took his uniform jacket off, rolled up his sleeves and sat on the edge of the tub, rubbing her shoulders with a washcloth with the look of a doctor treating his patient.

It seemed almost surreal to her, this whole scene that was unraveling in front of her eyes: him, suddenly so concerned about her well-being, and this strange feeling of intimacy, stemming from the very fingertips of the man who was everything but naturally gentle and caring.

"What is it with you tonight?" Giselle caught herself smiling against her better judgment.

The impenetrable mask of his cold, handsome face remained intact. "I told you that I couldn't have you sick."

"Why the sudden concern on my account?"

"You didn't think I cared about you?" He replied in the same emotionless tone that he always used. It was his hands that were warmer than his voice, sending strange, relaxing waves of pleasure through her body, even though he was treating her with the mindset of a therapist, not a lover.

"I didn't think you would choose me over your prisoner," she admitted at last.

Karl didn't bother with a reply and only proceeded to rub her forearms and chest in practiced, precise motions, relaxing her tense muscles.

"Why did you do it? Ordered his release, I mean?" Giselle pressed, in dire need to hear his reply for some reason.

He indulged her with a smile that didn't reach his eyes. His smiles never did actually. He just didn't know how to smile it seemed, in the way that most other people did.

"What if I told you that I had fallen deeply and irreversibly in love with you?"

She snorted, rolling her eyes.

"I'd call you a liar and demand the real reason."

"You don't think I love you?"

"Karl, we both know perfectly well that you don't. You are incapable of loving. Just like I am."

He paused for a moment, scrutinizing her eyes, and then renewed his cleaning motions.

"You're right. That's what attracts me to you. You think with your head, not with your heart, and it's a sign of superior intellect. We are intellectual beings; we aren't meant to be driven by instincts, as Darwin correctly stated in his works. You and I are representatives of such intellectual beings. We stand higher on the steps of evolution than those who aren't capable of controlling their urges. I worried about you at first; you seemed a little hot-headed to me with your defiance, but then I realized that it wasn't due to your temperament. You were simply fighting for your territory, that I took over as you thought, but as soon as you understood my motives and accepted me as your equal – you recognized the same nature in me that you possess. Then, you calmed down and became the partner I would like to have by my side. I decided that I would like to have you as my wife, Giselle."

She burst into a fit of chuckles.

"You're asking for my hand in marriage then? In a most romantic way, too, I should note."

"I'm not asking you. It's only logical, and you should see my reasoning behind it. Our union will benefit not only us personally but the strengthening of the relationship between our countries as well. You're a renowned novelist, and I'm the chief of the Gestapo in Paris. The union will show that we can coexist and cooperate on more levels than one."

"Isn't it illegal? Relationships between the occupying forces and the local population?" Giselle was observing him with a sense of amusement.

"For now it is. However, there can be exceptions in certain cases. I have already spoken to Reichsführer Himmler about the prospect of our marriage, and he found it to be a brilliant idea as well. After all, his Chief of the Intelligence Schellenberg married a woman of Polish descent. Surely, Himmler favors someone of French descent much better."

"Ah! So, you've not only thought everything through, but you've also weighed all the options, counted all pros and cons, and even asked your superior to marry me. Shouldn't you have gone down on your knee at some point and given me a ring? Or have I fallen behind the times, and that's not how it's done anymore?"

The irony was not lost on him, but Karl didn't seem to care to be offended by it.

"You're not a romantic type of a person, Giselle. Hence, I preferred to speak to you like to an equal partner, not some damsel from a cheap romance book that you find so distasteful – I remember you saying it yourself." He grinned, once again with his mouth only. "As for the ring, I have one that I bought after I got permission from Reichsführer. I wanted to give it to you on Christmas, but since we've started this conversation, I might as well give it to you now."

Giselle gave in to the soothing touch of his skillful hands as he shifted closer to the other end of the tub and started rubbing her feet, placing her heels on top of his uniform trousers. A sudden sense of disappointment filled her, the same type she would have experienced if she'd found out that a beautiful flower that she admired in someone's window was fake. That's exactly what he was, now she was sure of it, the last of her doubts disappearing together with the pain from her aching feet – he was a beautiful, almost breathtaking masterpiece of a man, in which some higher power forgot to put a soul.

Or maybe his highly praised Darwin was right, and they were representatives of a new, evolved species: utter nihilists, perceiving the outside world through the prism of a carefully organized thinking process and not through emotion like others used? But was he also right in his assumption that she was just like him, a cold-hearted creature who only acted out of rational thinking, and never with her heart? Didn't her father tell her that she was far too cynical for her age? Too calculated, too devoid of morals and principles, too practical and unable to understand that she could hurt people around her with that coldness... Could Karl truly see through her with the same eyes that she saw the world with, and recognize a kindred spirit in her? A partner... He didn't even make it sound like a marriage, but like a partnership, profitable for both sides. And the worst part about all that was the fact that for some reason she wasn't offended by his words, but had instead started weighing them in her mind, processing, calculating...

"So you aren't married after all," she said, just to say something, just to stop her mind from the constant *processing*.

"I told you before that I wasn't." He frowned slightly as if confused by her words.

"Well... I thought you might have been lying."

"Why would I?"

"Why did you never marry before?" she asked, following his practiced motions with her gaze.

"I was married. I divorced my wife two years ago."

"Why?"

"She couldn't have children."

"I'm sorry."

"No need to be. You and I are going to produce the finest offspring that can be desired. Just imagine how brilliant our children will be, combining the genes from both of us."

"How do you know that I will be able to produce

offspring?" Giselle inquired, with amusement at how certain he was on account of their future. "Maybe I also won't be able to have children?"

"I thoroughly checked your medical history before deciding on our marriage." He seemed to have an answer for everything. "You have had three abortions, according to your medical history. Abortions, not miscarriages. Not the best scenario, to be truthful, for it can cause some problems along the way due to the scarring of the tissue, but nothing drastic. I'll just monitor you closely, and you'll have the easiest pregnancy, I can guarantee it."

"Good to hear," Giselle mumbled, deep in her thoughts.

"We will raise our children in Germany, of course. I don't want any of that free-spirited French influence clouding their minds. Don't take it personally, but you could see for yourself through that escaped terrorist's example the damaging effect this influence can produce."

Giselle regarded Karl for some time before finally asking the question that had been nagging at the back of her mind since she'd met him. "Why do you hate French people so much?"

"I don't hate them." He carefully tried to feign indifference, but Giselle detected barely concealed emotion in his tone.

"Yes, you do," she pressed in a mild voice. "You even prohibit people from addressing you as *'Monsieur.'* You can't stand anything French. Except for me, I suppose."

"You're different."

"That's not an answer to my question."

"I have my reasons for it." Karl jerked his shoulder irritably.

"Still not an answer."

Karl gave her a pointed glare, went silent for a few long moments, and uttered at last, "Because of what they did to my family after the Great War, your highly praised compatriots."

"The soldiers?"

"Yes." He swallowed with difficulty, escaping Giselle's inquiring gaze. "Our house was in Alsace. My family settled there after the Franco-Prussian War, and, therefore, after the Treaty of Versailles had been signed in 1919, they were proclaimed to be 'enemy aliens,' unlike the French citizens or descendants of the French citizens, and we became subjects for forced deportation back to Germany. Only, the soldiers that came to our house to carry out these orders thought it would be amusing to physically throw us out in the street. My father was still a prisoner of war somewhere in the South, and I was only thirteen and far too young to protect my mother and siblings. They threw her down the stairs; thankfully she only suffered a couple of bruises, just as I did. However, my five-year-old sister and seven-year-old brother weren't so lucky. They threw them out of the window of the third floor."

Giselle gasped involuntarily, appalled by such atrocious treatment of innocent children. War made many men mad, but this was sheer bestiality even to her, who wasn't sensitive by any means.

"Did they die?" she whispered, noting how her voice faltered.

"Gretl did. The cobbled road on which she fell fractured her skull." Karl's unblinking gaze was full of long-forgotten emotions still brewing deep inside. "Friedrich, my little Fritz, was a bit more fortunate. He only broke his spine. Or maybe, not so fortunate after all... Such a lively, active boy, paralyzed from the neck down."

"I'm sorry," Giselle murmured, reaching for Karl's hand that was resting on top of her leg. He didn't remove it from under hers, much to her surprise. "Is that why you decided to become a neurosurgeon? To help your little brother?"

A scowl creased his forehead at the distasteful sentimentality of her words. A painful revelation flashed in Giselle's mind at how stubbornly this man detested every weakness of the human heart, even though in this case emotion was more than justified.

"*Ja*," he admitted at last, though with visible reluctance. "I thought I would make him walk again."

"Well?" Giselle encouraged Karl when he became immersed into his memories once again. "Did you?"

"*Nein.*" He slowly shook his head. "I graduated top of my class. I assisted the best Swiss surgeon, a true innovator in his field, while working in my practice. I did become an excellent surgeon eventually, yes. My success rate was almost ninety percent, and this is taking into consideration that spinal and brain surgery was such a new, barely studied field with few rare specialists working in it... I practiced for several years on others before putting Fritz on my operating table. I was sure of my success prior to the operation... And yet, he died. He died under my knife. I did everything right; it wasn't my mistake. It couldn't have been!"

Karl inhaled a full chest of air, bringing his emotions under control. Then he whispered, seemingly calm once again, "I never make mistakes."

"I'm sure it wasn't your doing," Giselle spoke, pressing his hand slightly. "You said it yourself; it was a complicated operation."

"The others lived though." There was audible resentment in his voice.

"Is that why you gave it up? Your whole practice?" This time it was Giselle's turn to scowl in disbelief.

"No." A detached, impenetrable mask had replaced the vulnerable man she had seen for a split second. "I gave it up to join the SS. The Führer promised us revenge... And it's not my fault that Fritz died. He would have lived, had those overzealous French nationalists not thrown him out of the window. Not my fault. But I can finally avenge him now. *Ja*, the tables have turned at last..."

He was saying something else, but Giselle moved her hand away gently, deep foreboding settling on her after learning his greatest secret, seeing him for what he really was and realizing with brutal clarity that there was no salvation for him anymore.

MARCEL'S HAND dropping hers brought her back to the reality of the cold basement room around her.

"You're getting married then?"

"Yes. In May. He says May has some special meaning for them, the SS." Giselle shrugged with a bored expression.

"You know, you women are strange creatures with a very short memory," she heard Philippe say. "Not that long ago you swore to kill him, but as soon as he dropped down to one knee, you forgot everything."

"He never dropped to one knee," Giselle replied with a lopsided grin. "And I never forget anything, Philippe."

26

Kamille stopped on the threshold of Charles's former study, her heart swelling with emotion at a sight that had never been common when her husband was still alive. Violette was sitting next to Jochen at his desk, biting the end of her pencil in deep concentration, as he patiently explained to her how to solve a math problem. Violette had never been good with numbers, but somehow he managed to tutor her so well that the girl's grades had improved noticeably, within just two short months. Charles, in contrast, had always prohibited his daughter from even entering "the sacred territory" of his study, leave alone "wasting his time" teaching the girl something that she would have no use for, in his eyes at least. Watching the two, Kamille smiled, recalling how one day Jochen had effortlessly comforted Violette, when he found her sobbing over her unfinished homework.

"Monsieur *Maître* will call me stupid again." She sniveled, wiping her face with a sleeve.

"What nonsense! You're not stupid at all," he replied with a reassuring smile, pulling her homework closer to take a look at it. "If you don't understand something, it only shows his failure as a teacher, not yours as a student. Now, let's try to solve this together, shall we?"

There was something bittersweet about it: that Violette had grown to love a mere stranger in a few short months more than she ever loved her own father. She didn't even cry when Kamille had sat her down and announced the news of Charles's death as gently as possible. Violette only pondered something for a moment and inquired if that meant that they could finally get a kitty. Her father was strictly against any animals in the house, citing that he didn't need any fur on his clothes, or any fleas from creatures that were infested by them.

The atmosphere of the house had visibly changed with the appearance of the uniform-clad lodger in their home.

"Can Monsieur Jochen be my *Papa* since my real *Papa* is dead?" Violette asked Kamille on the way home from school, a few days ago.

Kamille found herself at a loss, not knowing what to reply to such a straightforward question.

"*Chéri*, it's not so simple..." she started but didn't know what arguments to add.

"Why not? He loves us, and we love him." The little girl expressed her thoughts on the matter with the frankness that only children could afford. "Why can't you marry him?"

"He's a German officer, Violette. It's against the law."

"It's a stupid law then." Her daughter huffed and didn't utter a word the remainder of the way home.

What would happen to her little girl if Jochen disappeared soon, Kamille thought, feeling tears welling in her eyes again.

"If Wünsche only speaks a word, I'll be transferred to the front," he had confessed to her last night, when the two lay in bed, both unable to sleep. The metaphorical sword that was hanging above his head after Marcel's escape was still there, and Giselle's lover's silence only made the dreadful anticipation even more agonizing. "It's because I didn't hand over the prisoner when he demanded him. They think it made his escape possible. It's because I refused to go along with his wishes..."

"Don't blame yourself." Kamille hushed him, diving under his arm to press herself to his body, clinging to him while she still could. "You didn't do anything wrong. He's a monster, that man. You only acted like an honest man, and an officer, someone for whom human life still means something."

He was quiet for one very long minute, stroking Kamille's soft hair, deep in thought.

"Will you write to me if they send me to Africa?" he asked at last.

Kamille nodded, swallowing her hot tears before he could feel them spill on his skin.

All these thoughts crowded her mind while she greedily watched these precious moments of a life that could change very soon, while her daughter was still happy with a father, whom she considered Jochen to be despite all the "stupid laws"; while she still could meet him from work every evening and melt into his embraces despite the cold that he brought with him from the outside; while she could still bring him tea, just like she did now, and simply admire him silently, the man who had turned her whole world upside down and made her feel loved – for the first time in her life.

Sensing her gaze, Jochen lifted his head and smiled at her. He leaned to kiss Violette on top of her head and asked her if she would give him and her *Maman* a couple of minutes alone. Violette nodded readily and collected her notes and a textbook, solemnly promising him to try and finish everything by herself.

"I'll check everything later before you write it down in your notebook," he assured her and patted the chair next to him, inviting Kamille to sit down.

He was still dejected and tired but accepted the small porcelain cup of tea out of Kamille's hands with genuine gratitude.

"I spoke to Wünsche today." He took a sip while Kamille held her breath, her hands going cold at once. "The good news is that I'm not going to Africa just yet."

"That's wonderful!" Kamille pressed his arm, delighted by the news. But then her hands dropped back onto her lap; where was good news, there was also bad.

Jochen nodded as if reading her mind.

"The bad news is that he wants to shoot a man in retaliation. A man, whose only crime was to fly a flag from the bridge several months ago. I am to sign the authorization for surrendering that man into the custody of the Gestapo." Jochen took a deep breath, rubbing his forehead, creased with the exhaustion and worry of the last few days.

"And then… Then he won't press for your transfer to the front?" Kamille asked quietly.

"Yes. Wünsche has already gotten what he wanted. He

completely discredited the *Wehrmacht* in the eyes of Berlin and insisted on us handing over all cases of sabotage and terrorism to the Gestapo. That was the reason why he allowed your brother to escape so easily. He wanted to prove to the *Kommandant* and Berlin that the *Wehrmacht* are incapable of suppressing terror acts committed against the occupying forces. We are also, apparently, not capable of interrogating them thoroughly. I am to hand over all of the people, who are currently in my custody, to the Paris branch of the Gestapo tomorrow morning. If I refuse..." Jochen didn't finish, but Kamille understood everything.

"So hand them over then." She despised herself at how despicable and egoistic it sounded the very moment she uttered the words. But her Violette, her little Violette... How much she had grown to love Jochen! The same as how much she, Kamille, had become used to him being in the house... And those people were criminals, after all, weren't they? It wasn't like they were in jail for nothing. No, she couldn't lose Jochen over some terrorists. She felt for them, yes, but she was a woman in love, and a woman in love never thinks clearly.

"What if it comes to his mind to shoot them all?" Jochen asked quietly.

"So their blood will be on his hands, not yours."

Despicable, indeed. But, as long as her fingers were clasped around his forearm, as long as she could have him, this most precious possession of hers in her arms, despicable simply didn't matter to her.

MARCEL KEPT STARING at Philippe helplessly, waiting for him to say something, to come up with some plan like he always did, but the communist remained consumed by his moping, seemingly oblivious to Marcel's despairing stance.

"What shall we do?" Marcel tugged on Philippe's sleeve when he couldn't take the oppressive silence anymore, disturbed only by water, slowly dripping somewhere in the distance.

Philippe slowly let his fingers through his dark mane, his gaze dull and desolate.

"There's nothing we can do, Marcel." He released a long sigh, bringing his young comrade to terms with the situation that even he had rendered helpless. "They ran away, they're armed, and they're irate and desperate."

"Wouldn't you be, if you just found out that the *Boches* were about to execute your father for nothing?" Marcel grumbled gloomily.

How he wished now that something had gone differently this morning. How he wished that he and Philippe had gone to the Catacombs instead to get their food at the Black Market. How he wished that Philippe didn't take the boys with him, prohibiting Marcel to show his face to anyone outside, even to the profiteers, fearing that one of them could easily be a Gestapo mole. How he wished Pierre and Jerome didn't notice the poster with their father's face, haggard and almost unrecognizable after his incarceration, and how he wished they didn't have a gun on them, with which they might do something entirely irreversible and foolish that would only get them killed too. And how he wished all of this wasn't his fault.

"Eat." Philippe pushed an aluminum plate closer to the young man, not touching the contents himself.

"I can't eat," Marcel argued, throwing an almost disgusted glare at the chicken broth with some insides swimming in it.

Philippe had taught him a long time ago that nothing should go to waste in times like this. Marcel was used to the communist leader's simple cooking, and never questioned anything that was put in front of him, except these last few days had completely killed his appetite.

"You should. A lousy eater is a lousy fighter." Philippe muttered the unquestionable truth from his days in the Spanish Civil War, most likely.

"Why do you never eat then?" Marcel sulked, but picked up a spoon nevertheless. "Shouldn't a good leader show his men how to act by example?"

Philippe threw him a glare, but picked up his scratched, aluminum spoon and swallowed a mouthful of broth.

"A good leader shouldn't lose his men, too," he said, shaking his head at his own shortcomings. He blamed himself for everything, too.

"You couldn't possibly catch them once they took off," Marcel tried to reason with him.

Philippe only sighed again, for words always seemed worthless in situations like this.

A day later Michel Demarche came down to give them money and some wine to keep warm. When both men jumped to their feet to ask him for any news regarding the boys, he only placed a newspaper on top of the table in rueful silence. There were three bodies, tied to execution poles, instead of just one, for everyone to see right there, on the front page. A sinister warning to everyone, who would ever think to go against the regime. And next to them, the SS officials stood with their chief in charge, Sturmbannführer Karl Wünsche in his leather overcoat, a solemn, grim reaper with empty black eyes.

"The soldiers grabbed them before they could even open fire," Michel said, lowering his head in respect for the dead. "They rushed to their father as he was led to execution. So, the Nazis shot them all."

GISELLE STOOD in the middle of the reception hall, surrounded by green-gray uniforms and stared blankly ahead, obediently waiting for her new fiancé to bring yet another high-ranking dignitary from Berlin to her for a formal introduction. A seasoned socialite, who had never shied away from similar gatherings, she felt completely out of place here, amongst these men who spoke a language she didn't understand. They might have been talking about her for all she knew, and she would never have a clue. They all kissed her hand and expressed their "utmost pleasure" at meeting her, but who knew what they really thought?

Smoothing the material of her creamy silk gown self-consciously, Giselle brought the crystal champagne flute to her mouth, grateful that at least alcohol was flowing freely. Truth be told, everything flew freely wherever the Germans were: banquet halls were filled with music and dancing couples, the most exquisite appetizers were carried around by waiters in tuxedos, glasses with the best champagne were knocked off tables with almost appalling disregard, and the same uneaten, half-bitten-into appetizers would be collected by the same waiters to be brought home to their families. They were the lucky ones, who could serve the new masters of the country; they at least could feast on their leftovers. The rest of the country was slowly beginning to starve.

"*Gisela.*" Karl's voice distracted her from her gloomy thoughts as he caught her elbow and nudged her slightly towards yet another general in a uniform, almost bursting at the seams around his enormous waistline. "Allow me to introduce you to Herr Gruppenführer Schwartz. It's due to his interference that we'll finally be able to set law and order in this country. Herr Gruppenführer, this is my fiancé, *Gisela* Legrand."

"So you're the man who Karl always speaks so highly of." Giselle forgot how many times she'd pronounced the same phrase today with the same exact smile, offering the general her hand with the same practiced gesture. "It's a pleasure to finally meet you. How are you enjoying yourself on our French soil?"

"The pleasure is all mine, Mademoiselle." Giselle tried not to cringe when his wet lips touched her skin. "And it's our soil now, isn't it, Wünsche?"

The general was too busy winking at his compatriot to notice the glare that Giselle threw him after those words.

"It will be," Karl agreed with detached confidence. "As soon we rid it of the last partisan forces. But since you granted my office your authorization, I'm most confident that it will happen within the next few months."

"I granted you full freedom because I know that you're the best strategist in the whole of the Gestapo. Not counting Gruppenführer Heydrich, of course."

"Of course."

Both exchanged polite smiles.

"Sturmbannführer Wünsche told me you're a writer?" Schwartz switched his attention back to Giselle once again with the same indulging smile that she always despised in people who refused to take her profession seriously. Or literary critics, who sure had a lot to say on her account as well.

"Yes, I am, Monsieur Schwartz. A talentless plagiarist according to *"Le Journal,"* but my bank account states that the public actually reads my talentless plagiarism, and in rather impressive quantities."

A subtle but visible smirk curled Karl's lips upwards at his superior's look. The man was obviously taken aback by Giselle's sharp tongue and unapologetic attitude. Giselle replied to her fiancé with a slight nonchalant shrug. *He's not my superior; I'm not obliged to bow to him.*

"Interesting." The General quickly regained his composure. "And what are you working on now?"

"*Gisela* is writing a novel set in present day France," Karl replied in a rushed manner, giving her a warning look. "A wife kills her French husband and chooses her German lover instead."

Giselle brows shot up, but Karl only stared harder at her, imploring her silently not to argue with such perverted interpretation of her manuscript.

"That is rather… provocative." Schwartz chuckled nevertheless. "Not Hans Grimm, of course, but… I can see how it can pique the public's interest. You've certainly piqued mine, Mademoiselle."

Giselle's smile was almost genuine, even if it was tight-lipped.

"Now I see why Sturmbannführer became so interested in you. But you, Mademoiselle, have certainly chosen a fine future husband as well. He is one of the few men who invariably puts the interests of the Reich above all – something that the *Wehrmacht* apparently lacked."

"The *Wehrmacht* is an outdated organization," Karl declared, playing with the amber liquid in his glass. "Their time is over. The time of grand battles, sensitive officers burdened with morals and making those grand battles into some twisted poetry of warfare so that the future generations will later write noble stories about them... They're a thing of the past. The SS is the future; the future of the military, and of the moral health of the Reich, of everything. I assure you that I will prove it to you by my own personal example. Very soon I'll wipe the streets of Paris clean from that Resistance plague. After we have performed that execution, the people of Paris will understand at last that they should take us seriously, or there will be very grave consequences to any future foolish action."

"That's all fine and well, Sturmbannführer. I read the reports, and I am most satisfied with them. But -" The General rocked from his heels to his toes and back as Karl regarded him cautiously. "What about that little newspaper that is the very cause of spreading of all of this cancerous Resistance propaganda all over Paris? And not only Paris; there are reports from several other cities, in which *La Libération* is being distributed. And recently there were copies found even in the Free Zone."

"I am aware of that, Herr Gruppenführer." Karl cleared his throat. Giselle knew that any possible shortcomings for which he could be reproached unnerved him greatly, even if on the surface he remained absolutely calm.

"And?"

"I'm working on it."

"I know you are. In your latest report you attached that list of newspapers and magazines headquarters, in which your agents have conducted a search. They yielded no results, though?"

"That's correct, Herr Gruppenführer. So far they haven't, but we'll find the perpetrators, you have my word."

"You'd better move along with it then, Wünsche. Heydrich might be coming for an inspection soon; you don't want to present him no results in your report, do you?"

"I'll find them," Karl said sternly.

Giselle sipped her champagne, looking as bored as she possibly could. Inside, her stomach was churning.

On the way home she kept replaying the evening in her mind, strangely sober despite the amount of champagne that she had consumed.

"What's the story with the German lover?" She turned to Karl as if just remembering it. "There are no Germans in my manuscript."

"There should be," Karl spoke calmly. "It's good for business now."

"Business?"

"The publishing business, *ja*. It's business, isn't it? And you have to sell what's in now. The Germans are in. This way you'll be selling not only to the French public but the German as well. Maybe the Ministry of Propaganda will even approve it for publication on the territory of the Reich. Wouldn't it be just grand? You'll double your profits."

Giselle's face was twisted by a crooked grin. He was talking just like her, a male version of Giselle who thought only about profit. The love for writing was there, yes, but whatever she had written so far was almost all for money. Nothing came out from her pen just because she felt the need to say something about herself. She never spoke about herself in any of her novels. Even her very first one was just to argue with her father, to write his story but in such a way that she would have lived, the way she would have fought in the Great War and the person that she would have become upon her return. It was written out of hunger and defiance, not out of understanding and respect. She was indeed a terrible writer; terrible from a purely moral point of view, and she had just realized what sort of person she had become – she didn't like her. Giselle didn't like the famous Giselle Legrand, the novelist, at all.

"Maybe not everything in this world is about profit," she muttered quietly, speaking mostly to herself, and not to the man next to her, who looked at her strangely. "Maybe the thinking species aren't superior after all?"

"What are you talking about?"

"I'm talking about how maybe life isn't based on material things. Maybe there's more to it than money and power."

"And what would it be?"

"I don't know. I've never known. God, I sound just like my father, don't I?" Giselle rubbed her forehead in disbelief. "He was trying to tell me this my whole life, and I never listened."

"Are you all right?" This time his voice gave way to a shade of concern.

Giselle didn't blame him for it; she didn't sound like

herself and knew it perfectly well, but that sudden revelation struck her with such force that she felt an almost physical need to express it, to put it in words before it would slip through her fingers and disappear without a trace.

"I am all right, yes." She nodded slowly. "We are soulless creatures, Karl. You and I. So yes, I'm all right. I would never be if I were anything like him. He is a real man; I see it all so very clearly… His refusal to submit to the new order; his effort to live in a way that acknowledged all the lives he had taken; his desire to lead a good, honest life; his vexation with all that money that started flowing into the country, the bloody money as he had called it…"

She stopped abruptly, mid-sentence, quickly recomposing herself and smiled brightly at her scowling fiancé.

"Pardon my ramblings, will you? I'm trying out a monolog that my protagonist would say. How did it sound?"

"Rather insane. Don't write it down."

"That's what I thought."

She turned back to her window and spent the rest of the way with the most serene smile. The world that used to be so gray and useless, so base and disgusting, started suddenly making sense to her. Too bad that it had to turn upside down for it to happen.

2 7

The silence was driving Marcel mad. The silence, the same four walls, the same nauseating, moldy air, and what was worst of all – the impotence. Philippe was coming and going, organizing and managing the loyal comrades, to whom he was able to send word to through his contacts in *Le Marché Noir,* and the new recruits. Willingly or not, Marcel's example inspired more people to seek more Resistance cells, emboldened by the "Legend of the Ghost." That was the nickname with which his sister baptized him in her article – he saw it when he was helping Michel Demarche with the printing of new copies of *La Libération.* In that article, he was presented as something between a modern day Robin Hood and Jean d'Arc, a fearless national hero, the first one to throw a metaphoric glove right in the Germans' faces and escape their clutches – twice. No wonder the public went wild for him.

If only they knew that the real Marcel was nothing like a

national hero, but an ordinary young man, just consumed by fear which soon became replaced by desperation and eventually absolute numbness; if they knew the reality they wouldn't be cheering so loudly. Or maybe Giselle was right when she pointed out all too often that he was too hard on himself no matter what he did. But he was just like her – a perfectionist, who simply couldn't cope if something wasn't done right…

Only, while Giselle was a pragmatic perfectionist, Marcel was an idealist, striving for the world to be a better place. Maybe that's why he couldn't bring himself to pull the trigger during his very short-lived battle experience on the front, because the war itself went against his beliefs; maybe that's why he found himself so drawn to Philippe's teachings and ideas, because communism was a highly idealistic philosophy and that's why it found its way into his heart so easily.

Marcel sighed in irritation at all these thoughts crowding his restless mind, and lifted his head towards the stone ceiling, empathizing with wolves that felt the urge to howl at the moon in their solitude. He felt it in his bones that night, and especially with no Philippe around to talk some sense into him, to talk him out of his suicidal plans that his impaired mind conceived upon learning the news of the boys' fate. Marcel was slowly surrendering more and more to the grim power of those ideas.

He didn't share his plans with Philippe, for he knew all too well that the communist leader would refuse to even listen to them. He had expressed his position on account of such plans a long time ago, together with Général de Gaulle, who tried to manage the dispersed Resistance cells all over

France. But Général de Gaulle was too far, and he didn't just lose two of his comrades, just kids really, those little rascals who got shot for nothing, and to whom Marcel owed his life after they helped to rescue him without thinking twice about putting their lives on the line.

Maybe the time had come to be a hero, whom everyone considered him to be, then. Maybe the time had come to live up to his own expectations after all, so that if he managed to escape unscathed he would be able to look in the mirror without shame for once.

Marcel stood up from the thin mattress, thrown on top of simple wooden planks that formed a makeshift temporary cot for Philippe and himself. He unwrapped the layer of blankets that kept him warm in this stone dungeon, pulled the gun from his pocket and inspected it with the resolution of a man who had finally came to terms with his own decision. It was a *Boche* gun, the one that Philippe had taken from Horst that night and given to Marcel to keep. It only made sense to use it.

His steps echoed through the endless oppressing passage, with its darkness that was only disturbed by the dim light from his flashlight. Marcel's mind was surprisingly vacant, as if all the poisonous thoughts that had recently plagued him were exorcised, leaving him free and cleansed from self-inflicted shame that seemed to be etched into his very pores.

He turned the lock with a skeleton key, given to him by Michel Demarche, and put all of his weight against the heavy, unyielding door – the only obstacle separating him from freedom. He stepped into the infamous Catacombs leading to the Cemetery, somewhere far away from the *arrondissement* in which Demarche Publishing House was situated. He kept walking among its few habitants, who hardly paid any attention to his shadowy figure. They were all either criminals or other rejects of society, and felt safe and at home underground, in a place which the *Boches* were, so far, too reluctant to show their faces.

The infamous Parisian Catacombs spread out as far as the outskirts of the city and had so many dead ends, secret exits, and entrances that the whole army could wander around them, potentially ending up getting lost and perishing if they were without proper guidance. And so, the *Boches* let them be.

Marcel eventually made his way back into the city, exiting through one of the tunnels leading up to the Seine. He looked around, taking in his surroundings. It was a chilly but windless evening, with delicate snowflakes leisurely caressing his immobile face, invisible in the complete dark-ness. The blacked-out city was immersed in the moonless night, people cowering in their homes, herded into hiding by the uniform-clad men, who were the only ones who walked around in the dark after the curfew took its effect at nine. That suited Marcel just fine.

He allowed his eyes to get accustomed to the darkness, pulled the collar of his overcoat closer to his face and started to make his way soundlessly away from the bridge, just visible in the light of the glistening serpent of the river. Invisible and non-existent to the officers, whose boisterous laughter he could hear from the restaurant on the opposite side of the street, he merged with the wall, becoming what he was thought to be: a bodiless ghost, patiently awaiting his unfortunate victim.

Marcel noticed him first, a tall and slender figure in a

naval overcoat, lighting a cigarette outside, his young and noble face illuminated by the glow from his match for a few short seconds. The ray of bright light that spilled onto the street upon his arrival disappeared just as fast, as someone pulled the door to the bar closed behind him, in which the Germans were enjoying their pre-Christmas celebrations. Oblivious to Marcel's scrutinizing gaze, even though he stood barely within ten steps from him, the German took a long drag on his cigarette, peered into the distance for some time, and slowly turned in the direction of the bridge, from under which Marcel had appeared not that long ago.

As soon as he made the fateful decision to turn to the left, and not to the right, Marcel knew that this was his man, selected for his plan by providence itself. He wasn't looking for anyone in particular; the very first one who would take the road in front of him would do. It was only fair to rely on fate so it would be easier to blame it later, Marcel persuaded himself, as he noiselessly stepped behind the German, following him like a shadow in the deserted street. Otherwise, he would start peering into each face, scrutinizing every feature of every single *Boche*, trying to use crude selection to weed out the good ones from the bad ones just by studying them from his hideout.

And yet, a treacherous thought had already wormed its way into the back of Marcel's mind, which had been so resolute and serene in its determination just minutes ago, to begin gnawing on his conscience, quietly whispering its doubts: *what if he had just raised a toast to his newborn? What if he was a naval hero, who saved drowning men from the icy waters? What if he was getting ready for his leave to marry some girl who had been waiting for him for two long years? What if he was one of the good ones?*

Marcel cocked his gun before he could give in to the voice, which was becoming louder and louder in his mind, and called out to the German. As soon as he turned around, an expression of mild curiosity just visible on his young, handsome face, for he stood so very close to him, Marcel aimed steadily and shot several times.

"Please, forgive me," he breathed out on the verge of tears, dropping the gun next to his victim, and whispered, before taking off back to the tunnel, "the boys were innocent, too."

KAMILLE STEPPED through the doors of Augustine Marceau's house, Violette's former teacher, and for the first time didn't feel the relief of the warmth after the biting cold of the street. Augustine, wrapped in several layers of clothing and a blanket on top of her frail frame, seemed to have grown even paler and more exhausted than a week ago, with blackish shadows underlying her eyes. She managed a weak, apologetic smile at her guest, inviting Kamille inside with a gesture of her hand.

"Don't take your coat off," Augustine warned her and went to take the basket with food out of Kamille's strained hands. "We're out of wood, I'm afraid. Sorry it's so cold. The gas burner is all we have now, but that's for cooking only. Kerosene is so expensive nowadays…"

Her voice faltered after those last words.

"You should have told me last time, Augustine! I would have brought you some kerosene."

"No, no, I don't want to be an imposition. You're sparing me so much food as it is," Augustine pressed Kamille's hands, managing to smile with dry lips that had completely lost their color. "I wouldn't dare ask you for anything more."

"Ah, Augustine, you're saying such nonsense, really. You're not an imposition at all; you're my friend, and I can't imagine not helping you out. You're a mother like me... I know how hard it must be for you to feel so helpless around Lili..." Kamille looked around, just now noticing that Lili hadn't run out to greet her like she always did. "Where is she, by the way?"

"Oh, Kamille." Augustine's voice trembled. "She's sick. It's all this damned cold. She started coughing a few days ago, and then her fever started climbing higher and higher, and now she just lays in her bed moaning when she's not sleeping... She doesn't even recognize me, just whimpers something... I thought of taking her to the hospital, but they will just chase us away because the hospital is for gentiles only, and I don't know any Jewish doctors. I thought of going out and looking for one, but how can I leave her all alone here?"

"You should have found the phone booth and called me!"

"I was afraid that one of your lodgers might pick up the phone," Augustine admitted. "I didn't want to cause you any trouble."

"How silly you are! I told you they're good people."

"With you maybe."

Kamille thought of saying something in the two officers' defense but then realized that Augustine most likely had quite a different opinion on their account, and rightfully so. It was the Germans who had taken her job away and put her and her daughter onto such strict rationing, together with the rest of the Jewish population of Paris, so that they both would have been starving if Kamille didn't bring them baskets with food weekly. It was because of the Germans that they had no money to buy wood to warm their house, and it was because of the Germans that little Lili had become sick.

"Can I see her?" Kamille asked quietly instead.

Augustine nodded and led the way, the blanket dragging behind her. She opened the door to Lili's room, where the two girls loved to play dolls whenever Kamille brought Violette for a playdate. Kamille covered her mouth at the pitiful sight of Augustine's daughter. Her dark hair was wet where it touched her forehead, glistening with sweat despite the low temperature in the room, her skin was visibly burning, and she was breathing heavily in her sleep, her chest rising and falling with sounds that Kamille didn't like at all.

"I'll go get help," she merely whispered to the girl's mother, who stood at the head of Lili's bed with a dejected look on her face.

Augustine nodded faintly, but Kamille wasn't sure if she had heard her. Or maybe she simply didn't believe that Kamille would think of something to save her child.

Stepping outside, Kamille turned on her heels and headed resolutely towards the *Metro*. She bought a token, noting with condemnation that even the subway was warmer than Augustine's house, and rode the train, full of somber Parisians, straight to the *Opera* station – the nearest to the *Kommandatur*. Inside, before she reached the third floor where Jochen's office was situated, Kamille had to unwrap the scarf from her neck and unbutton her coat for her back had started to sweat. No wonder that people of

Paris had no wood: the Germans needed it more, as it seemed.

Upon reaching the doors of Jochen's anteroom, Kamille had to stop in front of the table behind which a secretary was working. The woman, who was also dressed in a uniform, was too busy chatting with a fellow co-worker to acknowledge her arrival, or they both intentionally ignored the visitor or simply didn't care enough to pay her any attention. It was only when Kamille cleared her throat and said a loud *Pardon* did they turn and gave her a somewhat annoyed glare.

"How can I help you?" the secretary inquired in a strong German accent.

"I need to see Hauptmann Hartmann, please."

"Do you have an appointment with him?" The blonde woman reached for her notebook to check her notes.

"No, I don't. It's a personal matter and I—"

"Herr Hauptmann doesn't do personal matters," the secretary interrupted her rather rudely, slamming the notebook shut. "Go to the second floor and ask for Hauptmann Bonn. He deals with civilians."

With those words, she turned back to her uniform-clad colleague, losing all interest in the woman in front of her table. Kamille felt her cheeks flare with anger at the dismissive manner of the secretary. It was Giselle, who always knew how to stand her ground, but she, quiet, meek Kamille, always tried to avoid confrontation, having adopted her mother's wisdom from an early age that no meant no, and arguing and behaving like a market woman was not worthy of a lady. But today she couldn't care less for manners or etiquette; a little girl, her daughter's best friend, was dying, and she wouldn't leave until she had spoken with Jochen about it.

"Pardon." Kamille surprised even herself with how firm and loud her voice sounded. Both women turned to her, this time scowling in discontent. "But I need to see him at once. Tell him that Madame Kamille Blanchard is here. He lives in my house, and the matter that I need to discuss with him is of utter urgency. I don't believe he will appreciate it if you refuse me the right to have a five minute talk with him."

The secretary said something in German to her friend, and they both snorted, exchanging knowing looks. Kamille tried to keep a handle on herself and to not react to the insult, even though she had a pretty good idea of what the two had said about her. Yet, in less than a minute she stood in front of Jochen's table, explaining the situation to him in all honesty.

He listened to her without interrupting, only biting his lip from time to time.

"So, it was them, who you were sneaking out the food for, not the church?"

Kamille lowered her eyes and nodded, expecting a reproachful speech. Jochen only regarded her and then grinned, shaking his head.

"What a good woman you are, Kamille."

"Is there anything that can be done for them?" She was ready to plead and beg so long as he agreed to do something.

"They're both Jewish, you're saying?"

"Yes."

"That's a problem. I can't think of anything right now, but I'll figure something out by the evening," he promised Kamille confidently. She smiled at him with renewed hope.

"For now, tell Horst to take the car and bring both the girl and the mother to your house. They can't stay in that cold; the girl will surely die there. And when I come back from work, we'll think of something together. I would go with you myself, but I can't leave my post…"

"I know, you don't need to explain yourself to me. You're already helping." Kamille closed her coat, getting ready to leave. "Thank you. I will be forever indebted to you for this."

"Just, please, be as discreet as possible. If someone finds out that I'm doing this…"

Jochen didn't finish the sentence, but Kamille nodded her understanding. "I will be careful, I promise."

Augustine was visibly nervous at the sight of Horst, stepping through her doors in his green-gray overcoat, and became even more anxious when he picked up Lili together with all her blankets from her bed.

"Don't worry. He's very good with kids. He won't hurt her," Kamille whispered to the distressed woman as they both followed Horst with a moaning Lili in his arms.

Augustine only relaxed a little when she climbed inside the car and sat next to her daughter, after Horst had lowered the girl onto the back seat with the utmost care.

"If some of the neighbors see us and ask you about it later, tell them it's your cousin from some farm or something credible of the same sort," Horst warned Kamille as they approached their house.

"We do have family who live on a farm not too far from the city," Kamille replied. "They never visit, but the neighbors know that we have cousins there. Yes, it'll work, I believe."

"You look somewhat alike." Horst glanced at Augustine in

the rearview mirror. "I don't think we will raise anyone's suspicions."

Jochen expressed the same sentiments later that evening when helping Kamille to prepare dinner.

"The doctor will come see her tomorrow morning." He spoke in a hushed tone, even though Augustine was upstairs with her daughter. Violette had begged Kamille to help Madame Marceau look after Lili, but both women decided that it would be better if the girls weren't in direct contact so that Violette wouldn't fall sick as well. "Everyone will think that they're your relatives from the countryside for now, but you'd still better find them new papers."

"I know. I'm sorry about all this. I know what consequences it may have for you if someone finds out that we're sheltering Jews, so I'll try my best to get them new papers as soon as possible."

"I'm not worried about myself," Jochen said in a mild voice. "I'll go to the front. There are worse things…So…"

He glanced over his shoulder and leaned even closer to Kamille.

"They'd better leave the Occupied Zone altogether as soon as the girl is healthy enough to travel."

"Why?" Kamille stopped stirring the potatoes, which were slowly obtaining an appetizing golden color together with the onions that she used to flavor them. "Can't they stay here with us until spring comes? They have their house to look after… Augustine's husband is a prisoner of war, even though he hasn't written to her yet, but she got an official letter saying that he was taken to Germany, and in case he writes to her and she—"

"Kamille." Jochen took her by the shoulders, making her

look him directly in the eye. "I'm very sorry to say it but Augustine's husband won't be writing to her. And she better leave before... Just tell her to leave, will you?"

"What are you saying?" Kamille tilted her head to one side slightly, an uneasy sense taking over her. "Why won't he be writing to her?"

"He's dead, Kamille."

"No, he was taken a prisoner of war, I just told you."

Jochen shook his head slowly, looking far too serious. Kamille dreaded what he was about to say next.

"Haven't you heard about how they treat Jews in Germany?" he continued in the same soft voice.

"I have, but..."

"The official order, which is unknown to the general public of course, prescribes that we should immediately execute all Jews or communists as soon as they fall in the hands of the German army. It's the SS that does the dirty work, but... The *Wehrmacht* is to stand by and not to interfere, as they call it. They probably shot him even before he reached the territory of Germany."

"But... But he's a soldier! Isn't it against some military code?"

"It most definitely is. And yet the SS still enforce this order. That's why I'm saying that Augustine and her little girl better run... While they still can."

"You think they're in danger here? In France?" Kamille inquired incredulously.

"So far, they're not in any direct danger. But I would rather not see it get to that point if you understand what I'm saying," he explained carefully. "There are lists, Kamille. Lists with names of all Jewish citizens, in every town, all over the

Occupied Zone. If the SS weren't planning something on their account, they wouldn't make those lists, would they?"

Kamille stood still, stunned to the core, until Jochen took the wooden spoon out of her limp hand and stirred the potatoes that were starting to get stuck to the bottom of the skillet.

Kamille looked around as if seeing her kitchen for the first time. Jochen pointed to a ceramic pot on the table – the object that she was obviously searching for to place the potatoes in it. She gave him a smile that was both miserable and grateful.

"I'll talk to her. When Lili gets better."

"Yes, when Lili gets better."

he Christmas mood that year was anything but celebratory. The dinner at the Prefect's was held in the most official manner, with invited German dignitaries and the representatives of the governing circles of Paris barely speaking to each other. The Germans eyed the French functionaries with disdain. The French were still recovering from shock after the drastic measures of retribution which followed the murder of the German naval officer. Sturmbannführer Karl Wünsche had personally signed the order for the execution of twenty hostages, most of which were members of the Communist Party.

Giselle glanced at Karl, who reminded her of a grim, morose statue even more than ever that evening. He hardly moved at all, leaving his plate untouched as he peered at a particular spot on the tablecloth, so deep in thought that his own colleagues wisely decided not to bother him.

"Eat something," Giselle whispered, covering his hand

with hers. He moved his hand from under hers and placed it on top of his lap. "We're celebrating Christmas after all. Stop sulking. You're insulting your hosts."

"My hosts?" he asked a little louder than she wished him to. "I owe nothing to my hosts after they allowed this atrocity to happen to one of our soldiers."

The conversation at the table became even more subdued. The French officials squirmed in their seats, lowering their heads as if by command.

"You shot those communists in retaliation, didn't you? I thought the subject was closed." Giselle spoke as quietly as she could and yet she was certain that the people around her could hear her perfectly.

"It's far from closed. It won't be closed until I find the perpetrator. It's very unfortunate that the administration of the city, which should be cooperating with us, seems to do nothing to help us find him. I wouldn't be surprised if all of them suddenly became de Gaulle's sympathizers and are hiding that terrorist from us on purpose."

"I assure you, it is not so in the slightest," the Prefect of the Police chimed in, desperately trying to hide the tremble from his voice. His brow, glistening with nervous sweat, was, however, telling another story. "We have pledged our allegiance to the German state, and we will stand by our promise. We are doing everything possible to find that man."

The gaze of Karl's charcoal eyes was so intense that the Prefect of the Police started sweating even more profusely, too fearful to even reach for his handkerchief.

"The *possible* doesn't seem to bring any results," Karl stated, with familiar calmness in his voice. This seemed to terrify the people around him far more than the most outraged shouts of some of his counterparts. He held the pause, making the Prefect squirm, and concluded pointedly, "Do the impossible then."

"I beg your pardon, Doctor Wünsche?" The Prefect shifted forward, awaiting some instructions to follow that would be more precise.

Karl lifted a knife from the table, which suddenly reminded Giselle of a scalpel in the hands of a mad scientist, studied it with the same immobile expression on his impenetrable, handsome face and placed it back, once again boring his black eyes into the man sitting across the table from him.

"Are you aware of the law prescribing that the civil servant in charge of the city should take the place of the hostages in situations like the one that we're currently facing?"

The Prefect of the Police swallowed with obvious difficulty, his face gradually turning a ghostly pale color. "I beg your pardon?"

"You heard me. If I don't get the results that I want from this investigation, you'll be the one ascending the gallows." After those words, Karl picked up his glass with red wine in it and rose from his chair. "I would like to honor the memory of our fallen comrade now. An innocent victim of the war, executed in cold blood by the terrorist who is still at large. But we won't sit idly until our own blood is avenged... Even if it means that I'll have to execute twenty people daily to make him finally show his face and take his punishment instead of his innocent fellow countrymen. To Oberbootsmann Rademacher."

"To Oberbootsmann Rademacher," everyone repeated in unison, holding their glasses high and heads low.

A VERY QUIET January had passed, during which all of the Resistance members seemed to lay low. Hardly any leaflets were reported, leave alone demonstrations or factory strikes. Both sides appeared to lick their wounds, rethinking their strategies. Giselle breathed out with relief when Michel Demarche announced the good news to her during one of their regular meetings: Marcel, who now sported a beard, a much shorter haircut and glasses, had successfully crossed the border with Etienne – Michel's late friend's son, who was in charge of the distribution of *La Libération* in the Free Zone.

Etienne himself possessed an *Ausweis*, allowing him to freely travel between the two parts of France, however he advised against Marcel using fake papers to try and cross the border by train. Luckily, Etienne had his own connection on the frontier, who smuggled both men through the forest within a couple of kilometers from an official check point. The territory was heavily guarded, and it was common practice among the Germans to shoot on the spot all those who tried to cross illegally. Fortunately, Etienne's smuggler proved himself worthy of the money he demanded for his services and had delivered them both safely to the Free Zone.

However, even though the legendary Ghost was long gone, Giselle was very aware of the fact that Karl hadn't given up on his obsessive search for him.

"How do you even know that it was the Ghost who shot that naval officer?" she asked him irritably one day. It was she who had written a new glorious article for *La Libération*, indicating with certainty that it was indeed the Ghost's doing.

The German gun – the weapon used for the officer's assassination – belonged to the *Boche* who was taken hostage during the Ghost's initial escape from prison, and this was enough proof to support the theory in the public's eyes. The article also highly praised the deed and stated with satisfaction that the innocent family that had been executed by the SS was now avenged. *Let it be a lesson to the Boches! We refuse to tolerate your violence and do nothing in response! For each innocent French life, we'll take a German one! Vive Général de Gaulle! Vive la France! Vive la Résistance!*

She probably should have toned it down a little, Giselle thought when she saw Karl's reaction to the newspaper. For the first time in her life she saw him lose his always perfectly calm composure, as he tore the paper into small pieces and swept them off his desk together with the rest of his neatly organized papers, folders, heavy golden penholders and even the phone.

The more disturbing part was that, since that fateful day, he had started studying every issue of *La Libération* with frightening meticulousness, spending hours with a magnifying glass on top of the text and making various marks in his papers. Soon, Giselle started noticing graphs and tables in his notes, in which he carefully separated different words and other markings. His diligence concerned Giselle, and finally she asked him, unable to feign indifference anymore, "What are you doing with all these issues?"

Karl leaned back in his chair, pushing the papers that he'd been perusing away from himself.

"You see, Giselle, I've always liked studying and analyzing

things. I was born with a very curious and inquisitive mind. It came in handy when I started studying medicine, and it came even handier when I became involved with investigations within the *Staatspolizei*." He paused, looking pensive, and then turned an issue of *La Libération* so it would face Giselle. "Come, take a look at this paper. What story does it tell you?"

Giselle leaned over the underground newspaper, which was well-known to her, but the concentration with which she scrutinized it this time was anything but fake. She genuinely tried to understand what story Karl was alluding to.

"I don't know." She straightened next to the desk, eventually admitting her defeat. "It tells the story of some liberals who are printing an underground paper."

"*Ja.*" Karl's eyes gleamed, as he grinned with a mysterious air about his face, a look she didn't like at all. "But what kind of liberals?"

"How do I know?" Giselle chuckled. "Communists, probably. Who else?"

"*Ach*, come now, Giselle, you can do better than that. They are in no way communists. Liberals, yes. But not communists. And they don't belong to the working class: the speech is too refined, not like in those leaflets that communists ordinarily spread."

Giselle felt her blouse getting slightly damp on her back.

"Try again," Karl encouraged her, still smiling. "What kind of refined liberals could write these articles?"

She faltered before responding, carefully weighing her reply. She couldn't just feign ignorance with him; Karl knew her too well by now.

"Um… Journalists?" she suggested.

"That was my guess as well, yes." Karl nodded in agreement. "But now we're facing a second dilemma. I have turned every single newspaper headquarters in the city upside down. Their printing presses were not used for printing this newspaper. And, after carefully studying each issue I finally realized my mistake. *La Libération* is not being printed on a big factory newspaper press. Here, take a look."

Giselle lowered her head above the paper together with Karl as he placed a looking glass on top of the text.

"Notice anything specific?"

Giselle thoroughly studied the text but ended up shaking her head again.

"Look closely at the letters *a, b, d,* and *e* in this issue." Karl moved another paper towards Giselle. "And now look at the same letters in this one."

"They're different."

"Different how?"

"In the first issue they're ink-filled in the middle, and in the second one they're clear."

"And why is that?"

"I don't know, I don't print newspapers." Giselle laughed, hoping to keep nervous notes away from her voice.

"That's the whole point." Karl gave her a pointed look with a victorious smile. "It's not a conventional rotary press that they're using. It's an ordinary mimeograph. The stencil that they're using is wearing out after producing several dozens of copies, which causes the letters to be ink-filled, and the text to appear lighter than in the beginning. See how it's fading slightly from black to dark-blue in this issue for example? It's not as bright as this one."

Giselle compared the papers again, inwardly cursing herself for not noticing anything before. To her they all appeared to be the same; how could she possibly know that Karl would examine them with such painstaking fastidiousness that he would notice the smallest details that she would never think to pay attention to.

"So what does it mean?" she asked, straightening out.

"It means that my job is getting more difficult. A mimeograph is such a small machine that it can easily be standing in one's apartment and no one would know that someone is printing something on it. It's portable and practically noiseless."

"So you've hit a kind of dead end?" Giselle inquired with a concerned look, silently cheering inside.

"I never hit dead ends," Karl proclaimed with confidence. "It only means that if I can't find the printing machine, I should find people who write for this newspaper. These Indigo Rebels."

"Indigo Rebels?"

"*Ja*. That's what I named them, after the ink that they're using."

"How are you planning to do this?"

"*Ach*, Giselle." Karl grinned again. "It's not as complicated as it looks. Just like these copies of the paper, people have their signature marks that I only have to study, classify and compare. Every single journalist – or a writer for that matter – has his or her own particular style, you see. Favorite words they use more often than others. Certain expressions. Metaphors. Sentence structure. Punctuation. Some love dashes and some semicolons. Some love ending their articles with question marks. Some are cold, some are indignant, some idealistic, and some are outright sarcastic. Every single article in this newspaper has its own, very distinctive voice."

Giselle's face took a guarded look against her intentions. Karl grinned wider and finished. "Now, I just have to find their owners."

Giselle forced a smile and turned to leave.

"Well, it's all very fascinating, but I'm already late for a meeting with Michel."

"Perfect." He rose from his chair as well. "I'll give you a ride."

"That is not necessary." She frantically tried to worm her way out of the situation, already sensing some malice behind his words. "It's such a beautiful day outside. I don't mind taking a walk."

But he was already opening the door of his study and making his way to the front door.

"Nonsense. It's freezing cold outside. Besides, I need to talk to Monsieur Demarche anyway."

Giselle could do nothing but follow him out of the study.

GISELLE FORCED herself to stop every time she noticed that she was biting her lips again. When their car pulled in front of the Demarche Publishing House, it was already dark out, and Giselle, to the last minute, nursed a hope that Michel wasn't there together with the rest; that maybe the weekly meeting had somehow been canceled. But after she had stepped out of the car with the help of Karl and his gallantly outstretched hand, Giselle saw the light coming from the top floor and hung her head in defeat.

They climbed the stairs in complete silence. Karl pushed the door open to let Giselle inside and nodded his acknowledgment to the stupefied doorman.

"Is Monsieur Demarche upstairs?" she asked, sliding her glance over the black phone next to the doorman, hoping that he would get the hint.

"Yes, he is, together with other gentlemen. I'll call him at once to let him know you're coming up."

"Merci." Giselle's smile was more of a grimace. Yet, she regained her composure before turning to her fiancé. "Well, you've seen my home away from home at last."

Karl only grinned enigmatically and gestured for her to lead the way. All these grins of his unnerved her, especially taking into consideration that this man hardly ever smiled. Now, he was beaming like a cat that had got the cream.

Giselle pushed the heavy iron cage of the elevator door open and stepped into the silence of the fourth floor. The walk along the corridor towards Michel's office felt like the walk to a scaffold. Giselle tried to pacify herself with the thought that the doorman had warned his boss of the unexpected visitor that she had brought with her.

The office met them with dead silence. Giselle tried to smile brightly at Michel and her colleagues, welcoming Karl inside. The Chief of the Gestapo removed his uniform cap and headed straight to Michel's desk, outstretching his arm. Giselle shook her head behind his back, indicating that there was nothing she could have done to prevent him from coming here.

"Monsieur Demarche, I believe?" Karl was at his best, ceremonious self, bowing slightly as the publisher encased his hand in his. "Karl Wünsche. It's my utmost pleasure to finally meet you."

"The pleasure is all mine, Monsieur Wünsche."

"Doctor Wünsche," Giselle corrected Michel before Karl would. "Karl is a surgeon."

"Please, pardon my ignorance, Doctor." Michel bowed his head again, playing the part of a perfect host.

"No need to apologize, Monsieur Demarche. I'm afraid the title remained only on paper after the Reich called me to begin a different duty. I haven't practiced medicine in a while."

A pause followed until Giselle remembered to act as naturally as possible and proceeded to exchange kisses with Michel and other men in the room. The look that Pascal gave her barely concealed his anger.

"Karl, allow me to introduce you to my esteemed colleagues and very good friends," she chirped, a bright smile plastered on her face despite an almost panicked look in her eyes. "This is Antoine Levy, my favorite novelist."

Again, Karl was the first one to hold out his arm, even though Giselle was almost confident that he would refuse to shake a Jew's hand.

"Monsieur Levy. My pleasure."

"As it is mine, Doctor." Antoine returned his polite smile.

"Excuse my curiosity, please." Karl slightly narrowed his eyes without releasing Antoine's hand. "Are you still holding a position here? I'm only asking because Giselle told me that this was a routine, scheduled meeting and you would be discussing your work."

"Your assumptions are absolutely justified, Doctor," Antoine replied, slightly uncomfortable with the German's prolonged grip still clasping his palm. "I'm afraid I was let go a few months ago, but I still come here from time to time to see my friends. I'm not breaking any law, I hope? If I am, I am terribly sorry; I was unaware of that."

"No, no, you aren't breaking anything," Karl rushed to reassure him. "Only the blackout law, but with this issue I should address Monsieur Demarche, I believe."

Karl chuckled almost kindheartedly.

Just now noticing that he had forgotten to lower the blackout drapes, Michel hurried to do so under the German's amused stare. Karl was visibly enjoying himself.

"I don't understand how I possibly overlooked it," Michel muttered, struggling with the thick material.

Karl walked over to him and pulled the drapes down with a precise, practiced move.

"*Merci, Docteur.*"

"Don't mention it." Karl turned to the other two men, who still stood by the chairs from which they had risen upon his arrival. "And these gentlemen are novelists as well, I suppose?"

"Yes, they also represent my finest. Monsieur Thierry and Monsieur Le Roux." Michel followed up with the introductions while Karl regarded every man closely, shaking their hands. "Now that we're all acquainted, may I ask how I can be of assistance, Doctor Wünsche? I don't believe Giselle mentioned anything to me…"

"Giselle had no time to mention anything to you."

Her heart sank against her will at those words. *He knew everything. He knew everything, and he was going to arrest them all.*

However, Karl proceeded with a strangely ordinary request.

"I need a list of your writers, Monsieur Demarche. It's routine procedure, and I'll be collecting those lists from all the publishing houses in Paris. I decided to start with yours solely because my fiancé works with you." He was all smiles and charm again.

"Are you... looking for someone in particular, perhaps?" Michel inquired carefully, fixing his glasses on the bridge of his nose. "In this case, I can probably help you. I've been working in this business for many years, and I know almost everyone in it."

"I am looking for some particular people, yes." Karl slid his glance over the tall redwood bookcase occupying the opposite wall. "Unfortunately, I don't know their names yet."

Michel scowled slightly, but proceeded to his safe, in which he kept all legal paperwork and documents. Karl, meanwhile, walked over to the impressive office library and traced his fingers along the top of the books, took one out and shuffled through the pages.

"Monsieur Demarche, do you have copies of your novelists' books here by any chance?"

"Of course, Doctor. Not all of them, but the most celebrated ones, yes."

Karl placed the book back on the shelf and turned back to his silent audience.

"Since I'm here and have made an acquaintance with all of these fine masters of the literary word, it would be my utmost honor to have their books in my collection," Karl said, smiling sweetly once again. "Would it be possible to arrange?"

"Bien sûr." Michel had already found the folder with the lists of his employees and went to hand it to Karl. "It's the only copy, I'm afraid… I would ask the secretary to copy them for you, but she has already left…"

"No need to worry. I'll have my adjutant duplicate them for me and have them returned to you next time Giselle comes to see you."

"Thank you, Doctor. Now, which books would you like?"

"Your most favorite works by these gentlemen." A slight nod in the direction of the three novelists followed.

Michel walked over to the bookcase and instantly pulled three copies from three different shelves, finding the books without any effort. After he had offered them to Karl with a slight bow, the latter studied the covers with a faint grin, and suddenly handed the first one to Antoine.

"Would you be so kind to sign it for me?"

Antoine wavered for a second, but then took the book from the German's hand and lowered it onto Michel's table, scribbling something.

"Gentlemen." Karl handed the other two books to their respective authors. "You would do me the utmost honor."

After the reluctant writers handed him the copies back, he almost beamed at their small company before bidding his farewell.

"Well, I won't bother you with my presence anymore. Discuss what you came here to discuss, and pardon my intrusion once again. A pleasure to meet you all and I'll be looking forward to reading your works, gentlemen." Karl bowed slightly to Giselle, passing her by. "I'll be waiting for you in the car, *Süße.*"

"I won't be long, *chéri.*"

"Take your time. Gentlemen."

The room remained silent until they heard the sound of the elevator door closing. After that Giselle turned back to the men, shaking her head vehemently.

"I did not invite him here, I swear! He told me that he was coming with me when I was already at the door of my house. There was no way I could prevent him from coming."

While Pascal Thierry eyed her with suspicion, Michel only sighed, dabbing his forehead with a handkerchief.

"That's all right, Giselle. I understand completely." He stood at his desk, his fists butting the surface while he tried to regain his composure, and then asked, "Why did he come though? Really, he acted mighty strange if you ask me. Not that I know him, but… I imagined him to be quite different from your words."

"He *was* acting strange," Giselle confirmed with a frown. "Far too strange. I think he suspects that it's us."

"What do you mean, he suspects?" Thierry exploded at last. "He wouldn't suspect because someone tipped him off, would he now?!"

"What are you implying, Pascal?!" Giselle took her stand as well, sounding indignant. "That I told him to come here and snoop around?! *Putain,* I write for this goddamned paper together with you!"

"Who knows if you've switched tables!" He squinted his eyes slightly. "Maybe he cut a deal with you to sell us out in exchange for the new position of *Madame Le Chef de la Gestapo!*"

"You pig," Giselle hissed, stepping closer as well despite Michel's and Antoine's efforts to pacify them both. "My brother is in the Resistance! He shot that naval officer, he's the man who Karl is hell-bent on finding! You think he cut a deal with me on that too?!"

"Enough!" Michel shouted with unusual emotion. "Do you not see what's happening?! We're going at each other's throats when we should bond together even tighter than before."

"I don't trust her," Pascal cut him off at once.

"I trust her." Antoine shifted closer to Giselle. "I've known her for years; she would never betray us."

"Legrand?" Thierry snorted with contempt. "Legrand would sell anything for money. Everybody knows that it's all she cares about. Even her own brother."

"Pascal, this is going too far," Michel spoke, with a sense of warning in his voice.

"I don't care anymore. I'm out of all this." Pascal jumped to his feet and headed to the exit, fumbling with his coat. "You can wait all you want until you hang together, while *Madame* watches you from beneath the scaffold, together with her new husband."

He slammed the door on his way out, leaving the room immersed in the gloomiest of atmospheres once again.

"I didn't invite him here, I swear," Giselle repeated softly once more.

Antoine reached out and pressed her hand in a reassuring gesture.

"We know you didn't. It's all right."

"Why did he ask for our books though?" Always quiet, Gilles Le Roux voiced his thoughts for the first time that evening. "Is he reading a lot?"

"Only what's useful for him," Giselle replied and gratefully accepted a cigarette that Antoine offered her. Her fingers shook slightly as she held it for him to light. "I'm afraid he's getting closer to the truth concerning *La Libéra-tion* than we thought. He knows what the paper is being printed on and he knows that it's educated liberals who are writing for it, and not communists. He also said today that each writer has their specific manner of writing and that he only has to compare their writing in the articles in *La Libéra-tion* with... other articles, written in different papers and magazines."

"Or books," Michel concluded, sounding strangely calm.

"Or books," Giselle took a long drag on her cigarette, immersed in her thoughts together with the men in the room.

"What shall we do?" Antoine inquired quietly. "Stop writing?"

"Not yet." Giselle shook her head, narrowing her gaze. "I know him. He won't act until he has all the facts in his hands and is one hundred percent sure of his theory. If he were certain that it was us, he wouldn't have come alone today; he would bring a small army with him to arrest us. No. We still have time. Let's use it wisely."

"Time until what?" Gilles frowned.

"Time until..." She sighed, shaking her head. "Until, I don't know. Until I find a way to stop him. Once and for all."

29

*K*amille kept blowing into her cupped hands even after she had removed her warm, fur lined gloves.

"The winter just won't go away," she complained to Jochen, who was warming her cheeks, rosy from the cold, with his palms. "And to think of it, it's almost March."

"Yes, indeed," he agreed, brushing melting snow off her dark locks that had been exposed to the storm outside. "Did you manage to get it?"

"Giselle's friend – I don't know who he is and I don't want to know – was a godsend." Kamille opened her bag and dug inside the lining, which she had purposely torn before leaving to see her sister. "He made papers for them both, and they're so good that I couldn't tell them from my own if I had to."

"Let me see."

Kamille finally found the carefully concealed documents

and handed them to Jochen. After studying both passports with thoroughness, he smiled at last, and Kamille let out a sigh of relief.

"They're really well done." He nodded in appreciation at the mastery with which the documents were executed. "I wouldn't know they were fake if I had to check them. The privates on the border definitely won't question them."

"That's good to know." Kamille beamed.

Lili had fully recovered from her illness weeks ago due to the gentle care of the doctor that Jochen initially brought to treat her. He was a military man, but having hardly any patients to treat he was more than glad to devote all of his attention to a little sick girl, who reminded him of his own daughter, whom he hadn't seen in over a year.

Violette was elated at the new living arrangements and having her best friend always available to play with. She didn't understand at first why Lili wasn't allowed to go to school with her, but when Kamille warned her that Lili was not Lili anymore, but Sabine Clemenceau, her distant cousin from a farm, and that she was not to mention her at school at all, Violette nodded solemnly and made a motion, imitating locking her lips. Jochen only chuckled at how fast she learned about keeping secrets. The children weren't children anymore, too; they were little adults now, carefully guarding their parents' secrets.

"How's Giselle?" Jochen inquired.

"She's fine."

"Was she alone?"

"Yes. Wünsche always dines with the Prefect on Sundays. He started taking Giselle along after they got engaged, but today she talked her way out of it, feigning illness."

"Is she really unwell?" Jochen frowned slightly.

"Of course not. She's just a first class actress, that's all. She did seem a little pale to me, but since she stopped using her rouge and wearing bright lipstick, she always looks pale to me. Maybe I'm just not used to seeing her like this."

"Is she still going to marry him?"

"That's what Horst always asks."

Jochen couldn't suppress a wry smile.

"I feel for him, the poor fellow." Kamille sighed, shaking her head. "She's breaking his heart."

"Horst is a hopeless romantic," Jochen retorted with a slight shrug. "He needs to suffer, otherwise he's not happy. He still dreams that she'll run away with him to Switzerland. A typical artist, I told you. She's doing him a favor, really. You should see the beautiful paintings he draws now. He already has a small gallery in his bedroom."

"Not her portraits, I hope?" Kamille smiled.

"No. He draws nature. Dark, gloomy skies and white snow. A lot of shimmering, stark white snow. Breathtaking, if you ask me. And you ignored my previous question."

Kamille fumbled with a glove in her hands, pondering her response.

"I don't know. That whole marriage affair… To be completely honest, I don't like Giselle right now. I mean, now she acts the same way she acted right before she ran away from home. Well, not ran away per se, but… She wouldn't talk to us, the whole family, for over six months. She broke *Papa's* heart when she ran off like that."

"She ran off with some boy?" Jochen asked.

"No, boys were never strictly on her list of priorities, believe it or not. Giselle has always been – how do I put it? –

a loner. She was perfectly happy in her own world. She would often sit with us at the table and ignore the conversation altogether, deep in her thoughts. And when *Maman* would ask her why she didn't want to participate in the conversation she would just shrug and say that she had no use in indulging in idle gossip. She sounded rude, but... Giselle's whole mindset differed from ours. She often complained that we didn't understand her. And she was right – we didn't. She always had these strange dreams, that she was destined to do some grand thing. It always frightened me when she would say something strange like that. What normal person declares openly that they were born to change the world? You know, I thought she was insane sometimes. But I was a little girl, and she was... This big, overwhelming figure for me. I was afraid of her sometimes. And then she ran off to put her dreams into reality. And what do you know? She became Giselle Legrand." Kamille smiled, but then got serious again, and added quietly after a pause, "She has the same detached look on her, like before, when she was contemplating her escape. And she's changed, too. There's something strange about her, something... I don't know. Maybe I'm just overthinking everything. Maybe she is a little unwell, and I didn't care to ask."

"When is the wedding?"

"May first. It's supposed to bear some special meaning for the members of the SS, or so I understood."

"It's just one of the German pagan traditions. In pagan times May was the preferred month for weddings, so after celebrating their union, the newlywed couple could go back to cultivating their land. Himmler's obsessed with paganism and rituals, so hence the date, I guess," Jochen explained.

Kamille chewed on her lip for some time and said in a barely audible voice, "I just hope she's not doing something she'll later regret."

KARL WAS SO IMMERSED in his reading that he didn't notice Giselle, who had stood next to his chair for over a minute already. She watched him mark something down in his notebook, like he had done for the past two weeks, diving into Antoine's novel with almost unnatural obsessiveness. But it was those notes of his, together with some sentences that he had underlined in several issues of *La Libération* already – in articles written by Antoine – that had bared her nerves to the point where she decided to act before it was too late.

"Karl," she called him softly. "I need to talk to you."

"What is it?" he asked without taking his eyes off the book, pen in hand.

Giselle fumbled with the ties of her belt, thinking how to start better.

"Karl, we need to change the date of the wedding."

That got his attention. Karl straightened in his chair, fixing the gaze of his onyx eyes on the woman in front of him.

"Why? What's wrong with the date that we chose?"

"Well… It's a little too far. We'll have to wait another two months."

He knitted his brows in confusion. "And?"

"It's just that…"

She hesitated a little longer before he urged her by asking, "What is it, Giselle? Say it already."

"I'm pregnant. It'll be embarrassing if I have this child only six months after the wedding. People talk as it is, and after that… Please, let's reschedule the date."

Karl rose from his chair, stepping closer to her. "You're pregnant?"

"Yes, that's what I just told you."

"How far along?"

"About a month I think. A little less than that. I went to my doctor this morning… He confirmed it."

Karl's lips slowly moved into a grin as he enclosed Giselle into a tight embrace. She stood with her face pressed into his shoulder, peering into the distance without blinking. *There was no turning back now. It was all going to end soon.*

"Giselle, my beautiful Giselle," he purred gently into her ear, covering her hair in soft kisses. "There isn't better news you could possibly tell me."

"I know how much you wanted a child."

She tried to smile through her unexpected tears, feeling a strange state of melancholy that choked her up despite her willingness to stay strong. She had gotten used to him, and no matter the arguments that she brought to herself during the sleepless nights, it wouldn't be so easy to do what she had set her mind on. But with the same certainty, Giselle knew that he wouldn't falter if it came to a decision like this, and so she couldn't either. So be it then, and to hell with all hesitation.

"I'll summon an excellent doctor from Berlin for you." Karl was back to his usual organizing self. "He'll live here in Paris until the baby is born. I want only the best care for you during the pregnancy. Unless you want to go to Germany? That would be an even better idea."

"Karl, I'm not going anywhere, and I don't want any other doctors except my own. He's been my doctor for over ten years, and I trust him like no one else. Believe me, he's one of the best ones in Paris. He knows what he's doing."

"All right then. But I still want to meet him to make sure he's not entirely incompetent."

"He's not, I promise." Giselle put her hands on top of his shoulders, smoothing out invisible wrinkles on his uniform jacket. He looked so handsome in it. She shook her head again, dispersing the wavering thoughts. "Just reschedule the date, will you?"

"What date do you want me to reschedule it to?"

"End of March at the latest."

"But Giselle! That's too soon! We will never be able to reorganize everything! And the invitations—"

"I haven't sent them out yet," she interrupted him with a somewhat feverish grin on her face. "I started to suspect something a week ago and decided to wait for a while. It turned out I was right."

She pressed her lips to his and then laughed softly, her green eyes shining with an unhealthy gleam. "Change the date, Karl. Do it for me, please. I'm carrying your child after all."

"But… With the preparations and everything I won't have time…" He threw a helpless look at the open book and his notes.

"Your investigation can wait a few weeks," Giselle promised, turning his face back to her. "Those journalists are still printing their stories. They aren't going anywhere."

"March 30th it is. No sooner."

"That'll do just fine."

There was no turning back indeed.

PHILIPPE STOOD with his arms crossed over his chest, eyeing Giselle apprehensively. He was more than surprised with her coming down to his temporary hideout in Demarche's cellar, but after the request that she had just voiced his indignation turned to suspicion.

"You need what?" he repeated, scrutinizing her face for clues. She seemed tired and dejected; only her eyes hadn't lost their glimmer and shone with determination like never before.

"You heard me."

"I did. And what exactly do you need rat poison for?"

"I have rats."

"You have rats? In your apartment?" Philippe arched his brow skeptically.

"Mhm." A slow, lazy grin curled her lips upwards. "Huge ones."

Philippe snorted. "Why didn't you go to the pharmacy then? They sell it."

"There are rats in pharmacies too, you see. Now, can you get it for me on *Le Marché Noir* or no?"

He didn't like that unhealthy gleam in her eyes at all. "What are you plotting, Giselle?"

"Me? Nothing," she replied calmly. "I have a pest problem, which needs to be solved, and the sooner, the better. Will you get it or not?"

"Not until you tell me what you really need it for."

"I have just told you. I want to get rid of the rats. I would go to the *Marché* myself, but people operating there have a certain problem with me. I'm the *Boche's* whore, you see. They will just scatter at the first sight of me."

Philippe cleared his throat, walking around his unexpected visitor. "When do you need it?"

"By tomorrow. I'm leaving for a weekend with Karl. We're going to spend a couple of days in the *Fontainebleau*. I need some fresh air, he says. I've been a little under the weather recently."

Philippe regarded her a little longer, but her face didn't give anything away.

"Tell me what you need it for." He decided to try again, softening his voice on purpose. "Maybe I can help."

"Why are you so concerned about me all of a sudden?" She burst into joyless laughter. "I need to kill my rats, what's not to understand? I'll leave the poison on the floor on Friday, so when I'm back on Monday, they'll be all dead."

"Giselle—"

"Will you get it or not?"

He took a deep breath, lowering his head in defeat. "Fine. Come tomorrow at the same time. I'll have it for you."

"Thank you." She reached inside her clutch and put the money on the table, together with a letter. Philippe's scowl deepened. "For your trouble. And this… This is for Marcel. Will you send it to him with Etienne, next time he comes? I don't want to drag Kamille into all this…"

Philippe nodded and watched her walk back to the door.

"Giselle!" he called out to her, just as she was at the threshold of the room.

"Yes?"

"Where exactly are you staying in the *Fontainebleau?*"

"Why?"

"Just curious."

She hesitated for a few moments, but then replied in a mild voice, "In a small hunter's house, near the lake. Do you know it?"

"Yes, I do."

She smiled at him once again before leaving. "See you tomorrow, Philippe."

"See you tomorrow."

30

The morning outside was painfully gorgeous. Giselle stepped onto the newly added terrace of a small one-story hunter's lodge. The lodge itself had been fully remodeled by some White Russian, who apparently missed his *dacha* so very much after the Bolsheviks had seized all his property in the former Russian Empire that he didn't want to spare any money to create something similar out of this rather simple cabin. Now, the terrace was covered with the intricate lace of shadows due to the sunbeams finding their way through the wooden carving of the railing. The snow was all but gone, the last few days being particularly warm.

Giselle took a seat on a bench and outstretched her legs, peering into the serene, pastoral forest in front of her. She found herself to be in the same restless state of excitement and heart-wrenching melancholia which had become her constant companion in the past few days. A small, worn out pocket copy of "Crime and Punishment" lay on her lap as her fingers gently stroked the cover. It was not the highly valued first edition that she had bought as soon as she signed her first contract with Michel Demarche. It was the one that she used to re-read time after time in her old apartment so she could later have heated discussions with her father, which only left them both frustrated at the other's inability to see their truth. Today she would finally solve that mystery for herself, which one of them was right after all. And yet, she was too afraid to open it, fearing to lose her courage.

Karl stepped out of the door, which groaned like the wood always did, swollen with the dampness of the changing season. Giselle's heart started thrashing like a wild animal inside her ribcage, while on the surface she remained completely unmoved.

"I thought you wanted to finish your manuscript while we were here," he spoke, noticing the book in her hands. "Not read other people's works."

"It's not other people," she replied with strange notes in her voice. "It's Dostoevsky. And I did finish my manuscript. I took it to Michel yesterday morning before we left."

"Now, that's not fair." Karl smiled, sitting next to her. "I thought you'd let me read it first. Now I won't know how it ends."

"You'll know. Very soon."

He looked at her closely. "You're not yourself today. Are you feeling all right?"

"I haven't been better, thank you. It's probably hormones." She took a ragged breath and turned to face the man in front of her as if memorizing every feature of his somber, handsome face. "We have a bottle of some remarkable wine if I remember correctly. How about you bring it here and we celebrate?"

"Isn't it a little too early for wine?" Karl chuckled softly.

Giselle slowly shook her head, smiling at him. *Murderer.*

"No. I think it's the perfect morning to share a glass of perfect wine. And celebrate."

"Celebrate what?"

"Life, *bien sûr, Charlie.* Life."

He grinned somewhat conceitedly, rested his hand on top of her stomach for a moment and went back inside. Giselle fumbled with something in her pocket, but he wasn't there to notice it. She tilted her head backward, willing the tears to dissolve and disappear, just like the last of her doubts.

"Here's to life then," Karl announced cheerfully, popping the bottle open with a corkscrew while standing in the door. Taking his place next to Giselle, he handed her one of the glasses and filled both, raising his in a toast.

Giselle lowered hers with a guilty grin. "You know, I don't think it was a good idea. For me at least. I shouldn't be drinking alcohol in my situation. That's irresponsible."

"One glass of wine won't harm anything."

"Probably. But I want this child to be perfect. No taking chances; not for our baby, you understand? Monsieur Darwin wouldn't approve." She grinned crookedly.

He smiled too. "I suppose. I'll go fetch you water then."

"Thank you, *chéri.*"

He disappeared behind the door, and Giselle stood up and splashed her wine onto the snow that remained outside – a bloody splatter on the pristine white sheet. She slowly turned back and took a small vial out of her pocket, eyeing the glass of wine that he had left there. *Yes. Let's drink to life,*

Charlie. She opened the vial and poured its contents into the wine.

Karl soon returned, holding a bottle of mineral water in his hand. He filled Giselle's glass again, and they both raised their glasses in a toast, after which Karl downed his wine while Giselle sipped her water, watching him closely above the rim.

"You know," he started, placing the empty glass on the bench between them. "I am quite convinced that one of the journalists writing for *La Libération* is your former colleague, that Jew Levy. The writing style is so very similar, and his…"

He choked suddenly, coughing a couple of times and apologized, clearing his throat.

"Excuse me. So much for the excellent French wine that burns your throat." He tugged on his collar slightly. "So I was saying, this Levy. Maybe he even instigated the other ones to conspire with him. Maybe all three of them work together. I'll soon get to the bottom of this, I promise. Do you know what they talk about before you go there? Maybe Demarche is in it, too."

He coughed again, more violently this time, a thin film of moisture forming on his brow.

"It doesn't matter anymore, Karl."

Struggling with breath, he moved away from Giselle, who remained oddly calm. He pulled on his collar with more force, grabbed the bottle of water and drank it greedily, only to bend in half as a new spasm twisted his stomach. Giselle jumped to her feet and stepped away after he had tried to catch her skirt.

"You…" His voice came out hoarse and strained. "You put something in that wine…"

"I'm sorry, Karl. I really am."

He tried to get up, but fell to his knees, clenching his stomach with his hand.

"I'll shoot you… I'll shoot you all…" He tried getting up again, but the searing pain only allowed him to move on all fours. Yet, he still slowly, but resolutely, turned back to the house, where he had left his belt with its holster, next to their bed.

Giselle swiftly moved towards the door, blocking him from entering. He clenched her skirt with one hand, and she willingly lowered to his level, but only to push him onto his back.

"Don't fight me, Karl." Giselle straddled him and placed both palms on top of his face, covering his mouth and nose, which had already started to bleed. "You'll die anyway. Strychnine is highly toxic, especially in such high dosages. I only want to make it easier for you so you won't suffer for too long. The pain will only grow stronger."

Writhing underneath her, he reached for her throat while trying to push away her hands with his other hand. Giselle twisted her head so that his nails only scratched the exposed skin on her neck.

"I didn't want to do this, Karl." She pressed her hands down with more force. "But you left me no choice. You can't just barge into someone else's house and start setting your own rules without expecting any resistance from the owner. You can't just march into someone else's country and not expect for us to resist you as well. What's not to understand? Why did you have to do this, Karl? Why couldn't you stay where you belonged, damn you?"

He managed to throw her hands off his face and coughed

up blood before Giselle replaced her palms back onto his mouth and nose with deadly determination.

"My French protagonist could never end up with a German, Karl. I don't care how good it would sell. The French girl killed her bastard collaborator husband and joined the Resistance, and that's the end of the story!" She didn't notice that she had started shouting, her tears falling onto his grayish face which glistened with sweat. His attempts to release himself were becoming feebler and feebler. "Why did you have to do this to yourself, Karl? What did you sell yourself for? Not even money... Ideas only. Ideas, written in books by people like me. And you were ready to die for those ideas? Why couldn't you stay a doctor, Karl? You were saving people's lives at some point. You returned hope to people. You could have been the man whose name was celebrated for many generations to come; why did you do this to yourself? Why, you fool, why?!"

Giselle took her hands away and hid her face in them, willing herself to stop sobbing. A few moments later she realized that the man under her wasn't moving anymore. Giselle lowered her hands slowly and looked at his face, still so unbearably handsome even in death, but finally at peace. She wiped the wetness from her cheeks with the back of her hand, frustrated at her emotional state and reached inside the pocket for a handkerchief.

She sat on the wooden floor of the terrace, leaning her back on the carved railing, and shifted Karl's body so that his head rested on her lap. She carefully cleaned the blood, sweat, and foam off his face, combed his tousled hair with her fingers and finally brought herself to close his eyes with their long, delicate eyelashes.

"Sleep well, my handsome prince. One day I'll write a story about you."

She had no idea how long she sat there in the same position, staring at the opposite wall with an unblinking gaze, gently stroking the hair of the corpse in her lap. It had been surprisingly easy to do it after all.

"I'm not a louse," she whispered and chuckled, quietly at first before bursting into loud laughter until the tears started forming in her eyes again.

Consumed by hysterical laughter, she didn't hear the steps on the wooden floor, and only frowned at Philippe's panting frame, confused by his sudden appearance.

"What on earth have you done?!" he shouted, after taking in the scene around him.

Giselle looked around as well, pausing with her gaze on Karl's body as if seeing it for the first time. She brushed the tips of her fingers on his cheek, seemingly at a loss, but at least her manic laughter had ceased for now.

"I did what we writers do the best, I suppose. Concocted a story for him, played on his emotions, developed a plot..." She raised her gaze, still clouded with tears, at the communist leader. "I told him that I was expecting so he would switch his attention from his investigation to the wedding and my fake pregnancy. I contemplated long and hard about the best way to proceed with my plan. I couldn't shoot him because I would only get arrested right away, and that was not in my plans. Neither could I stab him, for he's a strong fellow, you see... He would only end up stabbing and killing me instead. So, slipping the poison into his drink was my only option..."

"I meant, what have you done even coming up with

something like this?" Philippe glowered at her unexplainable serenity. "Do you realize the consequences that this assassination will have for the French people? For the Resistance? For you? You killed a man, Giselle!"

"I did. I had to protect my friends. And our little *Libération*. But that was only part of my reasoning, I admit." Giselle gave him a lopsided grin. "I proved myself right today, Philippe. I'm not a louse. I finally understand everything. I'm not a louse, but I'm not a criminal either. It's the war. That's what Raskolnikov's mistake was. He killed to try himself, not to pursue some noble goal. That's why he suffered so much. But I won't suffer, I know it. We're doing it for all the right reasons."

Philippe kept staring at her as if questioning her sanity. Giselle shook her head slightly.

"I haven't gone mad, don't worry. Just thinking out loud. How did you get here?"

"Last night I read your little manuscript that you left for Michel when you came to pick up the poison from me. Together with your previous request, it was rather easy to put two and two together."

"How did you like my ending?"

"Your ending? Your ending will be swift and painful unless we get out of here right this instant." Philippe pushed Karl's body off her lap and pulled Giselle, who he suspected was shell-shocked from the murder and therefore couldn't think straight, upwards. "Let's go. No one is expecting you two to come back until Monday, right? So, we have two days. I'll put you on a train to the Free Zone today. You said you had an *Ausweis*, didn't you?"

"I'm not going anywhere," Giselle spoke, collected and

calm, contrary to his previous assumption. She wasn't stunned; her gruesome deed simply didn't affect her that much it appeared. "I'm staying here to fight until the last one of them is gone. Before, I was reluctant to physically participate in Resistance activities, but now I know for a fact that my hand won't falter when it comes to taking another *Boche's* life. I can do it, and I will."

"Are you insane?! Your face will be on every wall Tuesday morning! The Gestapo will turn the city upside down looking for you!"

"I didn't say I was staying in Paris. I'm going to Dijon, and I'll join the Resistance there. Michel has his connections there through Etienne. I'll dye my hair and change my clothes. Giselle Legrand, as they know me now, will cease to exist." She paused for a moment and grinned again. "Do you want to join me?"

"Join you?"

"Why, yes." Her smile grew wider. "Couples generally don't raise suspicion. We can pretend to be husband and wife. What do you say?"

Philippe's glance slid over the corpse lying motionless at her feet. Apparently, he had been mistaken on her account after all. The communist leader peered into Giselle's eyes before making the fateful decision. There wasn't a trace of tears left in their hazel depth, only determination. He nodded slowly as an unfamiliar and exciting sense of anticipation started to take him over.

"Are you proposing to me then?"

"I'm proposing that you be my Resistance husband, yes. Till death do us part." She was smiling again.

Philippe chuckled, shook his head, but pressed her

outstretched palm nevertheless. "I hope the last part will happen later rather than sooner."

"Don't fret. I'm a formidable planner and an even better executor."

"Executioner," Philippe grumbled, eyeing the dead German again.

"No, Philippe, and that's the difference." Giselle regarded Karl's serene face as well. "He was one. I'm only protecting my land from the likes of him."

EPILOGUE

 *aris, June 1941*

KAMILLE STOOD IN THE HALLWAY, swallowing tears. This was
it then. The time to say goodbye had come. Jochen dropped
his suitcase on the floor and opened his arms to her again,
for the last time. Kamille pressed her wet face into his shoulder, not able to contain the devastating sense of loss tearing
her heart apart. It had only been a year, a short twelve
months during which she had fallen in love with the best
man on earth, who was now leaving for some far away land
that she had only heard about from geography lessons. The
war with the Soviet Union had been declared a few days ago,
and since then the city had become a buzzing beehive of
gray-green uniforms, which swarmed around and flooded
the streets, marching towards train stations to head east-

wards; who knew how soon they would return, and if they would return at all.

Jochen had been in the same state of distress for the past two days, until yesterday morning when he woke Kamille up and demanded her immediate answer to if she would agree to marry him before he had to leave to the front. Confused and still not completely awoken from her sleep, she didn't understand what he was saying at first.

"Well, my former fiancé left me after I went away last time. So, I figured if I make you my wife, you will wait for me," he explained with a hopeful grin.

"I will wait for you no matter what!" Kamille threw her arms around his neck, trying to stop the merciless time from reaching their inevitable separation.

They walked into a small church nearby, where Jochen almost threatened the priest into performing the rite that was prohibited both by German law and was more than frowned upon by the church for obvious reasons. Jochen wasn't afraid of breaking the law; the *Wehrmacht* was picking him up within twenty-four hours, and the priest would hardly head to the *Kommandatur* to report them without even knowing their last names. He would get arrested himself for agreeing to this, so Jochen didn't have to worry for Kamille's well-being either.

"Be strong, my love," he told her, holding his new wife by the shoulders to take one last look at her beautiful face, which was stained with tears. "I'll come back in no time."

"Swear that you will!" Kamille implored, clinging onto his uniform. It was a good thing, at least, that Violette was at school, having said her farewells to her newly adopted *Papa* earlier that morning. Kamille wouldn't be able to bear her crying; her own she could hardly stand. "Swear that you'll come back! Swear that you won't get yourself hurt."

Jochen gave her a long look but then nodded solemnly. "I swear."

With that, he was gone, after only twelve months of bringing the very reason of existence into her life. Kamille slid down onto the floor and cried until there were no tears left. After that, she rose to her feet, walked a little unsteadily into the living room and noticed the time starting a new countdown: a countdown to the day when he would return. She knew he would; he swore to it after all.

DIJON, June 1941

HORST STOOD ON THE PLATFORM, waiting to board the train together with his men. His superior, Hauptmann Hartmann, had given him a promotion before they had set off to the front, putting him in charge of a small group of soldiers, also heading to the East. His hands were itching to take his drawing album out and outline a quick sketch of the madness surrounding him. This was the last day before he would leave for the front. His desire to imprint it on paper before it would disappear from his memory, washed out and discolored by the new memories, was almost unmanageable, but he was a lieutenant now, and lieutenants didn't draw sketches in front of their men.

"Often we follow conventions that don't suit us personally, and slowly lose ourselves in the rotten swamp of public opinion, dissolving, falling apart until nothing is left of us."

He remembered her saying that on Sunday morning, in the forest, on one of the happiest days of his life. But, what had happened to her? The Gestapo were strangely quiet on her account after she had vanished, having disappeared without a trace as if she had never existed at all; a former socialite turned Resistance fighter. They only acknowledged that, and only during the first month while they still searched for her frantically all over the city. And then the new chief arrived from Germany, and soon the posters with her face on them and the bright red *Wanted* in both French and German were painted over, and new posters appeared, celebrating May First and praising Goebbels for something that he couldn't even recall now. But, a picture of her thoughtful face that he had drawn that Sunday while she sat there, next to him, contemplating something that he couldn't guess, reminded Horst that she did indeed exist and that he didn't dream her up like he often thought he did.

"Always stay true to yourself, Horst," she told him then with an unusually serious expression on her face. "And always remember to act according to your heart, not to what your commanders tell you. They're only men, and they make mistakes. Be a good man, and a good soldier. And after the war is over, go back home and draw your beautiful paintings. The world needs more artists, not soldiers."

She wasn't here so Horst could promise her that he was going to be a good soldier and that he would fight honorably, and, therefore, Horst promised it to himself instead, so she would be proud of him no matter where she was.

After ensuring that all of the men under his command

were seated inside, he climbed into the train himself and stood on the step in the doors, his new adjutant taking his usual position behind his back. A tall man with a cap pulled onto his face caught his attention, due to the sheer height of him, and then suddenly Horst's eyes widened as he saw the woman who stood next to him. He recognized her instantly, even though she looked anything but the portrait that he reverently carried in his pocket, right next to his heart. Dark hair reached down her shoulders, loose waves framing her face, which was completely devoid of any makeup. Her attire was that of a typical factory worker, with baggy corduroy pants and a shirt, also made of rough grayish cotton. Her lips curled upwards in an impish grin, and she winked at him, before turning around and disappearing together with her mysterious friend. Giselle Legrand, the former socialite turned Resistance fighter. Horst grinned too, pressing his hand on top of the portrait, carefully concealed under his uniform. So, she had decided to stay true to herself, too.

"Saw someone you know, Herr Unterfeldwebel?" his adjutant chimed, noticing Horst's beaming expression.

"Just an old friend saying goodbye."

"Maybe you'll meet someday?"

"Maybe. Someday. When the war is over."

ACKNOWLEDGMENTS

I would like to express my gratitude to the people who helped me with creating "The Indigo Rebels": to my fiancé for his encouragement and support throughout the process; to my amazing friend Audrey who helped me immensely with the research and who also made sure that my characters sounded authentic; to my wonderful and irreplaceable editor Alexandra whose suggestions, corrections and insights turn my manuscripts into novels; to my amazingly talented cover designer Melody who makes my books look so pretty; to my little "historical society" on Tumblr, who always have an answer to every question that even some history books can't provide — I can't thank you enough for your support, encouragement, humor and knowledge of your history. To all of my fellow authors who became my dearest friends: your talent and your stories always inspire me, and your support is truly invaluable. And finally, to my wonderful readers, who are the very reason why I write. Thank you for your continuous love and support!

FIND ELLIE ONLINE:

http://elliemidwood.com

http://www.goodreads.com/EllieMidwood

https://www.facebook.com/Ellie-Midwood-651390641631204/